Published 2001
Poolbeg Press Ltd.
123 Grange Hill, Baldoyle,
Dublin 13, Ireland
Email: poolbeg@poolbeg.com
www.poolbeg.com

© Gareth O'Callaghan 2001

The moral right of the author has been asserted.

Copyright for typesetting, layout, design
© Poolbeg Group Services Ltd.

13 5 7 9 10 8 6 4 2

A catalogue record for this book is available from the British Library.

ISBN 1 84223 032 8

Typeset by Patricia Hope in Palatino 10/14
Printed by
Omnia Books Ltd, Glasgow

ABOUT THE AUTHOR

Gareth O'Callaghan is one of Ireland's best-known radio personalities. His national daily radio show has continued to top listenership ratings for over ten years. He trained as a journalist in the mid-80s with the BBC in London. He is also a clinical psychotherapist and NLP practitioner. He lives in Dublin with his wife and three daughters. *The Limbo Vigil* is his third novel.

ACKNOWLEDGEMENTS

I have become a firm believer that, in whatever area of life you choose to find your feet, exist, learn and find contentment, you will be sent the spirit of guidance, resilience and foresight in the shape of individuals who can point you, guide you and inspire you, and above all love you for who and what you are. All we have to do is to watch for them and then to listen. These people are "true" friends.

So much has happened in my life since my last novel, *The Keeper*. So many of the memories have been happy ones, some not so. My special thanks goes out to a small group of people who have been with me through "thick and thin". I'm not often great at saying thank you when I should. These individuals are the people my life revolves around, without whom this story would never have been written. And I want each of you to know that I appreciate you.

~ My wife, Jacqui, who has been through the good and the bad, the happy and the sad, with me. She knows me better than I sometimes know myself. Some three millennia ago King Solomon asked, *"Ayshet chayal mi y'imtza?"* A Woman of valour, where is she to be found? I am blessed to have her with me.

~ Kerri, Katie and Aibhin, my three beautiful daughters: You make me so proud. I hope and pray for the very best of happiness, intuition, strength and gentleness for each one of you in the lifetime that stretches ahead.

~ My parents, Eileen and Joe, and my mother-in-law and close friend, Kathleen Nugent. Also my sister and brother, Amy and Dave, Amy's husband, Shay, and Dave's wife, Anne, and to Nicola and Bernard, and Cathy and Xavier. Thank you all for everything.

~ Breda Purcell, Micheál Moloney and Margaret Vaughan — towers of strength, each one of you, who recognised wrong turns and managed to steer me clear and give me a greater clarity and insight.

~ Maggie Stapleton, my former radio producer and close friend. If ever I need a second opinion on anything, Maggie's is always the best one to ask.

~ Geraldine Hall, a strong woman; Jim Daly, Fergal McDonagh, Val Devlin and Joe Connolly, Anthony and Joan McCarthy, Aileen and Paul O'Meara, Linda and Michael McNiffe. There's a danger here of forgetting names and accidentally leaving important individuals out. If I have done that, I am sorry! It wasn't intentional.

~ Carole Blake, my agent, for your friendship and prudent pointers, and everyone at Blake Friedmann.

~ To Gaye Shortland, my editor. Thank you for the care you have shown my work, and for your genuine compliments (which authors love to hear as often as possible). Your attention to detail and the way in which you open out a manuscript and "raise" it is unique and, considering that this was my manuscript, such a privilege to be part of. Thank you, Gaye.

~ My publishers, Poolbeg.

~ I reserve my final thank you, the big one, for the listeners to my radio show — old and new. I've been a part of the wireless décor now for almost twenty-three years, in various guises and on different networks, all over the world I suppose. It's been a truly amazing journey. It never ceases to amaze me and to lift me whenever I receive letters and e-mails from those of you who have trekked this road with me. This is for you . . .

Dedicated to the Memory of
David Hall
~ Fire-fighter, Neighbour, Friend ~
Peace, perfect peace . . .

HAIKU

"Nettles stinging weeds;
weeds are wrapped around nettles,
but nettles don't care."

Kerri O'Callaghan, aged 12

∾ ∾

I saw also that there was an ocean of
darkness and death.
But an infinite ocean of light and love
flowed over the ocean of darkness."

George Fox, the founder of
The Society of Friends
also known as The Quakers, 1647

1

Oak Bluffs, Martha's Vineyard, Massachusetts
Wednesday, November 23

Love and hatred co-exist, side by side, in a world where one is constantly outwitting the other, in equal parts, with equal passion. My parents always told me love wins out in the end.

Love is eternal. Forever.

My parents were wrong.

All of my life, I have tried to understand love and show kindness and affection to those close to me as hard and as best as I could. *Love Thy Neighbour*, they taught us in school. If knowledge is the food of the mind, then love must feed the heart.

Despite the physical, three-and-a-half-thousand-mile distance between us, my heart pounded madly each time the phone rang and an operator asked me if I would accept the charges, and that familiar, hesitant delay and crackly resonance reminded me unfailingly that love was very much alive, and thriving in the voice of the person who always ended her calls by saying, "Miss you, Dad".

Those three words broke my heart each time I heard them – her voice barely able to contain itself as she rang off. After hundreds of conversations they were the words I would always remember. Not because they had become the norm in conversations made up of flitters of events and "you won't believe who so-and-so has been going out with lately . . ." but because they told me she loved me. And in the ring of the spin she always put on "Dad", I could tell she knew how much I loved her. It's easy to believe that out of sight is out of mind. But no amount of distance could have come between my daughter and me once I knew she was thinking of me and, it goes without saying, me of her.

But all of that changed that night, which seems as if it was only yesterday. A sharp, savage reminder that love lives precariously in the awful black shadow of hate, like a tiny bird picking at crumbs, preyed upon by a huge, hungry cat.

The woman who called with the devastating news that night, whose voice still haunts me, was someone I never thought I would hear from again.

* * *

My name is David Freeman.

Ten years ago, I was accused of beating a young schoolboy, a thirteen-year-old pupil of mine, to within an inch of his life. There is no evidence to support this claim, which makes perfect sense since I didn't do it. To compound matters, the young boy disappeared later that afternoon. He vanished, literally.

Owen Durkin was a hyperactive kid who didn't take to discipline too easily. If an opportunity arose to give cheek or provoke a classmate, the whole class occasionally, he seized upon it every time and saw it through despite my protestations. His brazen bravado quickly turned him into a hero in the eyes of the other young impressionable pupils. To tell a teacher to fuck off was not uncommon for Owen Durkin. He quickly established himself in the role of class entertainer and, once inspired, any notion of education went right out the window, just like Owen did on occasions.

He was a gangly child with red hair and millions of freckles, and a pair of black-framed glasses held together with blue industrial insulation tape at the bridge of his nose. He was short of a few teeth; I couldn't decide whether this was a natural progression, or if he had decided to challenge some of the older boys, or girls, in the town. I had even mentioned to our local doctor that I felt Owen might have been suffering from Attention Deficit Disorder, a condition quite common among young children.

In reality I came to hate Owen Durkin. He made my life difficult and was slowly taking the enjoyment out of my profession. Much as I felt like pulverising him, it never happened.

The night I was accused by the local police of assault on a minor, I was at home. They questioned me and then arrested me. The next day, following my release, I received word that Owen Durkin had officially been listed as a missing person. I had been held and questioned for twenty-four hours, despite my innocence.

Smalltownsville being what it is, a small rumour rapidly grew into an unstoppable bogeyman, fuelled by gossip and cowardice, filled with lies and deceit. My only supporter, apart from my daughter, was a local journalist, a larger-than-life character called Josh Traynor. He was the only one who, I felt, believed my story.

More damning still, my wife supported the growing accusations.

On hearing her voice that night, ten years later, leaving the message she did, it felt like an old wound within had just been gashed open again with a red-hot knife.

* * *

Her message was logged at 8.04pm, almost as if she had known for certain there would be no one home – as I often refer to my shop – and the answerphone would record her call. It was as if my estranged wife didn't want to speak directly to me and had planned it that way – just said her few words behind my back and was gone – like she had done ten years before, the night she tried to kill me.

The store should have closed at eight, like it did every

Wednesday evening. It's not in my nature to be so punctual, not since I quit teaching. I just get bored most Wednesdays, asking myself why I should stay open late when no one ever crosses the threshold much beyond six. Tonight, though, would be different. I decided to stay open till nine. Schools were on an extended weekend for Thanksgiving, and families were exiting Boston, pouring onto the Cape for the final holiday weekend of the year.

Oak Bluffs had gradually been getting busier since early morning with an extra ferry every two hours, unloading people-carriers full of stressed fathers and patient mothers and small, weary backseat passengers onto Sea View Avenue for the short drive to Edgartown, all prim and proper with its freshly painted white clapboard colonial homes and manicured gardens.

Brady's Bed & Breakfast was booked out for a solid month now, always a sure sign that accommodation would be hard to come by anywhere along Nantucket Sound. It was always a popular time, particularly when Thanksgiving fell at the start of a weekend. It was a special time, especially for families: a time to make a concerted effort to travel, no matter how far, to be together, even if it was just for twenty-four hours. Feuds and fuelled opinions, dislikes and disagreements, no matter how execrated and extended, were all put aside for Thanksgiving Day. At least until someone began to choke on a turkey bone, or mother-in-law was at risk of being strangled during a game of charades.

* * *

I had become used, during the first couple of years I had lived on the Cape, to the simple task of spending the evenings alone each Thanksgiving Day in the quietness of my small room. I ate with the Bradys if I felt like it. Sometimes I ate alone in the bedroom that had become my miniature abode, with books in tilting, stacked bundles claiming every available nook and cranny, and a small work bureau, laden down with nothing of any importance. My room with its white wood-slat walls faced out onto the sea and the Atlantic waves, only a stone's throw from my window, spitting their salty spray across the back patio. And whenever I think of the evenings I stood gazing out through the open window at the changing tides, I remember how the smell of the night air was always tinged with a cocktail of salty drizzle and musty books, the abiding thoughts that always gave me peace in times of turmoil.

For six years now, Karen had been as much a part of my Thanksgiving as the turkey and cranberry sauce that she prepared so deliciously. She always insisted on a huge spread despite her tiny appetite, with the result that we ate meat sandwiches and drank flasks of turkey stock for a week afterwards. It was a day for quitting the old routine; a lazy opportunity spent thinking about doing nothing in particular, sweet Fanny Adams, and no fear of anyone invading our space and spoiling the experience.

No matter what happened it was our day, spent packed tightly together at one end of the huge settee until the hunger drove us back to the kitchen. Oddly enough the day, despite being intentionally sluggish, had its ritual. I would wake to the smells of herb and multigrain breads baking and coffee brewing while Karen went for her morning dip at the bottom of the garden in Nantucket Sound. Some mornings, if she had an hour, she'd take the wagon and drive to Herring Creek, on Lake Tashmoo, her favourite spot. Bad weather never bothered her. She loved the sea. I would stuff the turkey, while she put on my old Yankees sweat and prepared the veg and the roasties. We would both set the table. After dinner, it was back to the settee usually for the evening, and then finally we might venture across the street for a nightcap with Tom Brady and his wife, Thelma. They were the only close friends we had made on the Cape, preferring to do our own thing: "the only friends we needed," I always used to say to Karen. I loved my solitary existence. Or so I thought until that evening.

* * *

Business had been brisk since six, mainly small groups of twos and threes – children with their mothers, browsing and chatting, and disagreeing and arguing over who was getting what. By seven I needed a coffee.

"I'll watch the place if you want to nip over to Terry's," Karen said, with a soft smile. "Tired?" she asked, squeezing my hand in hers.

7

I nodded and yawned, winking to show my appreciation, struggling to smile back. I hugged her. "I'll be ten minutes. Do you want anything?"

"No, thanks."

* * *

Terry's Diner, on Sea View Avenue, framed by its knotty oak trees, was two up along the wide, windswept main street almost overlooking the old pier. The incoming tide was gathering the early darkness with it, the bitterly cold evening whipping up a stormy gale. The kites and parafoils and American flags and windsocks tied to the lampposts outside Dr Gravity's Kite Shop had been whipped into a frenzied, knotted mess by the wind. John McKane, the master stylist of Cape Cod, was busy next door, working through a small queue of elderly women, all waiting on blue rinses, which would see him there till nine at the earliest. In the distance, barely visible, the day's final car ferry signalled its approach to its overnight dock with three short hoots of its monotonous siren.

Oak Bluffs had just been transformed from a sleepy, "down-island" autumnal holiday hamlet. Now it was a mad, gridlocked, tourist-infested tow-away zone. "Down-island" refers to the easterly towns of Vineyard Haven, Oak Bluffs and Edgartown.

I recognised some of the old familiar faces at the bar. Bob, and his wife Nancy. They were from Newark. No surname. I suppose I had never bothered to ask each time they returned, since they didn't think it important to tell me. Perhaps it was friendlier that way. No grief, no ties. Just nice Bob and smiling, nodding Nancy. Bob gestured to a pint of lager Tom was pulling behind the bar. It was the same routine always: they arrived on a Wednesday, like the dozens of other friendly, smiling faces from Main Street America, and left at lunchtime Sunday.

"That's yours, David," he shouted above the heads at the counter. "Happy Holiday. See you over the weekend." Bob waved. Nancy smiled and nodded. "Tell Karen we said hello," and she nodded again.

Bob loved his fishing. They had a holiday home in Edgartown. Bob had been coming to Martha's Vineyard twice a year for twenty-eight years to catch the elusive bonito. We'd meet, talk about the latest gear at the local Fish 'n' Tackle. Next morning at first light Bob waited patiently, as he had done for twenty-eight years, for the tide to run out of Menemsha Pond, and the bonito to lurk off the jetties, and there he spent his weekend, manning these rows of huge rocks with a dozen other anglers.

Bob bored me. So I always made my excuse. See you later, I always said to them.

I knew they wouldn't see us. They never did, despite all the years they had been coming back to Martha's Vineyard – he just bought me a drink, waved as a neighbour does and disappeared.

I gestured with my thumb up. "Thanks, Bob. Hi,

Nancy. Great to see you." It was all so formal and insincere. I waved back with enthusiasm. "I'll have it later when I close up. Cheers." I picked up my coffee and gestured to Tom to get them another drink on me. "See you all later," I cheered.

* * *

I was keen to get back to the store. I was expecting an important phone call from a woman who, even my Karen knew, was the sole focus of, and the singular reason for – if there had to be a reason – my very being; for whom I lived my life every day, even though we had not seen each other for eight years now – my daughter, Molly. It was her twenty-first birthday on Thanksgiving Day, the twenty-fourth of November – the feast of Saint Andrew Dung-Lac, the patron saint of Vietnam veterans. Molly had always pointed out that I needed someone strong and, preferably, unwavering to watch over me. Since she occasionally ribbed me by calling me a martyr-for-the-cause – most likely I guess because of my predisposition for bitching and complaining – who better, she thought, than a genuine first-class martyr who shared her birthday to watch over me.

It was Molly's turn to call me. Despite the years and the distance between us, and a few scattered letters and our weekly phone call, and, more recently, the badly typed e-mails, we had developed a bond, much like two penpals who had struggled through similar harsh endurances, during our time away from each other. I often asked myself if this was not just my lame excuse for not getting in touch more often, this sixth sense that perhaps hid my shame for not writing like I had promised I would. But I knew she loved me. That was all that counted.

Tonight I was going to close up the store, switch off the outer lights, send Karen off to her friend's hen party and settle down in the small back-office for a long chinwag about nothing in particular with my young soul mate. I'd looked forward to it for days.

Molly had warned me in her e-mail, the previous week, that she would call on the dot of half eight with a number that I could phone her back on. She had just started a new job and I was dying to hear all the news. She was a second-year student of psychology, having drifted for a few years after school, scraping together college fees in and out of jobs. At least that's what she would have me believe.

I checked the clock above the diner door, as I pressed the lid down firmly on the disposable cup and faced into the defiant blizzard that had been brewing most of the afternoon.

It was just after twenty past eight. A sudden wave of urgency, almost panic, gripped me. I knew I had to rush, just in case she called early and thought I'd left. Karen might not hear the phone ringing if the store was busy.

A hand grabbed my shoulder. I spun around, losing

my grip on the cup, almost scalding Karen in the process.

She looked shocked. She had been crying, her eyes puffed and bloodshot.

"Jesus, Karen, I'm sorry." I wiped coffee off her sleeve with a paper napkin. "Are you OK? What's wrong?"

She ignored the questions. She seemed dumbstruck, out of breath, when she tried to speak. "David, you've got to come back to the shop."

Immediately I thought there had been a fire. Maybe a child had got hurt. "What's wrong?"

"It's Molly." She waited, anticipating that I might detect the awful dread in her voice if she spoke too quickly. "The phone rang. But I was looking for a book for . . ."

"*What's wrong?*" I yelled, so forcefully I scared her.

"She left a message."

"*Molly?*"

"No. A woman. Molly's in hospital." Karen wiped the tears off her face. "Dave, she tried to kill herself."

2

The sea scared me that night, its wild, thrashing brutality and its despairing havoc, crashing against the black dykes up and down Nantucket Sound for as far as I could see – the giant rollers, monstrous and almighty one moment, seemed to give up their might just seconds before flinging themselves with a deafening boom onto the flat sands, then beat a hasty retreat ahead of an even bigger roller.

I studied the waves for hours, counted them into the hundreds, tried to tell from the different sounds when the tide was about to turn, until a pasty softness, like a thin grey pencil line taking its time to turn into a sash of indigo blue, broke out across the horizon. I checked my watch against the fading light of a disappearing moon.

It was 6.30am on Thanksgiving Day. Thursday.

All I had to be thankful for was that somebody had found my daughter before she bled to death. Someone had saved her life. For that I would have given back my own. All through the night the darkness challenged me to the most torturous mindgames I had played in ten years. In between the tears and the anger, I must have reviewed my life a dozen times, retraced the steps that occasionally still gave me nightmares, forcing myself to think through the times I wanted to kill myself; trying to find a reason why she had wanted to give up: an emotional notion few of us want to entertain for longer than a few seconds.

I had kept watch over an angry sea for almost seven hours and countless mugs of tea. The bottle of Budweiser Karen had opened and placed beside me on the doorstep shortly after one before she had gone to bed was still chilled and untouched in the cold night air.

Now I heard her moving about in the kitchen.

I could hear her voice saying thank you and the phone being put back in the top drawer under the worktop. The door opened behind me. I could hear her breathing deeply; feel her shivering violently as a cold spate of salty spray blew in across the sandy, creaky-wooden porch.

"Have you slept?" she asked croakily and coughed.

"Couldn't." Even my voice sounded shattered. She sat down on the top step beside me and folded her arms around my knees, resting her head on my shoulders. "You're freezing. And soaked. You'll catch your death."

"Will I?" I didn't care. If it was going to be meaningless conversation for the sake of it, flim-flam, I wasn't interested. She could tell.

"A man called back from Logan. I booked a seat for you. You're on a flight to Shannon tonight. It leaves Boston at ten past eight, local time. Arrives Shannon at ten past seven tomorrow morning."

I knew she wasn't happy with the travel arrangements. I said nothing.

"You could fly direct to Dublin."

"I can't. I told Molly's mother I would collect her on the way."

"Why did you tell me that Molly's mother was dead if she wasn't?" Karen lifted her head and stared straight into my eyes with a pained, almost angry gaze that demanded an answer to a question she had asked every time I had set eyes on her during the early part of the night.

* * *

"Can I help you?" were Karen McQuillan's first words to me almost seven years ago, as I struggled to free an antique bookcase that I had fallen in love with from beneath a coat-stand jammed against the wood beams at the back of The Whippletree, a one hundred-and-twenty-five-year-old barn filled to the rafters with a vast selection of collectables and gifts, on Main Street, West Barnstable in the heart of Cape Cod. Come hell or high water, I was going to excavate it that Saturday morning and take it home. It was heavier than I first thought and my big toe was taking most of the weight.

I would have lain underneath the bookcase if it

15

meant I was going to get to chat with her. She was the most beautiful woman I had ever seen; her voice husky and sexy, her skin a natural tanned brown. She was so stunningly beautiful I instantly thought she had to be married, and very happily at that, or at least dating seriously enough to have moved in with her lover. Everything about her, I remember thinking, was perfect – all her different qualities complementing each other magically. I fell in love so quickly that Saturday morning I felt embarrassed. Within minutes I was reduced to a giggling child, repeating the things she was saying, finishing sentences for her and cracking stupid one-liners and telling ridiculous stories that hadn't a hint of truth. We both laughed about nothing in particular and all I could think of was that there was some other lucky bastard out there who had swept her off her feet long before I had ever spotted The Whippletree.

He was probably a quarterback with the Boston Red Sox. She probably got the best tickets in the house, the same front row seat every night to watch him break up the middle for five, sweep end for twenty, slant off tackle for eleven, and then down the sidelines for eighty yards. She was so beautiful I was certain he had to be a smouldering rock of perfectly chiselled beefcake with a naked photograph of her on the inside of his locker door. It was obvious, I guessed, the position wasn't open to tender.

"Do you like baseball?" I asked brazenly.

She shook her head. "Definitely not."

I tried not to show my pure rapture. Still, there were

hundreds of other dreamboat hunks she could be seeing. He was probably the top-paid disc jockey at WMJX; probably a smooth talker with a husky voice who played love songs late at night, and spoke in a way that melted women's hearts.

"What sort of music do you like?" I asked warily, praying that God in his kindness would afford another quick deletion.

"Classical."

"Beautiful." I grinned. "My name's Dave. Dave Freeman." I felt the time was right, having tried to create the impression that I was a virtuous, chivalrous, well-educated rock of sense with a side-splitting sense of humour and a sixth sense for good antiques, to shake her hand.

"Karen McQuillan." She nodded. "Nice to meet you."

"Are you new here?"

She shook her head. "I'm here now nearly twelve months. It's nice. I worked in Boston before that. I'm from Quincy. I'm a mature student. I'm only working here part-time. I just do it Saturdays and Sundays when I'm not in college. My mother lives upstairs. We split the shifts whenever I visit for a few days."

"I always said if I owned a place like this I'd get rid of a lot of the crap and give the nice antiques plenty of space to themselves. That way not only would the shop look a lot nicer, but you'd also be able to get a lot more people into the place. What do you think?"

"My mother owns this place. I'll tell her."

My face turned so red that morning I could feel it burning. I believed firmly at that moment that I had blown any hopes I might have nurtured that this woman liked me. So, logically, like any schoolteacher would assess a situation that called for quick thinking, I decided to ask all the questions I felt I should leave for another visit right there and then. She seemed to have that 'go on, ask me another' look about her. So I did.

"Are you married?" I braced myself.

"No."

"You must be seeing someone?"

"No." She shook her head. Two out of two. I detected by the dropped eye-line that she had been serious about someone in the not-too-distant past.

"That's a gorgeous tan. Been anywhere nice?"

"No. I suppose I'm always this dark. It's the Indian blood in me. My grandfather was a Sioux chief. The whole family is hazelnut brown."

I pitched in my final question for what it was worth. "I suppose I'd be wasting my time if I were to ask you out?"

She shook her head. "You wouldn't."

* * *

Karen's suggestion that we move in together took me by surprise. It was a May afternoon, a Sunday. She had called to say that Red Barn Antiques in Falmouth was off-loading some of its stock in preparation for a consignment of old valuables from a convent in New Hampshire that had just been sold to make way for a new housing development. She was going over with her mother's gold Amex to buy the lot. She sounded so excited on the phone that it never occurred to me to read between the lines.

I had been renting a small room in Tom Brady's Bed & Breakfast for almost three years by then, and I knew Tom wanted the room back. It just wasn't in his nature to throw me out.

Tom could make an extra few thousand a year if he let it out to tourists and business travellers, but he was just too nice to move beyond the occasional hint.

I was the world's greatest procrastinator – always tomorrow. But not that Sunday. She asked me if I could spare a few hours, since I seemed reasonably adept at shifting bookcases. I agreed, since the alternative was to stay in bed. Anyway I loved her company.

She had obviously researched the plan meticulously. Judging by how quickly she struck a deal with Red Barn – twenty minutes and the lot was paid for and ready to be shipped – antiques were furthest from her mind that afternoon. We drove off the ramp at Oak Bluffs gently so as not to damage the fragile cargo and turned left towards Edgartown. She had said a few times she'd been thinking of getting her own place, out from under her mother's feet, so to speak. She had intended to spend the summer decorating and employing a part-time dealer before college resumed in the fall.

"Where are we going?" I asked curiously.

She smiled, speeding up the old Bedford camper. "You'll see."

The back of the small house overlooked Eastville, one of the most beautiful beaches on Martha's Vineyard. The sheltered inlet with its bright, white sand gave off a magical, calming air in the late afternoon, creating a sentimentality all of its very own that I fell in love with immediately. The sea was calmer than I could ever remember, the sky touching the gently swirling, blue water on a seamless, invisible horizon like well-matched colours. As I stared outward towards the lighthouse I didn't want to leave.

"It's amazing, isn't it?" Karen said, utterly immersed in the view.

"Yes." It was all I could say. Anything else might have disturbed the perfect peace and this magnetic, secretive oasis that I just wanted to soak up in silence.

"Well?" she said.

"Well . . . what?" I expected she wanted to head back to the van and get her antiques unloaded. "We're not in any hurry," I said.

"That's what I like to hear." She slipped her hand into mine and I held it tightly. "Let's buy it."

The words took a moment to sink in: what they meant . . . what she was insinuating. My heart began to pound. "OK!" My answer came as a shock. I had always been so careful and calculated and predictable in everything I had done in recent years, never one for rash decisions – never one, I suppose, who liked to make important decisions. Then I realised what she was saying.

"I love you." And she kissed me and hugged me. They were words I never expected to hear from a stranger again; words I had relieved my toughened soul of many years before, that moment when I swore that I would never let my feelings get so irrevocably damaged and so inextricably confused again: three words that had almost caused my death.

"I love you too." I was glad to say them now, because I knew I loved her at that moment; and I decided, there and then on a Sunday afternoon looking out across Nantucket Sound, as she pressed her body harder against mine, that we had swapped something I thought I had lost forever.

* * *

The antiques remained in the van that night, while we spent the late hours making love for the first time, and sharing our pasts. I had already told Karen about my daughter. Now I wanted her to get to know her better – to paint a picture for her of what she looked like. I told her how I had a teenage daughter, Molly, at home in Ireland; and how Molly's mother had died tragically late one night two years before. She had been returning home from an extended day-shift in Saint Canice's Hospital. The weather had been particularly bad all that week, causing the Fedora River to burst its banks. Neasa missed the narrow turn for Claddagh Mines, on the treacherous Thurles road and skidded into eight feet of water, in a current that dragged her car downstream for almost a quarter of a mile. The rescue volunteers recovered her body the following day. What a liar.

"Why did the two of you break up?" Karen asked.

"We weren't in love any more," I replied.

"Who decided that?"

"We both did."

"But you can't just decide you're not in love any more."

"Why not?"

"Because it takes a long time to realise you're *in* love in the first place, doesn't it?"

"It didn't for you and me, did it?"

"I suppose not."

"I think it becomes pretty obvious to two people that they're not in love any more."

"How?"

Her questions were beginning to stretch my patience. She was being the psychologist now, probing and internalising. "Because life generally becomes a pain in the ass. I believe you can still love someone forever, but not be *in* love with that person. Does that make sense?"

She thought for a moment and shrugged. "Maybe. Were you upset when she died?"

"Not really."

"Jesus Christ!"

She was shocked by my attitude. "Let's change the subject," I insisted.

We argued for the rest of the evening until she staggered out to her van, having drunk too much champagne, and shouted back at me above the noisy, clanking sounds of the engine, that it might be better if we never saw each other again.

We closed the sale the following Friday and, despite the ominous proverb about the bad luck attached to moving into a new house on a Saturday, "Saturday's flittin', short sittin'," moved into the house. As I lifted her into my arms to carry her across the threshold, blissfully happy, at quarter past three, that Saturday afternoon, careful not to drop the champagne bottle, she touched her glass against the tip of my nose. "No secrets," she whispered.

"No secrets," I replied, and kissed her.

It was true to say I had no secrets. I had left them all behind me, three-and-a-half thousand miles away in a small town called Claddagh Mines, in County Tipperary, where my wife Neasa Maher was buried in a small graveyard beside the church of Saint John the Apostle, close to her family home, in a small plot tended to regularly by her broken-hearted mother and her three brothers.

It was a shameful lie and one that I would deeply regret telling. However, I will always argue that my reasons for telling such a lie were legitimate. Anyone who survived

23

the ordeal I had been subjected to will understand why I had to lie, and not for the first time. That said, I never thought for a moment that the darkest period of my life, a hellish existence I moved to the other side of the world to escape, would rear up on me again and try to destroy the two most important people in my life.

* * *

I slept for most of that Thanksgiving Day, and when I couldn't sleep I pretended to, occasionally opening an eye to check the time. Getting up would have meant talking, and explaining, and reasoning and disagreeing, and arguing. And the last thing I needed on a six-hour flight across the Atlantic was to end up a prisoner of my own conscience for hurting Karen's feelings.

Karen spent what seemed like a well-expressed lifetime on the phone that day. I counted at least eight conversations that I had become a third party to from the bedroom. She spoke to her mother in West Barnstable. She called her two sisters, one in Portland, the other in San Francisco. Each new conversation took the form of a chain letter, telling the next person what the previous one had said. Finally she phoned Thelma Brady across the street and spoke to her for two hours. She told Thelma I was going home to Ireland *on my own*.

"I want to go with you," she said again, as she sat back into the small, creaky rocking chair that Tom and Thelma had given to us as a house-warming gift.

24

"You can't. Who'll mind the business? It's bad enough closing up the bookshop. But there's no point closing up both stores."

"Why not? I think it's more important that I'm with you. I like to think I am *that* important to you, am I?"

"Of course you are. Anyway you said you're going to fly over next Tuesday. That's only four days away, Karen."

"Why did you tell me that Neasa was dead?"

I still hadn't explained properly why I had lied to her. The last time she had asked I simply replied that I didn't know. I owed it to her now.

"Because I hated her so much for the things she did. For the life I had to endure while I figured out how to get away from her. I wanted her dead so much that leaving her was almost like a period of recovery. I went through the anger and the grief. And eventually I knew that the only way I was going to close the door for the last time on that period was to believe that she was dead and buried!" I realised I was shouting. "Sorry."

I risked a glance across the room, dimly lit now as the dying fire threw long shadows across the floor. She wasn't rocking in the chair any more, but was perfectly still. She seemed to be studying me, waiting to hear more, resolved to give me the benefit of the doubt before telling me that I was the Mad Hatter. "What *things* did she do?"

"Ah, nothing. I'm sorry. I didn't mean to yell like that. Look, my head's all over the place. My daughter's on a life-support machine and I'm stranded half a world away from her."

"You're not stranded, David. You're going home tonight. You'll be with her tomorrow morning. You've got to try and relax."

She crossed the room and sat beside me. "You told me there'd be no secrets. I thought I was sharing my life with someone who had nothing to hide." She waited.

"But I *have* nothing to hide."

Secrets. I hated the word. It was a repulsive antagonist. It made me feel physically sick the more I dwelt on it. Secrets. If only Karen knew what lay in the past: if only she was aware of what would stare me in the face once that plane touched down. I always swore that I would do anything for Molly right down to looking death in the face. It seemed a strange contradiction that now death was holding out its cold hand, not to me but to her, and somewhere inside me was a selfish, greedy reluctance to pull her back; almost, as if I might have to give away my power and my freedom in order to claim her as rightfully mine. Even the notion shocked me. I wanted her, right here with me – now, but I was afraid of what I might have to endure in order to get her back. For years I had fooled myself that the phone calls were adequate for keeping in touch with the only individual in the world that I can safely say I ever loved and trusted unconditionally. So why in her hour of need was I hesitating? She told me each time we spoke, just before we said goodnight, that she loved me. I can still hear the sound of her voice packed full of daughterly love and pride for her old man. She reminded me, if I didn't say it, that I was forgetting to tell her something. I would laugh and say bumpily, 'I love you too'.

"What are you thinking?"

Karen's voice replaced Molly's in my tangled, fraught thoughts. I wasn't sure how to answer her question. "I don't know any more," I whispered, close to tears now. "I thought I had it all sussed. I really believed I had my life sorted out at long last, that I had finally been able to bury all the shit from the past. I thought when I had broken up with her that that would be it, that she'd finally get out of my life and let me start again."

"Who?"

"Neasa."

"Does she still love you?"

"No." I sighed and mulled hard over her question. "Maybe."

"And do you still love her?"

I could tell by the tone of her asking that she seemed prepared for my answer to go either way. Even the very idea made me baulk. "Of course I don't."

"Then why the bloody lies? Loads of people break up, David. Lots of couples go their separate ways. Most of them end up being friends, accepting that they couldn't stand each other and leaving it at that, not condemning each other to die, for God's sake!"

It was almost three in the afternoon on a Thanksgiving, when all my pain and bad luck, long dispelled, had come full-circle. I had to be at Logan airport before eight. That gave me almost two hours to kill.

There were no culinary smells in our kitchen that afternoon, nothing to turn the day into the pleasurable experience it had become over six years. "Would you like something to eat?" I suggested.

Karen recoiled in horror as if I had made some obscene proposition. "I'm not hungry."

I knew she wanted me to talk, wanted me to answer her questions honestly. And when they were answered she had more to ask. Because I could tell she didn't believe anything I was saying any more. I knew in my heart that, no matter how many questions I answered, nothing was going to prepare her for the real, undiluted truth, most of which she wouldn't believe anyway, until she came face to face with the reason I fled to Massachusetts all those years ago.

I went into the bedroom without saying any more and started to pack.

3

We met in Ibiza, in one of San Antonio's tackiest Irish bars, Dicey Riley's, on a sweltering August night. Everything about our week was classically holiday-packaged: the weather was too hot, the apartments were still under construction and the alcohol took its desired effect every night. I was celebrating the news from home that I had just passed my teaching exams. College was finally over, and the rather menial task of finding a job could wait until my wild summer vacation crashed to an end.

She told me her name was Neasa Maher, in between the tequila slammers. She had challenged me to a race. "It's happy-hour!" she hooted, in a thick, strong country accent. "This piss is dirt cheap at this time of the evening!"

I checked my watch, half-five, as I fried in the Mediterranean sunshine, weathering the alcoholic battering, watching the two mates I was on holiday with quit and drop away. They were, in every sense, out of the

29

game. And me? They say opposites attract. Neasa Maher's vivacious, outrageous, contagious behaviour was carrying Davey Freeman along on a wave of boldness. I was engrossed in her overpowering high spirits, all the time trying to impress this amazing woman who seemed to have the constitution of a brewery worker. Even without the alcohol, I could have got drunk on the woman's consuming intensity and indulgence. Little did I know that evening, as I fought to keep my eyes open, that she had already fallen for me, marked me for herself. "I knew I was going to marry you that evening," she told me on our wedding night, as she tried to unbuckle my trousers on the way to our hotel while I used the grassy ditches to keep the car steady and straight on the dark, narrow road between Thurles and Dundrum Country House, twenty miles away, in Tipperary.

Her persuasive convictions had overpowered my reluctance – thanks, mainly, to the combined efforts of her three older brothers: Turloch and Canice, two aggressive bastards; and Pius, a sad, twentysomething waster with the mental aptitude of a six-year-old. A little voice deep down inside me told me that day, as I was toasting the beautiful bride that I was calling "my wife", that I had made a bad mistake. All evening long I reasoned with the little voice that every man felt this way on his 'big day' and for a while after getting married. After all, I pointed out to myself, not long ago we were strangers. Later, however, after a lot of paranoid brain-bombing, the nagging voice proved itself to be more than a little prophetic when Neasa decided she wanted to say a few impromptu words before everyone got "pissed and laid", as she put it. I cringed, praying that God would spare me any further embarrassment, while watching the expressions on my parents' faces turn from quizzical to punished to hopelessly shattered. I knew by the way Neasa winked down at me and squeezed my shoulder that God couldn't accommodate my request that evening.

"And myself and David would just like you all to be the first to know that I'm pregnant!" She shrieked with wild laughter as my poor mother, God rest her, choked and spat her Baked Alaska back onto the plate.

Later, as the night porter signed us in at reception in Dundrum House, an old country home frequently visited by show business superstars and glitzy millionaires, Neasa shouted at the top of her best pissed, hoarse-raw voice: "It's a bit fuckin' quiet!"

"That's because it's half two in the morning, madam, and all the guests are fast asleep in their beddy-byes," the night porter spelled out slowly, trying hard to disguise his annoyance.

"Well, get them up. I want to *party*!"

When my ears eventually stopped ringing, I could hear dogs barking in the distance and doors opening on a landing upstairs.

We drove back to Claddagh Mines, having failed to get our deposit back, and spent our wedding night on two armchairs.

* * *

31

The Mahers were the most dysfunctional bunch of hard-drinking troublemakers it has been my scarce displeasure to encounter in my life. For a start they never did anything by halves. A drama in the life of any member of the Maher household was worthy of front-page news – which explains why, twenty-one years later, Blaise Maher still describes her sudden widowhood, six months before our wedding day, as if it had only happened.

Joe Maher always insisted on cycling home from The Bridge Bar in Claddagh Mines, on the darkest of nights, without a mudguard reflector or a headlamp for his bicycle, pissed as a newt and invisible as a ghost. Blaise recalls, "The night before Christmas Eve was the night in question. Joe Pa had called to say he'd be on his way home and to boil the kettle for his hot chocolate. And I'd have the mug steaming and a chocolate Goldgrain ready for him with his slippers opposite the TV. Well, he must never have seen the big truck – a forty-foot something, the boys called it. Sure it was so big and noisy that the driver never heard Joe Pa ringin' his little bell, never saw him ahead, as the huge truck bore down on him. Poor Joe Pa," Blaise would always say, "and didn't I have a lovely cardigan for him under the tree to wear to midnight Mass the following night, God rest him. The doctor said that God took him instantly."

Turloch Pa, who was assigned to Thurles garda station as a rookie cop at that time, never told his mother what happened to the truck driver. He was a Belgian who had just landed his first job in twelve years after a long stretch in a Turkish prison for trying to export enough heroin to fill a pallet of two-pound sugar bags. He had stopped off to ask directions in the Bridge. The police attempted to question him over an entire day. At first they suspected he had no English. It later materialised he had started to drink in my father-in-law's company at lunchtime, then decided at quarter past ten that night, in a stirring moment of hapless bravado, to try and make the 0300 hours sailing from Rosslare to Fishguard.

Joe Pa Maher's peacock-blue cardigan sat under the Christmas tree until Turloch threw it out the following March, one morning while his mother was praying at eight o'clock Mass.

* * *

The Mahers, or as their mother always insisted on calling them, the Ma-*ck*-ers, never fell short on stagecraft or spectacle when it came to life's crises. From the moment Blaise Maher's four children could link their monosyllables, and string their words together with a glossary of colourful expletives, their destiny became one of self-destruction; and they weren't short of incentive when it came to taking the occasional innocent bystander who got in their way down with them.

4

If I had to describe my wife's most inherent qualities as a human being, I can instantly recall three. Apart of course from her raven-haired good looks, one would have to be her natural capacity to display a magnetic and infectious love and affinity for other people. She just drew them in. Even strangers would feel like they had known her most of their lives after half an hour in her company. She had "time for everybody; even life's poor misfits," was how Blaise Maher frequently described her daughter's ability to bring out the best in some of the local oddballs. She just loved company, anybody's company, zooming in on their strengths and affections and quickly striking up a conversation, careful always to respect their disputes and problems, but equally unhesitating when the cue came to make them laugh. And, boy, did they laugh!

The sound of Neasa's laughter was contagious. There were nights I laughed for ten minutes, not sure what I was laughing at but aware that my stomach was in a knot and my ribs ached. There were times when I wished I could have bottled her laughter and the magic feeling of wellbeing she instilled, and the tangible elation that her public persona left in its wake, and kept it for later, releasing it into the atmosphere when things weren't so happy.

Murt Quigley, owner of The Bridge Bar for twenty-eight years – the third Murt to inherit the business in a long line of Quigleys – was always delighted to see Neasa Maher arrive in of a cold winter's night when the bar would be quiet and the few old men who had been there since lunchtime would be reluctant to stay. Her father, Joe Pa, would have kept an empty stool for her beside him. Murt would put up a large bottle of cider from the cooler – on the house – and Neasa would strike up her routine, with her accents and impersonations, and her Gloria Gaynor and Frank Sinatra songs – singing with an empty cola bottle to her lips – and a quick flirting jibe at each of the boozers who sat around her like flies around shite, aping old Battie Cleary in the corner sucking on his pipe, and Dimmy Neville, who had lost his dentures two weeks before, vomiting into a toilet bowl in the gents. Planting a kiss on Dimmy's cheek as he yawned, she told him that he looked like a corpse she had just laid out below in the hospital that morning. Eventually her mother would phone the bar and tell her that her father's dinner was ready. Neasa would finish her cider and give the old man a crossbar home.

To an outsider this behaviour might have seemed

erratic, but in Claddagh Mines Neasa Maher was regarded as a modern-day Florence Nightingale, the personification of virtue: a felicitous, big-hearted angel, who never had a bad word to say about anybody. I attributed this strange behaviour to her experiences of growing up in a house full of freaks.

And let's face it, Claddagh Mines never saw many strangers. I was to be the first in years.

The other characteristic that stands out in my mind, and will remain there till the day I die, no doubt leading on from this sad upbringing, was her affinity – mainly in private – to hate. A passion that possessed her, on occasions making her resemble a vicious animal, with an unprovoked talent, usually on a whim, for destroying you with a look that spelled revulsion, followed by a couple of well-chosen words that always succeeded in rapid annihilation. It was a knack she was proud of, a quickness she had perfected into a fine art over many years. It became a dangerous weapon she eventually lost control of; and one I saw for the first time over Christmas dinner: my one and only Christmas Day spent with the Mahers. It was an experience, like so many from a nightmarish litany, I will never forget.

* * *

Joe Pa might as well have been sitting at the head of the table that evening. Blaise Maher held a running conversation with the empty chair to my right, in between serving up the different courses, while Pius threatened to go up to Turloch's bedroom and get his .38 and blow Canice's head "clean fucking off" for pulling his cracker with Blaise.

"They're your father's favourite, them mince pies, so they are," Blaise said, nodding to the empty chair, bearing the well-worn cushion that had supported Joe Pa's lazy, fat arse for almost forty years.

She seemed oblivious to the lethal game being played out at the other end of the table.

"You don't believe me, do you, ye fuckin' alcoholic," Pius shouted at his older brother.

Canice laughed and gloated, waving the intact Christmas cracker in front of him, a pint glass half-full of Johnnie Walker malt whisky in the other. "I'd like to see ye try it, ye little spastic. You wouldn't know which end of the fuckin' gun to hold. You'd probably end up shootin' yourself in the forehead."

Turloch laughed as he manoeuvred the leg of the turkey into the left-hand cavity of his mouth, sucking and chewing, occasionally stopping to lick and rub his bushy moustache.

"What are you laughin' at, Turloch Pa? You're meant to be stickin' up for me," Pius spat, close to tears. "I swear to Jesus, Canice, if I bring the gun down here, they'll be wipin' the few brains you have off that fuckin' wall until Mammy takes down the Christmas tree."

"Jesus, did youse all hear that? Pius Maher has the

cheek to slag off my brains. Sure weren't you born with a hollow fuckin' head, not a brain cell in sight?" Canice pointed to the decoration-laden shrub in the corner of the room. "Why don't you start by shooting that fuckin' tree? It's the worst-looking heap of shite I've ever seen. I bet ye Sammy Toolin had that in the back of his shop since last Christmas, saw me poor fuckin' mother comin' a mile off, barely widowed, and robbed her, the miserable bastard."

"The gun's up in the drawer beside the bed. The bullets are in me leather jacket," Turloch Pa said calmly and nonchalantly in between mouthfuls of meat and stuffing. "Put it back when you're finished."

Pius stood up and kicked his chair back.

"Pius, get me more gravy like a good love if you're going out to the kitchen, pet," Blaise Maher smiled. "And don't be arguing with your brother. It's Christmas Day."

Pius left the room without saying anything and banged the door behind him. I looked across the table at Neasa as I listened to the creaking floorboards on the stairs, then the footsteps on the landing, then banging wooden drawers. "He wouldn't, would he?"

Neasa nodded and sighed, as if she had seen it all played out before. I watched the others. Blaise was trying to pick a hair off the tip of her tongue with her thumb and index finger. Canice was finishing off his whisky and Turloch Pa was stretching back in the chair, aligning himself for one of his famous, filthy after-dinner belches. The sound of the fast footsteps was closing in again now. I appeared to be the only one in the house who was giving the prospect of murder a top priority in the scheme of things.

The door swung open slowly. I could see the barrel of the gun, nothing else. Pius stepped forward and walked slowly towards the table and the back of Canice's head.

"Jesus Christ," were Blaise Maher's only words. She made the sign of the cross, then put her hand to her throat and held it there.

Turloch sat forward in his chair and brought his outstretched arms to table level. "Put it down, lad," he tutored his youngest brother.

"Fuck off," Pius replied, as he stood motionless and adamant, the tip of the gun's barrel a hair's breadth from the base of Canice's skull.

Canice sat frozen, the empty glass inches from his lips. "Jesus, Pius. *Please!* I'm sorry. Please don't shoot me."

I had always been useful with words, always assimilating situations, describing silently to myself interesting scenarios, digesting new experiences. I put it down to my short time as a trainee teacher with that newborn hunger to observe and learn. That afternoon, though, words failed me for the first time.

Time stood still in Blaise Maher's household that Christmas Day, over the turkey and ham and seven neatly-placed mince pies, each one alongside a shiny red Christmas cracker on each side plate. The decidedly dubious future of one of those crackers was now determining whether a young man would live or die. And he chose to play the game out further by putting down his empty glass and picking up the offending cracker yet again, in a fiddly sort of way, and pretending to pull both ends.

"You'll never do it, Pius. You don't have the guts to shoot me," Canice said with short breaths. "Turloch will lose his job in the cops. You're gonna go to prison. And Mammy won't come and visit you."

"What the fuck do you care? You'll be dead." The sound of sheer determination in Pius's voice made me close my eyes and clench my jaws with fear. The silence was palpable, like a gnawing toothache that eventually wears you down, as they both goaded each other on.

What happened next would change my life forever.

Neasa calmly stood up as if going to the bathroom, distracting Pius. She walked around to his side of the table and politely held out her hand. "Give it to me."

Pius shook his head.

"Give it to me," she said again, slightly louder and more deliberate this time.

Pius relaxed his grip and dropped his hand. He held out the gun and sighed softly. "Sorry."

Neasa carefully took the gun. Then, in the passing of a split second, she pushed him backward over the backstop of the armchair beside the fireplace. His legs were up in the air now, his head almost touching the ground. She followed him over the back of the chair, straddling him now, with a look of sheer disgust and revulsion in her eyes. She bent forward, careful not to lose her balance, and grabbed him by the cheek, forcing the top of the barrel into his mouth.

"How dare *you* spoil my Christmas dinner? Do you know how much arse-licking I had to do down at that fucking hospital to get today off? I've got to work New Year's Eve and every day for the next three weeks just so that I could spend today with my husband and daughter and you think you can spoil it just like that? Well, here," she grabbed his jaws and squeezed harder, "let's just see if this spoils your Christmas." She plunged the barrel of the gun deeper into the back of his mouth, until Pius started to gag, and pulled the trigger. We all jumped with the hollow click, with that same vicious snap of muscular shock that sends the body into an instantaneous spasm, sending plates and cutlery crashing. Blaise Maher screamed. Turloch cursed at the top of his voice. Canice knocked over his bottle of whisky. There was no loud bang. Just an earth-shattering click, and a childish, dog-like yelp from Pius, whose wide-stretched, bloodshot eyes stared into a space on the ceiling and then squeezed shut with tears as he pissed in his trousers.

Meanwhile, my one-month-old daughter, Molly – like the Nativity scene in the small crib beside her travel cot close to the warm hearth – gurgled and slept peacefully through the blind-drunk, earth-shattering consternation that followed, a scene that would earmark Christmas for all of us for many years to come. All of us except Neasa.

5

Logan airport on Thanksgiving Day looked like a huge, colourfully decorated ballroom that had just been evacuated; and someone had left all the lights on long after the party had ended and all the invited guests gone home. It bore all the trademarks of a warm peaceful haven that had witnessed a million tearful welcome-homes: a place that had counted thousands of passionate kisses and warm embraces, and intimate moments that had waited a whole year to burst out and couldn't wait any longer.

That was yesterday, I thought to myself, trying to configure my here and now, and what I could only imagine I was heading for, but the arrivals hall had somehow managed to retain a tiny whiff of that priceless moment when it comes to throwing your arms around someone who has been in the forefront of your thoughts and on the cusps of your heart for weeks before, and that indescribable anticipation of seeing them again after so long. How would they have changed? Will it be easy to spot them? Will they like their gifts? What did they get me? Why do I have to stay away so long when every year I promise them I'll make the journey every other month? It should have been what I was feeling. But in the departures hall that night there were no words of encouragement or reassurance for this reluctant passenger – no magic to relieve the dead weight of sadness, and the uncertainty of what lay ahead.

Small groups were squatting in corners, while young couples hugged and replaced damp tissues with fresh ones. One woman went hysterical as her boyfriend peeled himself away from her like pulling Velcro apart, and waved to her as he disappeared into the official boarding area beyond the point of no return.

The heating had been switched off. It made sense. There was only a handful of us waiting to board EI134, the 20.10 overnight service to Shannon, and a couple of cleaners mopping and muttering something about the overtime not being worth a sod.

"Happy holiday," one of them said to us as Karen kissed my chin and rubbed my arms, and sniffed and shivered. I was never one for long goodbyes; and since so much had been left unsaid, the atmosphere was brittle.

"I'll see you on Tuesday," she said with a tinge of resentment in her voice, intended as a protest because she couldn't come with me.

I kissed her on the lips and took my cue from the woman checking the tickets who nodded to me discreetly. "I love you," I said with as much warmth as I could muster.

"Do you?" she asked almost hopelessly, without changing that distant expression she'd used to punish me with all day because, she had claimed, I was holding back.

She was right. I had so much to tell her but I knew it had to be said in such a way that Karen McQuillan might still see some reason for loving me after she found out what had driven me to America in the first place.

* * *

I asked the woman checking my ticket what type of plane we would be travelling in. "An Airbus A330," she replied.

I froze. "Don't they use the Jumbo any more?"

"Not since I joined the company," she replied, in a conciliatory tone I am sure she reserved for silly passengers with ridiculous questions, like: "Have you ever seen a leprechaun?" Or: "Do only Irish people have freckles?"

I felt a stab of embarrassment. "I see," I replied.

I hadn't flown since I left Ireland, having decided that the next time I would return home would inevitably be for Molly's wedding. There were no other reasons for returning. At least none that bore thinking about. I had arrived in America on a gigantic Boeing 747 and simply assumed that the jets I looked up at in the late-night sky above Nantucket Sound, forty minutes out of Kennedy, as they climbed to their cruising altitude, on the start of their journeys across the world, were all Jumbos. I was concerned now. I had never been a good traveller and the notion of a flying-bus was making me very uneasy.

* * *

I tried to concentrate on thoughts of Molly as I packed my duty-free into the overhead locker, checking right and left to see if I could determine the back *and* front of the aircraft with one visual sweep. I could, just about. Nice thoughts weren't coming too easy. Instead I was creating a pageant of all the nice things a father might encourage his sick daughter to think of, to take her mind off the pain and the fever. I imagined her as a small child like I remembered her. The time she fell off Tom Brady's low garage roof, while refusing to come in for her dinner, and fractured her collarbone. I sat up with her that entire night, humming to her, promising her the pain would go away. "Any minute now," I kept on telling her. It amazed me how she trusted me to take away the pain. "I'll always love you the most, Daddy," she said to me. Despite the excruciating pain she was still able to tell me that I meant more to her than anything.

I turned my head to wipe my eyes, careful not to let any of the flight attendants see me.

A steady boyfriend popping the question and sweeping her off her feet seemed like an incomprehensible notion, mainly because marriage and happiness didn't come as an all-inclusive package for me. Consequently, while I wanted my daughter to find someone as kind – as I liked to think I was most of the time – and easy-going as I was, I always felt that I must have been partly to blame somewhere along the line for my short, but shocking, foray into marriage. I said a silent prayer to my mother and father, something I hadn't done for a long time, that she was having a peaceful night wherever she was, while, at the same time, I tried not to dwell on the possible consequences of what she had done or why she had done it.

My deep-rooted cynicism had never let me believe in the power of prayer so the sight of a young, attractive nun walking towards me I put down to pure coincidence. She seemed to be walking in my direction for ages. Something told me each time I looked up that she was going to sit down right next to me. I reasoned that there must have been some fifty empty seats around me and that, surely, she would prefer the extra legroom and privacy that tonight's flight would afford to all of us. Six hours in the company of a nun. I froze and picked an empty seat for her and imagined her sitting there.

She smiled and sat down beside me.

6

Blaise Maher stood in the doorway, adopting her usual statuesque pose – straight-backed and broad-shouldered – as the car drew up. She was a large woman with a round, rosy-coloured face, an addictive personality and a huge, infectious smile whenever she wanted you to like her. During the last few years that I knew her, shortly after Joe Pa's death, a form of depression had taken a firm hold on her, manifesting itself in the form of panic attacks, obsessive behaviours, and a type of agoraphobia that caused the woman terrible anxiety. As a result she stayed indoors a lot.

I was quite surprised that she should afford me a real quick wave and a broad smile as I fiddled to get the key out of the ignition. I watched her scrutinise the car, maintaining her cheesy grin as a thousand questions flooded her mind. I couldn't decide whether to tell her it was hired, or that I had bought it with cash as soon as I had got off the plane.

I didn't want her to approach the car until I got out. I needed a few seconds just to get used to this place again. Now that I was back, it hit me just how long the years had really been, remembering that the woman standing in front of the bonnet now was partly responsible for trying to destroy my life back then, calling me "a selfish, good-for-nothing, feckless bastard" the day before I left to begin a new life in Boston on my own, then spitting in my face when I courteously went to kiss her goodbye.

Now she was standing over me, her huge frame blocking out the beautiful mid-morning November sunshine. I had anticipated on and off, since leaving Shannon shortly after eight that morning, what her first words would be. I was wrong.

"Can I help you with anything?" she asked, with all the patience of a missionary addressing a bunch of pagans reluctant to convert.

I stepped out of the car. "I've only got the one bag, thanks."

"Only the one? I thought you'd have been stopping longer," she said smugly.

A direct hit before I had even a chance to catch my breath. I breathed deeply, reminding myself of the decision I'd made on the plane: I wasn't going to let her get to me. "What's that supposed to mean?" I asked calmly.

She quit smiling and tutted loud. "I would have thought you'd be staying for a good while."

"I *intend* to stay for as long as it takes."

48

"As long as *what* takes?"

I had almost forgotten how brilliant she was at her deadly mind games. "As long as it takes for Molly to get better."

"And then what? I suppose you'll disappear off again to yer fancy Yanky woman back in *Cape Cod*, or wherever it is you've been hiding away all these years. And leave us to look after her." She grabbed my bag out of my hand and walked back to the door. "I can barely remember how long it's been since you'd just gone . . . eight, nine . . . ten, twenty years . . . what's the difference? Sure who's counting at this stage? I don't think Molly even remembers the last time she saw you. And *you're* her father? I'm surprised you bothered to come back at all. God love that poor wee thing. I'm not surprised she's so confused."

"And when was the last time you saw her?" I asked.

She turned and stared me in the eyes, as if ready to correct me. Or hit me – I wasn't sure. "Last night, actually. *And* the one before that. Neasa and I took it in shifts. I went up during the evening. She set out early and spent the day with her."

She waited, looking out over the hilly-green rolling countryside above the small church and the tiny graveyard where Joe Pa was laid to rest, to see if I was willing to better that: to spark up a challenge. I wasn't. Those days were long gone. "I've just made some lunch." She disappeared into the house.

"How is she?" I asked, scanning the meticulously set table, laid for three.

"Who? Molly or Neasa?"

"Molly."

"She seems to be stable. Doctors say she's off the critical list. She was moved out of intensive care, thank God, into a nice room of her own. I brought up some fresh flowers from the florist's below. They've brightened up the room. I told the sister we'd take her down here for a few weeks when she's ready to come home until she's fully better. The fresh air and the open space will do her good."

"It didn't do me any good." I hadn't intended saying it. The words just came.

"We're not going to talk about the past, David."

It was the first time I'd heard her speak my name. Her words were filled with sensitive, interminable suffering and hostility. I could tell she wanted me to forget about all that had happened, and to sit down and admire her china and tell her how good her home-baking was, as always, as if nothing had happened. The concept that she was deigning to give me a second chance angered me. But now that I was back again, I was adamant that I was going to sort out my life, complete with all its drama and heartache and loose ends, once and for all, even if it killed me.

"I'm taking Molly back to the States with me," I said softly, my voice unwavering.

She almost dropped the teapot. "But you can't!"

"Why can't I?"

"Because she belongs here." She put the teapot on the table and, sitting opposite me, turned the china teacup and placed it gently in its matching saucer, as if she had carefully rehearsed it all before I arrived.

I was getting increasingly uneasy, almost panicky. I wanted to leave, drive to Dublin. I just wanted to be with Molly, more than anything. "Where's Neasa?"

"She just nipped to the shop for a card. The room was a bit bare last night when we were leaving."

"Leaving? Why didn't she stay with Molly?"

"Because she was tired."

I didn't hear the front door opening. When I looked around I almost didn't believe that the woman standing in the hall was Neasa. For a moment I couldn't comprehend how someone could physically change herself so radically that she was almost beyond recognising. Neasa Maher had reinvented herself.

She smiled as if she was about to be introduced for the first time. "Hello," she said, almost distrustfully.

I said nothing, just searched for signs of the old Neasa. Her hair was reddish brown, instead of jet black, more cropped now than its usual long, tossed style. Her face was thinner, her cheekbones more prominent, and her eyes deeper-set and sharper than I could remember. She seemed thinner overall, almost taller. "You look different," I said, continuing to inspect. "Do I look that different?" I asked curiously, baffled by how someone could change so utterly. I reminded myself that she was almost forty. Yet, with the afternoon sunshine pouring into the square-shaped hallway behind her, she could have passed for twenty-nine, thirty. She looked beautiful,

51

but the changes weren't natural. I was standing before an individual who had undergone a serious, carefully planned transformation. And I could tell it hadn't happened yesterday.

"Do *I* look that different?" she asked.

"Yes." My smile made me nervous. I couldn't help but feel that this was some sort of set-up. "Can we get going?" I asked. "I really want to see Molly. How is she?"

"Sick." Neasa studied me intensely, cramming everything in like last-minute homework. "How are you?"

"I'm good. At least, I was."

"I'll leave the two of you to get your lunch," Blaise Maher said as she adjusted her winter coat. "I'm just popping up to your daddy with a few flowers. I'll be back in twenty minutes." She was about to open the front door when she hesitated and turned. "David says he's going to bring Molly back to America with him."

"Did he?" Neasa kept staring at me. "Ah sure, he's a bit upset. I'm sure he doesn't know what to make of all this."

The front door closed. The silence of the house was broken by the slow, familiar ticking noise of Joe Pa's ancient grandfather clock. The snail-slow chomping sound of the ticking reminded me of the old clock Karen had never been able to sell in The Whippletree, taking up space at the back of the old barn all those months I was getting to know her.

Right now that memory felt like it belonged to another lifetime a million light-years away.

7

To this day I still don't know why I went to the graveyard that afternoon. Perhaps it was the suffocating closeness of a woman I had never wanted to see again that drove me out of the house to "stretch my legs," as I told Neasa in the most pleasant voice I could muster. We had nothing to say to each other, nothing in common whatsoever. So I had to get away from her – just to settle my mind: to allow it to acclimatise to accepting that she was going to be a part of my life again for a short period. As short as was humanly possible, if it was up to me.

Maybe it was just to look around the small, sleepy village I had fled for fear of losing my life some ten years earlier. It seemed this afternoon that that war had ended a long time ago. This could have been any market town anywhere. And I was just a visitor passing through, stopping to admire how the locals had taken a keen interest in beautifying their little village. There was nothing to remind me of how the locals had run me out of town that night, nothing physical to remind me of those dark days. But the atmosphere had remained the same.

I passed a woman outside the small minimart, Toolin's as it was back then. Now it was ValueMart, with a shopfront so colourful it would light up a small street. She was pushing her buggy, another small child in tow. I said hello, wondering if she would recognise me. She didn't obviously. I was just another of the many daily salesmen that the roaring economy brought to Claddagh Mines. I stood aside to let her pass on the narrow path and held my breath.

The town had changed: a metamorphosis that can only come about with wealthy newcomers, and strong investment in an infrastructure that only existed because people had stuck together and refused to let their small, inconsequential town disappear into the huge shadow of the mountain range it grew out of. Claddagh Mines was like a bothersome, recurring wart that kept drawing attention to itself on an otherwise low-ranking section of the body of everyday life. Houses were brightly painted. The parked cars signalled prosperity. I counted eight with the most recent registrations, all high-powered, gleaming saloons. Much as I hate the word, "cosmopolitan" rang through; even in this small outback town – population no more than two hundred – buried deep in a mountain range no one in Oak Bluffs had ever heard of.

I strolled past the church, its cold, granite walls recently stonewashed. The curates' houses – all three of them – were private dwellings now, redecorated and sold off, I gathered. They looked like family homes now. The parish priest lived on the other side of the church wall, in the hallowed ground that gave him respect and infallibility in the eyes of his people.

I stopped walking and dug my hands deep into my pockets to shield myself against the bitter northwesterly wind that whipped across the mountainside.

I could see Blaise Maher from the small green gate in the cold shadow of the grey edifice, her arse to me, huddled over the grave at the top of the winding, stony footpath, weeding, and then smoothing the small grey pebbles, as if they had just been laid hours before. The grave bore the remains of Maud Durkin, one of the friendliest and funniest, most pleasant, unselfish women I have ever met. She was also destined to become the saddest, most ill-fated citizen of Claddagh Mines ever. Her sadness eventually became too much for her to bear.

The priest spoke to a packed church from the pulpit the Sunday morning she was laid to rest. He told them that Maud Durkin had died of a broken heart. Life had become meaningless for her without her little Owen and she had gone to find him in God's care.

* * *

All the way across the Atlantic night-time sky I had kept so many painful memories at bay, refusing to entertain the past like some group of awkward distant relations who feel obliged to gatecrash your privacy each Christmas morning and spoil your precious holiday with their rankling conversation and disapproving observations. Now the carload of menacing faces had just rung my doorbell.

* * *

News of an Irish death has its own unique means of transporting itself around the world at varying degrees of speed and accuracy, depending on how well you knew the deceased. I didn't know Maud Durkin well, so she was dead a good two years before a tourist to Martha's Vineyard broke the news to me in The Meadows late one afternoon. I passed it off as one of life's certainties, saying something stupid like: she had a good innings! I excused myself and went into the back of the store and cried for almost half an hour. Maud Durkin had not received a good innings by any stretch of the imagination. She had endured a shit life. But I wasn't crying for Maud. The tears were for Owen, her thirteen-year-old son.

* * *

I can still see him at the back of the classroom, his bright red crop of hair mischievously ducked down behind

Jude Moran. No matter how often I moved him to the front row, he would have carefully manoeuvred his way to the back of the room in ten minutes. The rest of the children marvelled at his stealth. His brazen pluckiness and audacity made them jittery, so much so that they knew not to laugh out loud as he crept on all fours, under the furniture, from desk to desk, using a straight line of feet and ankles to cling on to and get back to "Owen Durkin's desk" as it became known throughout the school.

He wasn't a particularly attractive child with his freckled face and protruding buck teeth, and a huge egg-shaped head that made his wiry red hair look like a badly fitted wig. The dentist had applied a tamper-free brace, but Owny, as only his inner sanctum of apprentice bullies knew him, had managed to prise it free and flush it down a school toilet only hours after his mother had entered an instalment arrangement to pay for the appliance with the dentist. Now he was an even greater hero in the eyes of a class full of terrorised boys and girls who lived in a haunted twilight of fear and intimidation because they knew that Owen Durkin would "come and sort them" if they didn't live their lives to his liking.

Owen Durkin was the arch-bully of Claddagh Mines National School, a position he relished with great fervour. He was a dictator to forty-three students and ruled with an iron hand. His academic performance could only be described as brutal. On the other hand, his power and ability to scheme and manipulate and persuade and rouse was pure second to none: in short, pure evil. He capitalised on people's sympathy shown towards him. He realised early on that Claddagh Mines' folk felt sorry for him. He milked it for all it was worth. He made two hundred and eighty-four pounds on the day of his first Holy Communion, well in excess of anyone else's wildest dreams. For his confirmation he added another three hundred to the money he had deposited in the post office. When he tired of checking on the interest he was assured would be added annually to his account, he threw one of his famous tantrums in front of his mother and Nellie Gargan, the post office clerk, demanding to withdraw the lot. When he was told it would take ten working days to withdraw any amount over five hundred pounds for security reasons, he stormed out of the shop. Later that night the post office and the adjacent shop burned to the ground.

Owen Durkin was possibly the greatest networker I have ever encountered. It wasn't until long after I had settled in the United States and undertaken a network-marketing course to benefit our new bookstore that I learned more about this ingenious thirteen-year-old's penetrating powers over others – some of his admirers were three times his age.

For a bully to succeed he must be liked and his behaviour approved of on a wide scale – not just among his so-called friends but also among his peers. Owen Durkin was a certified Class A student at perfecting his pastime. No one crossed Owen Durkin a second time. They would come back from their experience with a new outlook and a greater allegiance to the boy they called "cool out".

His revenge tactics were savage and shocking, each serving needing to better the one dealt out before. As teacher in charge of Class 6.1 in Saint John the Apostle Primary School, Claddagh Mines, the admission that I didn't do enough to nip this "tomfoolery" in the bud, as one of my colleagues called it in the staffroom one morning, and prevent the traumatic damage and bitter resentment that followed was enough to haunt me for years of long nights after I left Ireland.

Owen Durkin's litany of reprisals ran into pages; most of them, when compared to the two ultimately savage attacks that he launched one autumn morning, two days after returning to school, could best be described as tasteless jokes. Unfortunately, his idea of a tasteless joke quickly leapt beyond the realms of acceptability.

Jacob Horgan was one of 6.1's best students, good-looking, softly spoken, well turned out and Protestant. For some reason Owen Durkin took exception to the young boy's religious background, and to the attention he received from the young girls in the school, and started to rob his lunch box on a daily basis. This went unnoticed for weeks until his mother met me at the school gates one morning. She was holding the lunch box. She handed it to me. I opened it. Its contents spilled over my hand and soaked my jacket sleeve and trousers. The stench was instantly recognisable. Urine. The lunch box had been filled to the brim with urine.

"If you don't do something about that little Durkin bastard, my husband will!" was all she said in her soft southern English accent.

Word had circulated long before my arrival in class. Mr Freeman was covered in pee. Owen Durkin didn't perform any of his attention-seeking stunts that day. Maybe he knew he had pushed just a little too hard. Then again, maybe he knew that he had proved his point.

The night I eventually cracked, consigning my famous laid-back demeanour to the past, came when Molly, our eleven-year-old daughter, didn't arrive home from school. The evenings were beginning to draw in – a thin dusk was settling earlier.

Molly had a punctilious routine: she would show up straight from school about three, have a late lunch, finish her homework and head for a friend's house until seven, the time Neasa insisted she was home by on a school night. That evening I had to go to a regional meeting of teachers and parents in Thurles. We had been campaigning to get a Careers Guidance Administrator assigned to the area and I was keen that she should visit Saint John's once a month. It was after ten when I arrived home. Neasa was hysterical. Blaise Maher had made enough tea and sandwiches to feed the reserve forces of the Irish army and had built a fire in the grate big enough to light up a dark hangar. Two of Neasa's brothers had been summoned from The Bridge Bar and were sprawled across two armchairs, pouring neat whiskey for each other each time one of them took a sip from his glass.

Molly usually visited Jude Moran's house. Jude's mother said she had never arrived that day. I called the police. They told me to give it another few hours. Midnight hour marked panic stations, as far as they were concerned. After that they were into a new day. Then they would consider her as a missing person. At five-to-eleven, I heard the key in the front door. I tore out into the hall and grabbed my chest and gasped at the vision that greeted me. Molly's eyes were red and swollen, her lips and jaws blue from the cold. That aside she still looked unusually different, utterly unlike her usual trendy self. I froze. It was her hair. Or lack of it, I should say.

Molly's beautiful, naturally curly, shoulder-length auburn hair that she took such young-womanly pride in was gone – completely vanished; in its place was a cropped mop, spiky and unevenly hacked. A blob of green dye streaked across one side of her head and down over her ear and jacket shoulder, as if she had been branded like a heifer. She couldn't talk, just shook and mumbled. And sobbed. Neasa pushed me aside and stepped into the hall. I tried to block her view but couldn't. She passed out. I panicked, tried to pick up the phone and dropped it, knocking over the small coffee table it sat upon.

I grabbed Molly and hugged her, squeezing her till I heard her crying into my overcoat. "It's OK," I kept whispering to her, looking down through her thin hair at her scratched, bleeding scalp. "It's OK, it's OK," I kept saying, marking time by rocking her and gently patting her poor, sore bare head nervously, waiting for her to say it *was* OK. But it wasn't OK.

Our little patchwork existence that we strove to make ourselves believe was a happy family unit would never be the same again after that awful night.

* * *

When I think back now on that moment in time when the gates of some hell opened up for a brief spell and gave us a glimpse inside, I still remember counting the cuts on her scalp and her neck where the scissors had cut deep, and smelling the pungent mixture of wet dye and the sweat of sheer terror. She disappeared into her bedroom with her mother. That was the last I saw of them until breakfast the next morning.

Molly sat at the table with a black skullcap on her head and a grey scarf wrapped around her neck. Her face was pale, her eyes roaring red-raw, and her voice hoarse. She reminded me of someone who was undergoing chemotherapy and had lost all of her beautiful hair and her self-respect and the dignity that goes with such a gentle commodity. Someone had robbed Molly's place at the table that morning, crept in and possessed her body like an unhappy spirit. It seemed like her will to live that morning had gone with the familiar tresses.

"How are you feeling?" I asked, pushing a bowl of porridge towards her.

She ignored the food. "I want to kill myself," she whispered softly. There was no anger, just pain, and a sadness I had never before seen in her.

I never again saw my daughter's old form: her corny little 'knock knock' jokes over breakfast, her bribes to get me to help her with her algebra and theorems; her expressive conversations over dinner that had me cracking up with laughter, her baffling theories on boyfriends and current news stories and her unique perception of life through the eyes of an inquiring, delightful, radiant eleven-year-old who wanted to be a grown-up woman; the future when she would "burn her schoolbooks for the last time and be free" and be a nurse like her mother; and most of all, the way she would collapse on top of me on the big settee every night for the last half-hour before she went to her bed. She would lock her arms around my neck until my shoulder muscles ached. But I never complained because I knew she loved me and needed me, and I wanted to think that someday she would bring as much happiness to a lucky young man somewhere as she brought to me so often throughout every day, but most of all in those final few moments before sleep offered her a chance to dream about beautiful places and wonderful people.

It was all gone. She had changed overnight, as if some putrid pervert had taken away her beautiful innocence while she went about her important business of enjoying the trustfulness and nescience of her essential, impenetrable world and what it should mean to be eleven years old. And happy.

I had always been a here-and-now sort of person, choosing subconsciously I suppose to live my life in the present, and never paying much heed to what went before and what we could expect after in the by-and-by. I always just got on with it, whatever it may have been, and tried to keep it simple. But late that night, hours after I had gone to bed and still couldn't sleep, I knew that whatever we had as a family 'before' was gone forever; we were now living, whether we wanted to or not, in that 'after' period that for many years to come I simply referred to as limbo.

8

Owen Durkin never answered during roll-call that morning. That was quite common. As usual I announced his name twice. An awkward silence made me look up.

His hands covered his face. His fingers were trembling. I watched him for a moment. His whole body was shaking. I shouted his name viciously. As he lowered one of his hands, I could tell he had been watching me between his fingers. *"Drop the other hand,"* I shouted.

His right hand clattered against the desktop. His ear looked red and swollen. A small red gash above his right eye had caused his eyelid to swell slightly. He stared at me, then looked away and shivered.

I remember whispering "little shit" when I called his name out a second time, wishing he had never existed.

It's not unreasonable for a teacher to hate a pupil. It

was dealt with briefly in training college, skimmed over –
like the emergency procedures prior to a passenger jet's
departure – then brushed aside quickly, like depression
and alcoholism. Claddagh Mines was a town built on
both such illustrious distinctions. The only occasion I
heard laughter during Sunday Mass was when our parish
priest advertised an inaugural meeting of Alcoholics
Anonymous in the school hall on Tuesday night; an open
meeting, he had called it. He might as well have
publicised a new leper colony. Disbelief was the reaction
of most of the congregation. Then the hilarity surfaced
when he urged families "to look deep within themselves,
and help the suffering boozer," as he put it so quaintly,
speaking as he did from experience. General George
Custer and his men died waiting for the US Cavalry to
come and save them. Custer had a better chance of
catching arrows with his right hand than AA had of
reforming the bad habits of Claddagh Mines.

The men of Claddagh Mines drank in The Bridge
Bar, and discussed with each other how their wives
didn't understand. They never specified what the
women couldn't cotton on to; they just "don't see
daylight" they all regularly agreed. The women drank
at home, secretly, and suffered their depression and
rejection unobserved, while their children were baby-
minded and prepared for the world beyond Claddagh
Mines by good old, reliable David Freeman.

Hating one of your pupils didn't mean you were
unsuitable for the job, the psychologist informed us

during our Higher Diploma year. "It simply requires a period of reassessment and perseverance."

I took the job to be near Neasa. By the end of my first term, I knew I had made a big mistake. Out of a class of twenty-three eleven-year-olds and one thirteen-year old that year, most of my pupils were above average performers, so different to many of their parents. Two of them were dyslexics, a problem I dealt with; another was a dreamer with the intellect of a university honours graduate, who did nothing but talk. And two others suffered from attention-deficit hyperactivity disorder, ADHD: Aidan Ferris and Owen Durkin, notorious around the school and town because of their brazen-faced boldness. In fairness, it should be said that Durkin was the ringleader. I often suspected that Aidan Ferris would have been more manageable and behave accordingly if it hadn't been for his older conspirator.

Owen Durkin was two years older than the rest of the class. He had been reprimanded so often, he was then kept back on two occasions at the end of the curriculum year. Like a dangerous, neglected, out-of-bounds beehive at the bottom of a neighbour's overrun back garden, the children were drawn to him to see what he was going to do next.

I started my 'hating' of Owen Durkin two years before when he stuck a lump of softly chewed bubblegum into the door-lock of my car. I later found out that he'd held a small six-year-old girl down on the grounds behind the bicycle shed and pulled the chewing-gum from her mouth. When he couldn't force it all into the lock's appliance, he came looking for her and pushed the remaining mess into her left ear. She required hospitalisation. Molly told me later that year, when I asked her not to eat chewing-gum at the dinner table, that she never told her parents what had happened. I thought about confessing it to the priest one Saturday night after Mass. The notion of it as a topic for his Sunday morning sermon forced a change of heart.

Owen Durkin eventually dominated my every waking hour. Soon he was invading my dreams at night. If I dreamt I was visiting Inchidony Strand in West Cork, with Molly and Neasa for an imaginary weekend, he would appear in my trance as an ice-cream vendor, refusing to give Molly her change, or sticking his fingers into her ice-cream cone, or spitting at her. In another dream he was a rabid Alsatian holding our baby in his jaws.

I couldn't escape this recurring nightmare and couldn't ask for help. Claddagh Mines was a network of prying eyes, pointed ears and gossiping potato-traps. I hated it almost as much as I despised Owen Durkin.

At first I marvelled at how a small child could openly stand up in class and discuss an operation whereby he planned to rob the local post office some day when he was old enough to get a gun in Dublin. His scheme seemed meticulous right down to his getaway. I thought about it for days, trying to pick a loophole. There was none. And yet here was a child who couldn't grasp simple algebra or fractions, couldn't recall pieces of poetry and was never able to get more than five correct in a twenty-word spell test. His daily news pieces were usually so violent and far-fetched they scared me.

I concluded that the only way to remain mentally intact throughout those two years, since Owen Durkin came to my class, was to accept that the boy was beyond help, and to regularly remind myself that he would be someone else's problem in a very short time.

* * *

My thoughts and every sharpened corner of my senses were with my daughter that morning; my poor, miserable, soul-stolen, heartbroken little girl.

Molly sat in her desk, two in front of Owen Durkin's, both of them trembling: her teeth chattering, his shoulders shaking. I had asked so often if she'd prefer to go home. She kept shaking her head each time I stooped to whisper. Eventually she just looked away each time I tried to catch her attention. Her mother – and I use the expression to create a distance between us – insisted she went to school that morning. I tried to reason but she told me, with a bread knife in her hand as she cut slices of toast into quarters and slid them across the breakfast table like a master chef dicing an onion, to "stay out of this!" I took her advice. I shouldn't have.

Looking back now, I am convinced that my wife's mind snapped that morning. Whatever thin, tight chord holds our rational minds together had come undone.

Like all partners in a two-way relationship, I had become used to brushing small unevennesses aside, ignoring snide remarks that could develop into full-blown confrontations if challenged. I gave up giving as well as I got. I took the shit when I knew the alternative meant not being spoken to for days on end, and watching my daughter being told her father was an ignorant bollox or a selfish pig. But this morning she was different. And she had every reason to be. Our daughter had been violently assaulted. We all needed answers to questions that were devouring us; the insatiable fury required immediate support and dissolution, police intervention, sound advice, professional counselling.

But this was bordering on farcical. Neasa's behaviour was clearly irrational. She was behaving like someone who'd had far too much to drink. She was boisterous, fuming, nonsensical, angry, and absurd. She was deranged. Mad.

Molly had been terrorised enough. Now she was being menaced again by this livid, dotty woman who seemed, in the space of a few short hours, to have gone from questionably eccentric to psychotically possessed.

She pointed the bread knife at me, as I watched for Molly's reaction to her mother's ranting. "Eat that *fucking toast!*" she roared. "Do you think I'm some sort of *skivvy?*" Even from where she was standing I could feel the spray of her spit on my cheeks. "Let's get things moving. Hurry up, Molly, or you'll be late!"

I felt obliged to say something. "I still think you should take Molly to see the doctor."

The safety net seemed to snap. She threw the knife and plate of fresh toast slices hard on to the tiled floor. The clattering smash of thin delph on the hard hollow surface made me jump. She made a run at the table and slammed her fist down hard. *"For the last time, no doctor, no hospital, and no fucking police! I don't want them bastards knowing our business. We'll deal with this ourselves, in our own way. Is that clear?"*

She was making herself quite clear, but, no, *it* wasn't clear at all. A crime had been committed. The perpetrator-bastard was at large. He had to be caught. I looked at my daughter stifling the mixture of pain and tears – a horrendous black hole of questions-with-no-answers. She gasped to keep her composure, watching her mother behave like a lunatic. I wanted to scream, to throttle the stupid bitch, but I knew that what my daughter needed right there and then – what she had to get – was a semblance of some strange sort of normality, the kind that exists in the eye of a hurricane when all around you balance and rationality are waving goodbye and leaving you behind to sort out a hell that is destroying you more quickly than you can breathe; the sixth sense that seems to buffer our last grasp of sanity against the unimaginable consequences of losing our grip completely when our minds feel like they want to explode. I wasn't sure why. It just seemed right. Maybe it was my mother's spirit taking over and reaching out to

Molly through me, since the bedlamite standing at the cooker had just declared herself berserk.

To this day I know I should have made myself part of Neasa's half-baked, home-cooked, consolation therapy that took place that night in Molly's room. A lot of talking was done; a lot of hysterical crying, and many silences in between the frenzied bouts. Things were said and discussed – never to be repeated. Not even under coercion. Not ever, no matter what.

I can be honest now with myself and say that in September of that year, our house lost its composure, my daughter lost her will to live, my wife her sanity which had been questionable for a long time before; and me? Considering that I still find it difficult to piece together precisely the events of that day, it's fair to say I lost my family.

* * *

I often tried to intercede in Owen Durkin's mad moments of delinquency, always believing that if I continued to discipline him with detention and extra homework, he would eventually see the error of his ways; that sooner or later, he would realize that there was an easier life waiting for him if would only learn to behave himself.

He liked Molly, but in the most peculiar, hurtful way, I always felt. He taunted her, pulled her hair, tripped her up and ripped her homework copies to shreds. That was only what I had witnessed. God knows what else he did to her.

Then, on other occasions, with a remarkable candour, he would place a Mars bar on her desk in full view of the other pupils. I can vividly still recall the morning they were all in their usual class line waiting for 8.45am when I would open the school door. Owen walked up to Molly and kissed her on the cheek, and apologized at the top of his voice for hiding her schoolbag the previous afternoon. Molly, in turn, liked Owen; or liked him back, I always thought.

As for me, the more I watched Owen Durkin, the more I became convinced he was a conniving, devious little bastard who courted evil with his twisted little mind. And yet, in confrontational situations in the school yard, he always rushed to Molly's defence, threatening in his own words to "knock the shite out of anyone who goes near her".

With hindsight, I can see now he was like her big brother. He thwarted her but she felt obliged at times to like him enough to forgive him.

If only I had known then what I know now, I would never have confronted him that morning. As I tried to carry on normal class work, my mind kept throwing up the same memory.

Owen had been going through a period of chasing Molly. When he caught her he would lift up her skirt and try to pull down her woollen tights, much to the screams of delight from some of the other children.

Such child's play made me see red. So it was only to be expected that I should have assumed that Owen Durkin had a hand in whatever had happened to Molly that September night ten years ago.

For whatever reason, my patience snapped that morning. I think it must have been close to lunchtime when it started in me.

I asked Owen Durkin to step out into the corridor. He had been ignoring my questions and had refused to take out a maths book when I had told the rest of the class to do so.

Once outside, a raging temper seemed to overtake me. I grabbed Owen Durkin by the shoulder and was about to demand that he tell me what had happened the previous night. In a fraction of a second, Owen Durkin tripped over my foot and fell against a steel heating pipe. He started to bleed heavily, I wasn't sure from where.

My first reaction was to get him to Neasa. She was on a day off. She would clean up the wound and bandage it. He was going to be fine, I told myself. For a moment he just lay there, motionless. I lifted him up and repeatedly called out his name until he blinked and focused on me. "It was just an accident, Owen. I'm sorry," I kept on telling him. "Just a stupid accident, that's all. You're going to be just fine. We'll have you right in no time." I searched through his matted, red hair with my shaking hands for the source of the cut.

The children went for their lunch. I told them to be

back at the usual time. I was forcing myself now to regard it all as inevitable; it was something that could have happened to any teacher. "Just a stupid, careless, bloody accident," I said again.

Deep down, a sad, confused voice told me my life, as I knew it, was over.

* * *

It was almost quarter-to-three in the afternoon when Maud Durkin arrived at the classroom door. I had always liked the woman, and felt sorry for her that her son's behaviour had made her life in Claddagh Mines so miserable in recent years. But she soldiered on. Today I felt sorry for a different reason. "Yes?"

She seemed surprised.

"Sorry for bothering you, David. Is Owen there?"

She tried to look beyond me into the classroom. I blocked her view. "No."

She seemed confused. "It's just that when he didn't come home at lunchtime, I thought maybe he'd got himself into trouble again."

"He's not here." It was all I could say.

She stood there looking at me.

"He had a small bit of an accident earlier, just before lunch. He fell but he was fine." I tried so hard to make light of the situation. "Neasa bandaged him up and he was grand. I'm a bit surprised he didn't head home to you for his lunch."

Her eyes filled with tears. She was becoming more and more agitated.

"If you'll excuse me, I'll have to get back to this gang; we're in the middle of an English test." I smiled and closed the door. Jesus Christ, what am I after doing? I asked. I squeezed my eyes shut and breathed deeply. "Now, where were we?" I asked the class. They had all changed. They were frightened. So was I.

* * *

Our house was quiet that night.

I was stretched out on the settee, my legs bent so Molly could lean comfortably against them with her arm wrapped around my knees. We watched a celebrity DIY expert on the television decorating a stranger's attic for free. He took such care over joining up two strips of wallpaper. Then he faced the camera and cracked a joke: "I said to my wife last night after finishing our hall, stairs and landing, 'Did you hear about the gynaecologist who wallpapered his hall through the letterbox?' She said to me, 'No. How did he manage that?'" The TV crew cracked up laughing in the background, their mocking horse laugh giving the impression that this celebrity was married to a moron. I wondered if he was in love with his wife, and would she be angry with him for making her look like a complete bonehead on national television. Or was it all a front? A sham. Like mine.

It was after ten when I heard the rap of the doorknocker. It seemed a very precise double-strike. Then another, as if to support the first blow. It had been so long since anyone had used the knocker I'd forgotten we had one.

Two uniformed policemen stood outside on the porch, looking awkward and contrite. They said nothing as if I'd been expecting their call. One of them took his cap off. They both stared at me, like they were expecting me to say something. They seemed almost winded, the cool night adding puffs of steam to their uneven breathing.

Turloch Maher stood behind them, his hands in his pockets.

9

I could tell Blaise Maher knew I was standing there, but she didn't look around. "Beautiful day," she said, casting off the withered petals of the older flowers, then snapping the stems of the fresh ones to make them fit and placing them around the outside of the discoloured, chipped vase that sat at the base of the modest headstone. I studied the inscription:

~

In memory of Maud Durkin
Hacketstown, Claddagh Mines
1948 – 1994
Also, her late husband, Charlie,
1942-1985

It was the last line that made me look again.

Jesus, protect our little boy, Owen, 13 years,
Lost to us September 1990. May the angels
keep him safe.

He was a lost boy. Not dead. Not an angel, nor a spirit. Just lost, somewhere in between two worlds: the one he disappeared from that morning, and a place that we try to protect our children from until they rebel and demand to be let go. I thought for a moment before saying anything. Owen Durkin would be twenty-three now, having shared my daughter's birthday. My mind still debated whether he was alive or dead, opting for the latter now that so many years had gone by without a trace of the little red-haired bastard.

"Did he ever come back?"

"Who?" I could tell she found the question silly.

"Owen Durkin."

"Of course he hasn't come back."

"You make it sound like you're sure he's dead."

Blaise Maher stood up, straightened her skirt and turned to face me. The sun hurt my eyes. The jetlag made me unsteady on the sloping path. "Well, if he's dead, his mother's there to take care of him. And if he's not, God will look after him." Her words had a cautionary tone about them, as if she was warning me not to go there. But I needed to now, after all those years, and a three-and-a-half-thousand-mile trip. "He's dead, isn't he?"

"How would I know?" She looked back at the grave. "She was a lovely woman. She brought up that boy as best she could."

"Why don't you just say it?"

"Say what?"

"Why don't you just tell me what a terrible bastard I've been, and how my daughter wouldn't be in intensive care today if I'd been a better father to her and stayed at home to look after her."

"Well, she wouldn't, would she?" A tone of sheer control smothered the sunshine.

I smiled and regretted going to the graveyard. "We've been through all this, Blaise. It's good to know that I wasn't wrong all along." I turned and started to walk.

"Wasn't wrong about *what*?" she snapped.

I looked back and nodded to the hills and fields behind her. "I couldn't imagine life changing too much here. Not like it does in the real world out there. You know, even though he was only thirteen, maybe this place was the reason he bullied people. Maybe it was his way of rebelling against a stagnant little hole full of alcoholic, paranoid, depressed misfits. It drove him mad. *That's it!* Maybe he'd had enough and just wanted to get out."

"Why are you so concerned with something that happened ten years ago when your daughter is lying in a hospital bed after trying to kill herself? Is she not telling you something, David?" Her voice was full of resentment.

"Oh, I am concerned. Because I believe that my daughter's suicide attempt has everything to do with what *happened* ten years ago, Blaise. And whether you like it or not, we're all to blame. We all have blood on our hands."

"*What* is that supposed to mean?" she said indignantly.

"It means that if we had all done the right things for Molly that night, given her the love and affection she needed, instead of worrying about what the neighbours and the local cops might think, and looking after our own selfish needs, she might have recovered and she mightn't have had such a shit life since then; and it's very doubtful she would have taken a blunt potato-peeler on Wednesday and *hacked her wrists to shit!*" My voice echoed I was shouting so hard. "And, *yes*, she is trying to tell me something; something she might have told me ten years ago if it hadn't been for your intrusive meddling. I know all about the affair Maud Durkin had with the local sergeant. I saw his patrol car outside her house. I know that Owen wasn't Charlie Durkin's son. Charlie had jet-black hair. The sergeant's was carrot-orange, for God's sake. Jesus Christ, you didn't need a Masters in gynaecology to see that. It was so fucking obvious all along. Why do you think Charlie drank so much? The poor bastard."

"Stop, please!"

The tears welling up in Blaise Maher's eyes were full of suppressed guilt and shame. I could tell that. My late-night walks along the deserted Nantucket Sound, with my haunted thoughts of the past and the ghost of Owen Durkin to keep me company, looking for answers on the incoming tides, had convinced me that whatever she had connived to hide with her daughter would eventually seep out through the cracks that come with time; doing life and sharing your cell with a hefty burden of guilt and shame eventually drives you to confession. I reckoned it was bursting to escape now. And I needed to hear it. She sobbed and pulled a tissue from her sleeve. It wasn't the time, but I hoped that the seed had been sown. I needed answers in order to string my two lives together, the old one aligned, for once and for all, with my new one. And I didn't give a damn about the casualties that would result and the bodies I was going to trample over in order to succeed.

I hesitated for a nano-second, but knew it had to be put on record. I had waited for this moment for ten years. "My daughter was raped that night, wasn't she?" My question caused a domino effect – a chilling vacuum of dark silence – in that small cemetery that afternoon. The flowers and branches that rustled in the stiff breeze seemed to stall, and the sun disappeared behind a cloud. The wind was gone now. Time stood still, and would only start to move again when I heard the answer I had suspected for a long time; the same answer I would have got if only I had cornered my wife ten years ago as she came out of my daughter's bedroom to make her a cup of tea, and I had asked her . . .

"Wasn't she . . . *raped* . . . wasn't she?"

Blaise Maher held the tissue over her nose and mouth and shook her head like a relieved jury foreman being asked if her colleagues had reached a majority verdict that she didn't agree with.

"No."

Her answer was barely audible.

My relief was palpable, indescribable. It was like finding out that the cancer was gone after being told previously that I had only six months to live.

So why then did she take a rusty skin-peeler from her kitchen drawer that afternoon and inflict such damage?

As the wind picked up again, sending a shiver down my spine, my suspicions were beginning to run amok.

10

The journey seemed to last an eternity. "Going nowhere quickly forever" was how Molly used to describe her life when I'd ask her on the phone how she had been, and if she'd got a job. I was only beginning to understand the plethora of significances of such a strange expression, and all her other quirky sayings that were coming back to me now.

I had quickly forgotten what traffic jams were, and how utterly and helplessly exasperated and wrecked they left you. I could count the number of times I'd driven a car of any description since moving to Oak Bluffs. I could have walked around the coastline of Martha's Vineyard in the time it took us to get from Claddagh Mines to where we were, a distance of thirty-five miles, firmly rooted in a gridlocked two-mile tailback. I missed the island. I missed Karen. Most of all I missed the sound of my daughter's voice. I recounted as many of Molly's phone calls as I could, and the marathon conversations we had, as I sat with my deathly-silent wife, shit-scared of what lay ahead of me, in heavy traffic in Abbeyleix, on the main N8 to Dublin.

Her silence unnerved me. Twice I had attempted to start a conversation by asking questions: How is your job going? "Shite," she replied. Half an hour later: You're looking well. Have you joined a gym? "No."

I wasn't sure if she was doing this intentionally. It was a favourite pastime years ago: Neasa would literally shut down for days and refuse to acknowledge my very existence if I had said or done something she didn't approve of. This behaviour reminded me so much of a life I was so relieved to leave behind, it was beginning to get to me in a very uncomfortable way. I knew, from experience, what she wanted: to talk about Molly. My heart wanted to, but my mind knew better; Neasa wanted to control the conversation about *her* daughter, not mine; she wanted to lord it over me by telling me what *she* thought was wrong, and how *I* naturally was to blame for Molly's suicide attempt. After all, as far as Neasa was concerned, I was the belligerent one in the relationship; I had pre-empted the separation by threatening to walk out. Therefore everything that followed was as a result of my freaky lifestyle, as she put it. Problem was, I could never figure out what was so "freaky" about it.

"She lost six pints of blood."

Neasa's voice, her sudden eagerness to be heard, startled me for moment. "Did she?" It was a start.

"They had to send out for more blood late on Wednesday night."

"From where?"

"How do I know? Wherever they get blood from I suppose."

She remained passive, almost sedated, as she spoke graphically about Molly's blood, as if she was back in uniform and discussing a casualty admission with a concerned parent. I had always assumed that the body held a gallon of blood: eight pints. "How could she lose six pints of blood? That's nearly all the blood she's got." I asked almost quizzically.

"I didn't ask. It didn't seem like a very relevant question at the time."

She seemed to be thinking of something else for that moment.

"What's she like? Is she beautiful?" she asked with a soft, almost uncertain tone of voice.

Classic Neasa, I thought to myself. The schizoid qualities were alive and well. She no longer wanted to talk about Molly. She knew all about Molly: suffice it to say she was on death's doorstep, her life in the balance, and six pints of blood packed into her like a good night on the beer. So what? We'd see her soon enough. What's the point in dwelling on it? And I knew how she would react if I insisted on hearing all about my daughter: "Sure, what do you care? You never saw her growing up." I never wanted to hear that expression again. If Neasa had dared to whisper it I would have dumped her on the side of the country road as quick as I could have shouted, *"Get Out!"*

Now her excessive selfishness needed to satisfy itself by delving into something she had been curious about for years: my girlfriend and partner Karen. When Neasa says, "Jump", the rest of us ask, "How high?" Not today.

"Who's that?" I asked as if confused.

"Your fancy-friend in A-*mir-ee-kay?*"

She aped a bastardised mid-Atlantic accent and rested her feet against the dashboard, which immediately set the tone of what was to come. I decided to play along.

"Karen? She's wonderful, thanks. She makes me very happy."

"How did you meet her?"

"In an antique shop."

"I hear she's a bit of an antique herself."

"I can't see how. She's thirty-three, five-foot nine. Quite the perfect partner actually."

Neasa kicked the dashboard, knocking the glove compartment open. I closed the door. Checkmate. I could get to like this. Now it was time to return to my daughter. "Has Molly been talking?"

"A few words. I couldn't make them out. She can hardly keep her eyes open."

"Who found her?"

"No one knows. Someone called 999. He didn't leave a name. The doctors reckoned she'd have died within the hour if they hadn't got to her."

"He?"

"Yeah, *he*."

"And he didn't leave his name?"

"Nope. Just explained that he'd dropped in to see how she was. She'd missed a few lectures over the previous days, and he thought she might have been sick, or something. The operator asked him to wait with her until the ambulance arrived. But he was gone when they got there."

"Have they been able to trace him?"

"They're not magicians, you know!"

I hated it when she treated me like a stubborn talking-parrot.

* * *

No one could have prepared me for Dublin City, Friday evening, rush hour traffic. The anger and teeth-grinding, brow-sweating frustration was tangible from the occupants of the cars that sat motionless around us, pure dead and going nowhere, in the last-ditch attempt to get out of the city for the weekend. At one point, I could have reached out of the window and felt the seething bad blood of the man to my right. If this had been California's Interstate, I dare say he might have reached for his gun and shot me.

We arrived at Beaumont Hospital – specialists in head injuries – at a few minutes after seven to be told by a girl with blocked sinuses, chewing gum, at the registration desk that our Molly had been transferred to the Mater Hospital – specialists in heart and lung procedures. When I asked why, I was told it was normal procedure. The nasally-chewing-gum-girl couldn't define normal procedure.

Shortly before eight, a helpful doctor in the Mater Casualty, who looked as if he could do with a stiff drink, found a manila folder with a single chart marked Molly Freeman. I choked back tears as the kind doctor explained she had been transferred yet again, this time to St Patrick's Hospital in James's Street, in Dublin's inner city.

Again, I asked why? He said it was the leading psychiatric hospital in the country. And they were best suited to Molly's needs.

I think I thanked him. The word 'psychiatric' had already dug in, and taken over my thinking within seconds. My daughter was in a mental asylum because she had tried to take her own life. Her statement that she'd had enough, her fancy Peregrine restaurant job, and her psychology studies, and her absent father, and her fanatical mother: her decision to stand still and say, "Stop this now. I'm getting off!" – meant she was considered unstable and unfit for anywhere except a psychiatric ward.

I looked at her mother. It seemed best not to say the obvious. I was now totally confused. The full impact hit me with a cruel wallop to the mind and heart. The implications of what Molly had done made me baulk, the nausea making me physically weak. I couldn't help feeling I was more than just partly responsible, because she was my daughter.

11

Saint Patrick's Hospital was preparing its patients for the night by the time we arrived. It was almost nine. In contrast to a city that was coming alive on a Friday night – bursting with packed buses and taxis, and visiting foreigners, and stag and hen parties, and nightclubs and late bars waiting to open, and wage packets wanting to be spent – all of life's mundane activities and daily chores, as we knew them and took for granted, in this hospital had been suspended; life hung in a delicate, threadbare balance of uncertainty.

This was a hostel for broken sanity. Its inmates were not sure why they were brought here. All they knew was that someone had taken the key out of the motor. They were just not *sure* any more. Other hospitals checked for symptoms, diagnosed conditions, illnesses, and administered treatments for sicknesses and infections that are mostly visible to the medical eye.

Here the doctors were psychiatrists; their main weapon of defence was time and patience and understanding; the drugs were Lithium and Parentravite and Tranxene and Erexit and Paxol. The disease was invisible and possessive. It took over and suffocated the senses, murdering willpower and enthusiasm; kidnapping self-worth and gagging self-confidence; creating a powerful need to die.

Alcoholics, manic-depressives, wet-brains, clapped-out crack-addicts and washed-out junkies; attempted suicides – rich man, poor man, beggarman, thief – it didn't matter what they came in with, they were all the same now: sick. Extremely sick. Here, God meant very little. The man or woman who signed your discharge papers was the giver of life – had made you better – and that was all that mattered. This place was akin to a lay-by I might have pulled into, and stopped and shut down my engine, if I thought I had taken a wrong road and was lost.

The people stopping here were utterly lost. Confusion and anxiety had turned to stress – had swung into deep, dark depression – their deadliest enemy. This was their ultimate stop; their last attempt to clutch the final straw that might give them the chance to reignite the will to take up where they had left off just before the "fog" finally became too hard to see through and they pushed themselves beyond the finish line.

And amid all this desolate sickness was Molly, my daughter. I had to get to her and take her away home with me to the island, as quickly as I could. Back to Karen, and the Bradys, and the good clean Nantucket Sound sea air. Or I too, I thought, would go insane. I stood at the reception desk and waited while the girl sitting at the computer terminal finished typing whatever it was that seemed so urgent and consuming.

"Can I help you?" she asked softly.

"My daughter was transferred from the Mater this evening. She's here." I wasn't sure what else to say.

"What's her name?" The young girl started flicking through a small roto-file system of handwritten cards.

"Molly, eh, Molly Freeman," I replied.

"Or Maher. Molly Maher. She might have been admitted under my name," Neasa sparked up, relishing great satisfaction at the prospect. Neasa used to ask Molly, prior to our separation, whom she loved the most, her mammy or her daddy? She answered: both.

The receptionist resorted to her computer screen. I watched her tap in M-o-l-l-y.

She waited.

We waited.

"Molly Freeman. Yeah, she's with us," as if she had just been accepted into a Girl Guide troop. "Who are you?" she asked authoritatively.

The tone of her question winded me. I was her father, for Christ's sake! Was it not obvious? "We're her parents. Why?"

"I'm only following instructions. That's all. Nearest and dearest only."

"Has anyone else been in to see her?"

The young girl picked up the phone and punched three numbers. "A fella came in with flowers. Youngish. Seemed nice. I assumed he was her boyfriend." She cut off and mentioned our names on the phone. "They're coming up to see Molly Freeman." She put the phone down. "She's in Rebecca. Second floor. Lift's just around the corner. Hit the buzzer and they'll let you in."

Hit the buzzer . . . they'll *let you in*. Molly was locked up. Jesus Christ.

I wandered down corridors, swerved around corners, my trainers squeaking on beautifully shiny floors that smelled to the high adenoids of wax polish, avoiding oncoming strangers like a car veering out of control. No one smiled here – all gaunt, long, worried-looking faces, as if they had all been given bad news. Spot the difference between patient and visitor. I couldn't. I wasn't sure how far behind me Neasa was. I didn't care. Every minute spent waiting for her to catch up was another minute I wouldn't be able to spend with my daughter. What time was it? I'd left my watch in the car. A bell would sound any minute. *Visiting hour is over!* a matronly voice would command. We climbed stairs, and more stairs, until we reached the second floor.

Rebecca.

An arrow pointed to the right.

Two steel doors, an electronic lock-box in the

middle. A buzzer and an intercom. *Close The Door Behind You When You Leave.* Behind the door, people who were ill in an unquestionable way; but how ill remained to be seen and diagnosed. Just for now they had to live in protective custody. They had brought our Molly to this place. I was gutted.

I pressed the buzzer and waited, smelling polish and listening to the sound of my beating heart. I wanted so much to take her in my arms and promise her that everything was going to be OK.

And it would be.

* * *

I had only taken my eyes off her for a split second and she was gone. We had laid out our towels – hers, a dayglo yellow and orange feast of bright colour, and mine, a navy-blue beach drape – and I was fixing the windbreak, positioning it so that I could spread out the picnic that Thelma Brady had prepared especially for us that morning. It was a rare treat of a very warm afternoon, about lunchtime, when we decided to close up the shop and sit on the beach for a couple of hours.

Molly was visiting me for a month. I had sent her mother the money for the trip and promised to take good care of her; I had been secretly hoping that she might ask to come and live with me in Massachusetts. Looking back now, it was a ridiculous notion to have taken seriously, expecting a young teenager to pack her bags, leave school and all her friends behind her, and move to America to live with her father – a man her mother hated. I missed Molly so much.

I remember vividly calling her name. *"Molly."* I flicked small flecks of sand off the peanut butter sandwiches and waited to hear her usual reply: *"Coming in a minute, Dad."* She didn't answer. When I looked around at the water's edge, and scanned the small, deserted beach at Miller's Cove, there was nothing. A few gulls swooping further out on the choppy water; but not a human soul between here and there. I panicked instantly. I couldn't swim. Yet I ran, thundering down the small stretch to the water, my feet barely touching the hot sand, and ploughing in until I was chest deep, thrashing the surface in the hope that I might notice her or touch her. My chest was going to explode – the pain of my heart thumping in the ice-cold water, and an agonising seizure of muscle in my gut and chest almost made me lose my balance. *"Molly!"* I ducked under and kept calling her name, gurgling, swallowing and choking; coughing to clear the sickening salt-water each time I threw my head back to catch more air and a deeper breath to hold before going further down each time. Then I saw her, hovering on the sea floor, her lifeless body swaying with the current, her camera strap limply clinging on around her arm, her camera some distance away dragging along the pebbly seabed. I thought she was dead, and then refused to accept it. I grabbed her and forced my way against the fierce undertow, the bashing waves falling back at me, covering my head, knocking me back, then beating me forward. Seconds later the sea was no longer a threat. I lay her on the wet sand.

She coughed and retched. And sobbed. All I could think of was that I had almost lost her.

* * *

Waiting to be admitted to the lock-up ward that night reminded me of how helpless I was that afternoon in Miller's Cove. The sea could have claimed her if I hadn't been so adamant to fight for her with my own life and win her back.

But tonight, life as I knew it – as I expected it should be for my twenty-one-year-old daughter who should have been celebrating her coming-of-age with close friends and family – was out of my reach; beyond my comprehension. I was standing at the front door to a strange world, unsure of what was waiting on the far side.

The buzz was short and discreet. That was all. I gripped the steel handle and pulled. The door opened. At first I thought I was in the wrong ward. I had expected a Victorian dungeon, with chains and metal buckles and black straps traversing narrow beds. Patients dancing with imaginary partners, having one-sided conversations, searching the floor for lost marbles;

others contorted in straitjackets, gagged and bound, muffling and sweating, their eyes protruding in horror – the dreaded "snakes running up the curtains" syndrome.

Instead I had walked into a large open-plan area with a plush, semi-circular reception desk in the centre, cosy and soothing on the eye and the mind, like a small motorway motel. Patients, in pyjamas and dressing-gowns, some wearing sweatshirts and jeans and sneakers, shuffled about busily, carrying books and Walkmans; others, slightly more distant, *were* looking for marbles.

Two women played pool. Another sat close to them reading the weekend supplement of *The Irish Times*.

A television blared at the far end of a corridor. I recognised the music from *Saturday Night Live*. A nurse smiled at me. The doctors didn't bother with white coats. They were smartly turned out in shirts and ties. They could have been looking at me across a bank counter. They could have been computer programmers. They could have been patients.

No charts, no stethoscopes or electric cathodes. No mountains of pills. No screaming or wailing; just peace and quiet while patients waited to be reconnected to the life they just couldn't seem to get a handle on.

"Where's Molly?" I found myself asking out loud.

Neasa pointed through an open door she was standing at. The room inside was dimly lit. She started to cry.

12

Molly smiled with all the effort of a weightlifter raising a set of dumbbells. She stretched out her hands and tried her hardest to sit up. Neasa grabbed one hand. I grabbed the other. I was afraid to let go in case I suddenly woke up and found myself still at thirty-eight thousand feet above the Atlantic and had all the confusion of that day's long journey to go through.

"Daddy," she whispered, her voice squeaky in pain. If she never said another word that night, or forever more, it wouldn't have mattered. She said it all in that one word. I kissed her forehead and her nose, careful that she wouldn't notice me observing the huge bruise above her left ear. But I could tell she knew. My tears dropped into her hair and onto her cheek. I put my hands gently behind her bony shoulders and hugged her until Neasa urged me to go easy.

"Go easy?" I thought. I was going to hug this child of mine until she was giggling and laughing and joking

and healthy again. I was going to get her into her warmest clothes and whisk her off that same night. And make plans to get her back to Boston once Karen arrived on Tuesday.

"How are you?" I asked, trying to make my question sound like it would during one of our trans-world telephone conversations.

I could see that the implications of my question were making her uncomfortable. "Besides what happened . . ." I added, in an effort to show that, if anything, I loved her more.

"OK. Tired." She yawned. "They have me on stuff that's making me sleepy." She casually gestured to the bruise below her left temple. "I walked into a door." I detected the shakiness in her voice.

I tried not to stare at the bandages. They were thickset and tightly bound, like protective wrist and elbow cycling pads, snow-white, running from the palm of each hand to below the elbow. One was slightly soiled. Her hair was cropped again. Jesus, I shivered. Her eyes were deep-set, her cheeks sunk, her lips chapped, pale-faced. She looked awful. "You're looking OK," I said, as if compelled to pay her some kind of compliment since I had not seen her for so long. Now that I had said it, it sounded farcical.

At least she smiled. "Liar."

It was a magic moment bearing the briefest of respite we all badly needed.

* * *

I sat perfectly still in case the slightest movement I might make would cause her to pull her hand away from mine. I wanted to hold onto it forever, its warm, small, helpless shape, safe for a time in my big clumsy, well-weathered fist. We didn't say a lot to each other. She kept her eyes closed most of the time, occasionally opening them and glancing at the window, or the lampshade, or the mirror on the wardrobe door – as if checking that everything was exactly where it was the last time she looked. "It's OK, love," I assured her each time she looked up at me. Again she smiled, as if reassured that I was staying. The tension in her wrist and arm relaxed each time she looked around, building again and making her twitch and spasm whenever she shut her eyes.

I, for my part, was a silent sentinel for her, shocked by her emaciated frame. She was skin-and-bone. At first, I thought it was just her skinny fingers and tiny hands. Then I noticed her shoulders and arms and elbows. Jesus, she was like a survivor from a concentration camp who had just been salvaged in the nick of time. A despairing mask had replaced her beautiful face, with all its classic features. Her gorgeous auburn hair had been hacked away. I rubbed the corners of my eyes each time she closed hers so that she wouldn't see me crying.

Neasa had gone in search of cigarettes. I was glad to have some time alone with my daughter. It reminded me yet again of that night I'd been robbed of crucial time with her ten years ago. And the following night:

that night after a day spent wondering where Owen Durkin was. The night *they* called.

* * *

Malachy Ward took off his sergeant's cap and told the younger garda to go back to the car and check the radio for messages: "In case they're lookin' for us," he told him. The boyish cop nodded.

Turloch ushered Malachy ahead of him, into the house. Out beyond them, outside the garden, a small group of children had gathered at the back of the police car.

Malachy treated me like a shifty stranger that evening with all the trappings of his recently appointed status of Garda Sergeant on Duty assigned to Nenagh garda station, in the district of Tipperary North Riding; unlike his familiar "How's things, Dave? Nice bit of weather we're havin'" greeting; or, "Jesus, your Molly is shootin' up into a gorgeous young woman. She'll be bossin' ye about in no time, Dave." Or, "You don't fancy swappin' jobs, Dave?" as he regularly joked as he tried to clear the pubs in Claddagh Mines during the Summer Festival each year.

That night he studied me, agitated, confused, uneasy – uncertain as to whether what he would eventually say was appropriate – from where he sat on the couch closest to the window, occasionally glancing over his shoulder, out to the driveway.

"Tea?" I asked.

"That won't be necessary, David." He looked across at Turloch who had picked a photo frame from the mantelpiece. My brother-in-law studied the photograph of his sister and niece. He remained silent, his left hand in his pocket, the frame resting on his beer gut.

Malachy Ward, with his red hair and his huge ears, was hurting that night. I could tell he'd taken a drink or two. His son was missing. No one was meant to know that Malachy Ward was Owen Durkin's father. Truth was, the dogs in the street had been barking the chorus for thirteen years ever since the day Maud Durkin appeared with her "bump". This was the gratitude she got for being vigilant, and taking her role as chairwoman of Neighbourhood Watch so seriously, and reporting her suspicions to the local police. The rest of Claddagh Mines kept their suspicions to themselves. Often nightly, the patrol car sat idle outside her house, while her husband sang rebel songs, and drank pints of porter, and borrowed a score from anyone who'd lend him just to stay out drinking a bit longer. If it hadn't been for the red hair, no one would have dared point a finger.

My brother-in-law was clearly uncomfortable about visiting me. His presence seemed to bring some relief to Malachy.

They were there to ask questions.

Turloch sat down opposite me next to the hearth. Malachy moved to the long settee to be closer to the conversation. Molly squeezed my hand. I could feel her heart beating as she moved closer to me. I could smell Turloch's dinner from where he was sitting – a Jumbo Dinner-box of Southern Fried Chicken and curry-chips. A blob of the sauce had spread out and soaked into his tie. His shirt was at least two sizes too small for him, two buttons open, the tie-knot sideways at chest level.

"Where is he?" Turloch asked with all the tact of a proverbial bulldozer.

"Where is *who*?" I replied.

"What'd ye do with young Owen?" He belched and spat into the dying fire. It sizzled.

Malachy Ward's eyes flitted between the two of us.

"Owen Durkin?"

He snorted like the fat pig he was, and cleared his throat. I waited for another long spit attempt. He didn't. This time he swallowed his phlegm and coughed on it. It made me feel queasy.

Neasa came into the room quietly and sat at the end of the long settee. She listened to the questions her brother was asking.

"What happened to Molly last night?" Turloch addressed Neasa. It was a sham. I could tell this whole charade had been carefully planned and rehearsed.

"You mean to say you didn't hear about Molly?" I wasn't going to let this continue. "You mean to say your mother didn't tell you while she was making your lunch for you today?"

He ignored me, waiting for Neasa to compose herself. I could tell Neasa was uncomfortable playing his game.

"She was attacked," she said softly, stroking the arm of the settee, her head bowed down.

"Stop this bullshit!" I shouted. *"What* is going on here, for God's sake?"

Turloch's face tensed up. "I'll tell you what's *going on here,* David. Owen Durkin has disappeared. His mother mentioned to us today that you'd been giving him a hard time in school. She told me he wasn't sleeping well at night. You were making a big deal out of little pranks he was playing on the other kids, and yet you appeared to be ignoring what they were doing to him. He spoke recently about running away from home, Maud says. When she asked him why, he said, 'Because Mr Freeman told me I was useless and he would be happier if I was on the other side of the world . . . as far away as possible.' Did you say that to Owen Durkin?"

"Of course I didn't."

"So you're telling me his mother is lying?"

"No, of course not. He's lying to his mother. She knows I wouldn't say something like that to a kid, bad an' all as he is."

"You laid into him this morning."

"I did not!"

Turloch Maher took a notebook from his undersized, shiny jacket and opened it at the most recently filled page. "These are Maud Durkin's exact words here. 'Two of the children told me that Mister Freeman knocked him unconscious. They told me he grabbed him by the throat and tried to choke him. They said he flung him down against the heating pipe and then he didn't move until Mister Freeman picked him up and started shaking him. There was blood everywhere.' Four pupils saw you standing over him while he was lying on the floor in the corridor outside the classroom." He closed the notebook and began to put it away. "Perhaps you'd like me to keep this out awhile. Maybe you'd like to make a statement?"

I was flabbergasted. "That's not true."

"And why would the children want to lie?"

"You know what kids are like when they get together."

Turloch shook his head. "Would you like to tell me what they're like?"

"They all rally together. Lord of the flies. Back up each other. One of them says one thing, another agrees and adds his bit to it. Another adds more. It's a hysterical reaction."

"But the kids would appear to be saying that you were the one behaving hysterically."

"I got a fright. I wasn't sure what to do. How was I to know he was going to trip?"

"Is that what you're saying happened?"

"That *is* what happened. I lost my balance. I was turning around and he tripped on my foot. Simple as that. He banged his head, hence the blood. He wasn't unconscious, just stunned. Neasa checked him over and bandaged him up." I looked across at my wife. She was now standing at the lounge room door, leaning against it, half in, half out, her arms folded. She listened with her head bowed.

"We'll have to get statements from the children who witnessed it."

"Suit yourself. Most of them hate me."

"Why?"

"I don't know. Because I'm a schoolteacher."

"Why do they hate you? Do you punish them? Are you violent towards them?"

"*Of course not!* They say I give them too much homework. I don't know why they give out; half of them never do the work I give them anyway."

"Will you give us a statement?"

"Of course I will. I've got nothing to hide." I looked at Molly. "Have I?" I squeezed her hand.

She smiled nervously. Her reaction worried me for a long time after that night had, as I thought, become a distant memory in the collective unconscious that was Claddagh Mines.

I stood accused of savagely assaulting a thirteen-year-old boy. "I had only meant it as a disciplinary measure. Yes, I grabbed him by the pullover. He tripped on my foot and fell. He banged his head. What's so criminal about that?"

No one seemed to want to answer my question.

Turloch was writing in his notebook. I had made a statement. I was in deep trouble. I knew that, if only by looking at Molly. And all along I watched this game being played out in front of my eyes. I was the whipping-boy in this set-up. Something awful had happened. I could reach out and touch the tension. A terrible accident of huge proportions, it seemed, and I was the fall guy.

There was a moment's silence, while Turloch Maher read back over his notes. He looked at me as he closed the pad. "Are you going to tell us what the conversation was about this morning?"

"*What* conversation? We had no conversation. I was simply reprimanding him in the corridor and he fell. That's all that happened. I didn't see Owen Durkin all afternoon. Neasa bandaged his cut forehead. He went home, or so I thought. The kids came back to school after lunch. He didn't. To be honest I was glad."

"Why?" Turloch seemed perplexed.

"After what he did to my daughter last night."

Molly stood up and left the room. There was a strange silence for a brief moment.

"Did you see him do anything to your daughter last night?"

"Just look at her hair. Look at the bruise on her face." I shook my head. I knew this conversation was already facing into a brick wall of farcical nonsense. "No. I didn't see him doing anything to her last night."

"Did you report this incident involving your daughter to the police last night?"

Neasa flashed through my mind: she was standing at the kitchen worktop, holding a bread knife. "No, we decided not to," I replied.

"Was that why you decided to reprimand him this morning?"

"Possibly."

"Taking your position of authority a bit too personally, aren't you?"

"I didn't think so. None of this would have happened if he hadn't tripped over my foot and cut his forehead, would it?"

The two men stood up.

"Is that it?" I had never felt so anxious as I did at that moment.

"We'd like you to come down to the station with us. Answer a few more questions," Malachy replied.

* * *

They held me for twenty-four hours. In and out, they came and went. Questions and more questions. Suggestions and theories. Then they said I could go. Nothing else. It was over.

I walked around Claddagh Mines for a couple of days in a shit-scared state of mind. My paranoia was in a state of self-reproduction – like a computer virus, growing and spreading throughout my system like some horrible mutant hybrid. Every time the phone rang, every knock on the door, my heart almost missed a beat. But why was I punishing myself like this? I had done nothing, absolutely *nothing*.

The posters went up in shop windows, in the dressing-rooms of the local football and camogie club, in the church porch; they were like wallpaper in the schoolhouse.

HAVE YOU SEEN THIS BOY?

The priests spoke about him for weeks during their Sunday sermons. The police unit that visited from Dublin spent time with each of the classes, individual pupils in some cases, including my Molly, urging them to come forward confidentially if they had seen anything peculiar. What they didn't realise was that none of St John the Apostle's pupils would say *boo* as far as Owen Durkin was concerned; not a cat's whisker if Owen Durkin was involved. Experience had proved to each of his victims that it paid dividends to keep quiet – *no matter what!* And this incident, in their eyes, was no different to any other they'd chosen to ignore. Owen Durkin had achieved his lifelong ambition.

He was famous.

13

Molly's apartment was what I would describe as tastefully upmarket; a *Desirable Residence* was how a property supplement editor might have classified it. Regardless of how swanky it looked, or how comfortably well off it made its owner appear, this apartment belonged to someone who wanted to die.

It was after one in the morning when the taxi dropped us off in a narrow side road close to the River Liffey. *The Cobbles*, the smart-looking brick plaque above the door read. I had been away from Ireland for ten years and so much of the old town was gone. Lack of familiarity with Dublin's inner-city web of back streets prompted me to leave my hired car in the grounds of the hospital and be driven. Molly's apartment was conveniently close, no more than ten minutes away, in the old markets area of Smithfield, in the shadow of the giant Guinness brewery, with its abiding aroma of hops and yeast, and its ancient cobbled lanes.

By the time I'd visited the bathroom and thrown cold water on my face and behind my ears, Neasa was asleep in bed, shattered from two long days and nights of despairing torment and uncertainty, her loud, uneven snoring breathing some life into an otherwise silent tomb. It was while I towelled off that I noticed the blood.

Just reddish-thin, vague streaks in a bed of dirt and sandy earth on the floor of the bath, left behind after a hasty, botched job at cleaning up by someone who visited Molly's apartment regularly; someone who, I felt, was more than just a weekly cleaner.

She must have climbed into the warm bath before letting her blood flow freely. She was evidently still wearing her shoes – hence the gravelly dirt – and most of her clothes, I assumed. This "someone" who cleaned up must have found her, dragged her near-lifeless body out of the cold water, and saved her life by calling for help. "Someone" must have pulled her out of the dark-red water and stemmed the flow. She'd lost pints and pints. I tried hard not to imagine the room and how it must have looked when "someone" discovered her, pale and unconscious. Small flecks of brownish blood – too small to be considered stains – like patches of dry rot, dotted the walls and ceiling.

I was glad to be alone. It meant I could cry for my daughter, without having to feel embarrassed in front of my wife who would have enjoyed seeing me cry; my daughter, who I admitted I didn't know, despite the phone calls and the cheery conversations that made me feel a false sense of wellbeing. Those special moments on the phone told me I wasn't such a bad father after all. I knew that evening I had been lying to myself. I was a worthless father, shit-scared by my own lifelong ineptitudes.

I lifted the lid of the dainty pedal-bin with a sticker of a big yellow sunflower on the side, stored neatly in a press beneath the small sink and immediately squeezed my nose, almost fearful of the once-white towel, now caked in a dark-brown mess. Stale blood stinks to high heaven after a couple of days, even in an apartment that hasn't felt heat for a long time. I sat back down on the toilet seat for a moment out of sheer sickness and shock. The tears came easily, and I cried hard, careful to stifle the need to bawl out and release my anger and frustration. The last thing I needed was Neasa performing her traditional headless-chicken act.

I found the kitchen, guided by Neasa's snoring. If her bull-like sounds were to the left, then the rest of the apartment was to the right. I decided against testing the light-switch arrangements. Anyway I preferred the soft beam of light from the bathroom. It diluted the impact of learning about a daughter I could easily have never met before.

Shelves were bare as if she had hidden the evidence. The more I checked cupboards and storage spaces, the more I realised that this wasn't so much a comfortably lived-in apartment as a holding-area; a temporary stopover for someone who simply needed a place to put her head down. Eating wasn't part of the plan. A saucepan and an egg-flip sat at the back of the cooker, still holding the aborted remnants of a small bag of half-boiled pasta shells. The fridge was dead. It could have been out of order. It could be that Molly just didn't feel it was worth plugging in: its contents would scarcely feed a family of hungry mice – two pots of *Petit Filou* yoghurts, a blackened banana, a half-eaten bar of whole-nut chocolate and a half-tin of congealed baked beans; the carton of milk had turned soggy: its sell-by date well over a month ago. The smell was putrid.

I found the plug and stabbed it angrily into its socket. The light in the fridge came on and it shuddered as it struck up a familiar hum. Maybe she was conserving electricity. Not Molly. She was a spend, spend, spend woman. Sure, look at this place. I glanced around the spacious kitchen, into the half-lit generous living-room area with its sumptuous armchairs and their expensive leather upholstery; the dining-table with its four matching pine chairs; the glass coffee table turned on its side; the plush, soft-ultramarine Warminster carpet; the matching full-length Berlin blue drapes; the kipskin hearth rug: nothing under five hundred pounds. At that moment I was aware of something that had been eluding me since I turned the key in the third-floor apartment. My daughter was paying a fortune to stay here, at least a thousand pounds a month, I estimated. I was panicking now, trawling through our transatlantic phone conversations, eight years since I had seen her, two or three hundred phone calls at least: listening back to her voice telling me about her myriad job history: each position she had taken hastily – her way of paying for something she needed quickly – and then quit like a bat out of hell. I always felt in the recesses of my mind that I didn't need to worry about my daughter: she had the right attitude, I believed. Careers, savings accounts, credit cards, pensions, security. . . none of them was important. "I'll get by, Dad!" she used always to say whenever I put on the fatherly concern-filled voice and asked her how long before she got another job. "A decent job this time?" I would always ask. Truth was, the whole notion of a "decent job" scared the shit out of me. I thought I had a decent job once; one that would see me comfortably through to retirement, with a pension that would allow me spend the quality time with my wife and daughter I'd been earning for forty relentless, brow-beating years like brownie points, when all along I should have been looking out for myself.

All I wanted for Molly: self-control, happiness and, above all, peace of mind. Fuck the establishment and its propensity for bullshit and what's expected of you as a child of the new millennium: my attitude through all the years I spent away, an attitude that had clouded the realities of life at home. Why did I feel that my daughter had been lying to me for months? Looking around this place at half one in the morning only served to reinforce my gut feeling that she had never been a dentist's assistant; or a website designer; or that she was studying psychology during the day and working in a pub at night. I tried to rationalise our conversations; tried to pinpoint where the word of truth had become confused by fabrication. But why would she want to tell me anything other than the truth?

Jesus Christ.

I felt there and then as if I was back, pacing up and down, in our sitting-room in Claddagh Mines that night her mother took her into her bedroom and struck up a scheme that would direct the rest of my daughter's life, one that locked me out of both of their lives.

Only this time I believed that Molly was flying solo.

* * *

I slept on the armchair and woke with a crippling crick in my neck. No time for coffee. We had to be at the hospital for ten to meet the consultant, a Mr Cruickshank. First name Arthur. It seemed to fit in perfectly with this whole surreal nightmare that a scholar called Arthur Cruickshank was caring for my suicidal daughter.

During the twenty-minute taxi journey back to St Patrick's, Arthur Cruickshank dominated my thoughts. Did he always want to be a psychiatrist? If he had grown up with a name like Tom Jones, or Jack Smith, would he have still turned out to be such an eminent physician? "Arthur Cruickshank," I muttered. I acknowledged the taxi driver's curiosity. "Did you ever want to be a psychiatrist?" I asked.

He afforded me a confused stare. Was this a patient or a visitor? "No," he replied.

14

Flowery drapes surrounded two of the beds. Bright sunlight showered the others, separating the spacious hospital ward into two triangles. Molly was in the bright half, propped up against two bolster-pillows. Her breakfast tray, untouched, remained at the bottom of her bed – a metal structure resembling a heap of old scaffolding arranged to accommodate a thin mattress and two immaculate white sheets.

Her smile when she saw me lifted my spirits.

"Daddy!" she shouted, her voice frail and hoarse, her bandaged arms reaching upwards.

I dropped the plastic bag and almost fell down on top of her in my effort to hug and hold her. *"Molly."* I squeezed her tightly and felt how bony and flimsy she seemed in my arms, almost like a malnourished child from a third-world-agency advertisement. We stayed like that until her mother pushed me aside and reclaimed her for herself.

Molly ignored her and reached out for my hand. *"Daddy!"* she kept saying, almost delirious with the excitement of seeing me. I kept sniffing, hoping that the tears would hold off. I coughed and laughed and clasped my two hands around hers, then sat myself awkwardly on the edge of the bed.

"I'm going to get some air," her mother said.

Molly stopped smiling and took a deep breath.

"Ssshhh!" At the same time I raised my finger to my lips, anticipating that whatever she was about to say should wait for another time and place, like when a four-year-old might plead for another bedtime story just before the light was switched off; just like she pleaded when she was four years old. "Don't say anything. It's OK." I grinned again and squeezed her small hand in a reassuring gesture that there was no need for anything even mildly complicated right now. I just wanted her to know that being here beside her was the most important thing in the world to me. "How are you feeling?"

She thought for a while, and watched me with those piercing eyes, her mother's eyes, blinking and sharpening her stare; almost afraid to look away. "Tired. Pretty awful, actually." She looked down at one of the bandages.

It was then that I remembered our transatlantic phone chats, and how she used to end all her sentences with *actually*. The more I drew her attention to it and teased her by mimicking her voice, the more self-conscious she became, and the more frequently she said it.

Actually.

The word had become an instant reminder to me of Molly. All a customer had to say was actually, and in an instant I could see Molly and hear her voice.

I raised my finger to my lips again. "It's all right."

"When did you get here?"

"Yesterday. I flew into Shannon and collected your mother. Then I came straight up here." Her blackened eyes were wide open taking in my every word. Her eyes looked enormous above her sunken, pale cheeks and thin lips. She didn't want me to stop. It was obvious from her slow, drowsy tone that she didn't remember our visit the previous evening. "We were here last night but you were asleep."

She seemed to hesitate over her next question. "How did you find out?"

"Your mother rang me." Even in a moment of such personal sharing I still couldn't bring myself to call Neasa by her name. It was as if she was simply an interpreter between two friends who were trying to break the ice after years spent apart.

"How did Mom find out?" Her face registered a curious stare with the question.

"I don't know," I said. "I haven't had a chance to ask her." I knew she could see through my lie.

"Are you two talking?"

"Yes." It was all I could say at that moment. We hated each other but, yes, we were 'talking', if you could call it that. We hadn't a civil word to say to each other for ten years. We only spoke now because our daughter had attempted to die on us – the one inextricable link that joined us together – and hated seeing us hating each other. I hated her and she me. I didn't want to talk about Neasa and our grimy past, or about our vicissitudes. I wanted to see my daughter smiling, happy that I was here: happy that she was still alive.

She squeezed my hand twice and grinned. "It's *so* nice to see you."

I wiped away a tear that had become lodged in the corner of her eye. "I missed you."

"I missed you too." She winked. "Why are we whispering?"

I looked around and smiled.

She laughed with me and dragged at my hand. "Can you stay long?" she asked.

"Now?"

"No. I mean here, in Ireland?"

"As long as it takes to get you well." She stopped smiling. It seemed as if all the demons that she had forgotten about in the thrilling few moments of realising that I had come home to her were tormenting her again. She knew that my answer to her question was a loaded one. It was loaded for all of us, but that was a smoking gun that could wait for that other time when other questions needed to be answered and powerful secrets needed to be addressed.

"I buried so many feelings," she said softly. "I didn't realise they'd been buried alive." Her hand shook as it squeezed mine.

"We'll be fine, Molly." I didn't know what I meant but it needed to be said. Those words had made my mind up for me. I wasn't going back to the Cape until I could stare my past straight in the face and walk away with an easy conscience and a sound peace of mind for both of us.

"Where's Mom?" She looked around uneasily.

"I think she's gone outside for a smoke." I was glad she was gone.

"You're not smoking, are you?"

I shook my head. "Five years."

She sighed. "I'm impressed."

The conversation expired. I felt awkward. I could tell Molly did too. We needed to talk. Not like our phone chats across thousands of miles. I needed to know why. "What happened?" I shouldn't have asked, but I couldn't resist it.

She shrugged her shoulders and let go of my hand. I went to take hers but she put them under the bed covers. I felt shut out.

She stared out at the sky and the bright morning sunshine. "I couldn't take any more of it."

I waited. Then, "Any more of what?"

"Any more of *this!*" She nodded at me. She was talking about me. "Of you and Mom. Of everything! Of what I went through."

She was raising her voice with each word. I was more confused than ever now. "What did you go through?"

120

She was shaking her head. *"It doesn't matter, Dad! It's over!"*

"What's over?"

She turned over in the bed and started to cry. *"Nothing!"*

"What's over, Molly?" I reached across and placed my hand on her shoulder. "Please tell me. I want to help you."

"What the *hell* do you think you're doing?" Neasa pulled me from behind, backwards and to one side. I lost my balance and fell sideways onto the floor. It brought back awful memories. "What the fuck do you think you're doing, upsetting her like that?" She hugged Molly and kissed her head, stroking her hair and whispering short, comforting words like, *"My baby . . . hush now . . . Mommy's here . . . it's all going to be OK!"*

In that terrifying moment, a ghostly, panic-stricken vision, I was standing outside her bedroom: a young man, scared for my child, unsettled by my wife's strange, violent tantrums, listening beyond a closed door, barred from paternal contact, to this voice comforting her young daughter with those same haunting words of reassurance. I had been shut out of my daughter's life then and lived to regret it.

And now, it was as if someone, or something, was giving me another chance to pick up the pieces right now, from that very moment here tonight, and mend my life.

Neasa held her, shielded her, and stared at me. "She

needs rest, for Christ's sake. You think you can just storm in here and behave like you've never been away? You think you can just get on a plane and come home an' expect everything to be all right? Who raised Molly while you lived it up with your fancy woman?"

I stood up. "Please, Neasa. Don't say any more." I looked at the door where a nurse stood silently, unsure of what she should do. "It's not the time or place."

Neasa seemed to regain her composure and sat down on the bed.

I picked up the flowers I had knocked over and put them back into the vase. "I think I'll go."

"No, Dad. Don't go. *Please* don't go!"

My daughter had spoken. I sat down on a chair at the end of the bed and waited. Molly was in charge now.

"Mom, I really need to speak to Dad. Alone."

Neasa nodded, and then swiped me with a look so hateful and full of nausea and revenge I felt angry. I had forgotten how bad things had become, way back when I had made my decision to go. She stooped and kissed Molly on her forehead. "I'll be in this afternoon to see you, love. I need to buy you a few things." She winked and waved. "I'll get you something nice." Then she added churlishly, "Maybe they'll have cleaned the ward by the time I get back. See you later."

She walked out of the ward with the cares of a woman whose daughter had just had her appendix removed successfully, and – as for me? – I didn't exist.

Just for a split second I longed to be back on the Cape – back in my island home – with Karen, safe and at a distance. More importantly, I wanted Molly there beside us, away from whatever madness had urged her to do this unthinkable damage to herself.

My instinct was telling me that common sense and rational thinking hadn't prevailed here for a very long time.

15

It was almost midday on a late November Saturday morning and Dublin was basking in an Indian summer. The air, normally damp and smoggy, was clammy from a strangely unwelcome, alien-like humidity; heavy with unusual sweet floral scents normally reserved for early spring. A few colourful flowers had perked up, misfired off-course; an orange rose-bud was opening prematurely.

A distant car honked its horn long and hard somewhere out beyond the sprawling grounds of this home of mental fatigue, its stress-filled driver unaware of our stress-free environment, behind a wall that was separating two different worlds completely at odds with sanity. Traffic and pollution, and the tension of nine-to-five existences, were prohibited from this small, timeless garden, beautifully pruned and organised like the map of a perfectly logical mind. All of the mortal coil's fast-moving animation was locked out behind the high parapets which protected this place of peace and tranquillity, where life moved only when it wanted to; only when it was ready to move by its own momentum, at its own rehabilitated pace.

This strange, misleading morning sunshine in the company of my daughter reminded me of my days teaching in the small schoolhouse in Claddagh Mines, occasionally strolling the hundred yards or so with a much tinier Molly straggling behind me, frequently disappearing from sight.

This morning, though, we were locked together, arm in arm. I wondered about what the other patients and visitors might have thought as they watched us taking small steps, making our way at snail's pace across the small pathway between Loricar, a convalescent ward Molly was due to be transferred to later that day, and the small, decoratively designed, wooden-like church, with its neat apex and its timbering exterior and its simple, striking cross above the miniature front door. It was a building I was familiar with, straight out of a New England landscape, which made me feel very much at home.

If she hadn't been wearing a knee-length, turquoise dressing-gown they might have thought I was the patient. Its sleeves came down over the palms of her hands, covering the tight, bulky, snowy-white bandages that hid gashes she wanted no one to see. I looked at her again, reassuring my own mind that such an error of mistaken identity would have been impossible to make that day. Molly looked ill ... very ill ... with her croppy matted, greasy hair and her ghostly paleness and her slow, short, painful strides. And I was here to make her well again. And I would.

Dandelions peeped out around the perimeters of the neatly tended lawns. Molly pointed out a queen bee hovering around the thick base of an ivy creeper, confused no doubt by this short, unexpected reversal of seasons. A ladybird landed on her shoulder and quickly flew off again, probably in a weather-headed state of uncertainty.

"The weather's mad," Molly said daftly, looking around this gentle orchard.

I agreed, and was so glad that the weather was mad, as she called it, because its brief clemency was giving her an obvious lift out of that awful black hole she seemed to have called home for quite some time now. Then again, it was only fitting that the weather was 'mad'. It had come out in sympathy with everything else, irrational and brainsick, which was besetting our sad, dysfunctional family unit.

"How's Karen?" Molly asked.

"She's very well." I was so pleased she asked. I missed being away from Karen.

"When do I get to meet her?"

"Tuesday." I said it in a nonchalant, satisfied sort of way.

"*This* Tuesday?" she asked with a rush of excitement.

I nodded. "Yep!"

"Why didn't you tell me?"

"I was keeping it as a surprise." That was a lie. At the time Karen was making arrangements to join me after a few days, neither of us was sure what we were walking into, or whether our trips would include a funeral or not. "She's coming over to see you. Flying straight into Dublin. Her flight gets in at 7.40, Tuesday morning."

Molly hugged me tightly. "Tell me what she looks like. *Please?* That way I'll be able to pick her out when she walks out into the arrivals hall."

The notion of describing the woman I loved came as a strange challenge to me. I'd only ever characterised her once before; that was on the phone to Molly, one month after I had met Karen. "Well, she's tall, hair cut short . . . kinda pageboy style, maybe a bit longer and not as straight, I suppose . . . very fit . . . jogs two-and-a-half miles along the beach every morning . . . swims, hail, rain or snow . . . gorgeous smile . . . loads of beautiful sparkling white teeth . . . Boston accent. Oh yeah . . . and gorgeous blue eyes like yours, as dark blue as Nantucket Sound on a clear day."

"And you love her?"

"I love her."

Molly laughed. "What's the Boston accent like?"

"Flat American. Real *yeaaa*-kind of talk. She sounds like one of the Kennedys."

"Go on . . . show me what she sounds like."

I coughed and thought for a while. "Well, instead of saying 'Park the car', Molly says *"Paaak the caaa!"*

"Oh my God!" Molly shrieked. She laughed warmly and squeezed my elbow with both of her arms. "I can't wait to meet her. How old is she?"

"Thirty-three."

"Cool."

"What do you mean cool?" I asked mischievously.

"'Cos thirty-three is pretty young."

"Young for what?"

"You!" She laughed again, teasingly this time. It was so comforting to hear my daughter laugh. As long as she could smile I knew she would be all right. It was as good a time as any to ask a few serious questions. "Would you like to come back with us?"

Silence. "Back to where?"

"Martha's Vineyard." I waited; unsure of what direction such a weighted question might take us.

"For a holiday?"

I knew she was fishing. Molly had always been a master inquisitor, always hiding her hand until everyone else had shown his or hers. "Not really. I was hoping that maybe you'd come and live there with us. You could work in the shop for a while until you found your feet. I think the air might do you good as well. Martha's is a small island; we're surrounded by the sea." I waited for some reaction. It was quite obvious she hadn't been expecting that question. "Well . . . ?" I added hopefully.

She let go of my arm. The short cheerfulness was gone. "I was hoping that maybe you'd move back here."

I knew I had to tread carefully now; perhaps this was one of the issues that her frailty was balancing on. "Molly, I've lived there for ten years. It's my life. I've carved out a little niche for Karen and me. We're happy there. I love my little shop. I don't really want much more. It's . . . nice, I suppose that's the word I'm looking for."

"And what about me?" she asked.

"There's room there for you too."

"What about Mom?"

I wasn't expecting that. It jolted me. I had to think fast and hard about what she was getting at. Was she hinting at a reunion? I felt confused and weak even entertaining the idea of trying to warm to that woman again. It would have been easier to breathe underwater. Could Neasa have persuaded Molly to talk to me about giving our nuked, long-butchered marriage another try? Surely not. "What about her?"

"Could she come as well?"

"To America? Your mother? *No!*"

"Why not?"

I couldn't believe she was asking such an unlikely question. "Because . . ." I was positively lost for an answer; one that might disguise the years of pain and abuse; one that might sound reasonable and caring. "Because it ended between us a long time ago, Molly."

"Do you still love her?"

I wished that I could have lied to her and said yes. "No, I don't."

"Do you hate her?"

I thought for a second of what the implications of saying yes might be. And while I had no idea why she had tried to kill herself I knew I had to be gentle but honest with her. "I don't hate her. I just don't love her."

"Why?"

I was surprised that she linked my arm again.

"Because . . ." I had to think, fumbling for words. It was like trying to open a door that had been locked for years without the key. "She hurt me so much."

"I'm sure you must have hurt each other."

Molly . . . my daughter: the great inquisitor. "Maybe we did. I often think that I must have hurt her in some way for her to do what she did to me."

Molly stepped aside and stopped me in my tracks. "What did she do to you?"

"We'll talk about it another time."

"I want to hear it now."

"You need to rest."

"No!"

"Yes!"

I had reached a point of no return. I was standing at a crossroads with my only child, my twenty-one-year-old daughter who had tried to take her own life. I knew, once I answered her question, I would have to tell her everything; all the skeletons I had spent years cramming into my cognitive cupboard like packed sardines would fall apart around our feet. Strangely, such a prospect didn't frighten me as I had always expected it might. Our crossroads that glorious November morning was a predestination that both of us had to arrive at sooner or later. Perhaps it was Providence that, now, we were both standing at that point together.

16

"Your mother tried to murder me one night, a long time ago." Once I had said it, my mind seemed to shift direction. "I'm still not sure if she had intended killing me but she came close to succeeding." I waited. I often wondered how it would sound when I eventually came to tell her the truth. What words would I use? Would she cry? Would she call me a liar? Would she accuse me of being the instigator, of doing something that forced her mother to knife me in order to protect her own life?

Molly seemed unmoved.

I nodded to a small white bench. "Let's sit down over there."

She eased herself into a seated position. She spoke slowly. "What happened?"

"She'd been out with a couple of her nurse friends. They'd gone to The Bridge for a drink and on to Thurles to a nightclub. It must have been nearly three when I heard her fumbling with her hall-door key. I was trying to cool you down with a cold cloth, I remember. You were five at the time. You'd had a cold for a few days and it eventually got into your chest. Your temperature jumped that night. I remember it was nearly a hundred and two by the time your mother got back. She couldn't get the door open so I opened it for her. She tripped on the doormat and fell into the hall. She was very drunk."

"What did you do?"

"I tried to help her up. But she kicked out at me . . . told me to fuck off. Like she always did when she got drunk. So I left her there and walked into the kitchen to ring the doctor. As soon as she heard me talking to him, she made a run at me. She pulled the phone off me and slammed it down."

Molly listened.

"She accused me of ringing the doctor so that he might come down to the house and witness the sort of condition she was in. 'Ye just want that bastard to see me drunk. Then ye can tell him I'm an unfit mother, isn't that right?' She hated everything and everybody whenever she got pissed. She started imagining that I had a plan to have her committed to the local psychiatric home; get her locked away. She really believed that the reason I rang Doctor Smith that night was because I thought she was an unfit mother."

"And did you?"

"At times, I did. There were times I knew she would do anything in her power for you, even die for you. But there were other times when I really wasn't sure what she was thinking and, worse still, what she was capable of doing." I looked at Molly, and the sharp concern that registered in her eyes. "I shouldn't be telling you this. You're meant to be relaxing, not getting upset."

"Who's getting upset? Anyway, I want to hear what happened. Go on."

I took a deep breath. I had just been given permission by my daughter to tell the whole story. Well, some of it. I'd know when the time came to stop. "She was carrying a bottle, I remember. A green bottle. Heineken, maybe. It seemed empty. When she slammed the phone down, there was a long silence. Then I could hear you calling for me.

"Daddy!" you were shouting. *"Is everything all right?"* I could hear you asking. *"Everything's fine, love, I'll be there in a second!"*

"Daddy, I don't feel well," I heard you saying in your room. I reached out for the phone again. Your mother slammed the base of the bottle hard down onto the back of my hand. It hit me like a blow from a hammer. The pain was excruciating. She tried it a second time, twice as hard, but I had pulled my hand back. The bottle smashed when it came down on the hard worktop surface. She'd cut her hand, I could see. I thought the fright of seeing blood might make her cop on to herself. I knew she was . . . very drunk. Her eyes were rolling around, and she was swaying, looking at the cut on the inside of her fingers. 'We need a doctor, Neasa,' I said to

her calmly. But she ignored me. Then she eyed me up and down and, before I knew anything about it, she raised the broken bottle neck that she was still holding, up over her head, and jabbed my shoulder so hard it stayed stuck in my flesh when she took her hand away."

"Jesus . . ." Molly held her hand to her mouth.

"I remember collapsing onto the cold kitchen tiles with the sheer agony. The pain shot right through me, all the way down to my toes. It blotted out all sound, all of the light. It was just pitch dark, I was dizzy from the pain. Then I went cold, almost went out . . . almost lost consciousness. I remember looking down at my shoulder, focusing my eyes on the green neck of this bottle, embedded in me; and the blood shooting up into my face and across onto Neasa's blouse. She started to scream, pulling paper tissues out of her handbag and pushing them into the raw flesh around the bottle. "I remember pleading with her, barely able to get my tongue around the words, *'Please, get the doctor . . . please . . . please . . . get the doctor!'*

"I could still hear your voice, getting closer and closer. Then I remember seeing you at the kitchen door, staring at me on the floor, your eyes following the trails of blood as they ran into the grouting between the black and white tiles. I remember your mother screaming at you, *'Get back to your bed, now!'* I remember you running back into the darkness crying, like I've never heard you crying."

Molly clung on to my jacket sleeve and pulled gently. "What did you do?"

"Well, she threatened to kill me if I tried to ring the doctor again. She told me she would swear in his presence and get you to do the same that I had stabbed myself in an effort to make it look like she had done it. She warned me, if I tried to make the phone call after she'd gone asleep, that she'd finally kill me in my sleep some night when I would least expect her to do it . . . if I called Doctor Moyne."

"And did you?"

"No. Your temperature came down very quickly, thank God, probably from the fright of what you saw. You fell asleep after that. And I nursed the hole in my shoulder for the rest of the night. I drove into Limerick the following morning and went to a casualty where I was sure no one knew me or, more importantly, your mother. They stitched it up there and gave me an antibiotic for an infection that had already started."

"What did you tell them happened to you?"

"I told them I was in a fight with a guy who tried to steal my car."

"Did they believe you?"

"In Limerick? Of course they believed me."

"And what happened?"

"Not a lot. Your mother never mentioned it after that night. It was like as if nothing ever happened. I'm not sure if she even remembered doing it, she was so drunk."

"And why didn't you report it to the police?"

"In Claddagh Mines? I might as well have stood up at Sunday Mass and disgraced myself."

"Did you ever try to talk to her about it since then?"

"I suppose I was afraid to mention it. It was over as far as I was concerned. I was fearful that reminding her of it would make her try it again. Anyway I was worried sick of what she might try to do to you if she ever took another turn."

I had said enough. I sat still and stared across the manicured lawn at the little church and its comforting stance in the scheme of things.

Molly glanced across at my watch. It was almost one. Her mother was due back shortly, and I didn't particularly want to be around for that.

17

Over the following few days Molly continued to make a steady recovery while I was rapidly enjoying the notion of being a Dubliner again. Cruickshank called to say they were relocating her to a small, airy room in Loricar, which housed most of the hospital's off-the-critical-list convalescents, overlooking the pleasant gardens that had become our very own private retreat.

Karen called late that Sunday night to confirm my worst suspicions. She wouldn't be able to travel Monday night. Business was booming because of the good weather they were enjoying in New England. She was on the verge of panic – I could hear it in her voice – as a result of stocks of most of our bestsellers becoming depleted. Thelma Brady had kindly offered to relieve her but couldn't get away from the Bed & Breakfast before Wednesday, at the earliest. I was delighted that Thelma had been so kind to offer; she loved books with a voracious appetite. I knew the shop would be in good hands. It gave me the option of staying in Ireland as long as was required. Karen left a message on Sunday night to say she had rebooked her flight to Ireland for overnight Friday, arriving in Dublin on Saturday morning.

I spent most of my days – from late morning to late afternoon – visiting Molly. Neasa had no choice but to return to work immediately in the hospital in Kilkenny; they were short-staffed, which meant she was out of the equation for the moment. I was so relieved not to have to face her on a daily basis. She commuted most evenings and returned home to Claddagh Mines after visiting hours ended: a five-hour round-trip. I suggested that she might stay in the second bedroom in Molly's apartment on the occasional night if the long return journey was proving too arduous. She told me, in no uncertain terms, that she would prefer to sleep with the snakes in Dublin zoo rather than share the same space as me.

It had to be said, in no uncertain terms, that suited me fine.

* * *

Molly's apartment became my temporary base from which to work. I enjoyed the freedom of being able to come and go as I pleased; the flexibility that goes hand-in-hand with living alone. While I missed Karen, I knew it would only be for a few days; and I was certain that

Molly was on her own way to full health again. She looked stronger and more resilient with each new visit.

Our conversations remained mostly inconsequential and harmonious. I told her about my time in teacher-training college and about life on the Cape, and some of the places I wanted her to visit with me after I returned there. I still hadn't broached the subject of her suicide attempt and what might have caused it. The consultant – his name had begun to infuriate me – advised me against jumping headlong into such a complication-fraught area. It was a no-go limbo for the moment until Molly saw fit to talk about it. He reassured me that if I stayed close to her, and vigilant, it would all become clear to me in its own good time. I accepted his superior judgement but there were two questions that plagued me constantly in the days following her incarceration and I was becoming more impatient by the hour to find answers: Who found her in the bath and rang for the ambulance? And how did she, or he, manage to get into the apartment at just that precise moment?

Of course there were other questions that sprang mainly from undiluted anxiety. I spent most of my waking hours convincing myself that they *would* be answered in due course. My priority now, and my catalyst to unlocking the secrets of the past, was to gain her confidence. After all, we hadn't set sight on each other for nearly eight years.

* * *

From day one, I rose early most mornings, about seven, washed and shaved, and went around the corner to a small coffee shop called Nell's Café, close to the Smithfield fruit markets, in the shadow of Chief O'Neill's with its huge cobble-bricked viewing tower, and beyond to the old brewery walls across the River Liffey.

Nell, a seventy-two-year-old chain-smoker she swore to me, quickly got used to seeing me and had a pot of black coffee and three thick slices of crisply burnt toast smothered with strawberry jam ready each morning when I arrived shortly after eight. I brought my *Irish Times* and read it from front to back, watching, over the top of each page, the sellers and truckers and taxi-drivers and building labourers come and go. It was as Dublinesque as you were likely to get anywhere.

Daylight was late to arrive those balmy November mornings. It was strange seeing people queuing for buses in the dark, wearing shorts and light sleeveless shirts. After breakfast, I strolled the half-mile or so to the hospital. Molly would ask what day it was, and I would tell her what Nell's outlook on life had been that morning.

I spent my evenings reading. I missed my bookstore on the Cape but made up for it by flashing my credit card each time I set foot in Waterstones or wandered back across town to Easons. I devoured books on depression, read insatiably about suicide, broken marriages, domestic violence, and scanned the shelves for anything to do with childhood trauma. I wasn't sure what I was looking for but I had developed an almost animated belief that, whatever it was, I would recognise it when I stumbled on it.

* * *

On Tuesday afternoon, Cruickshank took me aside and told me that I could take Molly out of the hospital for a few hours that evening if she felt up to it. "Nothing too energetic," he warned me. I was thrilled at the notion of being able to chauffeur my daughter around town, take her for a meal . . . maybe even a show.

I had noticed how despondent she was becoming with the hospital routine: a daily merry-go-round of tests . . . questions from junior interns, orientation, facilitation, antidepressants, tranquillisers and more questions.

I was also delighted when I recognised that familiar cynical sharpness that told me she was getting well. When I announced that I was taking her out for a meal, she asked if she would have to wear a leash for the duration of her "temporary release". On the other hand, I was gobsmacked when Neasa called from home to say she had managed to get the following day off work and would love to come. It occurred to me that Neasa never "loved" to do anything unless there was a pay-off in it for her.

Immediately I set about changing the plans. I wasn't going to sit opposite Neasa and listen to her moaning about her job all night, and about how exhausted she felt all the time, and picking faults with my new *Bon Homme* shirt, and telling me that none of this would have happened if I hadn't neglected my daughter for so long. I organised tickets for a live comedy show – Neasa hated comedy – and booked a late table for last orders at *Ristorante Bucci*, a cosy, intimate Italian place that Molly had raved about during one of our phone conversations. "I've got to take you there the next time you're home," she kept saying. I called Molly on her mobile and checked that she felt comfortable with the arrangements. When I told her I had tickets for *D'Unbelievables*, she screamed. I knew it was going to be a good night, if a little different.

My giddiness quickly evaporated that afternoon following a quick phone call to Cruickshank. I needed to know what time he expected me to drop Molly back to the hospital. I envisaged that the meal would drag on past midnight, provided Neasa didn't take one of her turns and spoil the evening.

"OK," he agreed, "no later than midnight. She really ought to be resting. No nightclubs, Dave," he quipped.

"Great," I said. "I'll collect her at seven."

"Before you go – Dave, you seem to like calling our switch."

I blanked. "Sorry?"

"Why did you ring the main switchboard to enquire about Molly when you could have spoken to her on her mobile? Is there something you need to ask me?"

I thought for a moment about my phone calls that day. "I didn't ring the switchboard."

"Fine. It must've been someone else then."

"Was it Neasa?"

"No, it was a man. The receptionist mentioned that he rang the main hospital number three or four times today enquiring about Molly. I assumed it was you."

"Did he leave a number?"

"Not that I know of. Oh, by the way, I'd like to have a chat with you at some stage tomorrow maybe about some aftercare therapy I've recommended for Molly. Give my secretary a call and we'll set up a meeting. Have a nice evening and make sure she doesn't drink the hard stuff. She's on some delicate medication. Bye bye."

He was gone.

My mind raced, so much so that I knocked the telephone off the glass coffee table. I stared at it as it lay upside down on the carpet, while something told me that the caller was the same man who called the ambulance for Molly that night. I grabbed the telephone directory and looked up hospitals. I scribbled the main number on the inside of the front cover. Recovering the phone, I dialled as quickly as my finger could punch the digits. It started to ring.

"Hello, Saint Patrick's Hospital, can I help you?" an innocuous voice asked.

"Yes, this is David Freeman. My daughter, Molly, is a patient with you there . . ."

"Hold please, and I'll transfer you. What ward is she . . . "

"*No!*" I yelled into the phone. "There's no need to transfer me. Listen," I said calmly and apologetically, "I was just wondering if you could maybe take a note of the names of anyone who might ring up asking about Molly?" I knew, as soon as I'd finished making my request, that no hospital would be receptive to such a ridiculous request. So now I just waited to be told politely.

"I'm sorry, Mr Freeman . . . that just wouldn't be possible, I'm afraid."

"Thank you." As I put the phone down, it occurred to me that, like me, someone out there that evening was agonising over my daughter's health and welfare; and that, more imperatively, that someone held the answers to most of my questions.

18

"David Freeman, I'm collecting my daughter," I told the security guard at the hospital gate. He waved me on and raised the barrier. I was feeling feisty and straitened for a reason I couldn't place. I had not seen Neasa for ten years – extenuating circumstances, I told people after explaining I was separated – and here we all were: my psychotic ex-wife, my deeply depressed daughter and me! Perhaps I was the one who should have been certified; maybe they were perfectly normal and I had unhinged their lives, and thrown their cosy, happy existences into complete chaos as a result of my selfishness. I straightened up in the seat. "You have to stop thinking like a madman, Freeman," I advised myself. We were sharing a meal, a family night out, in a swanky, top-drawer restaurant: *we*, a bunch of misplaced misfits! *Stop this now!* I said out loud, or you're asking for trouble.

I looked at the clock on the dashboard; I was almost

half an hour late. I knew I could expect a verbal roasting.

Karen had called, ecstatic. She had received a letter in the post that morning. She had passed her exams; she was now a fully qualified behavioural therapist. It was all she had ever wanted to be in the four years that we had come to know and to love each other. I was the one who had urged her on those long cold, winter nights to do something about it. "Don't just sit there imagining you can do it. Get off your ass and *do it!* Home study, why not?" She applied and was accepted immediately. I was the one who pushed her into the back office night after night while she pleaded with me to open another bottle of wine; I told her she would definitely fail her exams if she didn't read and work on her notes and essays for three hours every evening. Now she was only a year away from qualifying as a fully-fledged clinical psychologist. The world of the human mind was at her fingertips. Doctor Karen McQuillan; it had a nice ring to it. She'd clinked a glass of champagne against the phone and told me to crack open a bottle over dinner, and raise a glass to her success.

I was so pleased for her, but couldn't help worrying that she might leave the Cape . . . leave me. I could tell by her voice that she already had. She was already wearing the white coat. I could hear the diagnoses piling up in her excitement. Her final year in psychology meant full time intern work, possibly in Massachusetts Children's Hospital, in Boston. Commuting was not an option. Already she was talking about the two of us relocating to the city; I could get a job as a teacher. "You could study at night, Dave . . . graduate as a lecturer in Modern English . . . take charge of a college basketball team . . ."

"Hang on . . . wait, wait, *wait* a minute!" I howled. Her mind was running away on a farrago of wild woolgathering. I just laughed warmly as she cheered me on and thought all the while of what it would be like to lose her. I had already nearly lost my daughter. I couldn't cope with losing my other soul mate so soon.

While it was magnificent news, it was the last thing I needed to hear that night. At least she had booked her flight and bought her ticket. She would be in Dublin on Saturday, I kept telling myself. I had to put any upshots of her likely decision firmly to the back of my mind. Tonight I was Herr-Host to two strange guests whom I felt both close to and detached from.

* * *

At first I didn't recognise her.

I saw Molly instantly. She was dressed in a smart beige-brown-coloured jacket and matching trousers. She wore black high-heeled shoes, steel-tipped. I assumed the discreet peaked cap was to hide the cropped hair. A light dab of make-up highlighted her beautiful looks. The black rings under her eyes were gone, replaced by a peach-bloom glow.

I thought the woman standing slightly in front of

Molly, in the shade of the hospital entrance, was a stranger. Perhaps she was a friend hoping for a lift. I got a shock when I realised it was Neasa.

She had dyed her hair since last I saw her. Under the hospital porch-lights it seemed orange. She wore a black dress that looked three or four sizes too small. Her bare legs, although tanned, were fat and clumpy. The dress exposed her breasts, bunched together for optimum effect. The high-heels made her six inches taller, bringing her up to head-height with Molly.

When last I saw Neasa in such an outfit, we were holidaying in Ibiza and she was twenty years younger. I wasn't sure whether she had tarted herself up for my benefit, or perhaps she thought dressing young and outrageously would bridge her notion of a generation gap between Molly and her. Either way she looked like a cheap whore waiting for a truck driver who had reached the last resort.

She was caked in tacky make-up. Her lips looked swollen and her eyes black. A Prada handbag hung from her shoulder. I counted six rings and three wrist bracelets. I couldn't decide on genuine gold or cheap imitations.

Whatever, she was trying to prove a point. She was making a statement and I didn't give a rat's ass. I hadn't travelled three-and-a-half thousand miles to admire her sassy outfit.

They both waved, smiling. I waved back in absolute shock. I felt underdressed for the occasion, a pale blue

Burberry shirt and jeans, a brown bum-length leather jacket, black leather pointed boots. It was casual. Too casual now, I thought.

They didn't wait for me to get out, Molly slapping the bonnet as she ran around the front of the car shouting, "I bags the front seat." As I leaned across to open the door for her, Neasa was already capering across to the middle of the back seat, making herself comfortable. I could tell from the scent that they had shared perfumes.

"Hiya, Dad." Molly leaned across and kissed me on the cheek, hugging my neck with her hand. "You look great."

"So do the two of you," I replied warmly, not giving any thought to what I had just said. I looked in the rear-view mirror and caught Neasa smiling at me. My heart sank for a second. Her smile said so much and re-echoed times and places from the past that I had long forgotten about. I heard myself complimenting her. "You look lovely," I said into the mirror. *Jesus Christ! Did I really say that?* I shuddered and realised we were connected again.

Molly stroked my hair. "You look so handsome, Dad," she said.

I blushed. Then I grinned. My cheeks were on fire. I was glad it was dark. This time I avoided looking in the mirror. "We better get moving or we'll miss the show."

Molly piped up, like she did the Sunday afternoons we drove into the foothills of Sliabh na mBan as a family. "I'll navigate; considering I've got a culchie behind me and a blow-in half-Yank beside me, we might never find this place!"

I often wonder if they had a plan that night orchestrated accordingly against minute details thrashed out in advance; or was it purely just a coincidence that we were a family again?

* * *

It was a Berlin blue Mercedes 500SL, soft top. I'd recognise it anywhere; Ted Aitken had just bought one and shipped it to Martha's Vineyard. I noticed it pulling out behind me as I left the hospital car park and joined the traffic. I paid no attention to what was behind me after that, consumed and confused by Molly's lightning-sharp directions, with only seconds to react, through the heart of the old city, as she called each turn like a world-rally-class navigation champion. Fifteen minutes later we were parking in a side street close to the theatre. I glanced in my rear mirror twice, quite quickly, and found it odd that he was there on both occasions, a good distance behind us. Once we had parked, he sped past us without looking and disappeared into the evening traffic.

A coincidence? I was sure it was.

19

The show proved to be a tonic. Two comedians played off a combined audience reaction. Molly warned me beforehand not to even contemplate visiting the bathroom before the interval. "Don't even scratch your head," she warned the two of us.

From the moment the curtain went up, we laughed till our ribs ached at two professionals who knew their trade par excellence. Neasa laughed so much she disregarded Molly's advice and stood up half an hour into the first half to answer a call of nature. Molly pleaded with her not to but Neasa couldn't wait any longer.

"She's going to pay dearly for this," Molly whispered cautiously.

Pay dearly, she did. She was no sooner back in the main aisle of the theatre when one of the comedians jumped offstage and took her by the arm. He asked the audience to give "his mother" a nice round of applause, and Neasa spent the remainder of the first half of the show buttering slices of bread and making sandwiches in full view of a packed house, being referred to constantly by the two boys as "Mother", wearing an apron that bore the word, *DETENTION*, in big, bold letters and a tall dunce's hat.

The conversation over starters in *Bucci* was a mixture of hilarious horselaughing and choice lines from the show. Neasa didn't participate since she was the focus of our amusement. Eventually we had to stop ribbing her because she threatened to leave. The more we laughed at her the more she drank. Changing the subject became a commendable idea.

Bucci was an uncomplicated place, small yet charming. The aroma of the Italian menu made my stomach rumble. Molly was maître d' for the evening, ordering for the three of us. As I watched her reading so confidently off the menu in Italian, it occurred to me that I had missed all of this, all of my only daughter's teenage years when we could have been doing this together on a weekly basis. That very notion hit me like a blinding headache and stymied me for a short while in sheer disgust and heart-wrenching regret. I listened to her checking the year before she committed us to the wine. "Red or white?" she asked so masterfully. They were only little things but I noticed them because I had always felt I had been robbed of my daughter, but never more so than at that moment. She had grown up in a different world, a different culture, and I had been purposely excluded from marvelling at those magic moments and special years.

"Molly, you're not drinking. That shrink, Cruickshank, said no alcohol. You're on happy pills, and that's the way you're going to stay. Ye hear me?" I opened my eyes wide and stared at her. "She'll have water," I said to the waitress.

"*Ah, Dad!*" she yelled, sounding like a seven-year-old. "When do I get to go out for a meal with my parents?" She looked up at the waitress. "Chilean White, 1987, please. Don't listen to him; he's only my father."

"Water, p*lease!*" I emphasised.

"Wine," Molly replied.

"Water."

"*Wine!*" she said matter-of-factly, slapping the table.

"*Water*. . . and that's my final time to say it, Molly."

"*Wine*, Dad, or I'm leaving . . . *now!*"

She started to stare me down. That stubborn face hadn't changed in over ten years. I creased up laughing. In some ways, she was still only seven years old. "OK then, one glass of white wine, and not another drop. Do ye hear me?"

"Yes, Father. Thank you." She grinned at the waitress. "Make that two bottles."

"How have you been getting on?" Neasa asked.

I looked at her only to realise she was addressing the question at me. She gently sipped her vodka.

"Fine." I wasn't sure how to answer her question. How much do you tell a wife you don't like for lots of reasons that you haven't seen for ten years?

"Come on, Dad," Molly parried. "Tell us all about

Martha's Vineyard." She looked back at Neasa. "Mum, you would just adore this place. It's like paradise. Go on, Dad, tell her what it's like."

Neasa tapped the side of her glass. Her look said it all. It was a busy night in the restaurant. Since my voice carried quite naturally, I leaned forward so as not to sound too loud. "It's beautiful. I don't know another place like it on earth." I sipped my Southern Comfort. "It's home . . . to me."

Neasa nodded at my drink. "Did the Yanks teach you that?"

I knew that a row was brewing, curbed and suppressed by years of bitterness. I could tell, simply by the way she questioned my drink, that Neasa hadn't moved on anywhere. "I've always like Southern Comfort."

"No, you didn't. You never drank it while you lived here."

"Very few country pubs sold it while I lived here."

"Why don't you drink a gin . . . or a lager? Why do you have to be so particular?"

"I'm not being particular. I just like Southern Comfort, and they happen to sell it here. That's all."

Neasa bit her lip and drank her vodka. I noticed it was neat. "Want a mixer for that?" I asked, trying to be convivial.

"No, thanks. I just like it neat. Have you a problem with that?"

I shook my head and looked at Molly. "Why did you try to kill yourself?"

Molly froze. She played with the base of her glass, moving it onto the dead centre of the small white doily.

"What sort of a stupid fucking question is that to ask?" Neasa banged down her glass. "I thought we were meant to be going out as a family tonight. To try and forget about what happened for a while. What sort of a stupid freak are you, David?"

Hearing her calling me by my name just served to remind of all those times she physically tormented me. "I simply want to know what drove my daughter to such an extreme. That's all, Neasa, and I think we ought to get a couple of things straight here before we go any further. First, let's not be fooling ourselves about the family thing. We are *not* a family. You saw to that a long time ago. Second, if I choose to ask my daughter, whom I haven't *seen* in eight long years, a question, then I will. Don't you tell me what to do, OK? Let's not be fooling each other here. We're here tonight for her!" I pointed at Molly without looking at her, hoping she might step in and dissolve this smoking volcano. She said nothing.

"You haven't been here for her in over ten years." Her voice gradually rose, louder and louder. "You've been hiding away on that island over there, your little life of make-believe, imagining that everything is just fine. When was the last time you picked up the phone to see how I was?"

A dead-end conversation with an unanswerable question. "The reason I *ran away*, as you care to put it, was because I couldn't live with you any longer."

"So it was all my fault?"

"Well, since you asked, what did I do to provoke you all those times you tried to beat the crap out of me?"

Neasa looked to Molly for support. "Oh, do you hear this mild-mannered weakling, talking about a *woman* who's nearly twelve inches smaller than him, and weighs nearly five stone less than he does? *Ha!* He's probably even told you that I tried to kill him."

"Yes, he has," Molly answered, clearly in a state of disbelief.

"And do you believe him?"

Molly shrugged her shoulders. "Why should I have any reason *not* to believe him? He's my father, for God's sake. Why would my father tell me such a barefaced lie?"

"Because he wants you to feel sorry for him, Molly, that's why. It's perfectly reasonable to expect him to say anything, considering he hasn't given a damn about either of us for years, living in America with his fancy woman. Think of all the birthdays and all the Christmases he just ignored us . . . not a single bloody card or a phone call, like as if we never existed."

"I beg your pardon," I said sharply. "I have spoken to Molly on the phone every single Thursday night at half past eight for as long as I can remember. We took it in turns and I don't think there's a single Thursday that either of us has missed. Isn't that right?"

Molly nodded, clearly embarrassed now by this

painful, stripping ritual of denigration. "Except for the one when I was getting my appendix out," she said softly.

There was an almost admirable quality about Neasa's technique of wanton one-upmanship. She could have written a self-help bestseller on the subject she served it up so competently. I had had enough after ten years looking back on a painful lifetime of being walked over, I wasn't going to take any more.

"I mean just look at me." She drew back from the table and spread her arms, putting herself on display. "Do I look remotely like the sort of person that could successfully attack and kill someone like him?" She nodded at me. "A single belt from the back of one of his hands could leave me on the flat of my back." She tittered.

"*Stop!*" Molly said sharply.

I noticed that the people at the next table were absorbing the bickering with an almost raw relish. "Yes, please stop now," I said under my breath, "or I will personally pick you up by the scruff of your neck and fuck you through that window over there."

She froze. Molly looked at me, her mouth open.

"Am I making myself clear, Neasa?"

She nodded and grabbed her drink.

"Now let's get one thing straight here. I came over from America because my daughter wasn't well. That's the only reason I am here . . . not because of you, or your mother, or your brothers . . . but to see her." I pointed at

Molly. "You almost destroyed my life. That was the sole reason I left this country behind me, because, I didn't want to, I *needed* to get as far away from you as was humanly possible.

"I still don't know why I stuck by you for so long. What was it . . . ten years? I try not to think too much about it now. I guess I did it for Molly's sake. Not because I couldn't tear myself away from her, but because I was afraid of what you were capable of doing to her. You almost murdered me one night. I guess I was just terrified that you might do the same to her, some night she got upset because she couldn't figure out her homework? Some afternoon she came in from school with her socks dirty from playing hockey? You never needed any reason to have a go at me, so I reckoned why should you need a reason to slap your own daughter around?"

"Dad, please stop," Molly pleaded.

"Yes, I would like you to stop, please," Neasa echoed.

"You would *like* me to stop? Jesus, I don't believe what I'm hearing here. Molly, your mother is being civil and polite for the first time in her life!"

"Stop it!" Neasa demanded.

"Stop it? I've only just started. Hell, this Southern Comfort is good stuff. It's helping me to unwind. It's making me say all the things I've bottled up inside for fucking years. Jesus, I'm beginning to enjoy this."

"I'd like to go," Neasa insisted.

"You're not going anywhere until I've had my say.

I've waited ten long years for this opportunity. And considering it's crossed my mind what I would *like* to say to you if I ever saw you again, it's not going to take long because I suppose somewhere deep down in the dark recesses of my mind I've been rehearsing, unknown to myself. *Waiter, more vodka for my wife!*" I found myself shouting. "I think she's turning all shy on me just when I need her to fight back. Why don't you hit me, Neasa? Show our daughter the kind of stuff you're really made of." I leaned across the table toward her. "Right there." I pointed to my cheekbone. "Oh sorry, I almost forgot . . . Molly, your mother specialised in hitting me in places where no one would see the mark."

"Shut up, Dad, *now!* Or I'm leaving. Do you hear me?" Molly's eyes were filled with tears.

Suddenly I felt like shit. I raised my glass. "Right, I propose a toast. To our daughter who is twenty-one."

"*Was* twenty-one," Molly added.

"No thanks to you," Neasa muttered as she sipped her vodka, ignoring my gesture of a salute.

"And just what is that supposed to mean?" I asked rather foolishly.

"You're the one who's made a fool of himself tonight, Dave. You need help. I told you that before. You always did need help. Your trouble always was that you were too much of a *man* to admit it. You never grew up. For as long as I knew you, you were always a spoilt, arrogant, self-centred, self-righteous bastard."

"You know something, Neasa, I've always marvelled at the way you could turn everything around to suit yourself. You always had that uncanny knack of making everyone else out to be a piece of shit, and you were the shining diamond. You've spent your life lying through your fucking teeth. No matter what you've done wrong, someone else always ended up carrying the can."

Her lunge made me fall backwards off my chair. It brought back horrendous memories of that broken green bottleneck that ended up implanted in the flesh below my right shoulder. For a split second I could feel the searing hot pain again. The vodka on my face felt like fresh blood for a second: it stung my eyes. It got up my nose. It soaked my shirt and my trousers. For such a small glass, it felt like I was completely saturated. As she stood up and put her black cardigan around her shoulders, towering above me, I wanted to say something but she managed to beat me to it.

"You'll pay for this, Dave," she seethed. "And I don't mean the meal." Hate filled her whole face. She beckoned Molly to follow her to the door, then took her firmly by the arm and led her out.

She wanted my daughter to be in her gang. I could only imagine what she was saying to her as they waited out on the street for me. "What a clown . . . what a complete fucking idiot, with all his lies and all his bullshit. He's unstable. We're better off without him. Let him stay in America, as far away from us as possible. I'll look after you. I'll make you better."

Neasa was doing what she knew best. Each time she did it I cringed and begged that God might give me the strength and courage to run away from her. Now, ten years later, she had just done something that re-enforced my convictions as to why I despised her. I stood up and handed the waiter my VISA card. I turned to the audience. "Sorry for any inconvenience, folks. A lovers' tiff, that's all," I mouthed wryly.

I signed the chit and left.

* * *

We drove back to the hospital in silence. I was mad with myself for unleashing such a tirade of anger and abuse in front of Molly. Jesus Christ! Only days earlier, my daughter had tried to kill herself. She was recovering now, everything about her brittle and unpredictable, her future and stability uncertain. She needed to be told she was loved immeasurably and beyond doubt. We should have been hugging her, cosseting her in safety and wrapping her in our arms with words and gestures of reassurance. And what did we do? What we always did: we fought and argued and disagreed. And *hated!*

Of all the times I could have picked, that evening should never have been an option. During my flight across the Atlantic I had sworn to myself Molly would be my only concern. I hadn't allowed Neasa inside my mind for years and I was damned if she going to get there during this trip. My mercy mission, I had told myself, was Molly-focused, nothing else. I was worried now how she might be reacting. What if she turned suicidal again as a result of the bitter exchange she had witnessed in the restaurant? I tried to watch her without looking at her directly. She fiddled with the tips of the bandages that came to the ends of her sleeves. Now and then she contorted her face and pulled at her ear. I'd had it with Neasa. No more. We were through arguing. No, I thought. We were through, period.

"This must be what a hearse-driver's job is like," I said deliberately, tongue-in-cheek. The two women sat in the back seat. Occasionally I heard a sniffle, and a nose being rubbed with a dry paper tissue. It was a bit late for niceties; Neasa, one; Dave, nil, I kept thinking, the way she might see it; it was like a game to her, and tonight she was truly victorious. I needed to talk seriously with Molly. Tonight was not the right time.

As I eased the car through the hospital gates, slowing to allow the barrier to lift, I noticed the blue Mercedes pass behind us. It slowed as it passed behind us, then sped up as it continued on down to the bridge over the Liffey.

20

The apartment felt familiar to me now, in a way you expect a place won't become for years, like a new home takes on a strange intimacy after just a short stay. I knew where everything was, without having to look. The rumble of the fridge motor seemed to be years old by now. The light from the kitchen seemed inoffensive, compared to my first night there. It felt like my property, my retreat. I had even taken the liberty of moving things around, albeit a little at a time, until I felt comfortable with my surroundings.

I checked my watch. It was ten to two in the morning. I wanted more than anything, at that moment, to feel tired. I couldn't. Sleep had been chased away by the queue of painful conflicts and sharp-edged components that were battling it out against each other for space in my brain. I yawned, more out of sheer frustration.

I had been watching the reflection off the pale orange street-light outside the sitting-room window move slowly across the open floor space as the November full moon moved from right to left in the sky. I must have been staring at the window for an hour.

Neasa had barricaded herself into the master bedroom. It was only on that condition that she would agree to stay in Dublin that night – if she was given the key to the bedroom door so she could lock herself in. I'm not sure which possibility scared her more: the notion of me snuggling up beside her, butt-naked, suggesting a night of rampant, unbridled sexual athletics, or the equally unlikely prospect of her waking from a deep sleep to find me at the foot of her bed, foaming at the mouth, wielding a machete.

I suggested that she should leave the door unlocked if she was thinking of throwing herself from the bedroom window onto the street below; especially if she was hoping that the police might think I pushed her.

The silence was a gift, and would been absolute if it weren't for the loud, intermittent electrical hum that caused the fridge to shudder every few minutes, each time it stopped. On one occasion it practically swayed. I thought the fridge might fall off its narrow parapet onto the floor. It was while I was investigating the reason for this unbalance that I found a hardback copybook, jammed between the fridge's motor and the flaked wall. Judging by the coat of dust, it would appear to have been lodged there for a long time. I stood under the kitchen light and gently blew at the dust. Black handwritten, zigzag letters, over a dark-red background, were barely legible.

Molly Freeman. Strictly Private & Confidential.

I opened it. Written on the inside of the front cover in large, wavy, curling letters, were the words, *Things that make me happy;* on the next page, on the uppermost line, the words, *Things that make me sad.* The writing beneath each headline was tiny and fading. Her writing from line to line was uneven. Many of the sentences were unfinished, as if not properly thought out, with a thin red stroke of a biro to the left of each one that had been completed. A selection of reasons she was happy; some more why she was sad. Much of the writing was illegible, like tired scrawl. I tried to make sense of some of the longer words, the end of which just became flat lines. I turned the page. *Why I hate myself* was written across the top of another page packed with reasons. I turned the page again. *People I like who make me feel good.*

This was behaviour therapy. I remembered Karen raving about its benefits in counselling situations one night while she was studying for her psychology exams. She spoke about it until I had dozed off.

Behaviour therapists set specific goals for changing our behaviour and use a variety of learning techniques to help us achieve those goals. This therapy is often based on the principle of classical conditioning, the association between two things. This was Molly's book for a therapy known as *systematic desensitisation*, where she learns to pair a relaxation response with an anxiety-provoking situation. The more favoured, beneficial one overrules the harmful one.

My heart pounded hard as I sat down with a fresh mug of tea and started to study what I began to realise were my daughter's efforts to get help for, and get well from, something that had obviously plagued her for a long, long time and eventually driven her to the brink of life; something she had never told me about. I studied her writing. Some of the sentences seemed to be formulated as responses to specific searching questions. Other sentences made no sense whatsoever.

The things I could read properly that made Molly happy made me smile. I skipped through them quickly, looking for my name, hoping that I would account for plenty of her happiness.

> *Phone calls and e-mails from my dad*
> *Hearing my dad telling me that he loves me*
> *Shopping with Mum*

I threw my head back against the soft upholstery of the armchair and smiled. The joy of knowing I had made my daughter happy was worth all the pain I had come through. A smile outshone a thousand frowns.

It was a different story, though, when I turned the page and started to read the handwriting under the heading of what made her mad.

> *The times she told me she wished my dad was dead*
> *The times she brought men back from the pub and let*
> *them sleep in her bed*
> *The night J followed me home*

Suddenly I was angry, without warning. I felt as though I had no control whatsoever over the sheer thrust of bitterness and resentment I felt rising up inside me at that moment. I chose to stare at the window again, look at distant object and attempt to diffuse the dangerous unpredictability of what was going on inside my head at that moment.

It felt so instinctive. Kill . . . kill. . . kill, spontaneously. Find the bastard who had pushed my daughter over the edge and rip his fucking heart out.

Jesus Christ! She's my daughter.

I kept staring at the window, trying to see what was beyond it on the other side of the street, stretching my vision to see further still, trying to see something that might distract my swarmed, one-track mind at that moment, willing this to remain beyond me simply because it was farcical to even imagine, and appalling and sickening to think of, too much for any father to bear. But I wasn't just any father. I was *her* father, here, now. That young woman I argued foolishly in front of in a restaurant that she had recommended tonight. She was still only eleven years old in my heart. I was trembling with a rage, gallons of bad blood, I had never experienced before. I knew once I kept things beyond the window, I kept telling myself, I would cope until . . . until . . . until what? There were no answers. Jesus.

Just a burning, insatiable need to kill.

I tried to tell myself that she was twenty-one now. But all I could see was a twenty-one-year-old trying to kill herself. How lonely must she have been that she couldn't have picked up the phone that night and called me? What was it that had stolen her will to live? The letter, *J*, was burning me up now, consuming me to the point where I was no longer rational. Was I right to assume that *J* was responsible for her suicide attempt? Or had *J* something to do with that night long ago that lived on in me at that moment as if it had just happened a fraction of a second ago, when she was a mere eleven-year-old child? That night she arrived home with a bruised, cut-up face and a look of sheer terror in her eyes?

It took me a few glances back at the page to notice the scribbled writing in the bottom corner. It had been crossed out heavily. I held the page close to the light bulb. I could make out a few letters: *K and W*. Slowly I deciphered the block capitals in between.

21

Killcrow. The word made perfect sense. It played mercilessly on my mind. I watched the night's darkness change slowly, turning softly to a hazy greyish-blue dawn, to eventual, piercing daylight. Sleep had come unexpectedly and, with it, a dream I thought I'd rid my subconscious of, an ordeal I hadn't been haunted by for years. Only now, it took on a whole new life-form, transposed through the years, from the past to the present. I sat perfectly still in the armchair thinking back over each terrorising detail.

I was in the classroom, standing with my back to the children, chalking history notes on the blackboard. It must have been after eight because it was dark. Halloween, I remember. I offered private tuition on Tuesday and Thursday evenings, between October and December from seven to nine to the children I felt weren't capable of keeping up with the rest of the class during daytime studies, made up mostly of pupils in their final year of primary school. That evening there were six students learning history. I turned around and asked a question, "Can anyone tell me about the Vikings and what year they came to Ireland?"

One of the children, Olivia Fogarty, raised her hand. I nodded to her and she stood up, composing herself to begin her story. It was at that moment I became distracted. Her voice seemed to drift away to some distant, echo-charged corner of the room. My jaw dropped and I could feel the blood running from my face. I stared, rooted to the spot, at the window for as long as the face gazed back at me. It wasn't even a face. It was hideously evil; a mask with two piercing black holes where the eyes should have been. It was something out of hell, a grotesquely distorted nose and a small oval-shaped mouth. It was all I could see, set against the pitch-blackness behind and the brightness of the huge lights in the classroom.

Olivia Fogarty stopped her eulogy and screamed. Her screaming went on and on as she placed her hands over her eyes. I watched her peeping through occasionally and screaming louder. Then everyone was shouting and crying in the most hideous, panic-stricken din I can ever remember. I tried to calm them to no effect. It wasn't until I roared at the top of my voice, *"Shut up!"* that they started to calm down. I looked again. The face was gone.

I told the children not to leave the room. I ran as fast as I could, skating and sliding on the corridor tiles that had just been mopped, giving off that noxious, choking carbolic smell. Once outside, I could see nothing in the darkness. I waited for a few seconds until my eyes had adjusted to night sight. Still nothing. I ran over to the window and peered in, only causing the children to go back into convulsions of screaming. And all the time, as I turned around in circles, my body trembling like it would on a freezing cold night, looking out across the playground, and beyond into the cattle and sheep-laden fields that ran to the foothills of the Silvermine mountains, I knew that whatever, or whoever, had looked through my classroom window that night was still watching me. At that precise moment I was gripped with the worst jolt of uncontrollable fear that I can ever remember.

I spent the remainder of the lesson calming the children, until their parents arrived to collect them, telling them it was nothing; just a practical joker trying to frighten us on Halloween. My trivialising fell on deaf ears. Their eyes told me they were petrified, even after I had pulled down the roller-blinds on the three huge windows. It occurred to me then to ask the children if any of them had seen that mask before. My heart froze when, slowly, every one of them raised their hands. I looked at Olivia Fogarty. "Did you see it before, Olivia?"

She nodded, said nothing.

"When?"

Now she shook her head and squeezed her lips

together. She wasn't going to tell me. "Will someone please tell me what's going on?" I scanned the room slowly. All six children had bunched together now. They stared at me.

"Please don't ask us," Paul Branach whimpered from behind the two girls in the front row.

"Why not?" I asked gently.

Olivia Fogarty spoke this time. "Because he'll get us."

I waited, trying to digest beyond what they were telling me. "*Who* will get you?"

Two of the children nodded towards the curtained window.

"Him," Olivia sobbed.

"And who is he?"

Olivia was about to say something.

"*Don't tell him!*" Paul Branach shouted. "*Or he'll get you!*"

Olivia ignored the threat. "He's the Killcrow . . ."

I woke up at that moment, sweating and gasping, as if someone had two hands wrapped around my throat. A rancid, bitter bile rose up in my throat. I started to cough. My chest was heaving, my heart racing. I took slow deep breaths and sat up, counting to ten as I paced my breathing.

Saturday morning, December 3

It was dawn. I was happier than I had been in days. I rang the airport to check on the arrival time of Karen's flight from Boston. It had been delayed until ten. It was just after eight. I checked on Neasa. The bedroom door was still locked. I could hear the snoring. Leave her be, I thought.

I popped around to Nell's for breakfast, taking Molly's notebook with me. I fully believed that something in there, the smallest smidgeon, might tell me why life became too much.

I stepped out onto the street and was about to pull the main door behind me when I noticed it: the blue Mercedes that had followed us the previous Tuesday.

As I walked past the car I slowed down. The driver was hidden behind a copy of the *Irish Independent*. For the sake of peace of mind, I put it down to strange coincidence.

It was still bugging me after leaving Nell's half an hour later. And rightly so, I told myself; when I turned the corner he was still there. I checked my watch. 8.45am. Time for a spot of hoodwinking. I took out my keys and went to give the impression that I was opening the main door leading to the apartment-block foyer. Instead I ducked back and dipped down behind the front of the hired car, easing my way around on all fours to the driver's door. I killed the alarm. The doors unlocked automatically.

I opened my door and slid into the seat, fumbling to get the master key into the ignition. Engine started, I glanced in the rear-view. All I could see was a newspaper. I eased my way out into the main traffic lane and revved hard. Within seconds he was directly behind me. The bastard was right on my tail. But why?

I estimated I had fifty yards to the main junction that would bring me onto Smithfield fruit markets. There was nothing in front of me all the way to the traffic-lights. I accelerated, counted to five and, just as quickly, slammed my foot hard on the brake pedal. Hearing the screech of the Mercedes behind me getting closer, I braced myself for the impact. The damage was more than I had bargained for. The force of the Mercedes hitting the back of the hired Mondeo pushed my car forward. The actual thrust was deafening. I glanced into the back-seat area. The force of the impact had pushed everything forward a couple of feet, the back window smashed. But it was the only way to find out exactly who this stranger was and, more specifically, why he was following me. I staggered out of the car holding the back of my neck.

22

Karen scanned the multitudes of people outside the arrivals doors, most of them waiting to meet passengers from the transatlantic flight. Even her obvious tiredness couldn't detract from her stunning beauty. She was dragging her trolley-case behind her, wearing that familiar, heavyweight appearance called jet-lag. I needed her at that very moment to throw her arms around me and tell me that everything would be all right. I waved and forced myself to smile. She beamed back at me and broke into an awkward dash, throwing herself at me with wide-open arms.

We hugged and kissed.

"I missed you," was all I could say to her. She felt so good, the taste of her skin as I kissed her, the familiar scent of the Blue Water perfume that she always wore on special occasions. But the special moment had been marred by tragedy.

"I missed you too." She looked at me and knew. "Why the long face? Is everything OK, Dave?" She let her arms slide down into my hands. "What's wrong?" she asked, taking in the shocked look on my face.

"I had a bit of an accident while I was driving out to the airport this morning." I faked a smile, trying hard to undermine the seriousness of what had happened.

"Are you OK?" she asked in a concerned voice.

"Yeah, I'm fine."

"What happened?" She stood the trolley-bag to one side and put her arms around my waist.

"A guy in a car crashed into me as I was leaving the apartment to come out here to collect you."

"Did he stop?"

"Yeah, he stopped all right."

"Was it his fault?" she asked.

"Suppose it was. He drove into the back of my car."

"Well then, it *was* his fault. So it won't cost you any money to get the damage to your car fixed. Did you call the police?"

"Yes."

"And did they say whose fault it was?"

"Yes."

"And did they caution the guy who ran into you?"

"No."

"Why not?"

"Because he's dead."

* * *

Karen persuaded me to have a drink in the arrivals terminal bar; a stiff brandy, she said, would relax me. I sipped it, still shaking from the experience. I had told lie after lie to the police when they arrived at the scene. Within minutes there was an ambulance and the man driving the blue Mercedes was gone, out of my life as abruptly as he had entered. Karen sat opposite me, waiting patiently to hear more, reluctant to question as she could see that her curiosity was irritating me.

I shivered each time I sipped the Hennessy. I apologised each time I put my glass down. "I'm sorry, Karen."

"Don't keep saying sorry, Dave. I'm glad I got here. You will get over this. You're just suffering from shock right now, that's all. You're bound to feel traumatised after something like that. It's not your fault."

"It *is* my fault."

"It's *not* your fault," she insisted. "The police even told you that. He was driving too fast."

"I could have prevented it, Karen."

Karen took my hand and squeezed it between hers. "Dave, listen to me. These things happen. There is nothing you could have done to prevent that man from dying. For a start he wasn't wearing a seat-belt . . ."

"I jammed on," I shouted, cutting her short.

She looked at me. "At the traffic-lights?"

"No. He was following me. I braked, intending to get out of my car and go back and find out why he was tailing me."

"How do you know he was following you?" she asked in a surprised tone of voice.

"Because he sat behind me all night last Tuesday. He followed us into town to the theatre. He was there again when I dropped Molly back to the hospital. I'd seen him on and off at a distance. *And* he was even there when I stepped out for breakfast first thing this morning."

"And are you sure he was *following* you?"

Karen's question seemed absurd. "Well, of course he was following me! I doubt he was just relying on me to find his way around town."

"Did you tell the police?"

"Of course not. They would have looked for proof. That would be great, wouldn't it? 'That man was following me, Officer.' 'Oh, was he now? And why was that?' 'Well, actually I'm not sure. So I thought the best way to find out was to invite him into the backseat of my car for a few minutes.' For a start they'd do me for manslaughter most likely."

"It was an accident, for God's sake. You didn't intend to kill him," she pleaded.

"That's what manslaughter is: unlawful homicide without premeditation. I could still get eight years."

Karen laughed gently and pulled at my hand. "You are not going to go to prison." She stood up. "Did you get a look at him?"

I shook my head. "He was slumped over the steering wheel. The top of his head was face down on the dashboard. There were bits of glass everywhere. His head must have gone right through the windscreen. I couldn't see his face. I don't even know what he looked like. There was blood everywhere. It felt like the cops were there in seconds. I didn't even have a chance to see if he was still alive. Then they started questioning me. And before I knew it the doors of the ambulance were closed and he was gone." I downed what was left of my brandy, letting it warm my throat and gullet, and stood up and stretched. I felt like a bag of boiled shite.

* * *

I turned the key in the door to Molly's apartment and forced it open wide with my foot. I was just about to manoeuvre the trolley-bag through when Neasa stepped out into the hallway. My heart almost stopped. It was the last thing I would have expected. She had told me the night before that she would be returning to Kilkenny on the 9.05am train. She was still wearing a white nightdress and looked awful. I could tell she had been crying.

"Why are you still here?" I asked. "Did you sleep it out? Why aren't you at work?"

She sobbed and rubbed her nose. "I got a phone call from my mother. Turloch was killed in a car crash this morning."

"Where?" I asked.

"Here in Dublin," Neasa replied, sniffing and coughing.

At first her words were simply just that: words. I never felt anything personable for her brothers, not once regarding them as family. They were ruthless, conniving bastards who made the lives of other people, mostly decent folk, who came in contact with them miserable. "Whereabouts did it happen?" I asked, expecting to tell her afterwards about a coincidence.

"Just up the road from here." She pointed in the direction of my own incident. "He crashed into the back of another car and went through the windscreen. The police rang Mammy and she called me. She's in an awful state. She wants me to go to the city morgue to identify his body."

Dizzy and physically weakened, I sat down. Scatterbrained, I tried to rationalise what I had just heard. Another anxiety gripped me almost immediately. "What was your brother doing here in Dublin? I thought he was a cop down the bog."

Karen sat down beside me.

"I'm sorry, this is Karen," I explained somewhat awkwardly. "I meant to introduce her before now. She's just after getting off the plane from Boston."

Neasa blew her nose loud and long, as if to ignore the introduction. "He hasn't worked as a cop in over five years. He's a private operator now, moved to Dublin nearly four years ago . . . studied criminology at university in the evenings. He set himself up as a private investigator a couple of years ago. He was doing really well, making good money, he told me. I always thought some jealous two-timing bastard of a husband he was trying to find information on'd shoot him. I never thought he'd end up going through his own windscreen. " The two-timing bastard dig was aimed at me.

"What kind of surveillance work did he do?" Karen asked politely.

"Everything. Mostly domestic . . . a wife thinks her husband is having an affair; she calls Turloch and he watches the husband for as long as it takes to get enough information for the client."

If ever there was a predestined career that would have suited Turloch Maher, it was this one surely. A sleazy, pathetic existence, man and vocation perfectly matched. He was a fat, tactless, uncaring, cold-hearted bastard who always meddled and interfered in the lives of others, a nosey tyrant who deserved his come-uppance, I couldn't help thinking to myself. The job was tailor-made for him, hand in glove. My only regret was that I had to be involved. While Neasa continued her nervous twittering about Turloch, painting an image of a man who deserved honour and respect and every medal and award imaginable, I locked myself in the bathroom and sat on the bidet. I needed to be alone to consider my options: my *modus operandi*; I could come clean and tell Neasa right now what had happened; that it was my car that Turloch slammed into, and swear it was purely a coincidence. The notion amounted to hara-kiri in the cold light of day. It didn't survive more than a few seconds. I knew beyond a shadow of a doubt she wouldn't believe it.

Or I could ignore the whole nasty mishap and hope that the two strands of the story never got tied up together. The longer I turned a blind eye to the truth, the more likely I would be back in the States long before Neasa found out what actually happened that morning.

With hindsight, it's fair to say I wasn't thinking straight. If I had been I would have collected Molly from the hospital and, along with Karen, gone straight to Dublin airport that morning, the three of us boarding the first available flight back to Boston.

23

Stephen's Green looked exquisite in the warm late-afternoon December sunshine. The trees were bare, adding a quaint expansion to the neatly tended walkways and avenues. Karen and I walked slowly, hand in hand, across O'Connell Bridge to the edge of the small lake. We sat on a park bench and watched two black swans glide across the still waters with such hush and unflappability.

Karen squeezed my hand. I knew she was happy here. I had spent years telling her about all I had planned for her first visit to Dublin. It was all I had dreamed of for so long, to show her off to my favourite city. I prayed for this very moment every night I wandered down Nantucket Sound, kicking the sand while looking out towards the dark horizon, wondering if we would ever get the opportunity to travel there together. And while I prayed, I also asked whoever might be charged with directing our destiny that the past would remain dormant.

It wasn't to be.

Karen had stepped off a plane that morning right into Pandora's box. I leaned across and kissed her while she studied the gracefulness of the swans.

She smiled. "What are you thinking?" she asked. It was Karen's favourite question, one that often ended in arguments.

"I'm afraid," I said.

She moved closer and put her arm around my shoulder. "I'm here now. Whatever is going to happen, we'll just face it together."

Her words meant everything to me. "I didn't mean you to walk into the middle of all this."

"How were you to know this was going to happen?" she asked.

"I can't believe I did what I did this morning. I was responsible for killing her brother."

"But nobody has to know that that's what happened. You didn't set out with the intention of killing him."

"Karen, there was obviously a reason why he sat outside that apartment all night. He knew Molly was in hospital. So what was he doing?"

"Maybe he didn't know you were staying there. Maybe he was looking after the pad in case someone tried to break into it."

"Why would anyone want to break into Molly's apartment? It's on the first floor for a start. Anyway it's just one of a thousand small apartments along that strip. And why did he follow us across town and back? There's got to be a reason why he was doing that. After all, if he was a private investigator, there must be more to it."

"Hang on, Dave. Let's not get too deep about this. He was Neasa's brother. Maybe she asked him to keep an eye."

"On who? Me? Thanks a bloody lot, Karen."

"Calm down, Dave. This is the first time you've seen Neasa in ten years. Maybe she was nervous about meeting you. Maybe she just asked him to stay in the background. I don't know what happened between the two of you so I can't tell you if your brother-in-law was spying on you. I sometimes wish you'd bloody well tell me, because, as far as I'm concerned, there's a whole chunk of your life that just doesn't exist."

There was both concern and anger in her voice. I looked at her. She was perfect in every way. And I loved her. But deep down within, something was telling me that I could lose her as a result of this trip. "How much do you love me?"

She stretched out her arms and stood up to face me. "This much!" she shouted. She tapped my knee with her boot and sat down again. "There's loads of things on your mind, Dave. Loads of stuff you haven't told me."

I nodded sufficiently to let her know she was right. "Have you ever heard of the Killcrow?"

She frowned and squeezed her lips together. "The Killcrow." She walked away from me slowly toward the edge of the lake and stood with her back to me. "The

Killcrow," I heard her say. She turned. "Why do you ask?"

"I don't know. I thought maybe you might have come across it in your studies. It just strikes me as something you'd see in tribal dances, or something like that. Did the Indians have anything like that?"

"Like what?"

"Like the Killcrow? Did your mother ever mention anything about it?"

"Yes."

Her answer shocked me. I wasn't expecting it.

"My mother is very proud of her background, She's a direct descendant of the Sioux Indians. Her father was an Indian chief. He lived until he was one hundred and three."

I mimicked her speech because I had heard it so often. ". . . I know, I know, and he lived in the Dakotas with a wigwam in his back garden. You told me."

"The Killcrow was treated by many of the tribe as someone pure in heart, putting it simply." She spoke slowly, with a strong reminiscence and great reverence. "Killcrow was usually a man, with simple intelligence, revered by everyone. He might have been a slow learner, or slightly handicapped or deformed at birth. My grandfather always despised the way the younger Sioux poked fun at the Killcrow. He used to shout at them to stop calling him names. He chased and chastised them and often took them home to their parents with a stern warning that he would report their conduct to their schoolteachers the next morning."

"Your grandfather sounds like he was a wonderful man."

She sighed. "My grandfather was the most wonderfully kind, free-spirited man I ever knew. I loved him so much I wanted to marry him when I grew up. He was one in a million."

She walked back to the bench and sat down. "Some people use the word 'killcrow' to describe a bully . . . like a kill-joy. It's not like that at all. Folklore has got a bit twisted down through the years. It's not a very common expression though. Why did you want to know?"

I took the red exercise book out of my pocket and handed it to Karen. "It belongs to Molly. I found it behind the fridge yesterday. She'd kill me if she thought I had read it."

Karen flicked through the pages. "What is it?"

"It seems to be some kind of therapy exercise book, like she was making notes of things she was instructed to do."

"By a psychiatrist?"

"By some sort of professional, I presume."

Karen opened the first page. Her lips moved quickly as she read. "This looks like rational-emotive therapy. I studied it for a while last year. It's very interesting because it's based on the idea that psychological problems develop because of people's irrational beliefs. And the therapist works to change those beliefs by confronting the person about them when they pop up in conversation. Normally the therapist gives you assigned homework exercises, which hopefully combat those beliefs. Therapists tend to encourage their patients to keep diaries of thoughts and events. Most young girls keep diaries anyway. These can be helpful in age-regression therapy."

"Did they help Molly?"

"Unlikely, considering . . ."

"Is that what this is?" I nodded to the copybook.

"It definitely looks like rational-emotive therapy. I'd need to have a good read through the stuff in here to be sure."

"Can this notebook tell you why Molly tried to kill herself?" I asked.

Karen shrugged. "It's unlikely. There might be some indication if she was being perfectly honest with her therapist. That's *if* she was seeing a therapist lately. This doesn't look very recent. Any idea how old it is?"

"It could be a month old. It could be five years old."

"I'll see what I can find . . . try and read between the lines, if I can. But I could be miles off the mark, Dave. There are so many new therapies being tried out these days. And don't forget I'm only starting off in this business." She held up the notebook.

I nodded. "I had a dream last night. More a nightmare actually, based on something that really did happen. I was in school with the kids late one evening, ten years ago. I was giving some extra lessons in history and English, and this horrible mask . . . like a distorted face . . . so frightening . . . like nothing I'd ever seen before, appeared at the window. One of the kids called it the Killcrow. When

I asked them to tell me more, they all bunched together and refused to speak. It was like as if they were afraid of something happening to them if they told me. I was as petrified as they were. I spent days afterwards walking around local shops and supermarkets asking if they had any old Halloween masks in the storeroom. Half of them thought I was mad. I found the name, Killcrow, in that book I gave you but I don't understand why Molly should mention it. That's probably what made me dream about it that morning. Am I mad?"

"No, you're not mad." Karen smiled. "Neurotic? Yes!" She kissed me. "You're terribly confused. And you're going to have to sort that out soon, David." She stood up and stretched. "Come on, it's getting chilly. Let's walk and talk." She pulled me with her. I knew she wanted to hear more. "What have I just walked into?" she asked like a lawyer cross-questioning.

I thought. "Hell?"

"Would that be accurate?" she asked.

"Now that I'm back after ten years and it all feels exactly like it was then, yes."

She stared at the tiny ducklings following their mother in single formation. "I said to you last week that I knew you were holding things back from me. Have you any idea how that feels – when someone you love is concealing something?" She looked at me. "I decided before I left, Dave, that if you don't tell me about the side of David Freeman I know nothing about, I'm going back home tomorrow."

Her ultimatum almost winded me. It was time to deliver. I knew what she was saying: if you don't tell me, it's all over. "I was accused of beating one of my pupils almost to death ten years ago. It's a long story." I looked at her.

"I'm not in any hurry."

"Ten years ago Molly went missing. It was the 8th of September. Shortly before midnight she turned up. Her face was scratched and bruised. Her hair had been hacked so badly, her scalp was bleeding. One of her eyes was swollen. Whoever had attacked her had daubed her from head to toe with streaks of green dye. She was shaking, in a state of horrible shock.

"I suspected it was Owen Durkin. He was one of my pupils, thirteen years old, completely unpredictable, with the strength of a bull. He'd started playing up to me during maths. I told him to step outside the classroom for a minute so that I could have a word with him."

"Where was Molly?"

"In the classroom. She didn't want to come to school that day. Her mother forced her to go. Anyway, once the classroom door was closed, I grabbed him by the shoulder." I raised my hands. "I know I shouldn't have touched him, but, after what had happened, I couldn't stop myself. But that's *all* I did, Karen, I swear. He tripped over my foot and fell down onto a steel radiator pipe that ran at floor level for the length of the corridor. He lay there real still. Jesus, I thought he was dead for a second. His face was so pale, white as a sheet. I lifted him up real slowly. His face was covered in blood. I'll never forget that scene for as long as I live. He had a nasty gash on his forehead, just under his hairline. There was blood everywhere, all over my shirt, all over his uniform.

"I didn't realise that the classroom door had swung open and we were now in full view of twenty-three pupils. To them it must have looked like I'd thrown him down against the metal pipe."

"And did you?" She stopped walking and let go of my hand.

"Of course not!" I could understand why anyone would want to ask the question. "To someone who might have just arrived on the scene, it must have looked like I had been hammering the kid." It was the tone of her superior voice – the psychotherapist – that pissed me off.

"So what happened?" she asked more benevolently.

"It was nearly lunchtime. The other kids went home while I brought Owen Durkin to Neasa to have the cut patched up. She's a nurse so I reckoned we might be able to avoid bringing him to Doctor Moyne and causing a big scene. I thought that might have been the end of it. It never struck me that it would get out of hand."

"But it did?"

"Get out of hand? You bet. Within half-an-hour all of Claddagh Mines had heard that Dave Freeman, the schoolteacher, had beaten the crap out of a defenceless kid who most people thought was more than a little bit odd anyway.

"Oh, there were all sorts of rumours. I had fractured

his skull with a kick to his head; I had broken his neck; he was unconscious; he was dead. You name it, someone was talking about it."

"And how was he?" Karen was engrossed at this stage. I wondered whose side she had taken.

"He was fine, once Neasa washed it with antiseptic and bandaged him up. He was even smiling, so he knew it was an accident."

"And then?"

"And then he disappeared."

"What do you mean disappeared?"

"Exactly what it sounds like, Karen – he disappeared. He just walked out the door and that was the last ever seen of Owen Durkin."

Karen shook her head. "How could someone just disappear like that? Surely he went home after he left your house?"

"He didn't. He just vanished, literally, off the face of the earth like he never existed. His mother turned up at the school just before three that afternoon, wondering why he hadn't been home for his lunch."

"And how were you after all this?"

"Once school finished, I spent the evening at home. I just sat in the sitting-room with the curtains closed. I just wanted to die. Molly came in from her room and sat beside me on the settee and we stayed there together for hours, watching the TV. I didn't realise he'd disappeared at that stage. It was dark, about ten. We hadn't turned on the lights at all so the house was in complete darkness.

Just Molly and me, in the sitting-room. Neasa was ironing in the kitchen. She always ironed when she got mad. The police called. Turloch was with them. It was like he was gloating – watching me squirm."

"What did they say?"

"They told me that Owen's mother had reported an assault on her son and that he was missing. They questioned me. They didn't seem to know what they were doing. Then they decided that they needed me to come to the police station to answer more questions."

"Then what?"

"They let me go after twenty-four hours. Usual bullshit: 'You're not thinking of leaving Claddagh Mines in the next few days, Mr Freeman?' I assured them I was not. Then I went home."

"And where was your wife during all this?"

"She was there while the police asked me questions. Then when they were taking me away in the back of the car, she just waved to her brother and closed the hall door."

"Surely there was a search?" Karen said.

"The police combed the area for nearly two weeks. It was on television news bulletins. Helicopters, tracker-dogs, sub-aqua units, volunteers. You name it, they camped here."

"And . . . nothing?"

I raised my hands in disbelief. "Nothing. I was on the TV news every hour for three days. Claddagh Mines became like a carnival town. Hot-dog vans, sandwich stalls, civil defence. Sunday drivers came by for a look, even started taking pictures of us all trying to co-ordinate the search. It was sick. They were only short of selling T-shirts. Sad, really."

The park was filling up with commuters heading for home, catching a short cut across the green. I pointed to an empty bench. We sat down.

"Eventually it all ground to a halt and life returned to some strange sense of normality. Locals seemed to readjust. It was only mentioned on the news every other day. Then it became once a week. 'No sign of missing schoolboy, Owen Durkin'. Then nothing at all." I could hear Karen sighing slowly.

"And what happened you?" she asked.

"I was run out of town. Out of the country, actually, if the truth were known. And I went to Boston. And I finally settled down in Oak Bluffs where no one had ever heard of me. And it was nice for a change not to have people staring at you like as if you were an escaped knife-wielding lunatic who ate small children for supper."

"And did you ever find out what happened to him?"

"Owen Durkin?" I asked, for a moment longing for the safeness of Oak Bluffs. "No. Initially the hatred was so intense, I had to get away from the town itself. I packed a couple of bags and went and stayed in a bed and breakfast in Dublin. Eventually the woman who ran the house found out who I was. I found my cases packed and on the doorstep half an hour later."

"And did your wife not stand up for you?"

I looked at Karen. "You've got to be joking."

She said nothing.

"I was buying a newspaper one morning. I think it was four, maybe five, days after Owen Durkin had disappeared. A father of one of the children that I taught turned around to me in the corner shop and head-butted me. Nearly broke my nose. It bled for hours."

"Did you go to the police? That's assault, for God's sake!" Karen slammed.

"Well, there was a slight problem. Owen's mother, Maud, had been having an affair with the local sergeant. Young Owen was the outcome of that little liaison. Anyway, to cut a long story short, I was a disgrace to my profession. I knew my teaching days were over. Corporal punishment had been outlawed a few years before that. It was still a very tenuous issue among teachers. Parents were relieved. Teachers were becoming frustrated. Their hands were tied when it came to simple matters of class discipline.

"The whole class could launch a revolt against the teacher and all we could do was stand there and watch. If you raised a hand, you could expect a solicitor's letter from the parent involved.

"So when the rumour machine got going after what I was perceived as having done, the teaching authority said they were faced with no choice. They had to be seen to be setting an example and laying down the law. So they publicly made *me* look like an uncontrollable bully. Then they dumped me."

"Jesus, Dave. Has anyone any idea where he disappeared? He was only thirteen years old."

I shrugged. "There are loads of stories, down through the years. The journalists camped out for a fortnight down the local pub, The Bridge. All the hardened drinkers from all over the area congregated there, all trading their stories about what they thought had happened to Owen Durkin for free drink. One guy from the *Sunday World* used to just stick his credit card behind the bar and fill them full of beer for as long as they kept talking."

Karen dragged her boots along the ground. "And what do you think happened him?"

I smiled wryly. "Do you really want to know?

"Yes."

"His mother used to give out to him for hanging around a halting site just outside the town on the road to Thurles. Six travelling families. They all had small kids, a couple of them Owen's age. They were harmless, just went about doing their own thing. They never seemed to bother anybody. The local publicans all got together and barred them from their premises. The local town committee wanted them out of the area. Everyone hated them. Everyone except Owen. He used to play with three young fellas out at the site, sitting around the fire with them, each of them telling stories and throwing bits of sticks and rubbish onto the flames. They disappeared two days after he vanished. Sometime during that night into the early hours of the following morning, six travelling families packed up their belongings and moved away from Claddagh Mines."

Karen looked confused. "Do you think they kidnapped him?"

"They wouldn't be so stupid. They were hated enough as it was. They were a blot on the landscape, one woman said to me. They were even warned to stay away from Mass on Sundays. It was pathetic. I'm sure the cops were already breathing down their necks to get them out of the townland."

"And did the police interrogate them?"

"They kept calling back to the site every couple of hours. They found nothing, or no one. Then after they left the area, the police followed them."

"Did they catch up with them?"

"Oh sure they caught up with them. Turned them upside down. Stripped their caravans. Questioned the kids. Searched the vans. Nothing."

Karen stood up. "And do you really think he went off with them?"

I nodded. "It makes sense. They accepted him. He didn't see anything different or wrong in them. Sure, they lived in caravans, but a young kid would be fascinated by that. That would be like an adventure to him. Everyone in town thought he was a troublemaker. Did you ever hear the old wives' tale that if you don't eat up all your dinner, the tinkers will come while you're asleep and steal you away?"

Karen baulked. "That's awful. How could anyone tell a young child that?"

"Well, some of the old wives around the town started to believe their own story. I think he just hitched up with them when they were getting ready to leave the area and went without a second thought."

"And what about his mother?"

"She was always giving out to him. Always sending him to school with letters explaining that he hadn't done his homework properly because he wasn't paying attention the previous day. That's bound to impact on a young boy." I looked at Karen. She was deep in thought. "Can you think of a better solution?"

She looked out across the pond. It was still now, the reflection of the streetlights softly shimmering on its surface. The duck family had disappeared into the rushes, well out of harm's way. An evening chill made Karen shiver. "So where is he now?" she asked.

"He's twenty-three. God knows. He could be anywhere."

"So he was older than the other children?"

"Yeah. Two years older. He was kept back twice. I sometimes think that made him more rebellious." I shrugged and breathed the heavy, smoggy air. "Anyway," I said, placing my hands over hers, "that's my life in a nutshell."

Karen still shook her head in disbelief. "Why didn't you tell me all this earlier?"

"Why should I? There was no need for you to know any of this earlier. Once I'd left here ten years ago, all I wanted to do was forget about what happened. If I'd told you, you would always have questioned it in your mind."

"Questioned what?"

"Whether I did hit him or not. Whether or not I had something to do with his disappearance. I just wanted to consign it to the wastebasket forever. That's all. Do you ever get that feeling that someone is watching you? And when you look around there's no one there?"

She ignored my question. "How long did you hang around for before leaving the country?"

"About three weeks. I stayed with an old college friend of mine in Dublin. Eventually I just wanted to get out here. It made me sick, the double standards . . . the attitudes. I just wanted a clean break . . . a fresh start. Somewhere no one knew me."

"David, do you ever wonder where you'd be now if . . ."

I cut her question short. "If I hadn't been responsible for injuring him that morning? Not any more. Not since I met you."

That wasn't exactly true, but for the moment Karen didn't need to know that.

"When do I get to meet Molly?" Karen asked.

"This evening. She's getting out of hospital."

"What time?"

"Whenever we collect her. I haven't told her about Neasa's brother."

"Don't worry. Leave that to me," Karen said. "I've got an idea."

24

Karen and Molly spent the night chatting in front of the small gas fire. It was such a relief and a treat to hear Molly laughing heartily again. They spoke about college, boyfriends, old jobs; Karen talked about The Whippletree, and her antiques collections, and the prospect of moving to Boston to start her internship at the children's hospital. My heart sank listening to how much she revelled in the prospect of being a professional counsellor. I had come to accept that Karen was very much like her grandfather: a free spirit. If she stayed cooped up on the island, our relationship might suffer. She needed her own space; a routine through which she could express herself freely. At least this way – while long-distance relationships rarely work – we had a chance, slim as it was.

My intention, I had definitely decided, was to ask Molly to come back to Martha's Vineyard with the two of us. That way, she could look after The Meadows for me, while I commuted to Boston three times a week. Or she could transfer her studies to Harvard if she wished to. I reckoned Thelma Brady would jump at the offer of a job in The Meadows.

The idea of coaching and teaching part-time had begun to appeal to me again. It also meant I would get to see Karen every other day, instead of just a scrambled, fleeting few hours each weekend.

However, Boston and Martha's Vineyard, antiques and books, all seemed light-years away at that moment. Forced between us and our home that night was a funeral, a cauldron of old skeletons and a bogey journey down memory lane. I knew that the funeral would force me to face my past. In doing so, I might lose everything. In failing to do so, I knew I would be haunted forever more by the restless ghosts of an incident I had tried for years to disregard. Now it was staring me in the face.

As I sat at the small study table in the bedroom that evening, listening to the two most important people in my life, I hung on at a distance to every word of the two women who had just met, and realised they were already soul mates. I could only hope and pray that the strength and power of their combined love for me might pull me through the days to follow, and my return to a time in my life I had spent ten years recovering from – most of those trying to forget.

* * *

201

It was after twelve when Neasa arrived back at the apartment. She was very drunk. Molly and Karen had retired for the night. I had organised sleeping arrangements in the event that Neasa did return, instead of going back to Claddagh Mines, as she said she might. Molly and Karen shared a room. Neasa could have the spare bed. I could kip down on the settee. On taking her brown leather jacket off, she did something I wasn't expecting; she put her arms around me and hugged me tightly. As she stood there, with her head against my chest, I listened to her sobbing. Then she looked up at me.

"My life's in fucking bits, Dave," she whispered.

"No, it's not," I said. "You're just in shock after what happened today." Her emotions had always confused me utterly, so why should I be shocked by this rare gesture?

She kicked her jacket off the settee and plonked herself into the middle of it. "I'm pissed."

"That's OK," I said. "Would you like a coffee?"

She grappled with a box of matches and eventually lit a cigarette. She took a long drag and blew small, wobbling circles of smoke into the glow from the fire. "What the fuck would I want coffee for? Is that your way of telling me I should be sober?"

I hated when she was drunk. She became paranoid and obnoxious. "That wasn't what I was thinking. I was just going to make myself a cup and I thought you might like one."

"Well, I wouldn't fucking like one, all right?"

I busied myself in the kitchen, filling the kettle. "Where did you go tonight?"

There was a long pause. "Well, I arranged bits and pieces for the funeral. I identified his body and I needed a couple of stiff drinks after that. He was in bits. I suppose he was an ugly-looking bastard most of his life. There's no point tryin' to turn him into an oil painting now, is there?" She shrieked and laughed. She got serious again. "Still it wasn't a nice way to go. So what did I do then? I went to the funeral home and made the arrangements with them."

She was paralytic, her 't's were 'd's; her 's's had become 'ch's. Everything was slurred and elongated. Her eyes were crossed; her cigarette had started to burn her index finger.

"Anyway, he's dead. No point talking about him. Respect to the dead. Let's talk about the living, will we?"

"OK," I replied.

"Your girlfriend seems very nice . . . very pretty. I hate her accent though. Can't stand that put-on American shite!"

"Keep your voice down. Molly's asleep. She needs plenty of rest."

"Don't you tell me to keep my voice down. I am as entitled as you are to be sitting here tonight. While you were sitting on some fucking island in the middle of the Atlantic, I was sitting at your daughter's bedside, willing her to live."

I'd had enough of this crap. I slammed the kettle down on the kitchen worktop and walked back to the sitting-room area. "Listen here, you witch. I'm sick of your patronising shite and your emotional blackmail. *You* broke up this family ten years ago; *you* put our daughter in hospital. And it was *you* who left me with no choice but to get out of this country as fast as I could. You took away my confidence and my dignity. Jesus, you stripped me bare, left me with fuck all!"

"How dare you!" she slurred.

"How dare me nothing! Now you shut your fucking mouth for a minute or two and listen to me for once in your life. I've waited a long time to say this. I hadn't bargained on saying it tonight, but I know now that I'm likely to do something I'll regret if I can't get this off my chest. You terrorised me for years. I was just too much of a gentleman, as my mother saw fit to make me, to stand up to you. I should have beaten the crap out of you a couple of times, but I probably would never have been able to forgive myself. You see, my mother taught me never to raise a hand to a woman. You knew I wasn't going to retaliate, didn't you? You squeezed me; you held me to ransom . . . you bled me dry until there was nothing left. And then – the final nail in my coffin – you spread that goddamn awful story . . . you told everyone that I had beaten up a thirteen-year-old boy . . . *one of my own pupils!* How could you even contemplate such an appalling heap of shit? You told the cops ten years ago that I beat the shit out of him. Didn't you?"

She shook her head.

I grabbed her arm. *"Didn't you?"* I shouted.

"Yes!" she replied.

The sheer relief of hearing her admit the truth for the very first time was weakening. I sat on the armchair opposite and caught my breath. "Thank you," I gasped. "I don't know why I'm saying thank you. I should be trying to resuscitate you after beating you unconscious for all the things you did to me." I studied her for a moment, looked her up and down, and wondered what possessed me to propose marriage? I must have loved her once. I couldn't remember what it was like. Unfortunately that once had been buried like a small shining spade in a sandstorm. Whatever it was – love? – it was gone forever. Now I just felt sorry for her. I jumped up from the armchair and took my hands out of my pockets.

"Please don't hit me," she pleaded, her hands standing out in front of her face, like a 1st Dan Japanese martial arts expert who hasn't found the knack yet.

I laughed at the notion; it was a loud cynical laughter. *"Me* hit *you?* That would be a first. Of course that's what you'd like everyone to think, isn't it? That I always beat you up. Dave Freeman, schoolteacher and wife-beater. That'd look good in the local paper, wouldn't it? You'd get plenty of sympathy out of that, Neasa. Hell, it'd probably get you free groceries out of the local shops.

"You had it well sussed those nights you had a go at

me. Do you remember the night you fucked the chip-pan at me? Molten-hot vegetable oil? That would've left a few marks all right. I pleaded with you not to make chips, remember; you were too drunk . . . we *both* were pissed! We'd had a great night in the pub. We could have bought a single of chips like most other normal people do. But, no . . . not my Neasa. She had to come home and take the most dangerous fucking cooking implement out of the press and plug it in. Most couples would have just switched off the cooker and gone to bed for a screw. But not you; *oh no!* You picked up the pan . . . three hundred fucking degrees of bubbling boiling fat and fucked it at me. Only that I ducked, I'd have looked like the elephant man for the last twelve years. Then there was the night you crept into the spare bedroom where I'd gone for some peace and quiet. I thought you were tiptoeing in for a quick shag. I thought we were about to make up like other *normal* couples resolve their arguments. You thought I was asleep, didn't you? Thought I was asleep as you held the kettle full of boiling water over my legs. You wanted to pour it all over my balls. Lucky I was awake."

She smoked her cigarette, defenceless, listening to the stories I was afraid to mention, too scared to even contemplate, all those years ago.

"You thought you were being very clever. And I suppose you were. The chip-pan . . . the boiling water . . . the broken-bottle incident . . . You knew that you couldn't be blamed for what you did. They all looked

like accidents I could have been responsible for myself.
So if I *did* call the police, you could have denied
everything. 'That's not true, Officer. He was in a fight
outside the pub. Someone else stabbed him. I was here
all night minding my daughter like a good mother and
wife.' I could easily have knocked the boiling kettle off
the kitchen worktop, spilling the hot water all over my
balls. I could easily have tripped carrying the chip-pan.
Fair play, Neasa, you had it all worked out very
methodically. Foolproof . . . there was no way any of
this would ever have found its way back to you. Isn't
that what you were thinking?"

She lit another cigarette and stared at the gas-flame
with tears in her eyes.

"All I want to know . . . to this day, I still haven't
been able to find out . . . why did you do those things?
How could you have hated someone so much, someone
who told you that he loved you, that you wanted to
torture him to death? And you know what was harder
to take? The never-ending emotional blackmail. Most
parents tuck their kids up with a bedtime story. You
used to spend the nights filling Molly's mind with lies,
pure *junk*, telling her how 'silly' her daddy was . . . how
'useless and lazy' he was. You could have destroyed her
mind as well as mine. For all I know you might have.
Why did you do it? Did you set out all those years ago
with the sole intention of annihilating me? Did you
really want to be a young widow? I know how country
villages look after their young widows. They all rally

together around her. 'Isn't she marvellous . . . so brave . . . rearing a child all on her own . . . she's better off without him . . . have you heard the stories?' Did you really want to hurt me so bad? I'd appreciate an answer, because I've spent ten fucking years of my life trying to figure this whole thing out. Either you're mad or I am. And I've got to be fairly honest, I feel pretty damn sane at the moment. So that leaves you. If I was your solicitor right now, and this was America, I'd be asking you if you thought you were up to taking a lie-detector test. And you know what my gut feeling would be to that? You're *not* up to it. You would fail abysmally. So why don't you just give me a fucking answer for once in your sad life . . . why did want to hurt me so much?"

I knew there wasn't going to be an answer.

It was the gentle cough that made me turn around. Karen stood in the small landing area between the main sitting-room and the bedrooms.

"I'm sorry, but I need to get a glass of water," she said politely.

I knew by the tone of her voice that she had heard everything. It wouldn't have been difficult. Deep down I was relieved.

25

A schoolteacher, like a priest or a doctor, ranks high in the pecking order of any small rural community. That afternoon, as I watched six uniformed policemen carry Turloch Maher's coffin up the centre aisle of Saint John the Apostle's Church, I knew I ranked somewhere between a conman and a sewer rat.

Mourners – the entire population of Claddagh Mines – had come to pay their final respects to the local boy made good. They stared me down, watching me as if they expected me at any moment to turn into Satan himself. Younger parents I didn't recognise pulled their small children close to them as I followed the bereaved family, looking for a seat midway. They had heard the stories.

Karen squeezed my arm, a gesture of solidarity, and stared back. We left the church just as Father Ted Murphy was extolling the virtues of a former garda officer who had "sensed danger and hadn't been afraid to stare it in the face". Turloch Maher had as many skeletons in the cupboard as there were Mass-cards in his name on the altar that evening.

The locals were good at staring. They had moulded the pastime into quite a fine art. The Claddagh Mines Bridge Bar was where you learned the art of staring, proudly carrying it on your person at all times like a secret weapon.

A stare could mean a number of things: 1). I'm right. You're wrong. 2). That's mine. Give it back. 3). You're not welcome here. 4). What are you staring at? And 5). Why isn't my dinner on the table?

It was important to remember not to stare unless you were very familiar with the procedure and, more important, the repercussions.

* * *

One of the few faces I was overjoyed to see that day belonged to Josh Traynor. He waved to me from the opposite side of the churchyard, across the top of Turloch Maher's coffin, then made the shape of a T with his index fingers. For as long as I had known Josh Traynor it could mean only one thing: a pint afterwards. I nodded and smiled discreetly, relieved that someone still loved me.

Josh Traynor had always worn a permanent, dark suntan, despite the inclement Irish weather, from the first day I was introduced to him at a school football game. I just assumed the pigment in his skin lent itself to the rusty brown colour that kept him looking well and, despite his heavy drinking, fit and rugged. He never told me his age. I reckoned early fifties. A baseball cap covered his balding head. The little bit of hair he had to show off was a rusty brown, tipping his shoulders at the back, neatly complementing his rich tan. I could imagine him wearing combats, carrying a weapon slung over his shoulder, beating his way through the Pantanal in darkest Brazil, and feeling quite at home.

He had worked as a journalist for *The Thurles Tribune* for as long as we had known each other. He was an adroit social diarist, talented and gifted with words. His articles could extol or extinguish, flatter or flatten, depending on what humour he was in the night he arrived at a function.

Home for Josh was a one-bedroom fleapit above a butcher's shop in Kilkenny city centre, out of bounds to most, except when he had had too much to drink, and company on the home journey was a leggy, busty blonde with an ass like chiselled marble, he once told me.

Traynor was as sexist as they come. He had a way with women. They were like bees round a honeypot. "Women love a sense of humour, Dave," he frequently preached to me.

A native of Nebraska, he came to Ireland to find his ancestors and stayed for another beer. He told the women who chose to listen he was an author-in-waiting, on the verge of writing that elusive bestseller. He got his job at the *Tribune* because of the weekly letters he wrote to the editor. "A Yank's Journey in Ireland", he called them. Within weeks, his letters had become so popular the weekly paper's circulation doubled. Traynor was offered a job.

His throaty, gravelly laugh betrayed a habit of eighty cigarettes a day. He told me how he flew helicopters in and out of Cambodia in the mid-seventies on search-and-rescue missions behind enemy lines. He spoke with a surreal conviction, which made most topics he discussed eloquently, utterly believable.

That was the secret to Josh Traynor's success. Everyone believed him. Everyone was terrified not to. This was his infectious appeal. He had monstrous ambitions, magnified through the bottom of a pint glass and inevitably drowned in beer before they ever saw the light of day.

"You know what I love about the Irish, Dave?" he'd often say. "The way they don't label you 'alcoholic' just because you ask for a late drink."

Josh detested good news. Heavily divorced – three times, he told me – he lived for the day, notebook in the car, that two packed trains would collide on his patch and his face would be beamed all over the world. He warmed to individuals only when he recognised they were useful for some reason. He would regularly quote Groucho Marx when in female company: "If I'd known I was gonna live this long, I'd have taken better care of myself!"

Within five minutes of harnessing their attention, Josh lifted his shirt and showed them the scars. "A great white tried to have my ribs for lunch one day I was diving off Long Island. I swam ashore with that big bastard chewing me up, five sets of razor-sharp teeth! Eyes like black holes. He knew eventually he wasn't gonna get Josh. He just gave up and let go." Then he would perform his magic trick on the woman he wanted. He would say to her, "Here, touch the scars with your fingertips." He would look deep into her eyes and hold the palm of his hand twelve inches from her face and say, "Do you know that by slapping a shark hard on its rubbery snout, you can hypnotise it?" Then, gently, he would quickly tap his selected woman on the nose. Usually she nearly jumped out of her skin with the fright. "When you've been through an experience like that, nothing scares you any more," he'd tell them. Everyone laughed and Josh was set up.

He regularly bragged about his threesomes and the cocaine and the joints they smoked in between sex. Josh was a high-flyer in his own peculiar world where there was only room for one. Yet I liked him. A lot. Maybe it was his personality, or part of it. He had a joke for every occasion. He had the last word of the night. He told wonderful stories, most of them untrue I was certain. I wanted his self-confidence, his ease in the company of strangers; his eloquence, and how he could switch to being bold and pithy. He was always friendly towards me. He always had time. His laugh was unique, a gruff chortle that went on and on, that could be heard in even the noisiest bars. No one was addressed by his real name. His female girlfriends were called "babes", their married partners, "smucks" and I became known as Teacher.

I still can't quite put my finger on exactly what I liked about Josh Traynor. Maybe it was his incalculable energy, maybe his unpredictability. Or maybe it was just whatever qualities made him so different to everybody else in Claddagh Mines.

We sat in the corner of Nora's Bar, on the outskirts of Thurles. He insisted on buying the first round. No half measures, he bought two of everything.

"So Karen, what do you do?" Josh asked politely. He threw the well-worn leather jacket onto the windowsill directly behind her.

"I'm a psychologist," she said.

"A *psychologist*? Well, well, Teacher," he gushed, looking at me and winking, "we are coming up in the world. How long have you two been an item?"

"Nearly seven years," I said, smiling.

"Have you done any work on the teacher here? I reckon you could spend years trying to find out what the fuck is wrong with him and still be asking questions!" Josh laughed.

Karen laughed.

I laughed.

Josh raised his glass. "To you, Teacher, and to your beautiful girlfriend."

We clinked glasses and I drank my stout. I had forgotten just how good it tasted.

"How long is it since we've seen each other, Teacher?"

I thought for a moment. "Must be ten years, Josh."

"We used to be good ol' drinking buddies, Karen. I used to pour him in home through his letterbox most Friday nights." Josh finished his first whiskey and exhaled. "Ooh, that tastes good." He took a deep breath and whistled. "So what brings you back to Claddagh Mines, Teacher?"

"Molly had an accident. I flew back from Boston a couple of weeks back. I spent the first week and a bit in Dublin with her."

"Nothing serious, I hope."

I considered telling him but decided against it. I didn't want the gossips of Claddagh Mines and Thurles talking about my daughter as if she was some sort of suicidal neurotic freak. "No, nothing much. She had a bit of a car accident, that's all. She's fine now. It was more the shock of it all that upset her."

Josh looked at me for a moment. "Nothing to do with her uncle, I hope?"

I shook my head. "No. That was tragic. An accident, I hear. He just ran into the back of some other guy's car apparently"

Josh grinned. "Come on, Teacher. We all know what happened to Turloch Maher."

I froze. Karen looked at me. "What do you mean by that, Josh?"

Traynor looked about the near empty pub and leaned across the table. "You rammed his car," he whispered and smiled. "I heard. One of my contacts on the inside told me that you reversed into his car as he was driving behind you. He broke his neck because the silly bugger wasn't wearing his seat belt. That's what I was officially told. Does that tally with what you remember?" He sat back and bolted the second whiskey, growling as he swallowed.

My Guinness had lost its appeal. "That's not what happened. That's bullshit," I said softly.

"Well then, do you want to tell me exactly what happened, off the record like? It's nothing to do with me, Teacher. I hated the fat bastard. Told me he'd get me off a couple of small misdemeanours. He didn't even bother telling me he couldn't. He was a lazy son of a bitch." He leaned forward again. "You never liked him either."

"Yes, I did."

"Don't lie to me, Teacher. I remember only too well the night you sat here with me in this very seat and spent an hour cursing that fat bastard from a height, telling me how much you hated him, and how much you wished he was dead. If I'd given you a gun that evening you would have shot him dead." He finished the whiskey. "Well, now your dream's come true."

I was getting angry. "Josh, can we change the subject, please?"

"Sure, what would you like to talk about?"

"I didn't see Doctor Moyne at the removal this afternoon," I said.

Josh sighed. "Yeah. Ivan Moyne. Now there's an interesting one, all right. He retired from medical practice about . . . eight years ago? Maybe longer. You wouldn't have been too long gone yourself when he quit. You know he split up with the wife."

"Ingrid and Ivan Moyne split up?" I was stunned. They were a doting couple any time I saw them together. Most uncharacteristic for a professional couple, but they couldn't keep their hands off each other. Both doctors.

"Yeah, he was spending more and more time across at that pharmaceutical plant he bought into years ago. What was it called?"

"Blaine Odox," I said.

Josh clicked his fingers and nodded. "Blaine Odox, that's what it was called. You've got a great memory, Teacher. But then again," he said for Karen's benefit, "you never drank as much as me."

"Is that place still running, Josh?"

He looked around at the barman. *"Same again, Jack,"* he shouted, and threw a twenty on the table. "Blaine Odox? Let me think . . . eh, that closed down about a year after you ran out . . . sorry. About a year after you went to the States, Blaine Odox was relocated to some town in Tunisia, or one of those nigger countries."

Karen coughed.

"Josh, do you have to be so uncouth?" I said.

"Fuck that, Teacher. Political correctness is something that I'm not really familiar with just yet. Unless of course I'm writing an article for the weekly; in which case, I excel myself."

The drinks arrived. Josh insisted on paying: two of each, again.

"Why Tunisia?"

"Cheap labour, I expect."

"What happened to the employees in Clonmel?"

"They each got lump-sum settlements – fifty grand apiece, I was told. The shop closed its doors inside of six weeks of the announcement. Some huge Internet bigwig moved in there a couple of years back. Vartech, they call themselves – no, Varsene Technology, or something like that. The mother ship is in Dakota, I hear. Most of the local folks managed to get jobs."

"Tell us more about Ivan Moyne," I said.

Traynor seemed reluctant. "What do you want to know, Teacher? That was an awful long time ago. He retired from general practice around here and went to live somewhere abroad, I hear."

"Where?"

Josh threw his hands in the air. "How the hell do I know? I find it hard enough to pick up local stories in a twenty-mile radius around here, without having to track down some crazy doctor who's gone to live somewhere else."

"Did you say crazy?"

"Sorry?" Josh raised his glass and sipped it this time.

"You just said *track down some crazy doctor* . . . what makes Ivan Moyne crazy?"

"I never said he was crazy."

"Yes, you did."

"Well, that's not what I meant to say. I didn't mean it literally, for fuck's sake. OK? Look, Teacher, excuse me, Karen, I've had a long day today. I've covered two mayors switching on Christmas-tree lights. I've interviewed four Santa Clauses, and I've been to two hospitals to report on what they expect to be doing with patients on Christmas Day. And it's only the fourth of December. So why can't we all just enjoy our drinks in peace, without this turning into some hair-brained debate about nothing. All I know is that Ivan Moyne doesn't live around here any more."

"And what about Ingrid Moyne?" I asked.

Josh stared at me and put his drink down. "Jesus, I'm beginning to regret your homecoming. Can you not relax, for God's sake? You're still as paranoid and jumpy as you were ten years ago."

I was beginning to think he was right.

26

Monday morning started cold and damp.

The street below our hotel room was alive with traffic and a cacophony of noises I hadn't been familiar with for many years. Oak Bluffs came alive in May each year. It was mainly a tourist trade made up of visitors who like to sleep late. Traffic on Martha's Vineyard – the little there was of it – was insignificant compared to the busy, narrow bustling streets of Kilkenny.

The sun broke through shortly after eleven.

We decided against going to the burial that morning. We accepted we were not welcome.

Karen wanted to do some window-shopping. I plumped for a swim in the pool and a sauna. While she was gone, I called the porter and asked him to drop up a bottle of medium dry Chardonnay and a hamper of sandwiches. I had decided from the moment I awoke to surprise Karen with a picnic at my favourite spot,

Crator's Gap, in the Silvermine mountains. Molly was attending the funeral. We were going to collect her from her grandmother's at five.

By half past one we were firmly ensconced on our blanket in a small lee at the top of a sweeping pasture, overlooking the South Riding of Tipperary. The scene was breathtaking. It had rained heavily over the previous few days, heightening the richness of the colours of the foliage and the hedgerows, and the fields and fields of green grass that surrounded us.

"This is where we used to come at lunchtime," I said, taking in the view.

"Who?" Karen seemed puzzled.

Then I realised she thought I meant Neasa when I said 'we'. "I used to wait for Molly on sunny days. If her friends were going home for their lunches, we used to make up a packed lunch and sit up here for half an hour. It's beautiful, isn't it?"

"Stunning. Did you love living here?" she asked.

"Yes. And no." I breathed in the air and waited for the right answer. "I loved living here. It's a wonderful place for bringing up small children, I always thought. It's so different from the city. Here, you can leave your car open without the fear of having it stolen. Everyone knows everyone. It was nice for a long time. I wouldn't have had it any other way. Then it all fell apart."

"Did your wife beat you often?" Karen said it softly. I knew then she had heard every word two nights previously in Molly's apartment. I was glad she asked.

"Six, maybe seven occasions that left me in pretty bad states."

"Why?"

"Because she was in a bad humour."

"That was the *only* reason?"

I nodded. "After a couple of weeks, I couldn't sleep at all. I was afraid to close my eyes in case I dozed off and she crept upstairs with some crazy scheme to get at me. I started to drink coffee at night. I'd have three or four cups before going to bed, if she was out with her friends. She'd come in with a few drinks on her and, for no reason other than I smiled at her, she'd go absolutely berserk. So I wouldn't smile. And she'd go mad because I was putting her into, as she used to say, a dog's humour."

"When did she start attacking you?"

"I suppose if I were to be honest, I'd say before we got married. But I used to think she was just clowning around. She was my first serious girlfriend, so I wasn't too familiar with how women behaved behind closed doors. She'd start an argument, and push me around a bit. One night she pushed me over a chair in her mother's kitchen. It broke and she gave me a dig in the shoulder and told me it was my fault."

"And you thought this was regular carry-on for married couples?"

"I didn't know otherwise, Karen. Most of the time it wasn't very serious."

"And when did it get serious?"

"I always knew she had a temper. I remember the

night, Christmas night in her gran's house – we had all just finished dinner – and she stuck her brother's gun into her youngest brother's mouth and pulled the trigger. Luckily it wasn't loaded. Although I sometimes wonder . . ."

"What do you mean?"

"Well, if it had been loaded, she would have been charged with manslaughter. Mind you, I suppose she'd be well out of prison by now, having done ten years."

Karen looked at me in amazement.

I laughed.

She punched me in the shoulder and then put her hand up to her mouth. "Jesus, Dave, I didn't mean to hit you."

I hugged her and we both laughed.

"Why didn't you go to the police and report her?"

"Are you serious . . . around here? I'd be the laughing-stock of the countryside. I can just imagine what they'd be saying: 'His wife, a woman who is nine inches smaller than him and weighs sixty pounds less than he does, beats up Dave Freeman regularly.'"

Karen threw her arms around me and knocked me back onto the ground. "You know something?"

"What?" I said, looking up her as she lay on my chest.

"I just realised we have never made love in the great outdoors."

I roared laughing. "Make love here? Karen, even the sheep and cows gossip around here."

She sniggered and looked around. She started to open my shirt buttons.

The slamming of a door a short distance behind us caused me to jump. A car was parked close to mine. The man standing on the driver's side had blackened his face, it seemed. Then another door shut. And another. I counted three men. They all wore nylon tights pulled down over their faces. I stood up, pulling Karen quickly up onto her feet, and stood in front of her. "Don't say anything. Let me do the talking." I didn't know what I was saying.

The man who had stepped out of the front passenger seat opened the boot and took out a carjack and a cricket bat. He threw the bat to the driver. The back-seat passenger leaned against the car, his hands in his worn, torn jeans. I started to look for identification markings. Belts. Shoe-buckles. Rings. Watches. Studs. Any jewellery.

Carjack man wore a flashy gold watch. It seemed too big for his wrist. Cricket-bat man had a moustache and dark, heavy eyebrows.

"What do you want?" I tried to be calm. My words caught on my sharp breaths. I squeezed Karen's hand and pulled her close to me, putting my arm around her. I looked around for a house. I couldn't see one. I knew how remote this spot was. Not a living soul for at least three-quarters of a mile in any direction. It was for that very reason I came here. It was beautiful. Molly loved it. She called it Molly's Gap. I remembered all these things now in fast flashes, tumbling out of my mind like quick-pick holiday snaps. My life was flashing before me. These men wanted me. Not Karen. They wanted to injure me. Kill me.

27

My car was maybe fifteen feet away from me. "Get into the car," I said to Karen. She refused. I said it again and pushed her away. "Get into the car. Here's the key. Start the engine and wait," I said slowly.

She inched her way to the bonnet of the car. The three men didn't seem interested in her. They watched me. The one holding the bat clapped it in his hand.

"You were warned never to come back here, Freeman," the driver said.

"By whom?" I tried to appear calm. My stomach turned over and knotted. My heart pounded.

"By the folks down there." He waved the carjack at the small village at the bottom of the hilly pasture. "You're not welcome here, son."

I took a couple of steps closer to my car. They moved a few steps closer to me. I watched Karen as she slid into the driver's seat and positioned herself. I wasn't sure whether they were moving towards her. "I came here to bury my brother-in-law. Am I not entitled to do that?"

The men looked at each other and laughed.

"You came all the way back from America to bury a man you hate?" the driver said.

"I didn't hate him."

"Well, that's not what I heard." The driver seemed to be the one chosen to speak. His shirtsleeves were rolled up to the point above his elbow. His arms were freckled and chubby. His gold watch reflected against the sun. The gold-coloured watchstrap let the timepiece hang loosely around his arm.

"When you left here ten years ago, you were told never to set foot in these parts again," he said.

The three men stood motionless now, their feet spread apart, their large guts hanging out over their dirty denims. I looked around again for a house, anything that I could shout at. A jet went overhead, its distant roar quickly fading. The numbing silence returned.

I cased each of the men, sizing them up and guessing which of them was the strongest. They all looked bulky and lethal in their taut nylon masks. Their faces were distorted beyond any recognition. I wondered who had told them I was here.

"I'm leaving for the States tomorrow," I said, hoping it might dissuade them.

"You're leaving in a few minutes, Freeman. Leaving in a wooden box if we've got anything to do with it."

The driver looked to his companions. When they saw he was laughing at me, they laughed too.

"Let's not let this situation get out of control," I said. Once I had said it, it sounded ridiculous. They laughed again.

"Oh, we won't, Mr Freeman, *sir!* We're very much in control of the situation, as you put it. Isn't that what you demanded all those young kids called you . . . *sir?*"

Karen was fumbling, head down. There were eight or nine keys on the key ring. *Come on!* What the hell is keeping you? Seconds were beginning to feel like hours. "Why don't you just get back in your car and no one will ever have to know that any of this happened?"

"No one's ever going to know this happened, *sir.*" He waved the rusty carjack at my windscreen. "Nice car. You must be making a few dollars to be able to afford a top of the range rental, Freeman. Tell your lady-friend to get out of the car."

I nodded at Karen. She had one hand low down to the ignition, fumbling with the other to unlock the steering wheel. She was starting to panic. "Pull the wheel hard to the left and turn the key, Karen." I edged closer to the bonnet. The men moved a few steps closer, gripping their weapons.

"Tell her to get out, Freeman," the driver said again.

"Stay where you are, Karen," I shouted. They were only a few yards away from me now, almost within striking distance. The one carrying the bat raised his weapon and rested it on his shoulder. They moved closer again. I was edging sideways now, feeling the front of my car bonnet behind me. They seemed to gloat as I resisted the urge to run. With my back to them, I was as good as dead.

"What do you want from me? Money? I can arrange to give you money."

The driver spat at my shoes. "I don't want your money, Freeman. A life for a life, that's fair."

I didn't know what he was talking about. "A life for a life? What do you mean? Are you talking about Turloch Maher?"

"I'm talking about the schoolchildren you destroyed," the spokesman said.

"Who?"

"The kids you destroyed? My son for one. And the four kids who died. They were all in your class, Freeman. What did you do to them?"

My mind couldn't keep track of the conversation. It was tripping in and out. I was afraid and becoming confused. "I don't know what you're talking about."

"Six months to a year after you left Claddagh Mines it started."

"What started?"

"The madness. They all started acted weird. Sick. Hallucinating. My son was the last. The kids who died, it took them years. It was horrible. And you know why no one pointed the finger at you, Freeman? Because they all died in different ways. Four of them, one after the other. All young boys who had everything to look forward to. A slow, horrible death that took everything away from them."

"I really haven't a clue what you're talking about," I implored. I edged my way backwards now to the passenger door. They followed me. Karen started the engine and revved hard. "But let me help you. I'll find out what happened to them. It's not too late." My pleas were falling on deaf ears. They moved closer until I could smell the stale tobacco and alcohol of the driver's breath. I purged my mind in the hope that I could put a name to this distorted disguise.

"My son is twenty-one. He used to love playing football. He's got medals. Trophies. That's all I got to remember him by. He doesn't talk to me any more. He doesn't talk to anybody. He can't. I get to read him bedtime stories now. Doctor says he's got the mentality of a five-year-old. My wife's got to feed him with a plastic baby spoon. He eats baby food. He wears nappies. If he doesn't he craps all over the place. He dribbles all the time. All he can do now is cry, Mama . . . Dada . . . That's all he says. All he can say."

Before it could register, he had raised the carjack over his shoulder and swung it hard. It slammed into my ribs, winding me. I became so dizzy I don't remember hitting the ground. My head thumped off the corner of the passenger door, which I must have been opening when he struck the blow. I raised my hands and prayed that I wouldn't die. Somewhere in the distance I could hear Karen's voice, screaming at them to stop. An engine revved close to me. I opened my eyes and realised that my head was only inches from the front wheel of the car. If Karen's foot should slip off the clutch, I knew I was dead. I heard myself shouting, *"Please. . . stop!"* I could feel heavy boots and my ribs aching. I tried to draw breath but couldn't. Then I heard the loud, powerful gunshot – its thump re-echoed and bounced off the hilly valley. The beating stopped. Then the pain came. It was excruciating. In the distance I could hear another car revving. I looked up and squinted my eyes, feeling the blood trickling down my forehead onto my eyelids. I could barely focus on the two men who dragged the man who'd been wielding the carjack. They pulled him backwards across the gravely surface to their car. His body was limp. His shirt, hoisted up over his gut, was heavily bloodstained.

I blacked out.

* * *

Two broken ribs and a suspected ruptured colon, I heard them saying somewhere in the distance. I told the Indian surgeon in the white coat that my car had collapsed on top of me while I was changing the sump.

They had pumped me full of pethidine. I was floating, neatly packed in styrofoam. My eyes felt like great big velvety stage curtains, resting on a cushion of warm air. I was invisibly suspended. My brain felt like a warm sponge in a hairnet, my lips and tongue and fingers belonged to someone else. My ribs, once I lay perfectly still, felt parcelled in soft crepe paper. My toes tingled. I was hallucinating. It was magic once I kept my eyes closed.

When I eventually came to my senses, I could feel the fresh linen resting lightly on my chest. I moved my legs. They were bare. I opened one eye. Sunlight streamed in through the window on my left like the giant white beam of a floodlight. The air was scented with disinfectant. As I took a long, slow deep breath the pain jabbed me like a red-hot poker. I winced and coiled up. It was an atrocious agony.

Then I remembered the severe beating I had taken. I immediately remembered that Karen was with me. *"Karen!"* I roared out loud. A hand grabbed mine and squeezed it.

"I'm here. I'm OK, Dave."

I recognised her voice and relaxed in so far as I could. I opened my eyes fully but couldn't focus. Everything was blurred and discoloured. I could see two images of Karen as she shielded my eyes from the bright sunshine. Someone stood beside her. It was a man.

"You OK, Teacher?" he asked.

I could instantly place the voice. "Hi, Josh," I said. My tongue was dry and swollen. It hurt to swallow. In fact, it ached to move anything at all, in any small way.

"Jesus, Teacher, you fighting a herd o'wild buffalo? You took one hell of a beating. Looking at you now, I'd have said you came face to face with a hungry mountain bear. They stitched you up good, Teacher. What the hell did they want from you?"

It hurt to speak, so I shook my head. My ribs ached so much I tried only to breathe every few seconds. "Doug Ferris," I whispered.

"Who?" Josh asked.

"Dougy Ferris. He was the one with the carjack, Josh. I couldn't place the other men. But I remember now. I can see his face. The one who did all the talking – he was holding a carjack – his name is Dougy Ferris. I used to teach his kid. I can't remember the kid's name. It'll come to me." I'd spoken for too long. My ribs felt like they were ripping my lungs to shreds each time I took a breath. "Ah, *Jesus!*" I whispered in agony. "Who shot him?"

Josh looked at Karen.

They both stared at me.

"Don't know. I didn't hear about it until Karen rang me from the casualty ward. She said someone shot the main man in the group. He went down like a felled tree. He's bound to turn up here at some stage this evening. If his injury is as bad as Karen said it looked, he'll need medical attention pretty urgently. So I guess the police will be able to identify him officially as soon as he comes crawling in here."

I took a long, slow breath, jerking with the darts of pain. "I don't want the police to know anything about what happened." I could see the shocked reactions on both of their faces.

"You *what?*" Josh said. "These guys nearly finished

you off, Teacher. Only Ferris got shot they were gonna kill you. You've got to give a statement to the police. If you don't . . . what if they try it again?"

"No police," was all I could say without writhing from pain jabs.

"Why?" Karen asked.

I wasn't going to explain anything at that moment. The discomfort was so bad I couldn't concentrate. I needed time to think about what Doug Ferris had said. If possible I needed to talk to him. I ran my fingers down the stiff bandage, which encased my ribs. My right leg ached and my head throbbed. Ferris had mentioned deaths. Four children . . . one after another . . . all ending differently. I couldn't stop thinking about what he had said. My pupils, he said. I had taught them all.

I could hear the consternation on the corridor outside the small ward, the panicked voice of a young woman, then rushing footsteps. I looked at the door just as Molly appeared. She had been crying, her eyes puffed, her cheeks red. She held a white tissue. She ran towards me. *"Daddy, I only just heard . . ."* She threw her arms around my neck and squeezed. I grimaced. The pain was unbearable, but I clenched my teeth and reassured her, "It's OK, Molly. It looks worse that it really is. I'll be fine."

28

Sunday morning.

The bells from a local church woke me.

The painkillers the consultant something-or-other had given me when I asked to discharge myself late Friday night had helped me to sleep an hour here and there over those last couple of days. He told me I should stay for a couple more. Let the damage heal, he said.

I had turned down his advice.

I needed to get up and wander for a while. The hotel bed was too hard for my damaged ribcage. I felt stretched on the tough, solid mattress. I checked the small alarm clock. It was half seven and still dark. My mind was muzzy, still charging with images after what Doug Ferris had said.

Karen slept soundly beside me.

Aidan Ferris was his name. I stared at the curtains, watching the colours change slowly from a bluish darkness to a grey dawn. I could see him in the fourth row of my class, another hyperactive child, always neatly turned out. Maths was his weakness. Nothing to be too concerned about, I'd told his mother.

I eased myself out of the bed, and swung slowly into a sitting position. The pain made me weak, robbing my breaths and sending a tingling sensation through my feet and toes. I sat there for a while, afraid to move, hoping the agony would subside, even just for a few seconds.

"How are you feeling?" Karen asked sleepily.

I couldn't bear to turn around. "I'll be fine," I said as cheerfully as I could muster.

"Why don't you stay in bed?" she said. "I'll organise to get breakfast to the room."

"I can't stay in that bed. It's better when I move about . . . take the pressure off my ribs," I grunted. "I need you to drive," I said.

"Where?"

"Claddagh Mines. I need to do something this morning."

"What?" Karen sounded annoyed. "I thought you told me we weren't going back there, Dave."

"I have to. There's something I need to do, Karen. And I have to do it this morning." I stood up slowly and straightened my back. The pain wasn't as bad once I kept my torso straight. "We should go as soon as we can," I said to her. I went into the bathroom and closed the door. I had a speech I needed to practise.

* * *

Father Ted Murphy was a small rotund man with a large nose and a double chin. He had been parish priest in Claddagh Mines for as long as I could recall. I imagined somewhere, in some distant diocesan office, his file had been lost and he had now unofficially become a priest in limbo, left to serve out his time in this small community until he retired and went to wherever retired priests go.

No one really knew how he passed the time outside of his daily celebration of Mass and his other parochial duties. Visitation was high on his list. He had five houses he visited on strict rotation for Sunday dinner, I remember. Blaise Maher's was one of them.

I called on him that Sunday morning shortly after ten, requesting a special favour. A white towel was draped around his neck.

He looked at me for a moment, recognising the face but trying to recall my name, staring at the pair of steel crutches I leaned heavily on.

"Morning, Father. Dave Freeman . . ." I waited.

His eyes opened wide. He threw the towel across the banisters and nodded to me to step inside. "What are you doing back here?" I could detect by the tone of his voice that he hoped it would be a short visit.

I didn't answer his question. "Father, I'm sorry for bothering you. I know you're probably busy preparing for Mass. But I have a huge favour I need to ask of you."

He shrugged as if to say, try me.

"I need to address the congregation at eleven Mass this morning," I said.

He looked surprised, then appalled. "I'm sorry, David, I can't allow you to do that. You'd need written permission from the Archbishop to address any congregation from the altar of a church, especially during holy Mass."

"Father, it's important that I talk to them. I've thought about this, and I really think it's the most appropriate time and place to do it. They'll be in the right frame of mind and they'll listen to me."

"What's it about?" he asked. He glanced over the bruises and scratches on my face and forehead. "What happened to you?"

"I fell." I wasn't interested in explaining. "Please, Father. It's of the utmost importance to me that you allow me to do this. It'll take no longer than five minutes . . ."

He raised his hand, reached past me and opened the door. "My answer is no. Not unless you have a letter signed by a higher church authority can I grant you such a request. Now, if you don't mind." He nodded towards the door. "Thank you."

"Father," I implored, "I have questions I need answers to. I've been asking these questions for ten years. If God can't supply the answers then I'm damn certain someone sitting in that church this morning can."

"Listen to me, the sanctuary is a sacred place, Mr Freeman, reserved for people who speak the divine word. I can't accede to your demand. Now please keep your investigation, whatever it involves, off my altar and out of my church." He nodded firmly and pointed to the door.

As I hobbled down onto the doorstep and thanked him for his time, he closed the door firmly behind me.

It was a dainty church, I always remembered, a place of great peace and tranquility. I occasionally nipped in for five minutes during lunch if I was staying at the school during the break. Two hundred worshippers and it was packed to capacity. I sat with Karen about midway, watching individuals and couples and young families taking up their regular seats. Blaise Maher led the mourners, dressed in black and huddled together in a small posse towards the front.

I closed my eyes and asked for guidance. I hadn't prayed properly in over ten years. I asked God, wherever he was, to help me with the words I chose and, once chosen, how I delivered them. I had told Karen of Murphy's refusal. She seemed relieved. I decided against telling her that I was still going to address the congregation that morning, one way or another.

After communion had been distributed, Murphy sat back into his mahogany throne-like chair, facing his flock. I found myself walking, without the aid of my crutches, towards the lectern. Murphy's head remained bowed. Then he saw me. He stood quickly, adjusting his vestments, and hurried towards me, his hand extended.

"Please, Father, I *have* to do this," I said quietly, looking at him.

He stopped and closed his eyes, and gently bowed.

"Five minutes," he whispered. "I hope you know what you're doing, Mr Freeman." He bowed to the crucifix and sat down again.

I stepped up to the tall lectern and adjusted the microphone. I waited a few moments, noticing, one by one, heads towards the back of the packed church craning and moving from left to right to get a better view. I counted eight people as they stood up and left the building. I coughed and breathed gently, and stood so that my aching ribs were comfortable.

"My name is David Freeman." I paused and fortified myself for what was coming. "Many of you know who I am."

"Oh we know who you are all right, Freeman . . ."

The voice tailed off. I searched the front rows for the source. It was Doug Ferris, his arm supported in a white sling.

"I haven't come here today to ask for forgiveness . . ."

Molly dropped her head into her hands and slumped down in the seat.

"I don't believe I've done anything wrong to anyone in this community, young or old . . ."

Doug Ferris stood up, hurriedly blessed himself with his left hand, and left by a side door close to where Murphy was sitting.

"I learned yesterday, in unfortunate circumstances, that some of the children I taught in this parish have . . . passed away. I also found out that some of my other pupils are very sick." I paused again and took the weight off my ribs by leaning on the lectern. "I loved teaching your children. I would have laid my life down to protect each and every one of them from harm. I still would today." I could detect a snigger and some comments. "Your children were as important to me as my daughter was. Still is. I was forced to leave Claddagh Mines because I was accused of beating one of my own pupils . . . to within an inch of his life. Some of you were silent accusers. Some of you told others that I had murdered him."

A strong, tangible reaction of whispering and growling comments washed, like a wave, over the congregation.

I looked down at Molly, sitting beside her mother. I wondered for a minute how many of these people knew about the injuries Neasa Maher had inflicted on me . . . *for better or worse*, I couldn't help thinking.

"My daughter will vouch for me. I am not a murderer. I have never so much as laid a hand on any of your children, and would have been the first to seek out anyone who did. I never laid a hand on my own . . ." I looked down at Neasa sitting next to her mother. She looked away. "It's more than I can say for some people who are in this church this morning.

"I left because my life as I knew it was over here. The national teaching body, to which I was affiliated, struck me off. I was informed." I waited again to catch my breath. The church was so silent it could have been empty.

"Owen Durkin disappeared on the ninth of September ten years ago. I helped in the official and unofficial searches that went on and on. He has never been found. I was questioned for twenty-four hours, which led me to understand that I was the chief suspect." I spoke slowly now, aware that they were hanging on my every word. "When the police released me, I also understood that I was no longer part of their investigation. Neither did I harm or kill Owen Durkin, nor do I believe he is dead."

My last remark caused a storm of mutterings again.

I looked at Karen as I spoke now. "I intend to remain here in Claddagh Mines until such time as I can uncover the reasons why four of my former pupils died, and why another young man whom I taught is now distressingly and incomprehensibly ill and disabled beyond recall." Somewhere in the silent church I could hear sobbing.

As my eyes scanned the packed congregation, I spotted Josh Taylor. He was leaning against a wall close to the back, his elbow resting in his hand, his other hand covering his mouth. He listened and watched. When he realised I was looking at him, he smiled and stuck his thumb into the air.

"You took our children to the Lastec plant," an angry voice broke the silence. The woman was dressed in black, from head to toe. She wore a mesh veil over her face. I didn't recognise her. Her son had been the first of the four teenagers to die, I learned later.

The school outing flashed across my mind. I had organised the trip to Lastec for two classes. The plant was located outside Thurles. It was a chemical detergent plant, manufacturing domestic disinfectants for the European market. Our trip took place on the same day that hundreds of gallons of toxic waste had escaped accidentally into a nearby river, resulting in a widespread fish-kill. The management accepted responsibility. Eventually, due to major local opposition, the plant was relocated to east Cork.

"Their deaths had nothing to do with the Lastec plant," I insisted.

"How do you know? You're not a doctor," a man shouted from the back.

Others nodded and agreed with him.

"Doctor Moyne told us their deaths were related to that outbreak," the woman in black protested.

"To *what* outbreak? There was *no* outbreak at Lastec. No toxic poisonings, apart from the fish, no vapour emissions. It never affected the drinking water. There were no recorded casualties in any of the local hospitals. Claddagh Mines is fourteen miles from where the Lastec plant used to be situated. There are three towns and at least a hundred houses between here and there. How come none of them reported any casualties?"

"Over three hundred cattle had to be destroyed," another man objected.

"They drank from the river."

They were clutching at straws, figments of their long-starved imaginations, I could tell; akin to the words of a desperate liar trying to wriggle his way out of a situation with language he doesn't understand. I said nothing for a couple of moments, allowing a stiff, uncomfortable silence to fall on the hushed crowd. "This has got nothing to do with Lastec, has it?" I spoke softly. "Our class visit to Lastec that day had nothing to do with the deaths of those four young boys. If it had been responsible, I wouldn't be standing here this morning. I'd have become a victim also. It would have affected the entire class.

"You still *want* to believe that I beat up Owen Durkin. But most of you know now that I didn't. I think it's fair to say I taught most of the children in this area in the years I was here. And each one of you knows that I would have died for every single one of those children.

"So why are you all so afraid of me? You weren't afraid of me ten years ago. Some of you would have been happy to throw a rope around my neck and hang me in the town square, given half a chance.

"So why . . . are you afraid of me? Is it because . . . I came back? I was run out of this parish ten years ago, having been accused of a crime I never committed. That crime had nothing to do with taking a bunch of school-kids to a chemical factory as part of a chemistry exercise. And this argument here this morning has nothing to do with the Lastec incident, has it?" I suddenly had a flash of inspiration. I nodded to the members of the congregation who were waiting for the opportunity to rile me again. "You people know what this is all about. You're hiding a secret. You're afraid that I'm going to unearth that secret. I don't know what that secret is, but

I can assure you of this: if it helps me to clear my name and gives me back what I lost ten years ago, then you can all be damn sure that I'll find out what's really going on around here, and why a number of people here in this church this morning would rather see me dead than standing here addressing you."

I was getting nervous now, quite surprised and overcome by my own words, which had been spontaneous. I looked for Josh Traynor. He was busy taking notes. He looked up. I caught his attention, beckoning him to join me at the lectern. "The journalist who covered the Lastec incident is here this morning. He'll tell you more." I stood aside and let Josh past me.

He leaned over to me, covering his mouth with his hand. "I knew it was a bad idea coming here this morning, Teacher. Something told me something like this could happen. Does trouble always follow you wherever you go?" He turned to the congregation.

"My name is Josh Traynor. I write for *The Thurles Tribune*. I've been living in these parts for nearly fifteen years."

The dissent had stopped. People were listening again. Josh was liked and highly thought of in Claddagh Mines.

"It is my belief that Lastec was not responsible for what happened to our children. I am not a doctor. I am a journalist. Occasionally my journalism falls into investigative areas and I do my best to report as accurately as I can. Whatever happened to your children was not, *not*, David Freeman's fault. It's ridiculous even to entertain such a notion. I know my newspaper wrote a number of stories about Owen Durkin's disappearance and the events leading up to that. One journalist who no longer works for the newspaper may even have incriminated Dave Freeman in the matter of the young boy's disappearance. Maybe that journalist was ultimately responsible for forcing this good man out of Claddagh Mines and out of the country." Josh looked at me. "If the newspaper I work for did that, then I apologise personally. I've had ten years to think back over the events of that time and I now believe the way this man was treated by the people whom he loved and worked for was totally unwarranted and completely out of order."

Josh stepped back and turned around. In full view of his audience he extended his hand.

I shook it.

The silence remained. The doubt, and the mistrust and resentment, was deep-rooted. Ten years of blame wasn't easily overturned.

He moved down the steps to the edge of the sanctuary. "It's good to have him back among us," he shouted. "Maybe you'll find it in your hearts to accept him, like we all used to, as one of our own again. I hope he considers staying." Josh looked around at me and winked.

It was a brave speech. He was courageous to say the things he had said.

Father Ted Murphy took me aside as I left the church that morning, unashamedly linking Karen on one side,

Molly on the other. He paused, head bowed, before he said what he wanted to say, a nasty stink off his nervous breath.

"What do you think that achieved this morning?" he asked.

I tried to see the motive in his question. "I needed to clear my name, Father. That was the only reason I did what I did."

"Let me explain something to you, Mr Freeman. It's taken this small community a long, long time to get over what happened to those children. Some of these families are still grieving their losses. What you did this morning was pure selfish. You have a blatant disregard for the feelings of others. And I just want you to know that I am not associating myself with what you did in there."

He spoke loudly and slowly, putting his message across to the worshippers who strolled past us.

I was livid. Karen tried to coax me away by pulling at my arm. I wasn't moving. "Let me say something to you, Father. I've waited for ten years to say some of what I said from that altar this morning. I forgive those people who drove me away from my school and almost destroyed *my* life. I was brought up to believe that God forgives. I did nothing wrong in this town, as God is my witness, so in that respect I have nothing to ask forgiveness for. I've made a lot of mistakes in my lifetime, but teaching the children of Claddagh Mines was not one of them.

"And maybe someday, if you ever come down from

your high and bloody mighty self-righteous ivory tower, you might realise that you too have made a few mistakes. Canonical errors, let's call them." I stood and stared at this pitiful man, his red whiskey nose and his ridiculous lick of black hair that took the bareness off his forehead.

"I-I-I *beg* your p-pardon!" he stuttered

"This town looks up to you, Father. *You*, because of your vocation, dictate the pace and style of life in this small rural community for so many people in there. Those people live by your every word and move. I saw it when I lived here. And you know what? I resented you for having that much power. Therefore, you are partly responsible for covering up this scandal!"

"What scandal?" he babbled.

"Four young boys dead? *Jesus*, Father, why didn't you do something about it?"

"What could I do? It was the will of God that they died. There's nothing I can do about the will of the Lord, Mr Freeman."

"The will of God?" I shouted. "God had no hand in it, Father. Not my God. He doesn't behave like that. Those *children* died in suspicious circumstances. Surely you thought the same. Unless of course you know something that none of your flock knows!"

"What are you insinuating?"

"I'm not interested in insinuations, Father. That sort of talk belongs to the gossips in Claddagh Mines. You wouldn't be one of them now, would you?" I lowered my voice now. "I meant every word I said in there this morning, whether they all still hate me or not. It doesn't bother me any more. You know something, Father? A couple of weeks ago, thirty thousand feet above the Atlantic, I was petrified at the prospect of coming back to this town. Today I'm glad I came back. And I don't intend leaving until I find out exactly what happened to those four boys that I taught ten years ago." I turned to look for Karen. She was standing with Molly, a good distance away. I decided I had more to say. I turned again. "One other thing, Father. I took a severe beating last Monday from three men who I can only assume are your parishioners. They broke two of my ribs and put me in hospital. I discharged myself because I have too much to do and not a lot of time to do it all. I don't intend letting the grass grow beneath my feet for the next couple of weeks. The reason I mention these men? I presume, like good Christians, they'll come to you and confess what they did. I suggest you ask each one of them why they are so afraid of me. And why they resent me setting foot in Claddagh Mines after ten years. If they are true to their religion they're not going to lie to a priest, are they? After all, Father, you're a holy man, not easily swayed by small town corruption and small-minded ignorance." I waited for his answer. None came. He looked away into the distance.

"If I ever find out that you knew anything whatsoever about the causes of those deaths and you didn't come forward, I'll go to the police with whatever I find out. And *your* name will be on my written statement. Good day, *Father* Murphy."

Molly and Karen were speechless when I caught up with them. They had been watching silently with Josh Traynor.

"I don't feel like having that nice lunch you promised me," Karen said scornfully. "You had no right to speak to that priest like that, Dave. Who the *hell* do you think you are? You're behaving like some sort of crusader. I didn't realise you were going to walk up there this morning. I would have stopped you if I'd known!"

"Really?" I said. "And how would you have done that, Karen?" I looked around. People were staring. Again. Molly said nothing. I knew from the way she looked at me that she agreed. My outburst was unnecessary, they were saying. Maybe they were right. If they were, I would apologise later. But I didn't think I would have to. "Josh, will you drop the girls off?"

Josh nodded, confused. "Where will we meet you?"

"Back at the hotel. I have a call I need to make. I might as well do it now while I'm here." I looked at Karen. "I'm sorry I didn't do it ten years ago."

They walked away towards Josh's old clapped-out green Jeep. Karen glanced back. I could tell she was seeing a different side of me that she never knew existed. The call I had to make was within walking distance. The look of sheer terror in Father Ted

Murphy's eyes stayed with me for the remainder of the day.

As I walked briskly, I knew without doubt that Doctor Ivan Moyne had a lot to answer for – wherever he was.

Steven Broderick was the town's doctor.

He had replaced Ivan Moyne in Claddagh Mines nine years ago, Josh had told me. He was a young man, early forties, Protestant and very private, I was informed. His religious preference meant he would have missed my performance that morning.

His house was the grandest in Claddagh Mines, painstakingly restored with great affection and lots of money, after he had bought it from Ivan and Ingrid Moyne in a somewhat dilapidated state, and renewed it to its original Victorian glory. It was situated on the outskirts of Claddagh Mines where the trees bend over on each side of the road to give an evergreen tunnel effect, blocking out the sunlight.

The front wall of the house was painted aubergine, with wooden shutters, a deep brown colour, nailed back on each side of four windows. The garden was separated from the staring strollers on the road outside by a ten-foot-high privet hedge. The lawn was manicured, with a wooden birdhouse grounded next to a massive stone fountain.

The grey stone-pebbled driveway crunched beneath my feet. A brand-new shining black Lexus was parked outside the conservatory. The doorbell played Elgar's *Chanson de Matin*. A dog barked somewhere inside.

I waited nervously, expecting a servant to appear. Instead, a fit-looking man in a Nike tracksuit opened the door. He was out of breath and sweating. His glasses were partly steamed up. He dabbed his face with a thin white towel that hung around his shoulders.

He smiled. "What can I do for you?"

"Doctor Broderick?" I said.

He caught his breath. And laughed. "That's me. I'm sorry." He wiped his forehead. "I have an exercise machine that's been taking up space upstairs. My wife's been giving me a hard time about it. So I decided to surprise her this morning by using it." He gasped. "Right now I'm expecting to collapse and die." He took his glasses off and wiped them.

"Doctor Broderick. I'm sorry for bothering you on a Sunday, but I was wondering if I could talk to you for five minutes."

He smiled. "No problem. Locals call here day and night. It's kind of an open house. I'm used to the disruptions by now. Come in, please."

He showed me into a small study and excused himself for a couple of minutes. As soon as I heard footsteps on the stairs moving into a room at the top of the house, I moved over to his bookshelves. Medical manuals. Psychopathology. Freud and Jung. Self-Help books. Psychology. Psychotherapy. Neuro-Linguistic Programming. Three books by Deepak Chopra. An entire bookcase dedicated to better health. Against another wall, a feast of fiction.

As I started to thumb through familiar titles, the door opened behind me. Broderick came in fast, wiping his chin with a tissue. "Sorry about that, I'm not as fit as I thought."

"You've got some great books here," I said, putting *The Prince of Tides* back in its place.

"That's one of my favourite books of all time," he said. "Pat Conroy is a genius. It's a pity he can't write a bit faster. I'm looking forward to his next. Do you read a lot?"

"I sell books, actually. I have a shop in the States. Martha's Vineyard."

"*Martha's Vineyard?* One of the most beautiful places on earth. You know I proposed to my wife on Martha's Vineyard, close to where they made that film, *On Golden Pond*. Do you remember it?"

"Yeah . . . Peter Fonda and Jane, the daughter. Mill Pond. I know the spot well." He was no older than forty-two or -three, fair-haired and tall. He wore a polo-neck sweater and brown baggy corduroys.

"Anyway, what can I do for you? The chemist here is closed on Sundays, so you may have to travel to Thurles if you need a prescription." He watched me, looking concerned, as I moved awkwardly across the room, adjusting the tight corset that was supporting my ribs.

I smiled, encouraged by his easy manner. "No, the health is fine so far. Apart from this." I pointed to my chest. "I took a tumble. Nothing major. I was hoping actually you might be able to help me with some information."

He sat down behind his desk and pointed to the chair opposite. "I'll see what I can do."

"My name is Dave Freeman." I waited to see if it registered. I was relieved when it didn't. He extended his hand. "Steve. Steve Broderick. Nice to meet you, Dave."

"Am I right in assuming that you took over from Ivan Moyne?"

He frowned for a split second. "That's right, I did. But I only met him once. And that was for no more than an hour. We just went over some medical histories, a few of the locals whom Doctor Moyne paid special attention to. Why do you ask?"

"Well, it's a twofold question. I'm trying to locate Doctor Moyne. And I'm also trying to find out about four young adults who died in strange circumstances between five and ten years ago."

"I can tell you straight off, I have no idea where Doctor Moyne is these days. To put the record straight, Dave, I took over here six years ago. Doctor Moyne used a locum when he wasn't here for morning and afternoon surgery before that. In fact there were a couple of different doctors who shared this room between them until such time as the position was officially advertised. I had had my eye on the house here for some time while on temporary assignment as a paediatrician in a hospital in Naas. And to cut a long story short, I got it," he said, full of pride.

"Do you know who those doctors were?" I asked.

"The locum placements? I haven't a clue. They could be from anywhere in the world. A lot of international students who work as interns here would usually follow up their hospital attachments by taking up positions as locum tenentes to increase their required general practice-hours quotas. I could find out names for you, Dave. But you could find that if a Nigerian was a locum here six years ago, he might have gone back to his native country to practise. Students do that a lot." He watched me, unsure of what to say next.

I was staring at a brick wall. "Did you hear anything about four young boys who died in suspicious circumstances?"

He seemed surprised by my question. "No. If their deaths occurred before my tenancy, I wouldn't be too familiar with their cases. There were certainly no medical records passed on to me of such deaths. If I had them, I'd tell you. I tend not to socialise locally, so I don't get to hear much local gossip. One thing I noticed very quickly, within a few weeks of taking the position here, is that Claddagh Mines is a very private community. They stick very close together and very much to themselves around here. I hope you understand. I can't be of any more help than that unfortunately." He smiled in a sympathetic way.

"Have you ever heard of a local called Doug Ferris?"

Steve Broderick thought for a moment, tapping his index finger against his bottom lip. "Ferris . . . Ferris . . ." he said over. "Name rings a bell. Why?"

"He lives out the road here, about eight or nine miles. Someone shot him during the week. I just thought perhaps he might have come to you for help."

"With a *gunshot* wound?" Broderick laughed. He put back on his glasses and studied me. "It's unlikely if he was shot, Mr Freeman, that he'd go to a local doctor's surgery. I would imagine he went straight to the hospital. Who shot him?" he asked in disbelief.

"I don't know. Here, let me give you this." I jotted down my mobile phone number and placed it on his desk. "If anyone's asking about me, or if you hear anything about Ivan Moyne, maybe you'd give me a call?"

The doctor nodded, studying the number.

"You don't have medical records for an Aidan Ferris, do you? He'd be Doug's son?" I asked brazenly.

Broderick thought for a moment, saying the boy's name to himself, over and over. "Wait here for a minute," he said, leaving the room.

My heart surged. Something positive, at long last.

He was gone less than a minute. He was shaking his head as he walked into the study. "Sorry, nothing." He shrugged.

The frustration came back with a vengeance. I stood

up, disappointed. I knew I'd been expecting too much. Even if he had information on file, he was hardly going to divulge it. Anyway, I suspected he knew nothing. And yet, I still wasn't sure what I'd been hoping he might have told me.

"Have you talked to the local priest at all?" he asked.

"Father Murphy? Yes," I said. "We don't see eye to eye on a couple of things. He's not that forthcoming."

Broderick smiled sympathetically. "Indeed." He held out his hand. "Well, if you need me for anything, you know where to find me. Are you home on holidays?"

"You could say that, I suppose."

"Do you mind me asking why you need this information?"

"I used to teach the four boys who died. Ten years ago, I was the head teacher in the local school here."

His mouth opened. His eyes widened. *"Yes!"* he said eagerly. "I've heard your name mentioned a couple of times. Freeman, yes!" He looked at the number. "Are you staying locally?"

"Kilkenny. Langton's."

"Fair drive from here. Could you not have found somewhere close by?"

"Not really. I'm not very welcome in these parts." I left it at that. I thanked him and walked down his pebbly driveway, looking back as I reached the road. He was standing in the doorway to the conservatory speaking into his mobile phone.

30

Slán Abhaile, the small road sign said on the outskirts of the town. Safe Home.

I was both relieved and annoyed to be leaving Claddagh Mines behind me for another day. It had become like an office I felt uncomfortable in, a place where work was required to be done, in a location that was increasingly irritating me; I felt like a squatter.

Relieved, because I could now step back from the pain and anguish it had caused me in the recent past, safe in the knowledge that I had confronted it. It was a ghost that had refused to leave me in peace. Speaking out to a full church that morning had given me back my peace. And annoyed, because of what those people had held back from reporting for ten years. For all I knew, they were all accessories to some grossly indecent crime against humanity they had chosen to lay at my doorstep.

In return for being given back my peace, it was

almost like I was being asked to do something of great importance. Important to whom, I wasn't sure.

My thinking had become divided like I knew it would. As I drove that afternoon I was torn apart by the temptation to throw it all back in their faces. Let them sort out their own vile mess and take full responsibility for their ghastly secret, the seriousness of which would inevitably come to light some day. And when it did I would read about it in the *Vineyard Gazette*, or I'd meet someone while strolling along Katama Strand who'd stop me and say, "You used to work in that little town where that awful scandal took place, didn't you?" But I knew that would never happen. If it did I would spend a lifetime blaming myself for not having done something for the children I taught. Which brought me to the second option: search for the truth myself.

For some strange reason that afternoon, I was convinced that something sinister had been frozen over with time, buried beneath the ice. My problem was finding the right spot in the ice to poke a hole through to find out the truth.

A shower was long overdue, followed by a nice pint. The pain made me sweat more. I wanted to rest my ribs in a cosy armchair in front of a crackling log fire for a couple of hours. I needed to breathe without aching. I wanted to see Molly.

I had booked a table at Crossan's restaurant for seven that evening for the four of us. Our hotel receptionist had recommended it. I hoped against hope that Karen might have mellowed; that Josh might have worked some of his old, standard magic on her, extolling my virtues and telling her what a nice guy I really was. Lying through his teeth. Josh was good at that.

At the small field where the travellers had settled during my final months in Claddagh Mines, I slowed down, pulled in off the road, and stopped. I stepped out onto the grass verge. A stone wall guarded the land now, broken by a pretty red gate. A tarmac driveway and a dormer bungalow had grown up out of the long grass and hedgerows at the far end of the field of ten years ago.

I remembered the evening I had pulled my car onto the grass verge and knocked on a caravan. It was the 10th of September, the day after Owen Durkin had disappeared. The air was smoky, smelling of burnt tinder and rubber tyres. It was getting late, after ten, on that dusky summer's evening. Children and teenagers eyed me up suspiciously from behind the flames of a fire burning in a red and white barrel.

A woman opened the door. She was breastfeeding, the tiny baby dwarfed by the size of her huge breast. "Is Owen here?" I asked.

She shook her head. "Owen who? Who's this Owen lad you all keep lookin' for? I don't know any boy from the town. Sure none of the town kids play down here. Has the wee boy gone missing?"

I was about to answer her when a man's voice bellowed from behind her, "Never heard of him. Get lost!"

I had seen him, on lots of occasions, playing with the

travellers' children in the field. He would duck in and hide with the other children behind a caravan when he'd see my car. He always denied it at school the following day.

They had played the hiding game right up to the end. Then they left with their dogs and their clotheslines and caravans and four-by-four Honda CRVs and Jeeps under the cover of darkness. And I would bet my bookshop on it to this day that Owen Durkin left with them.

I had been driving too fast. I didn't even remember turning out onto the main N9 Kilkenny road, which was busy that Sunday afternoon. The bike cop could have been following me for miles, for all I knew. It was the siren that caused me to look in the rear-view. He was right on my tail, blue lights flashing. He waved me onto the hard shoulder and overtook me, stopping his bike a good distance ahead. I turned off the engine and waited. He took his time, securing the bike, taking off his gloves, radioing in my number, getting his notepad out of the pannier. He strolled back, a Goliath in his leathers and knee-buckled boots.

Bastard, I thought. I wound down the window. "Afternoon," I said pleasantly.

"This your car?" he said.

"It's a hired car. I'm on holidays."

He flipped his notebook. "Name?"

"David Freeman."

"Address."

"Here or where I live?"

"Where you live," he said smugly.

"Oak Bluffs, Martha's Vineyard, Massachusetts, USA."

He looked at me. "You being smart?" he muttered over the chin-bridge of his helmet.

"No. Why should I be smart to you? You asked for my address. That's where I live."

I knew he hadn't heard it properly but he wrote anyway. "May I ask what the offence is?"

"Speeding. Turning onto a main without due care to indicate. One of your brake-lights isn't functioning."

"What speed was I doing?"

"In excess of the speed *I* was doing."

"And what speed was that?"

"Fifty-five miles per hour."

"So that means you were breaking the speed limit also, Officer," I suggested.

"So what?" He put his hands on his hips. "I can do whatever speed I like. It's because of cheeky bastards like you that I occasionally have to break it."

"And it's because of cheeky bastards like you that this country is the way it is. Isn't that right?" I was now eligible for arrest.

"And what's that supposed to mean?" He started to raise the two-way radio.

"At least where I live – in the States – the cops treat you like an intelligent human being with a name and the understanding that they might just be talking to someone with manners and education as distinct from an animal."

"I could arrest you, you know that?"

"I'm sure you could. But let's face it, what would that achieve? You'd have to radio for a patrol car. Then you'd have to wait here with me for half an hour until they freed one up. And, be honest, on a Sunday afternoon, I'm sure your mates could think of better things to be doing than filling out forms and organising to bring me a hot meal in my cell. Anyway, what offence are you charging me with that requires you to arrest me?"

His eyes stared out through his helmet. I was gambling dangerously, doubting that he came across many motorists who gave him such unadulterated cheek. I knew I would either pay dearly or be let off with a warning. I stared back at him and smiled.

"You're that teacher from Claddagh Mines," he said.

"You must have the wrong person, Officer."

He scribbled in his pad and ripped the page off. "Here," he handed it to me, "fifty pounds for speeding, on-the-spot. You've three weeks to pay it or you'll go to court."

"Thank you, Officer. Sorry for keeping you." I started the engine and indicated right. "Have a nice day, y'hear?" I shouted in my best Boston accent and drove past his bike. I scrunched the fine in my fist and popped it out the open window, watching him through the rear-view.

31

Jean, the hotel receptionist, told me very graciously that I had been upgraded for the remainder of my stay. Room 47, she said with a smile. "All of your belongings have been moved for you."

Room 47, compared to our old room, was like a luxury penthouse that would accommodate a sheik's extended family. The others had beaten me to it for the grand tour. Josh lay in a cloud of smoke, blowing circles, stretched out on the brown leather-upholstered chaise-longue.

Karen called me from the bathroom. "I'll be there in a minute. I'm in the Jacuzzi."

Molly sat at an ornate rectangular table, complete with six matching chairs, close to the window.

I stood in the centre of the drawing-room and scratched my head. "I can't afford this. What's going on?" I asked.

"Don't fret, Teacher. I organised it for you," Josh muttered from behind the Sunday newspaper.

"Do you know the owner?" I said.

"No," he replied. "The receptionist. We have a little thing, Jean and me. She knows the owner. No problem. Say 'thank you, Josh' . . ."

"Thank you, Josh," I said boyishly.

"Hi, Dad," Molly said quietly. She didn't look up. The table was covered in paper. Pages. I sat down opposite her. Photocopies, in three neat piles. "What are they?"

"These are the articles that were written about you after you left for America." She concentrated on the page she was reading.

I fingered one of the pages close to me nervously. "What articles?"

"I asked Josh if there was any way we could access the *Tribune* archives today. There's no point going in during the week when the office is busy because they all know who I am . . ." She looked up at me and smiled. "Well, I *am* your daughter, after all. And I remembered a conversation we had a long, long time ago, years back, when you told me that the *Tribune* had written something about you after all that business ten years ago . . ."

She stopped, as if she was waiting for me to object. "Go on," I said.

"So, I asked Josh if it would be possible to get into his office today, Sunday. He said he had a key and he didn't see a problem. We spent a couple of hours going back through the old files of newspapers and . . ." She slid a photocopy of a front-page story across the table. "Look what I found."

I stared at the headline, frozen with amazement.

HEADTEACHER FLEES FOLLOWING ASSAULT ON PUPIL

I felt a lump in my throat. I swallowed hard. My fingers twitched as I picked up the article. It was a lengthy story, three columns, about a quarter of the front page. One particular paragraph caught my attention.

> "According to other pupils who witnessed the beating, Freeman threw his pupil against a steel radiator pipe after savagely striking the boy about the head a number of times."

I was livid. "Jesus Christ, I never read this." My eyes felt watery. My mouth dried. I felt weak. I slammed the article down on the table and grabbed another page. My hand was trembling so badly I couldn't focus on the headline. "What does this one say?"

Karen came out of the bathroom in her dressing-gown. "What's wrong?"

Molly reached over and put her hand down firmly on mine, so I couldn't see the print. "Dad, please, it's all right. This all happened ten years ago."

"That's just it, Molly. It didn't happen ten years ago. It never happened!"

Next I knew she was hugging me. "It's OK, Dad. Don't get mad. We're going to get to the bottom of this.

I didn't realise you hadn't seen these articles. I thought, the way you'd spoken about them years ago, that you had seen them. I'm sorry. I wouldn't have just casually shown you if I'd known that. Really, Dad, I'm sorry. I'm sorry," she kept saying.

I shook my head and took a deep breath till it felt like my ribs were stabbing me. "No, I've never seen them. I heard someone wrote something, but I didn't realise that it was this nasty."

"Listen, Teacher, this is all in the past," Josh said, coming to the table and sitting with us.

"That's just it, Josh! It's not in the past. *Nothing* is in the past. Nothing ever was. It's been bubbling under the surface for ten years. And it's all come back to life again in the last couple of days," I said. "You heard those people this morning, Josh." I looked at Molly. "You heard them too. They want answers. But they're afraid of asking the questions. I don't care if they hate me any more." I looked at Karen. She was watching me, I knew by her expression, convinced that I was going mad. I banged my finger down on the newspaper article. "Someone got these kids to lie . . . brainwashed them to say this." I picked up the page again. "Who wrote this article? Some journalist must have written this crap! What's his name?"

"Her," Josh muttered.

"Her, what?" I said.

"It was a woman who wrote it. Her name is above the third column. There." He pointed. "Just to the right, under the headline."

"Sharon T Jory," I read aloud. "Who the hell is *Sharon T Jory?*"

"She was a young journalist. Just qualified from a college in Dublin. It was her first job. That, I guess, was one of her first big stories. She was probably trying to impress the editor with her brash, brazen in-your-face style."

"Brash?" I shouted. *"Brazen?* This is defamation. Pure *libel!"* I waved the page. "This, Josh, is worth at least one hundred grand in a court of law to me. Do you know that?" I was furious. "This destroyed my career, *this* article. I reckon that if I was to take this to any half-decent lawyer and get him to take *Sharon T Jory* to court, I could clean both her and your newspaper out of it. *Completely!"* I waited.

Josh took a long drag of his cigarette and scratched his chin. "Yes, you could. Under normal circumstances."

"Are you telling me that these circumstances aren't *normal?"* I said.

Josh turned his chair back-to-front and sat down, resting his arms on the frame. "Well, we have a couple of problems here. Problem number one, it's ten years since these articles were written. First of all, your solicitor is gonna want to know why you haven't taken action against the publication before this."

"Because I didn't know these articles existed before this," I reasoned.

"Yeah, but wait a minute, Teacher. Most people in your predicament are gonna keep an eye on what's goin' on behind their back while they're out of town. You left Claddagh Mines and went to America. Everyone in Claddagh Mines saw these articles so any judge and jury is gonna want to know how come you weren't told that these articles existed." Josh lit another cigarette.

"Because I wanted to leave it all behind me," I explained.

Josh pointed at me. *"Guilty as sin, Your Honour!"* he shouted.

"How dare you!" I shouted back.

"Wait a minute, Teacher. See it from our point of view here." Josh pointed to Molly and Karen. "Just suppose for a minute that we are the jury. We don't really know you at all. We've been selected at random, so we don't know each other. I have never seen these two women in my life." He looked at Molly, then at Karen. "Have I?" he asked.

They shook their heads.

"And they have never met me. We are sitting here having read those articles about you some time before. We are trying to decide whether or not you are guilty of assaulting Owen Durkin. The prosecution stands before us and says, 'Ladies and gentlemen of the jury, this man you see here before you ran away to America after assaulting a young boy in his care; a defenceless thirteen-year old pupil in the care of a *responsible* school teacher. He beat him savagely and then knocked him unconscious by throwing him down onto a metal radiator pipe using all the power he could muster. He denies doing it. Yet a classroom of young schoolchildren, also in his care, witnessed him doing it. This man, ladies and gentlemen, even had the gall to try and sue a local newspaper for printing an article he didn't realise existed for ten years. His excuse for not doing it before? He wanted to forget about the whole incident . . . '" Josh stared into my eyes. He frightened me by what he had just said. He made it sound so true and vivid, as if it could have easily happened all those years ago. As if it could have easily happened to anyone. He also made me realise I had been very wrong to do what I had done.

"Teacher, if you were on the jury, and you were trying the man I had just described, conscious of the fact that he had no witnesses, *none whatsoever*, to substantiate his case, how would you find him?" Josh let the cigarette burn his fingers as he waited for me to answer.

"Guilty," I said. "But it didn't happen like that," I shouted and banged the table.

"I *know* that." Josh looked around. "We all know that, Teacher. But all those people out there don't. Well, at least they didn't until this morning."

"Well then, let's get Sharon T Jory, or whatever her name is, to retract the stories she printed. Make her tell the truth. Force her to undo the damage she's done, Josh. I'm sure your editor would allow her write an apology."

Josh nudged his cap with his wrist. "Ah, that's the

second problem. You won't get much satisfaction from Sharon Jory. She's dead."

My heart almost missed a beat. "Dead?" I felt winded. Beat.

"She was killed in a car accident in London. Died instantly. Six years ago." Josh smiled sympathetically. "Sorry, Teacher."

I studied the way Josh watched me for a moment, his eyes flitting between the two women and me. He watched for their reactions as he spoke, then looked to me to see how I was reacting to them. But he never looked me straight in the eye. "You bastard," I said.

Josh stopped speaking. "What did you say?"

"I said, you bastard. You think I did it, don't you?"

"Did what?"

"You really think I beat up that kid, don't you?"

Josh shook his head. He waved his hands like a boxing referee. "Hang on a minute, Teacher. I can understand how difficult this all must be for you right now. It hasn't been easy coming back here, what with Molly's little accident, and then her uncle crashing into your car. And this whole business with that mad bastard, Doug Ferris. You're bound to be a little freaked out."

Molly stood up. She looked pale. She stared straight at me, disbelief written all over her face.

"Molly, what's wrong?" I said.

"You never told me Turloch drove into your car."

I looked at Karen. She had her two hands up,

covering her face, shaking her head. "Karen, you told me you were going to tell her."

"Tell me *what*, for Christ sake!" Molly shouted.

"I'm sorry. I was waiting for the right moment, Dave. I was going to tell her this evening. I'm so sorry," Karen muttered through her hands.

"Oh, Jesus, what have I done?" Josh leaned over the arm of the sofa and covered his eyes. "Teacher, I'm sorry. I thought Molly knew."

"Will someone pleeease tell me what the hell is going on here?" Molly screamed.

The clamour in the room was more than I could take. Karen was berating Josh for saying what he had said. Josh was shouting at her that he didn't realise it was all such a hush-hush secret. Molly was pleading with them to shut up and explain.

"OK! Calm down, *everyone. Shut up!*" I yelled.

Silence.

"Molly, your uncle was following us the night we went to the theatre. He sat outside the restaurant and followed us all the way back to the hospital. He was parked outside your apartment when I got into my car to go and collect Karen from the airport." This was where I had to change the story. "I was so busy watching him in my rear-view mirror, I didn't realise that the traffic-lights had changed to red at the junction I was approaching. I slammed on my brakes and . . . he ploughed into the back of my car . . ." I looked away, afraid of how she might react. She had been through so much stress and anxiety that I was suddenly terrified that what I had just said could be too much for her.

"Thank you," she said quite punctually. She picked up her coat.

"Where are you going?" I stood up quickly and reached out to grab her arm. She sidestepped me. *"Wait, please!"* She ignored me. She opened the door and left.

Karen waved her hand. "I'll go after her. She'll be OK."

The door swished shut behind her.

I slumped back into the chair, reached into my pocket and took two Ponstan capsules out of a small plastic jar. I reached for the mineral water and washed them down. I looked at Josh.

"I'm sorry. That was all my fault," he said. He pulled the peak of his cap down over his eyes and rolled over into the corner of the settee. "So what happens now, Teacher?"

I threw up my hands. "I've a good mind to drive to the airport, leave the rental back and fly home to Boston."

Josh sniggered. "That's like something you would have done ten years ago."

I turned my head and looked at him. "Are you trying to be smart?"

"Nope."

"Josh, this might mean nothing to you. But I need to know that you don't believe that I beat that young Durkin kid ten years ago." I waited for his answer, watching him playing with the matchstick that seemed to eternally to be stuck between his bottom front teeth. "Well?"

"Would it make any difference if I did think you did it?"

I pondered his question. "Most likely it would, yes. And do you believe that I did it?"

He smiled and shook his head. "No, of course I don't believe that." He pointed his finger at me. "You wanna know something, Teacher?" His warm, friendly tone was gone. "If I thought for a minute that you lifted a finger to that kid, I'd have told the whole church." He held his arm straight, pointing at me.

I was so relieved to know that he trusted me. I could smile again.

"Now, are we going downstairs to the bar? I'm thirsty and I'd like to buy you a drink."

"Sounds good. Let me check on Molly and Karen. I've booked a table for seven o'clock this evening. The four of us. Crossans."

"I love that place. There's this really cute little French waitress in there who wears a little tight dress and nothing else." Josh blew a kiss.

As I stood up, my mobile phone rang. "Hello?" I said.

"David Freeman?"

"Speaking."

"This is Steven Broderick. You called to see me earlier this afternoon."

"Yes, Steven, how can I help you?"

"Well, actually, I may be able to help you. You asked me to call if I heard anything about Ivan Moyne?"

"Yes?" I said eagerly.

"Well, nothing about Ivan, I'm afraid. But I did do some checking with a friend of mine. He's a doctor in Nenagh. It's about fifteen miles from Claddagh Mines. I remember him telling me some time back that Ivan Moyne's wife, eh . . . estranged wife, actually, is in the same nursing home as his mother, if you follow me. Have you got a pen?"

Music to my ears. "Excellent," I said, fumbling in my inside pockets for a pen and paper. Josh handed me both. I laid the pad on the table and aimed the pen. "OK, I've got one."

"She's in a home called Sunny Hall House. Three words. It's in Summerhill, in County Meath. I think he mentioned it was quite close to Trim."

"That's fantastic," I enthused. "Does your friend visit her when he goes to see his mother?"

"No, I'm afraid not. He simply just mentioned it to me some time back, because of the connection with my predecessor and Claddagh Mines. That's all. I hope it's of some help to you."

I thanked him. "Before you go, Doctor Broderick, do you mind me asking you another question?"

"No, of course not."

"We don't know each other. You've never met me before. So why did you bother going to all that trouble to find out this stuff for me?"

He sounded polite in his reply. "Because after you'd left I remembered meeting your young daughter many years ago. In the course of the conversation she told me how you had saved her life in a swimming accident." He stopped and seemed to hesitate. "I suppose I admire you for having had the guts to put your own life at risk. My daughter drowned in similar circumstances some years back. All I could do was watch. You see, I was afraid of the water, Mr Freeman." He stopped. "It was a pleasure meeting you. You lived up to the wonderful description your daughter gave me of you that day."

The line went dead.

"What's going on, Teacher? You look like you've just won the lotto," Josh said wryly.

"You know that feeling where you think you're getting absolutely nowhere for days and days, and then suddenly you get your first piece of the jigsaw?"

"All the time," Josh mumbled.

"Well, for what it's worth, I've just found my first piece of the jigsaw. I think that calls for a drink," I said triumphantly.

32

Molly and Karen compared credit cards and giggled like two schoolgirls on a trip to the city. I dropped them at Kildare railway station at 9.30am. Molly had a 10.30 appointment with the consultant at the hospital. They had planned a shopping day in Grafton Street once she had finished.

My streetwise knowledge of Dublin was out of date by ten years. So, following a heated debate as to where we should rendezvous, I arranged to meet them in the late afternoon, half-three, maybe four, I said, in Café Mocha, one of Molly's trendy hang-outs close to the Westbury Hotel.

The journey across country to Sunny Hall took me little over an hour. It was easy to find, a pleasant enough place, as you might expect of a retirement home, secluded and well in from the main road. A single-level series of creamy-coloured, interconnected buildings like perfectly placed pieces on a scrabble board, surrounded by a sprawling, lush garden with black tarmac winding pathways, bordered by small flower beds and hydrangeas, and wall creepers around most windows, and three pretty redwood birdhouses marking the triangular perimeter. A hospital without all the fuss, I thought as I parked the car. The silence struck me as pervasive.

Visitors must ring the bell. I rang it. Somewhere deep in the bowels of Sunny Hall, a loud intrusive school-like bell rang. I could hear the footsteps. I checked my watch. It was just after eleven. It was still too early for Christmas at Sunny Hall. No tree. No Santa.

A middle-aged woman with jet-black hair walked towards me. She smiled and fingered a bunch of keys that jangled noisily from a loop on her belt. She was a large woman, wearing a white uniform under a dark-blue cardigan. Her hair was perfectly straight, tied back with hairpins. A pair of spectacles hung from a chord. She wore a gold cross and chain around her neck. As she turned the key in the door, I smiled back and nodded. Her badge said *Day Care Manager*. A blast of heat hit as she opened back the door.

"Can I help you?" she asked cheerfully.

"My name is David Freeman. I'm hoping to see Ingrid Moyne. I believe she's a patient here," I said graciously. I stepped inside.

"Ingrid? Are you her nephew?" she asked, as if half-expecting me.

"No. I'm just a friend."

"Oh, I see."

"Were you expecting her nephew?" I asked in the hope of adding to my jigsaw.

"No, not really. We just thought, coming close to Christmas like, that someone might call. She asks a lot about her nephew . . . well, it's kind of hard to explain." She looked at me warily. "Ingrid has been deteriorating at a pretty fast rate over the past few months. And it's getting a wee bit difficult knowing what to believe every time she starts her talking."

"I'm sorry?"

"Well, she told me about a month ago after one of her phone calls that her nephew was coming home from America to see her. But I didn't know whether it was another one of her made-up stories or the truth."

Coincidence, I thought. "Well, I'm actually home from America for a couple of weeks, but we're not related." I paused.

She nodded ruefully.

"Would it be possible to see her?" I asked.

"Of course it would. And your name again?"

"David." I held out my hand. "David Freeman."

"Lovely to meet you, David. I'm Vera Tubridy, the Day Care Manager. If you'd like to follow me, I'll show you to her room." She led the way, clomping her sandals like horses' hooves, like the sound of a dull whip-crack on the shiny linoleum floor. "I'm here from eight to eight, four days a week. Every second week,

I'm here five days. And twice a year I do a week of nights, one week on, one week off, for two months. And, *believe me*, I hate the nights. It's like a morgue around here . . ." She glanced back at me and giggled, putting her hand to her mouth. "Oh, you'll have to forgive me, David. I didn't mean that literally."

"That's OK," I said. I couldn't see her reason for telling me her schedule. Then I thought of the patients and how she must sometimes long for two-way conversation.

We walked slowly past the day room, its occupants in dressinggowns and slippers, Zimmer frames parked conveniently at an arm's length. Two of them eyed me eagerly. One of them hid a cigarette and waved at the smoke.

We passed the staff bay; two nurses standing next to an open window were devouring a quick cigarette. Then came the wards; four- and five-bed rooms, like a general hospital, their residents sleeping or reading. Beyond that point the doors on either side were closed.

"These are the private rooms, the clients with money," Vera Tubridy explained. "These are for our long-term residents. The bigger wards are for osteopathy and arthroplasty. Do you have arthritis, Mr Freeman?" Vera Tubridy asked me curiously.

"No, thankfully, I don't."

She looked back and examined me up and down. "I'd say you're fairly healthy."

"Fairly, thanks."

"Many of our clients here would be in for short-term care, following hip replacements, and more serious rehabilitation following cardiac surgery if they're considered a bit on the elderly side for the general hospitals. Here they tend to get a bit more TLC."

"*Clients?*" I mused. The word felt cold and impersonal. I could see it used to describe judges and barrister.

"We don't call them patients, Mr Freeman. Most of these poor people don't want to be here. Most of the long-term residents have been put here by their families. Some people would call it institutionalisation."

"And what do you call it?" I said.

"Desertion," she replied without a moment of hesitation. "There's nothing wrong with seventy-five per cent of the people in these private rooms, so why should they be labelled *patients?*"

Vera Tubridy knocked on a door. Number 7. She walked in ahead of me and half-closed the door behind her. "You have a guest, Ingrid." She spoke slowly and stridently. I couldn't hear an answer.

Vera opened the door wide. "Ingrid will see you now," she said with a cemented smile.

"Before you leave," I said quickly, "I meant to ask you a few things. I haven't seen Ingrid for nearly ten years. Even before that time, I didn't know her too well. Has she been abandoned too?"

"By who?" Vera Tubridy seemed confused by my question.

"By her husband?"

"Vera Tubridy has been abandoned by her mind." She lowered her voice. "She has Alzheimer's." She laid on the dead smile again and closed the door behind me.

She might as well have slammed it hard on my face. My heart sank the second she had said it. My hopes of finding out what I needed to know felt shredded.

I smiled before turning around.

I wasn't sure if the face looking at me could see me clearly. Her eyes had a glazed, uncertain stare about them. Ingrid Moyne looked dead, her body withered and deflated, her cheeks sunken into the frilly neckline of her flowery nightie, her eyes sore and blackened. "Hello," I said softly.

"You're not my nephew," she said, almost whispering. Her head seemed to shake permanently, more pronounced when she spoke, tilted to the right.

"I'm David Freeman, from Claddagh Mines. I knew you a long time ago, Mrs Moyne, when I was a teacher at St John's primary school."

Her eyes never moved, never blinked. She looked away from me and stared up at the television sitting on an angle-poised stand at the top of the wall, directly in front of her. She raised her right hand slowly and pointed to the screen. A chat-show audience was driving on their host. *Trisha* was her name, in the bottom left-hand corner of the screen, in fancy handwriting. She was berating some woman, asking her if she thought there was nothing wrong with sleeping with her daughter's boyfriend. The audience booed her, and cheered Trisha on harder with every question she asked.

"What kinds of idiots watch that sort of tripe?" Ingrid Moyne said. Then she smiled. "Turn that off and sit down, please."

I did as I was told. I pulled my chair close to the bed, watching her hand as it said closer, and closer still.

"My hearing isn't too good. My brain isn't too good either. But my mind is fine," she said, coughing and catching her breath between sentences. "They look at me here as if I'm some sort of retard."

She studied me, rubbing her cheek against the pillow to steady her head. "Who are you?" she asked again.

"David. David Freeman. How long are you here?" It felt like a foolish question.

"I don't know and I don't care, David," she said. "*David, David, David . . .*" She looked out at the sunny day, trying to place my name. "You were a schoolteacher, weren't you?"

I nodded.

"And you went away, didn't you?"

"I did." I spoke softly and patiently. "I went to America, ten years ago. I've been there ever since."

"So why did you come back here?"

"My daughter . . . she tried to commit suicide." For some reason I felt comfortable sharing this with the old woman. Yet she wasn't saddened by what I had just said. "How old is she? Your daughter?"

"Twenty-one."

"Is she an attractive girl?"

"Stunningly beautiful," I said, and smiled.

"Then why did she want to do such a terrible thing?"

"I don't really know. I hope she'll tell me someday."

Her chest wheezed as she breathed. "I'm a doctor. Or, at least, I *was* a doctor. I loved being a doctor. Did you know me when I was a doctor, David?"

I nodded. "Yes, very well. You were a brilliant doctor."

"Rubbish!" she said. "I suppose I wasn't such a bad doctor. Doctors tend to look at things very differently from the way our patients would. Do you know what I mean? Doctors train for so long that I used to think we traded our minds for the education we were given. Once you started learning about medicine, you eat, sleep and drink it. From the moment you wake up till the moment you fall into an exhausted sleep late at night you see the world and everything in it as a doctor of medicine. Even when you are eating your meals, you're questioning yourself about the morsels of food you're chewing with your teeth." She stopped talking and focused on me. "I'm wandering now . . . I'm sorry."

"No, please, continue. Go on."

She sighed. "I've often thought about ending it all." She laughed. "What's left of it; sure it's nearly all over anyway."

"They say it takes a lot of courage to do it," I said.

"To do what? Kill yourself?" she asked, resentful

that I had interrupted her. "It doesn't take any courage to kill one's self, Mr Freeman. I often think, and I've told my patients this, that it takes a lot more courage to stay alive and face up to the awful demons in your head that drive you on to attempt such a terrible thing."

She watched to see if I would argue with her. "You're right," I said. "I agree with you. That's why I'm so happy that my daughter is still alive. At least, now, we can get her the help she needs."

"Do you know something, Mr Freeman. It's been proven by research that *ninety-five* per cent of people who attempt suicide but who are caught just before the moment of no-return, and that's a very small window, Mr Freeman, ninety-five per cent of those would-be victims are grateful that someone saved their lives. And ninety per cent of those usually go on to live long and happy lives, once they've sorted out their neuroses." She smiled. "Look after your daughter, Mr Freeman."

"Dave, I'd prefer if you would call me Dave," I said.

"David!" she replied. "I shall call you David. I hate these clipped names that young people like to be known by today." She sighed again. "There's something intrinsically evil about what lies in store for young people trying to find their way in the world today. There's no trust. Even their friends sell them drugs. They have no confidence in themselves. There's no happiness any more, David. Everyone is trying to outdo the other. No one does a good turn for you any more. People only like you for what you might be able to give

them." She watched me. "Isn't that why you're here today, David?"

"You're a good person, Mrs Moyne. Actually I came to talk to you."

"Ingrid. Call me Ingrid. And no you *didn't!* You came here like the others. Like my nephew. You heard I had Alzheimer's, or something ridiculous like that. You heard I was losing my marbles and you wanted to check if I was going to leave you some money. You want to know what's in it for you, don't you?"

"Of course not. I don't want your money."

"You're no better than my nephew. Thank God my husband is dead."

I froze. It was exactly what I didn't want to hear. Ivan Moyne was dead.

"Sorry, Mrs Moyne, did you say your husband was dead?" I asked, in the hope that I had heard her wrong.

"Yes. He's dead. *Dead!* Thank God I don't have to leave him a damn penny in my will. I'd turn in my grave if I thought that man had benefited from the paltry few pounds I have saved."

Someone coughed behind me. I looked around. Vera Tubridy stood discreetly outside the almost closed door. She shook her head and urged me to come outside.

"I'll have to go, Mrs Moyne . . ."

"*Ingrid*. Please call me Ingrid. No one calls me *Mrs* Moyne. Will you come back again and visit me?"

I nodded and stood up. "I promise I will."

"When?" she asked.

I wasn't expecting the question. Today was Monday. "Next Friday."

"I'll be expecting you." She held out her small, frail hand.

I held it and shook it gently. It felt like a china teacup, narrow and bony and cold. I placed it gently back on the bedclothes. "Next Friday."

33

Vera Tubridy closed the door gently. She beckoned me silently, with her index finger, to follow her to the small office at the end of the corridor. She pointed to a chair. I sat down. She sat behind the desk. "I wasn't eavesdropping on your conversation, Mr Freeman, but I feel there are some things you should know about Ingrid."

"Well, if you weren't eavesdropping, how do you know there are things I should know?"

Eye contact stopped. She looked at the scribbling-pad on her desk and drew a diamond shape. "Ingrid has been a client here at Sunny Hall for almost four years. Doctor Moyne left her for another woman he had been seeing, I'm afraid." Vera stared at me as if she was just after breaking some terrible news that would upset me deeply. "Anyway, Ingrid had a nervous breakdown. She was found wandering along the main Dublin to

Cork road hysterical at three o'clock one morning by the local police. Her husband paid for her to stay here, following a short period in a psychiatric unit, for as long as she wanted. And, well, she's still here."

"Has she always just lain there in her bed?" I asked.

"For the past few months, yes. Before that she used to regularly walk in the gardens. She even enjoyed helping our gardener, Tom, with the rose pruning. But for the past few months, since the end of the summer, she's shown no real interest in going outdoors. She occasionally comes down to the TV room. But she doesn't like talking with the other clients, so she stopped that as well."

I was beginning to dislike the word *clients*. It smelt mercenary. "How long has she had Alzheimer's?" I asked.

"How long is a piece of string?" Vera Tubridy asked, obviously gloating behind her medical knowledge. "It's hard to know when Alzheimer's starts. It's only when the patient starts to display signs and symptoms that tests begin. Three years. Maybe more. Who's to say she didn't have it in some mild form for a long time before that? It could be possible that you and I could be nurturing the condition and we may not be aware of it for years to come."

I wanted to tell the woman to shut up. "She seems quite lucid to me."

"You haven't been talking to her for long enough."

"She told me her husband was dead."

Vera Tubridy laughed, and then apologised. "If I hear that one more time . . . Ivan Moyne calls here once a fortnight, by phone, often once a week, to enquire how Ingrid is. He normally asks if she needs anything and tells us to buy it, whatever it might be, if she does. Then he sends a banker's draft." She joined her hands and rested them on the scribbler.

"Where does the draft come from?"

She seemed surprised by my question. "I don't know. Our accounts section would deal with all end of it. *And* it is confidential."

"Of course. Where does he live?" I asked.

"I've no idea," she replied pompously. "I've only spoken to him twice. *No,* actually, three times. He normally calls late at night. Lovely man. Always has something nice to say about the staff."

"And his wife?"

"Sorry?"

"What does he have to say about his wife?" I said.

"His *ex*-wife, you mean." She paused after correcting me.

I could tell she was enjoying this. I tried to concentrate on Vera Tubridy's slick, smart-alec answers, while wondering almost unconsciously about her mental health, and its stability, and whether she had been bottling up countless neuroses herself over the years. Madness is contagious, I had been told somewhere before.

"Doctor Moyne has always sounded very concerned

about Ingrid's health any time he's been on the phone. He just wants to make sure she's getting the best care. He knows we look after her well here. She's in good hands."

I looked around the office, comfortably furnished, cosily decorated. "How much does it cost per day to stay here?" I asked.

Vera Tubridy shook her head. "I've no idea. We leave all that to the accounts people. They work on the other side of the building. I can make an appointment with them for you if you wish?" She went to pick up the phone. She was playing her game beautifully. She didn't want me there. She wanted me off the premises. Her tactics were admirable. I stood up. "That won't be necessary." I put on my jacket. "I think I've a few years left in me yet."

"I'll show you to the door," she said, moving past me and out into the corridor, her hand sweeping in the direction of the exit.

"Does she have any family, apart from her nephew?" I asked.

"I don't think so. No one has ever called in the four years she's been here. She has no immediate children of her own. She talks about this nephew in America. He owns a bar in Buffalo, upstate New York, it seems. Stan is his name."

"Stan?"

"Yes."

"As distinct from Stanley?"

Vera Tubridy was confused again. "Yes, why."

"Nothing," I said. "Did she mention who he's related to? Doctor Moyne's side of the family, or hers?"

"She never mentioned. All she says is that he's after her money. She reckons he's going to come back as soon as she gets helpless and rob her."

I tried to conjure up such a picture. "What a hideous way to be forced to live out her life." I said. "I told Ingrid I'd call again to see her next Friday."

Vera Tubridy forced a smile. "She'll be delighted, Mr Freeman. It's very good of you to come all this way for someone you haven't seen for so long." She unlocked the front door and opened it just enough for me to squeeze out. "We'll see you Friday then?"

"Yes. Thank you." I stood on the step. "Oh, one more thing, Mrs Tubridy."

She stopped short of closing the door. "Yes?" she said, her impatience finally showing through.

"Would there be a problem if I wanted to take Ingrid Moyne out to dinner Friday evening?"

She stared at me, unsure of how to answer. "Well, most likely there won't be a problem . . . provided she's accompanied by a member of staff, and that's provided one of our staff nurses agrees to give up her night to go with her. It's an unusual request, Mr Freeman, but Doctor Moyne has been generous with his donations, and we wouldn't like to upset him in any way. It should be OK, provided . . . once the consultant thinks it fine."

I nodded to her, waiting for her to lock the door, and

turned and smelt the ice-cold, crisp country air. It stung my nostrils, freezing them for a moment. The bright midday sunshine felt warm on my forehead. A cow mooed in the distance.

I smiled.

34

Winter arrived that afternoon with a vengeance, making up for the time we had conned ourselves into believing the sunshine was there to stay. The first downpour soaked me. I cursed myself for pretending to know my 'streets'. I was lost. The coffee-shop business was booming, I concluded, after finding myself back outside the same pedestrian exit, where I had parked my car, three times. The corner of South King Street and South William Street was where I should find Café Mocha, Molly told me. It seemed quite straightforward until I emerged from the multi-storey car park. On foot, everything seemed different. Side streets were bigger. Small cafés jumped up at me from refurbished basements. Bistros and restaurants of every nationality I could think of: Thai, Lebanese and Japanese, right next door to each other. Diners that looked so small I questioned the profitability of such a venture. For every one pub I had noticed while sitting in the heavy traffic, now there were three. It was half four.

Christmas had come to Grafton Street and its surroundings. A cacophony of seasonal music filled the busy street, assaulting my ears from all sides. Every few steps produced a different carol. Out of a sports shop, Wham, "Last Christmas".

A bearded busker stood over his open guitar case, belting out "The Twelve Days Of Christmas", strumming the strings hard in an effort to drown out Bing Crosby's "Little Drummer Boy", playing in the chemist behind him.

A dejected-looking Santa Claus rang his bell and wished me Happy Christmas. His beard, soaked and dishevelled, hung around his chin like a baby bib.

An elderly woman with white wisps of hair tucked in under a blue headscarf pointed to her wrapped bunches of flowers. "Two for a pound, love," she almost implored me, as the rain grew heavier, its thick drops cold on the back of my neck. She seemed to know Santa. She shouted to him, "See ye later, Tommy." He disappeared into a pub as she reached into her pram for the flowers. I bought four bunches and asked her to make them look like two big ones.

She smiled. "Did ye have an argument with her?" she asked.

"With who?"

"Your girlfriend . . ."

"Why do you think I had an argument with my girlfriend?" I said curiously.

"'Cos no one buys that many flowers unless they've been fighting like cats 'n' dogs . . ." She chuckled and pushed the two bulky bunches under my arm. As she took the coins in the palm of her hand, she felt the rain. "That's down for the night, love. Ye'd better get movin', or she'll be giving out to you for getting soaked." She laughed heartily and pocketed my money. Then she set about covering her old pram and its dwindling consignment of flowers.

I hadn't a clue what the flowers were called. I was more impressed by their colours. "Where's Café Mocha?" I asked.

She turned away from me and faced the Westbury Hotel at the bottom of the street. Her hand zigzagged through the small side streets she mentioned. I feared I was going to get lost again. I didn't even bother taking in the instructions. Then I remembered my mobile phone, something I had never bothered much with before coming home, but knew now I couldn't do without it. I thanked the woman. The way she wished me luck reminded me for an instant of Ingrid Moyne, and how she had spoken to me, slowly, with such a deep, resonant voice for someone who was so thin and frail-looking.

Perhaps if I hadn't been so consumed, thinking about Ingrid so much, and the debate that raged in my head since leaving Sunny Hall earlier that afternoon as to whether Ivan Moyne was dead or not, and the consequences that might follow on as a result of finding out that he *was* alive, I wouldn't have got lost.

My mind was restless, trying to piece together a confounding jigsaw while wearing a blindfold. Even without the delusions, I was still in the dark as to what had taken place in Claddagh Mines in my absence. Just like I had tormented myself all the way across the Atlantic that night over what might have been, and what I would have done, if I had spotted the smallest hint that could have prevented Molly's suicide attempt, now I was haunted by what I believed to be my own absent-mindedness; almost like visiting the hallowed scene of a great historical battle that had been fought out many years before, when all that lies in front of you is an empty, green field – the rest is left up to your imagination.

On finding Café Mocha, a friendly waiter, a Tunisian I guessed, shattered my relief by telling me there were in fact four Café Mochas, all situated within a one-mile radius.

I sipped my cappuccino, hoping the girls hadn't got here before me and assumed I had got my Mochas mixed up, and then gone elsewhere to find me. I watched curiously the array of umbrellas passing outside the steamed-up window. A strong wind had whipped up, turning the gentle rain of the early afternoon into a spitting downpour of hailstones. The battle of avoiding other umbrellas while managing to prevent your own from blowing inside out had begun in earnest. I looked at my watch. It was ten past five. Rush hour had begun.

I watched people as they came in out of the elements. A man and a woman eyed up my large table. My look said *Reserved* as I stretched out my arms to lay claim to what was mine, placing two identical bunches of flowers on the table, one at each end. I must have looked like an idiot. They sat elsewhere.

It was now half-five, pitch-dark. The rain continued to lash down, unabated. There was no sign of Molly and Karen.

My mind wandered as I watched the chocolate-covered frothy bubbles of my second cappuccino dispersing.

Today was the twelfth of December. Monday. I had been home eighteen days. Almost three weeks. And already I could have written a book based on what had happened to my family. My mind threw up faces from the past.

I watched Aidan Ferris from the top of the classroom. He recited a poem I had asked them all to learn the night before. I glanced at Owen Durkin, defeated in his rebellious attempts now that I had moved him into the middle of the front row of desks. He stared back stubbornly.

I could pick out four other faces, dotted here and there, as if for some reason it were yesterday. In the back row, closest to the cloakroom: Colin Harris. Seated next to the middle window: James Dowling. Another boisterous rebel, in the front row beside the main door:

Michael Furlong. Directly under the statue of the Blessed Virgin: Paul McHugh. I remember the class photograph, and how I had separated the four of them, strategically placing them, each one apart, in the four corners of the photo frame to keep them away from each other. I remember how I had to persistently remind Paul McHugh to smile. I must have shouted at him a dozen times. He just ignored me.

Dead. Every one of them. Not even twenty-one yet. They were all dead.

I remembered how Owen Durkin hated them all. He thwarted each one of them so much, that they would gang up on him and chase him.

Durkin always outlasted the four of them at everything. He could trick them, cajole them, con them and finally lose them in the chase.

Was he dead? I asked myself, waving for another cappuccino. I didn't believe he was dead. I never had. He was too clever. If he could run rings round his mother, his teacher and four of the most antagonistic boys I have ever met, he could survive. Anywhere, I was convinced.

Aidan Ferris came to mind again. I could see his father's face in the church, cowering to avoid my glances, his arm in a sling.

For a few moments I imagined all these young boys together, standing in a line. My mind swept across them, from left to right, remembering their young faces. My memory, however, kept coming back to focus on one of them: Owen Durkin. I was convinced he was the key that would unlock the true account of whatever it was that had happened the others. Something subconsciously told me, whenever I doubted it, that Durkin was alive, and that, sooner or later, I would come face to face with him. How? I didn't know the answer. Even the question seemed ridiculous. One thing I did believe now was that, even though he was only thirteen at the time, Owen Durkin knew something, or had seen something, that had driven him away from Claddagh Mines.

I could hear a mobile ringing somewhere in the distance. I watched customers checking their coats and bags, pulling out their phones and then putting them away again. That was when I realised it was my phone. Expecting to hear Karen or Molly on the other end, I answered simply with, "Where are you?"

A man spoke. "Hello?" he said. "Dave, is that you?"

It was Tom Brady. It was wonderful to hear his voice, someone familiar sent to rescue you in a sea of confusion. *"Tom, how are you?"* I shouted. *"You sound like you're in the room next door. The line is really clear . . ."* I looked around. People watched me, amused by my comments. They looked at me as if I had just discovered some new form of innovative telecommunication.

"I'm fine, Dave. How are you? How is your daughter?" Tom asked.

"She's fine, Tom. We're all fine, thanks." As I

enjoyed the sound of his voice, it occurred to me that there might be something wrong. Maybe the shop had burnt down. "Is everything OK, Tom?" I asked, trying not to sound panicky.

"Yeah, sure, everything is fine, Dave. It's just we haven't heard from you in a few days. We wanted to make sure you were OK. How's Karen?"

"She's fine. Enjoying playing with her Amex card. Is the shop OK, Tom?"

"Couldn't be better. It's done some powerful business over Thanksgiving. You're gonna need to restock when you get back. You are coming back, aren't you?"

I detected the sarcasm in his voice. I laughed. "Yes, of course we're coming back. It's just that things have been happening here and I haven't really had a chance to call you to see how you're getting on. How's Thelma?"

"She's great. You might find it hard getting rid of her out of the shop when you get back. She loves the books. She chats to every customer for at least fifteen minutes. I reckon she mightn't give back the shop at all." Tom gave a husky Brady laugh. It was so comforting to hear him. I missed my shop, listening to him on the phone. I missed my home. "Have you been doing any fishing while I've been away, Tom?"

"You bet!" he shouted. "You're not gonna believe what I landed last Tuesday, Dave . . ."

"Bonito?"

Tom screamed with excitement. "Not just one, *two bonitos!*" He whooped and laughed. "I caught the first one off East Chop. Then about three hours later, I caught the other off Squibnocket. I even got a phone call from Bill Narkiewicz on WMVY. They want me to review some blues CDs . . . just for catching a couple of bonitos. The *Gazette* wants to do a double-spread on me, Dave. Can you believe that? I'm a legend."

He laughed again. I was so happy for Tom Brady. He had, just six months before, undergone a quadruple heart bypass. He made a quick recovery, but since the day he left Boston General, Thelma refused to take her eye off him. All she said for weeks afterwards was, *"Don't lift that!"* She was delighted the night I asked Tom to look after The Meadows for a few days.

"What did Thelma say when you told her you'd caught two bonitos?" I asked.

Tom roared laughing. "She said, 'I hope you didn't lift them into the boat by yourself!'."

We both laughed. I missed him. I missed Thelma. For years they had been like parents to me. They had put me up in a small room. Thelma cooked my meals and washed my clothes. She cut my hair whenever she thought it needed a trim. She bought me shirts when she shopped for Tom. Tom had employed me as a handyman around the B&B. I mended the roof. I painted and did the plumbing. And all the time I lived with them and worked for them, they never once asked about where I had come from and why.

I don't know what I would have done, or how my sanity would have remained intact, without Tom and Thelma Brady. They were gifts from God. And I never forgot that for a moment.

To this day I still haven't told them my story. Someday, maybe, I will.

"Any idea when you're coming back here?" Tom asked.

I detected urgency his voice. "I should be back by the end of next week. Is that OK?" I said.

"No problem." He stopped. "Is everything OK there, Dave?"

There was a huge difference now in the tone of his voice. His question was filled with concern and sympathy. I could tell they were worried about us.

"Everything is *fine*, Tom. Don't be worrying."

"Oh, I'm not worrying. But you know what Thelma is like. A mountain out of a molehill. She worries about everything, does Thelma. You take your time, son. Come back when you're ready to come back. Everything here is just fine."

I could hear a familiar voice in the background.

"Thelma sends her love," Tom repeated her instructions in his henpecked mocking, exasperated voice.

"Tell her I love her too, Tom. Thanks for calling."

"Talk to you later, son. Bye."

I pressed *end* on the phone menu, remembering how Tom had treated me like a son for years, and suddenly felt alone again.

As I looked up, Karen was flapping her closed umbrella; being chastised by Molly for opening it up indoors. "That's bad luck," Molly scolded.

I counted at least ten bags. Karen's new Amex had been through the fire.

They both chattered away excitedly about their shopping experiences. I smiled, and nodded, and sipped my fourth cappuccino. Molly told me about her appointment with the consultant. He was very happy with her progress. I knew by the way Karen watched her that they had something to tell me. When they had run out of shops to talk about, and clothes and gifts they had bought, they looked at each other and smiled. Their eyes opened wider. Karen nodded, prompting Molly to say it. I held my breath and waited.

"Molly's got something she wants to tell you," Karen said.

"I gathered that," I replied, unsure as to whether I should be excited or terrified. I looked at Molly and nodded. "Well?"

She took a deep breath and held it. Then . . . "I have decided to come back to America with you two."

My heart began to pound. Before I realised it I had grabbed her hand and reached out with my other arm and hugged her tightly. I could hear cups being knocked over somewhere below me. I didn't care. I could hear Karen's laughter. Molly's words were like a Christmas gift that I thought I would never have been able to afford. Unexpectedly, someone had just bought it for me.

Somewhere in a distant coat or pocket a mobile phone rang, just at that precise moment. In hindsight, I will always associate that moment of elation with an expression my mother used to come out with every Stephen's Day in our house when I was a boy; when the turkey was gone and the Christmas carols sounded old and jaded. she said, 'All good things must come to an end'.

And for a while, after the indescribable joy of that moment when Molly told us she wanted to come home to Martha's Vineyard with us and be part of our family, it seemed like our happiness was doomed.

The message on Molly's mobile phone was from her grandmother. Blaise Maher wanted to see me that night.

The message was brief and to the point. "Tell your father I would like to see him at nine. Please tell him to call then."

35

Molly suggested we get something to eat in Dublin, and then head back to Kilkenny, stopping en route to find out what her grandmother wanted. We grabbed a McDonald's and ate silently in the gridlocked traffic, while we watched carol singers outside the main gate to Stephen's Green.

It was close to nine when I pulled up outside Blaise Maher's house. Christmas lights flickered around the sitting-room window. A flashing Santa had been lashed to the side of the chimney with a mooring rope. A Christmas tree sat in the porch, bolstered against the windy gusts by a huge wooden log, resting on the prongs of its small metal tripod.

Pius opened the door. I never felt comfortable in his company. I could never decide whether he liked me or not. I had always been kind to him, and felt that, unlike his other two brothers, he had eventually warmed to me. He nodded to the open sitting-room door.

The jury was waiting to deliver its verdict by the time we all shuffled silently into the room. In fact there was no jury, no fair trial, only judges – predominantly biased judges, namely the Maher family and friends.

They were all sitting around the long teak dining-table as Pius ushered us to different soft chairs around the room. I was told to sit in the armchair that directly faced Blaise Maher and Father Ted Murphy. I looked at the table, the same one I had sat at for Christmas dinner all those years ago. I glanced around the room. Nothing much had changed. I recognised the small porcelain ornaments on the mantelpiece, oddities and knick-knacks. The three ducks were still hanging on the wall above the mahogany bureau with only three legs.

Someone had made a half-hearted attempt at repapering the walls, and had obviously quit in the early stages, leaving a wide, scotched blank space over the fireplace. A few rolls of lilac-patterned wallpaper lay in the corner of the room, beside the old Bush TV set, with its rabbit's ears for an antenna and its gyratory knobs.

Blaise Maher must have noticed me staring at the blank spot over the fire. "Turloch had just started to decorate the house for me. He would have been working at it right now on his weekend off. He told me he was going to have it finished for Christmas Eve. But then you . . ."

I waited for her to tell me that I had killed her son. She didn't. She turned, sobbed into a napkin while

Canice and Pius stared at me, and Father Ted, as he was known affectionately to the chosen few – those he called to for dinner – glowered at me.

"The sergeant told us that Turloch had hit the back of your car, or rather that you had reversed into him." She raised the tissue to her nose and then poked it gently into the corners of her eyes. "You killed my son." She spoke softly, watching the tissue as she folded it on the table.

They watched us, eyeing Karen and me up and down, disdaining us, condemning us with their eyes, like vultures waiting to swoop. I reached across and took Karen's hand. She was terrified.

"My father didn't kill Turloch," Molly said softly, almost inaudibly.

"What did you say?" her grandmother seethed.

"I said my father didn't kill Turloch!" Her voice showed no emotion. She stared at the collective sitting.

"Don't be upsetting yourself, child," Blaise Maher said, in a patronising tone of voice.

"Shut up!" Molly said. "Don't interrupt me while I'm talking. Isn't that what you used to always say to me, Gran, whenever I spoke out of turn at the dinner-table?"

"This doesn't concern you, child," Blaise Maher said, looking past Molly to me.

"Don't you patronise me, you self-righteous bitch!" Molly shouted, stepping closer to the table.

"Don't talk to your grandmother like that!" Father Ted Murphy said, sitting forward in his chair.

Molly looked at him. "Who are you?" she asked. "What right have you to come into this house and hold court over a private matter such as my uncle's death?"

Murphy went to speak. Molly cut across him. "You call yourself a holy man? You're evil. And you're a liar. You sit here in the middle of this family and play God. It's a great big game with you. *Isn't it?*"

I tried to reach Molly with my hand, to coax her away from what had turned into a serious confrontation. She moved out of my reach, closer to the table.

"I have decided to go back to America with my father," she said succinctly. "I hate this family. I want out of this charade." She pointed to the priest. "You knew all along. Didn't you, *Father?*"

Murphy shook his head frantically. He waved his hands around. "I don't know what you're talking about." He stared at Blaise Maher. "She's been drinking, Blaise. Your granddaughter has lost her senses. Tell her to stop this at once."

Blaise stood up. "Molly, I order you to stop. How dare you speak to Father Murphy like that. Apologise. *Now!*" she shouted.

"*Shut up and sit down, you witch!*" Molly roared, her voice almost hoarse. She watched Murphy. He squirmed about in his chair. "You knew about those boys, didn't you?"

I sat forward, terrified by what she had just said, uncertain of what was coming next.

The priest shook his head again. He squeezed his eyes close and frowned.

"You knew something had happened to them. Aidan Ferris's mother sat in that very chair . . ." Molly pointed to where Karen was sitting. "Just sat there for a whole hour and cried her eyes out like a little baby, begging and pleading with you to help her. But you ignored her. You told her to go home and pray to God. You told her there was nothing you could do, that if God wanted to see her child right, then so it would be. 'Trust in God,' were the words you used to her that night." Molly stood inches from the table, towering over the crumpled priest, his hands outstretched on the table, his head bowed down. "Why?" she asked.

"Why *what?*" he asked irritably.

"Why didn't you help her?" Molly asked.

Ted Murphy stood up, like a man quitting a card game, having lost his shirt. "I have to go. It's getting on. I have to be up early." He looked at Blaise to say goodnight. She was staring at her granddaughter.

"Are you going to answer my question, Father?"

He ignored her. "Goodnight, Blaise." He took a cap from his side pocket and put it on, adjusting it by pulling at the peak.

"Wait just a minute," Blaise Maher instructed the priest. He sat down again, clearly relieved that she was speaking now. She raised her hand. "I had never intended for this situation to get so out of hand. I apologise to you, Father, for my granddaughter's outburst. It will never happen again, certainly not in *my* house."

Blaise looked at me, affording Karen a quick glance also and a sneer. "The reason I asked you to come here tonight . . . you are no longer welcome here in Claddagh Mines. My family would be grateful if you left immediately and, please, don't come back!" Her eyes flitted between the two of us as she served her sentence. "I am speaking on behalf of most of the residents of this peaceful town, following your disrespectful outburst from the altar."

Her words were rich and distasteful, coming from a woman who had made a vocation out of hiding and protecting a family of alcoholics and neurotics.

"I feel I have a right to say something here," Karen said politely.

Blaise Maher stared her down. "*You*, of all people, have *no* right to be in this house, you adultress! You are both guilty of the sin of fornication." She looked to the priest for verification.

He nodded.

"You're hiding something, all of you. Aren't you?" I said. I knew by the way the priest suddenly fiddled with his pioneer pin that a raw nerve had been painfully touched. "Whatever it is you're all hiding, it's quite clear you're deeply ashamed of it."

"Son, I think you should go now, like the woman of the house has asked you to," the priest said indignantly.

"With due respect, Father, I was about to say to you

that this is none of your business. But maybe it is." I watched them all now, sitting around the table, uneasy in their chairs, anxious and apprehensive. "I intend to go to the police first thing tomorrow morning."

Blaise Maher sat bolt upright in her chair. The others watched her protectively, waiting to hear how she would react to my threat. *"Get out of my house!"* she spat.

I put my arm around Karen. Molly was at the front door before I had even realised she was no longer in the room.

We sat into the car and said nothing, each of us alone in our thoughts about what had just happened.

* * *

Monday night, twelfth of December, was the last time I saw Blaise Maher and her two sons.

Once back at the hotel that night, I drank myself into a state of oblivion and had to be put to bed by my daughter and my girlfriend – something I hadn't done since I was married to Neasa. Karen and Molly tried to make me see sense. There was no point. I just wanted to be alone.

Molly returned to Dublin on Tuesday. She wanted to put her apartment up for sale. She had decided to get out and start afresh in the States. In the days that followed I just drank and slept, occasionally stopping off for a small meal. I fought non-stop with Karen, over silly things usually. By Wednesday, she had had enough. We decided to go our separate ways for a while. She caught the train to Dublin to stay with Molly.

I had left hourly messages on Josh's answering machine. I couldn't understand why he hadn't called me. I missed Karen, within half an hour of her leaving with two hastily packed bags. I wanted to apologise for all that had happened. I kept phoning her. Her mobile was switched off.

It was time to get off the merry-go-round and bail out.

At lunchtime, Wednesday, my phone rang. I answered it, assuming it was Josh.

"David?"

It was a woman's voice. Neasa. "What do you want?" I said.

"Where's Molly?" she asked.

"She's gone back to Dublin. She's putting the apartment on the market." I realised then that I shouldn't have said what I said.

"My mother tells me that Molly's going back to the States with you. Is that true?"

I thought about her question for a moment, and the conversation she had obviously had with her mother. "Yes, it is true. And before you jump to any conclusions, I had nothing to do with her decision. In fact I was quite surprised when she told me."

"I bet you were. Well, I've got news for you . . . she's not going."

"What?"

"You heard me. I don't care about you or what you do with your life, you and your little slapper of a college student. I haven't given you a single thought since you walked out on me ten years ago. But I will *not* let you take my daughter away from me, is that clear?"

"For God's sake, she's not a child any more. She's twenty-one and she's well capable of deciding for herself what she wants to do with her life. If she wants to come back to the States with me, then so be it."

"I won't let you take her away from me, do you hear me? *Won't!*"

"And how do you propose to stop me?"

There was an awkward silence for a few seconds. "I will kill you rather than let you take my daughter away from me. Do you hear me?"

"Like those three men you sent to kill me the other day?"

"I don't know what you're talking about."

"Dougy Ferris and his friends? They broke my ribs. Is that what you told them to do? 'Just give him a tough warning, boys, a real frightener. Maybe beat the crap out of him. That should send him running back to where he came from.' Is that what you told them?"

"If I really wanted to kill you I'd do it myself."

"Well, if past experience is anything to go by, I wouldn't doubt you for a moment."

The line went dead.

36

On Friday morning I decided, while staring at the ceiling and counting the peals of the church bell, to get out of bed for the first time in three days. If it hadn't been for a call from Karen, I might have stayed there till the money ran out.

"Have you grown up yet?" she said.

"Yes, I think so."

"I'll be there about eleven."

"I'm sorry about the other day," I said, pushing last evening's dinner tray to the bottom of the bed.

"So am I," she said. "I suppose I shouldn't have walked out like that. You really need people who like you around you right now. I just felt that, since there doesn't seem to be too many of them breaking down your door at the minute, maybe you could do with a friendly face."

I smiled. "Thanks." I counted three different meal trays on the floor. It was time to come out of hibernation. I felt rested but weak. My ribs felt a lot better.

"I'm in Carlow. Traffic is light. The bus seems to be making up a bit of time. I should be at the hotel in an hour. Meet me in reception."

"Why don't you come straight up to the room?" I asked.

"Because the girls on reception saw me leaving on Wednesday with my bags packed. It's going to look peculiar if I walk past the desk carrying the same bags, isn't it?"

"You know something? A bloke would never have come up with a scenario like that. That is classic woman's paranoia. Am I not right, Doctor?" I said teasingly.

"You are *not* right, Teacher. And *I* am not a doctor. OK?"

And she was gone.

I checked my mobile for messages. Just one.

"Hey, Teacher, it's Josh. How ya doin? I hate speakin' to voice mails so I'll keep this short. I'm back in town tomorrow morning. See ya for breakfast in the hotel. You're buyin'."

The message had been left on Thursday at 4.15pm.

I cleaned up the room, left a stack of trays and a million stale smells out in the corridor, and opened the windows. My suite felt too big and impersonal to be comfortable. I wasn't used to opulence, feeling more at home in a hotel room where my suitcase takes up most of the space.

I sat on the side of the bed and reached into the

drawer. I placed a sheet of the hotel stationery on the cramped top of the bedside locker and drew a line down the middle. I wasn't sure why, but my head was becoming so cluttered it was important now to start making notes and keeping a written tab on what I had arranged to do on one side of the cardboard, and what I wanted to do on the other.

At the bottom of the grey page on the left-hand side, I wrote down Ingrid Moyne's name. I had an appointment with her that night. I had no idea what I wanted to talk to her about, but something was telling me she was important in all this. All what? I asked myself. Hopefully it would become clear very soon.

I wanted to go back to Steve Broderick, and find out from the doctor what exactly might have caused Aidan Ferris's retardation. I needed to squeeze Broderick a little more on what he knew about Ivan Moyne and his work with the pharmaceutical company. Then I needed to track down someone who worked at the plant directly with Moyne, on a par with the sort of work Moyne would have been involved in. There must have been a right-hand man. If Moyne was chief executive of this company, who was the company secretary? Then again, if Moyne was only a humble sleeping-partner, what was his connection? There must have been a bank manager, or a personal assistant who typed letters for him, or a gofer who delivered the post.

I sat back on the bed and stared at the window. Where do you start looking for someone who worked with a man whose ex-wife claims he is dead? Then again, *who* am I looking for?

My hotel room phone rang.

"Hello?"

"Hey, Teacher, it's me!"

"Josh, where the hell have *you* been? I've been trying to contact you all week!"

"Where have *I* been? Where have *you* been? I've been calling the hotel. They're telling me they can't contact you. I rang your mobile. It was switched off. I hate leaving messages on them damn things. I had no choice yesterday. Did you get my message?"

"Yes. Did you get all of mine?" I asked.

"Yeah."

"Well, where were you, Josh?"

He seemed to hesitate for a moment. Then, with a smile in his voice, "I was entertaining a lady-friend. I just took off for a few days. Man's allowed to do that now and again, ain't he? Anyway, where were you?"

"In bed."

"For *three* days, you were in bed?" he shouted.

"Yeah, I was tired. Where are you right now?"

"Right now I'm downstairs in the lobby. I'm goin' in for some breakfast. You coming down?"

"Yeah. I'll see you in ten minutes."

I finished making notes, packed a waterproof and a map, and went downstairs.

* * *

"There is no argument, Teacher," Josh argued over peppered scrambled eggs and toast, washed down with a Bloody Mary. "The man retired. He wasn't running from anything. What makes you think he was?"

I threw my hands up in the air. "I don't know, Josh. I just get a nasty smell about the whole thing. Ingrid Moyne says her husband is dead. Yet the Day Care Manager claims he phones the place every couple of weeks to check on her. She told me he sends a banker's draft."

"Where from?"

"She wouldn't say."

"Did she mention where he is?"

"No, she doesn't know. She just gets the money sent on."

"Did you ask her where the money order comes from?" Josh mumbled with his mouth half-full.

"Yeah. She wouldn't say."

"They're not obliged to tell you anything, Teacher, just because you're looking for someone you haven't seen for ten years."

"But they might be obliged if we brought the police in on the case, wouldn't they?"

Josh looked at me warily. He munched on the toast, ignoring the trails of melted butter in both corners of his mouth. "Two questions, Teacher. One, what *case* exactly are you talking about here? I didn't hear about any case being looked into. Two, what the hell have you told the police?"

I sat back and took a deep breath. "OK then, in answer to your two questions . . . One, we don't have a case yet, but we might have very shortly. Two, I haven't gone to the police yet but I believe already we have good grounds on which to get them involved."

"Such as?"

"Such as four deaths. Let's get hold of the death certificates, Josh. Let's find out what these kids supposedly died from. Let's find out who declared each one of them dead. Were they taken to hospital? Who performed the postmortem? How come Steve Broderick, Ivan Moyne's successor in Claddagh Mines, knows nothing about the case of Aidan Ferris?" I watched Josh as he stopped eating, taking in all I was saying. "I mean it's kinda strange that a kid who's so badly handicapped is not known by the local town doctor. Does that not sound strange to you, Josh?"

He nodded. "Very strange." He wiped his mouth with the napkin and sipped his Bloody Mary. "I hate to shatter your hopes, but I have this picture in my head of you going into a police station and the duty sergeant asking what exactly he can do for you. Now, if you don't mind taking up the story from there, you might just convince me that you haven't gone completely nuts since I last saw you!"

"Right. Four deaths. Almost secretive in the way death claimed the young boys. People in Claddagh Mines refusing to talk about it . . ."

Josh cut across me. "Hang on. Wait a minute. What

you're saying is nonsense. These kids died in different parts of the area, Teacher. You know how big that area is. They didn't all die together. They died over five years, one at a time. Their deaths were *not* linked." He stared at me, thinking me down, getting me settled for the final blow. "You've got nothing, Teacher, *nothing* that is going to make a local police force sit up and get scared." He sat back and drank hard.

The thought of a vodka turned my stomach. "Well, I'm still gonna go ahead with my investigation, Josh. So what are you gonna do?" I waited, feeling foolish and premature, still hoping and praying he'd agree to support me. I needed Josh Traynor's backing, an endorsement by Traynor guaranteed to open all those doors that otherwise would be slammed in my face.

He swallowed and lit a cigarette, clearing his throat while blowing out the first drag. "Let's just look at what we've got here again, Teacher." He placed his elbows heavily on the table. "We've got four dead kids. Therefore we've four families who are going to be so grateful to you for dragging up some God-awful painful memories. Memories they might just have about managed, after all these years, to come to terms with."

My heart sank. His sarcasm had always precluded his interest in doing something. He went on. "Then we've got a retired doctor, who rings his ex-wife every whenever to see if she's OK. She's got Alzheimer's so she can't recall him calling her so she assumes he's dead. And then you've got a retarded kid in a wheelchair whose daddy tried to beat the crap out of you with a wheel brace and got shot. Stephen King might be interested in that kind of story, but you . . . ?" He sighed. "What exactly is it you want to achieve here, Teacher?"

"I want to find out what happened to the four boys who died. I want to know exactly what role Ivan Moyne had in all of this, if any. And I want to find Owen Durkin."

Josh Traynor started to laugh, louder and louder, shaking his head harder and harder. "You're asking for a lot of prayers here, Teacher. You've got nothing substantial to base your theories on. Imagine you're writing a good thriller, OK? You need a beginning, middle and one hell of an ass-kicking end. Your problem is that even with a hazy beginning that you weren't really around here for, and a middle section that you can't seem to find, and even with all your characters missing, you're still expecting fireworks as a finale." Josh leaned across the table and grabbed my arm. He whispered with his drink-stinking breath, "Owen Durkin is dead. I've been a reporter around here for nearly fifteen years, Teacher. Tell the truth, you believe he's dead too. Don't you?"

I shook my head. "I refuse to believe that, Josh. He's alive."

"He's *not* alive. He's as dead as that sausage on your plate in front of you. Deep down you believe that. Don't tell me otherwise."

"I an convinced, on my parents' grave, that Owen Durkin is alive. For all I know he could be listening to this conversation now."

Josh laughed and shook his head wildly. "You haven't a hope in hell of sorting this mess out. There's not the slightest possibility that you'll find out anything outside of what people know around here. And they're never gonna let you in on their little secrets, Teacher. Not after what they believe you did, sermon from the altar or no sermon."

My heart sank. It was over. I knew it.

Josh sat back and finished his drink. He threw his head back and gurgled. He swallowed and flew forward again. "*Unless . . . you got Josh Traynor on your side,*" he yelled. "Then things could be *very* different." He stuck out his hand. "Count me in!"

I stood up and threw my arms around Traynor's shoulders, pulling the tablecloth, food, plates, cups and cutlery, onto the floor. "Thank you," I said.

37

Following a short debate and a lot of cursing, Josh Traynor agreed to drop us out to Doug Ferris's house.

Josh had always made a point of driving his twenty-four-year old camouflage-marked Safari Jeep flat out, whether he was on the wide-open road, or on a narrow dirt track. It made no difference. The noise was insufferable. As a result, conversation between driver and passenger was pointless. Yet, Josh insisted on talking. A two-way conversation became a bellowing match.

The gears crunched painfully and the engine squealed like a pig being slaughtered slowly. It was a rust-bucket, like something I'd seen in *Bridge Over The River Kwai*. Shocks and springs hadn't worked for years. Seat belts, if you could get them to work, were optional. I always maintained that passengers with a fear of flying would happily walk across the wing of a jet at thirty-five thousand feet rather than take a lift from Josh Traynor.

"Every one should be forced to drive an animal like this before they pass a driving test!" Josh shouted above the deafening din. "This requires great skill."

"Is it insured?" I yelled back.

He shook his head and urged the beast to move faster by bobbing back and forth in his seat each time he climbed a gear. "I'm a careful driver. Want to buy it?" He looked across, at me and back at Karen, and grinned, taking his eyes off the windy road for a good ten seconds. "You know, you lovers just make me want to be sick. First you split up and say it's forever and go your separate ways. Then I turn my back for a day or so and when I look around again you are all over each other like a bad rash." He laughed and we narrowly missed the Turnpike Bridge. "You should see my other car."

"Oh yeah?" I said. "What is it?"

"A sleek black Audi convertible, 2.5 litre. She's a babe!"

"I believe you." I smiled. "Keep your eyes on the road." I watched the surface of the road through a gaping hole in the floor of the Jeep, careful not to drop my foot into it. I checked that Karen was OK. She sat midway on a bench that had replaced the back seat years ago, leaning on the tops of the front seats with her elbows for support.

"Tell me again, Teacher. What are we going out here for?"

"Like I said, I want to see Ferris's kid."

"For as long as I've known Dougy Ferris, no one's been welcome at his place," Josh said.

"Why?" Karen asked, her voice barely audible.

"You gotta understand. These are simple country folk. They get on with their lives in a very private sort of way. They just do their own thing, and let other folk get on with their lives."

"And what do you think he'll do when he sees me turning up today?" I said.

Josh shrugged. "I'm not sure. I doubt he's gonna walk over to you and hug you, if you know what I mean." Josh laughed.

I felt a cold shiver and touched the spot on my ribcage that hurt most.

"Do you believe what those folk were saying about the Lastec plant and the toxic waste?" Josh asked.

"No way."

"So what do you think happened?" Josh said, his eyes permanently away from the road now.

"*Jesus*, Josh, watch where you're going, *please!*" Karen implored, as we watched a tree's heavy branches shaving the Jeep's bonnet.

"I haven't a clue what happened," I said, pretending to ignore his driving. "That's why I thought it might be helpful if Karen was there. Moyne told these people that the toxic emission was responsible for killing their children. Now I can't find it in me to believe that these people could be that stupid."

"How do you mean?" Josh said.

"Well, how can a massive leak of toxic waste just isolate four people and kill them while everyone else gets away without as much as an itchy rash?"

"Figures, I suppose," Josh said.

Karen shook her head. "I'm not a doctor. I really don't know what you expect me to see out here today."

"No, but you *are* a qualified psychologist," I said.

Josh slapped the steering wheel and straightened his baseball cap. "God, I love this investigative stuff. It sure as hell fires me up!"

"You're a sick man, Traynor," Karen said, thumping his shoulder.

Josh Traynor threw his head back and laughed. And, by the skin of his teeth, avoided another tree.

38

Nature was slowly swallowing up Dougy Ferris's small cottage. From the narrow road that ran parallel to what was once a gleaming, whitewashed façade, all I could see was a roof badly in need of new slates. Small rusty sheets of corrugated iron covered up what appeared to be gaping holes where slates once were. The roof had partly subsided.

Behind the long, unkempt grass was a grey wall, cracked and dirty, with two small square windows. In places, an ivy creeper hid the crumbling neglect. The creeper seemed to have a stranglehold on the front door; it was more like the entrance to a cave now. Apart from a tilting, triangular clothes-line, dotted with wooden pegs, the garden was empty and overrun. The pretty wooden fence that once surrounded the property had collapsed like a starved, tired animal. It lay partly buried.

A passing stranger would simply assume that the property was derelict, and had been so for many years. All it lacked was a *For Sale* sign.

Josh kept the noisy engine running, as we each silently formed our own impressions. Out here in the remote countryside, watching the sharp December wind doing its best to rotate the ramshackle clothesline, with its tea cloths and bedclothes, I couldn't help thinking we'd left the world behind us. When Josh did eventually kill the engine, the silence was eerie. A light rain fell. I looked around at the empty acres, fields and fields of lush green. Nothing else. Ten years ago, Doug Ferris grew barley and wheat, and the bales of hay dotted the horizon, all neatly squared and tied. This was the end of the road. Directly in front of us, a sign: *Trespassers will be shot.*

"Right," Josh said, "who's gonna go in first?" His voice trembled slightly.

"Well, I guess since you've been to Cambodia in a helicopter, maybe you should," I said quietly, my ears still ringing from the noise of the engine. My joke was lost on the unmistakable sound of a hunting rifle being cranked and cocked, akin to the turning, clicking sound of a ratchet-wheel.

Dougy Ferris stood at the gable end of the house, in a corner, nestling the weapon across his chest, the butt of the shotgun resting in the bandaged sling supporting his right arm. He watched, eyes squinted, from under the peak of an old, dirty-brown boater.

Josh raised his right hand and pushed it out through the open window, as he opened the door slowly with his other hand. "Hey, Dougy, what's happenin'?" he said, with the same enthusiasm he would have if he had just arrived at a party. He climbed out and stood on the roadside.

Dougy pointed the shotgun, keeping it at chest level. "I got nothin' against you, Traynor. It's that bastard beside you. If he sets one foot on my property, I'll blow his head clean off."

Josh leaned against the front of the Jeep and nodded at the long grass. "You could do with a couple of boy scouts around here, Doug. Maybe next Bob-A-Job, they could give this place a good goin' over for you. What do you think?" He bent down and picked up a plank of wood.

"Easy, Traynor," Doug Ferris warned. "Don't do anything stupid."

Josh straightened up and tossed the plank aside. "Don't *you* be doing anything stupid, Doug. This is a big enough mess already without you killing somebody." Josh surveyed the land. "Your kid used to be in the Boy Scouts, wasn't he, Doug?"

Ferris nodded and tightened his grip on the wood of the shotgun. "He was. But we had to take him out. Scout leader told us he was wild. Uncontrollable." The shotgun did a figure-of-eight, as Doug swayed and spoke. "He loved goin' huntin' with me. But most of all, he loved his hurling. He took such pride in it. The chairman of the county board told me one day we were out huntin' for rabbits, when Aidan was twelve years old – 'Doug,' he said to me, 'that young lad of yours, Aidan, is going to win a gold medal in Croke Park for the Tipperary Senior Hurling Team someday.' And I agreed with him. I knew he wouldn't. But it made me feel good. 'Twas one of the only times anyone ever had a decent word to say about my son." Doug bowed his head and looked at the barrel of his gun.

"How old is Aidan now, Doug?" Josh continued, inching his way past the rickety, lopsided gate.

"He should be at an age where he's playing for the senior team," Doug said. He sniffed angrily.

Josh was inside the garden now. "And why isn't he?"

Ferris drew up his rifle in a flash, level with Josh Traynor's eyes. "What kind of a smart, insensitive gobshite are you, Traynor?"

Josh kept moving, arms outstretched. "I didn't mean to be insensitive, Dougy. We've known each other too long to be fighting like this. What are you pointing that thing at me for? I haven't done anything to hurt you *or* your family."

Doug Ferris lowered the weapon gradually. "I know that." He pointed it towards me, as if he was poking a hot fire. "It's because of that bastard that my boy is not playin' hurling. It's because of him that my son can't be like the other young fellas around here. They're all out laughin' and drinkin' with their girlfriends, goin' to the local discos, planning decent careers for themselves. They don't even bother to call by to see how my boy is.

"The younger kids jeer at him. You want to know what they call him?" He was looking at me again, shouting loudly. "Ye want to know, Freeman. *SPASTIC*! That's what they call him. Behind his back, when his mother's pushin' him in that horrible chair. They call my son Spastic. They sing it and they laugh and torment him. Laugh at him.

"Do you want to know what I pray for, Freeman? First thing in the morning, last thing at night, I beg the Lord Jesus Christ that he'll spare my son any more of this agony and punishment. I pray that he'll take him in his sleep some night. Maybe tonight is what I'm praying for at this very moment. Tonight wouldn't be a moment too soon, as far as I'm concerned. May God punish you, Freeman, the same way my young boy is being punished. I hope you rot slowly in hell. I hope God punishes you with ten times the pain my poor boy is enduring every second of the day, *every* day!" he snapped.

Before I had realised it, Karen was out of the Jeep, standing behind Josh. The gun was on her now. Josh raised his arm behind his back, tucking Karen in behind him, out of view.

"Who are you?" Ferris shouted at her.

Karen pushed Josh's arm aside and stepped out into full view. "I'm a friend of Josh. My name is Karen. Karen McQuillan. I think we might have met before . . . briefly . . ."

"What the hell do you want?" Ferris lowered the shotgun slightly. "I supposed you've come to gawk, eh? Like all them little brats from town. I used to think they cared for my Aidan. I used to think they were his friends. But all they wanted was to look, like they were looking at animals in a zoo. They looked at him like he was some sort of circus freak, half-expecting him to jump out of that chair and start doin' tricks for them."

"I'm a psychologist," Karen said kindly.

Ferris squealed with laughter. *"A psychologist? You don't say?"* He frowned and tucked up the shotgun high in his arm. "We've had loads of your type here. Psychologists, physiotherapists . . . you name it, I've seen them come and go. They came to talk to us about helping my young boy. And then they stopped coming. One by one, they never came back. They promised us they'd make him better. We spent every penny we had on their promises. They built up our hopes and then . . . *bang!*" He thumped the butt of the shotgun against the window ledge.

Karen jumped.

Josh reached out for her and placed his hand on her shoulder.

Ferris laughed like a madman. "Yippp! They took our money. Robbed us and disappeared. You're no different, so get back in that Jeep and get off my land before I shoot the lot of you." He waved the rifle and shook it in Karen's direction. "Can't you people see? We just wanna be left alone?"

"You weren't thinking like that the other day," Karen said.

"What are you talking about?" Ferris said.

"The other day. You and your *friends* tried to kill David. That *was* you, Mr Ferris. I know it was you. I still haven't decided whether or not to go to the police about it."

Ferris cackled. "The *police?* They're not gonna bother with me. They think I'm mad. 'Ferris?' they'll say to you. 'Sure he's barking mad. Stay well away from him!' they'll tell you."

"Not if I get my lawyer to file charges against you. Then they'll put you away for grievous bodily harm." Karen nodded to the weapon. "How do think they'll react if I tell them you threatened us with a loaded shotgun?"

"Trespassing on my land. Harassment. That's what I'll tell them," Ferris said defiantly.

"I came out here today to see your son, Mr Ferris," Karen said softly.

"Why do you want to see my son?" Ferris raised the weapon. "You can't see my son."

Karen watched, hands in pockets. "You want to know what I know?" she said.

"What d'you know?" Ferris replied.

"I know that the trip to the chemical plant had nothing to do with Aidan's decline, Mr Ferris. You really ought to stop blaming David Freeman for your son's misfortune."

"Well, if he ain't responsible, who the hell is?" Ferris waved the rifle at me.

"I don't know, yet."

I grimaced at her determination, knowing that Ferris might snap at any second.

"My son is incapable of going to the toilet on his own, lady. On paper he might be twenty-one. In reality he's no more than a helpless baby who needs to be put to bed, dressed in the morning and bottle-fed like a six-month-old child. My son doesn't want to see you."

"I'd still like to meet him, Mr Ferris."

Ferris was becoming addled and confused, a dangerous state of mind to be in when brandishing a weapon that could kill us all with one clumsy shot.

He lowered the weapon. I held my breath. Karen's patience and politeness had visibly stunned Dougy Ferris. He put his hands in his pockets, resting the snout of the shotgun barrel on the ground beside him.

"Let her meet him, Dougie," Josh implored.

"Where are you from?" Ferris asked Karen.

"Boston. I work with sick children in a hospital in the city. MCH . . . it's one of the biggest children's hospitals in the States."

"Do you work with children who are . . ."

"Mentally handicapped? Yes. All sorts of handicaps."

"Can you help my son?"

"I'd like to try."

"She's not here to take your money, Doug. I asked her to come along with me today. You know me a long time, Dougy. I wouldn't trick you. You know that, don't you?" Josh piled on the charity. It was working.

Ferris shook his head and ran the back of his hand across his forehead. "I don't know nothing any more, Josh. You hanging around with that bastard . . ." Ferris nodded to me. "I don't know whether I should trust you any more, Josh."

"Will you let Karen meet Aidan?" Josh said.

Ferris watched me, and then studied Karen. "Only if *he* stays in the Jeep."

* * *

It was close to four, cold and getting dark, when Karen and Josh emerged through the creeper-cramped door of the cottage. Throughout the visit, Doug Ferris had stood, sentry-like, exactly where he'd been standing when I first spotted him earlier. The shotgun stayed trained on me throughout. My fingers and toes were numb from the cold, my breath carried steam each time I exhaled, fogging up the windscreen.

I could only imagine how cold Ferris must have been. Yet he never budged once. My back ached now, my ribs were sore and my knees had locked from sitting so rigidly for almost three hours.

Josh stopped for a moment and said something to Ferris. A handshake was declined. Karen climbed into the back seat and slumped sideways. I could feel the warmth of the indoors off her as she lay down across the seat.

"Are you OK?" I said. My teeth chattered.

"Yeah," she sighed. "Nothing a brandy won't cure."

Josh climbed into the driver's seat and slammed the door hard. "God, I need a drink."

"What happened?" I asked

"Alcohol first, Teacher. I'd say Karen has a fair bit to tell you." Josh started the engine and waved to Dougie Ferris.

Once we had turned, I watched out through my window. He looked like a lifeless scarecrow standing in the long grass, as the light from the small window silhouetted him in the darkness. I watched as he stepped out onto the dirt track, his ghostly stance making me shiver even more, the shotgun trailing behind him, until the dusk of that December evening swallowed him up.

Josh drove aimlessly for the next hour, it seemed. When I asked him where we were going, he shrugged aimlessly and muttered, "Don't know yet, but I'll know when we get there." Every time I asked him what they had seen and talked about while at the Ferris house, he raised his finger to lips. "Later," was all he would say to me.

Rain pounded against the windscreen, a howling wind rocking the car side on each time we slowed down.

Karen dozed. Either that or she wasn't interested in talking. I threw my jacket over her to keep her warm. I watched her carefully, wondering what she was making of all this. It seemed worlds away since Thanksgiving night when I watched her sleeping in my lap. I couldn't believe that that was only a couple of weeks ago. It felt like years. I knew that, without her, I couldn't have taken too much of this insanity.

"Are you lusting over her?" Josh quipped. "I'm watching you, Teacher."

A sense of humour so wickedly bent and corrupt I couldn't help laughing.

39

We sat in a deserted pub in a place called Paulstown, not far from Kilkenny. The owner, a burly, bald-headed man took our jackets and draped them over three chairs in front of the fire. The mere sight of three bowls of steaming hot, homemade vegetable soup eased the cramps in my chest, and the numbness that was eating at my hands and feet. As soon as our host had left the order, he went back to hanging paper decorations along the front of the bar. I had to keep reminding myself that it was only one week to Christmas.

Karen sipped her brandy, Josh his treble vodka.

While they acclimatised and chatted with the owner, I found a private spot and phoned Sunny Hall. Even if I left at that moment, allowing for the horrendous driving conditions, it would have been close to midnight before I reached Ingrid Moyne.

Vera Tubridy answered the phone.

I could tell by the rushed, staccato tone of voice that she was going off shift shortly. She sounded quite abrupt. I asked her to explain to Ingrid Moyne that I had got held up and would drop up to see her the following day instead. "Please pile on the apologies," I said eagerly.

"She'll be very disappointed," Vera Tubridy said curtly. "She hasn't talked about anything else all week. But I'll pass on your message."

"Thanks. Before you go . . ." I waited.

"Yes?" she said.

"Has Doctor Moyne called yet this evening?" I said.

There was silence for a moment. "Why do you think he'll call this evening?" she asked curtly.

"Just by the way you said he phoned every couple of weeks . . . I just thought he might have called. That's all," I said.

"No, he hasn't called yet. We'll be expecting you tomorrow."

"Just one more thing," I added.

"Yes?"

"As I said last time we spoke, I'd like to take Ingrid out for dinner tomorrow night, if your boss doesn't mind . . ."

"I might as well be the boss as far as the clients' welfare is concerned, Mr Freeman. That doesn't create a problem provided one of the staff accompanies her. We don't know you. You've visited once and all of a sudden you want to take one of our patients out to dinner."

"Are you suggesting I might kidnap her?"

"Don't be ridiculous, Mr Freeman. What time will you be collecting her?"

"Seven."

"Thank you, Mr Freeman."

The phone clicked. No goodbyes.

Karen was still tense. She hadn't touched her soup. She was sipping her second brandy when I sat down. For someone with a well-tanned complexion, Josh Traynor looked pale. He seemed uneasy.

"Do you want to tell me what happened?" I asked Karen.

Karen pursed her lips and sat back in her chair. "Do you want the official psychologist's report on the visit, or do you want it straight from the heart?"

"Give me the official brief first," I said.

"The boy is severely physically disabled. He is severely cataleptic."

"What's that?" I asked.

"It's like a total muscular rigidity. No control, no movement. His hands and fingers are closed tightly and rigidly stiff, almost claw-like. He's suffering from a curvature of the spine, so he's bent over in his chair all the time, possibly caused by damage to the flocculonodular lobe. I would suspect there's serious damage to the spinal canal, which carries the cerebrospinal fluids. And I'd hazard a guess and say that the reticulothalamic system is also malfunctioning. And that would be just to start with. We could go on to emotional deprivation . . ."

"What does all that mean?" I said sheepishly.

Karen sipped her drink. I noticed her hands were trembling, despite the warm glow off the fire beside us.

"It means basically that someone who was, ten years ago, a young, perfectly healthy and active boy with no apparent brain damage, is now a seriously ill, chronically mentally deformed one, beyond any hope and scope of recovery."

"He could have had a stroke, couldn't he?" Josh suggested.

Karen stared at him. "It's highly unlikely for a ten-year-old boy to have a stroke, Josh. The rupture of a blood vessel in the brain causes a stroke. What Aidan Ferris suffered was not a stroke."

"Then what was it?" I asked.

"I'm not a doctor, Dave. And even if I was it would take a lot more than a doctor to come up with an explanation for what happened to that boy."

"Well what, in your opinion, does it look like?"

"Catastrophic and irrevocable brain damage."

"Caused by *what*?"

She raised her hands and dropped them into her lap. "I haven't a clue. If it came about as suddenly as his father seems to think, it could be blood-related."

"Like something that got into his bloodstream?"

"Yes. But that's as far as any of us can hazard a guess. And that's all it is, Dave, a very rough guess. Ten years on, today, I'm not sure whether anybody, and I mean the greatest medical minds and the most highly educated physicians at our disposal, could tell you precisely what happened to Aidan Ferris."

"What do you think could give us a clearer understanding?" Josh asked.

Karen shook her head. "I'm not sure if there's any point in carrying out tests at this stage. Brain scans, pattern analysis, multiple correlation, EEG tests, you could spend years just running round in circles. It would all be blind analysis if you ask me."

"What does that mean?" I said.

"Aidan Ferris is incapable of speaking, thinking, reacting. He ought to be in a special home where his needs could be catered for appropriately. From what I can gather, David, on a brain-damage scale of one to ten, he scores an eight-and-a-half. Maybe a nine. He probably has another two or three years to live. And then he'll die. And that's when someone might be able to answer your questions, Dave. Only then."

"What exactly will he die of?" Josh said.

"Pneumonia . . . brain haemorrhage . . . massive stroke. Possibly a massive heart attack; a combination of conflicts usually; most times caused by complications such as a chronic respiratory virus. High temperature leading to kidney failure."

"Will it be quick?" Josh asked.

"Are you calling what he's going through now quick? He's dying a little bit each day. I don't know if he's in pain. He just sits there and groans and makes these awful, plaintive sounds. His mother sits with him in an armchair, when he's not in his wheelchair. She puts her arm around him and strokes his cheeks. 'Now, now, Aidan, you're all right,' was all she said to him while we were there."

"And what did she say to you?" I asked.

Karen stared into the fire. "Nothing. But her face told me a lot."

"Such as?"

"She's petrified of her husband. She hates him, although she told me he's a decent man, generous to a fault, and a caring father. She's dying to talk. I could feel that the minute I sat down beside Aidan. I'd say only for 'husband of the year' standing guard outside with the shotgun, she would have spoken to me a lot more."

"Will you go back and see if she'll talk?" I said.

"I don't think that's going to be necessary," Karen said.

"Why not?"

"Before we left the house, she asked me how long more we were staying here. I told her a few days; that I wasn't sure. She asked me if there was any way she might contact you before you returned to the States, privately. I gave her the hotel phone number and told her to call you tonight. If you ask me, that woman is going through hell out there, Dave. You've got to do something to help her."

"What do you suggest, Karen?" I said.

"You've got to find out what happened to her son."

Karen was right. I checked the time. It was almost nine. I desperately wanted to rush back to Langton's at that very moment, hopeful that Maura Ferris might have left her number, along with a message. "Come on," I said, "let's get moving."

"Wait a minute, Teacher. Hold your horses," Josh said, flapping his arm. "Sit down and have a drink. I think we should just talk about this for a few minutes longer."

I sat down. "What's there to talk about, Josh?"

"I'm gonna be the devil's advocate here just for a moment, OK?"

I looked at Karen. She seemed surprised. She nodded to me. "OK," I said. "What's on your mind?"

"First of all, Teacher, what exactly are you lookin' to achieve here?" Josh asked, signalling to our host to bring another round.

"I want to vindicate myself, clear my name and, if there's even the remotest chance of finding out what happened to Aidan Ferris, while hooking up a possible connection to the deaths of four other young boys whom I taught ten years ago, then I want to find it."

Josh shook his head hard. He took off his cap and threw it on the table. "If you don't mind me saying so, Teacher, it sounds like you might be treading on some mighty big corns here."

"Such as . . . ?" I said.

Josh sighed and scratched his head. "I know you're digging for the truth. I respect your desire to see justice done. I'd probably be doing the exact same thing if I were in your shoes. But I just sometimes think that some things are better off left alone, like where they belong . . . in the past."

"Have you ever heard of the expression, 'Buried feelings are buried alive?'" Karen said softly. Her eyes were closed.

Josh shrugged his shoulders. "Beats me. You're the expert. I just feel I know people's depth a bit better than you do, Teacher. I just wonder what's gonna be achieved by raking up all this bad news and sadness as if it all had only happened yesterday." He smiled. "But I want you both to know that I'm with you all the way." He looked at me. "Teacher, whatever you intend doing, I will back you up one hundred per cent, whether I agree with the principle or not. I hope you know you can trust me. Don't you?"

I nodded. "Thanks, Josh. I don't think I know what I'm meant to be doing any more. Maybe if I caught the next flight back to Boston, it'd be better for everybody."

Josh raised his eyebrows. "Or would it? I don't think so. All I know is that I'm gonna have one hell of a front-page story when this is all over." He raised his glass and grinned. "Bless you both. You're very special to me, both of you."

I was glad he said those last few words. "Whatever's destined to happen, we can't do a lot more tonight. Let me get you both another drink, then I'll treat you to dinner back at the hotel."

My urgency had turned to exhaustion. I needed to rest for a while . . . to forget. I was in good company for the night, I reminded myself. I felt safe and relaxed with these two people; Traynor, with his happy-go-lucky, life's-a-bitch attitude, and Karen, with her simple, inquisitive, all-in-its-own-good-time nature, a quality that made me fall in love the second I laid eyes on her.

If Providence was playing a role in how my life was continuing to evolve that night, I could easily have believed that I had been destined to meet up with these two extremely lovable yet different people. That said, if the same Providence had predestined what was about to happen to us all shortly after that evening, I would still be unsure as to whether or not there was anything spiritually worthwhile believing in.

40

Maura Ferris was waiting for me, sitting nervously on the edge of a luxurious deep-blue armchair in the reception of Langton's Hotel, when we arrived back that evening. I froze as soon as I spotted her. She stood up quickly as soon as she recognised me.

She seemed hunched under a weight of despair and sadness. She was a skinny, starved-looking woman, elderly in appearance for such a young age. I imagined her to be in her forties now; yet, I would have placed her in her late fifties. Her face, despite the touch of make-up, seemed ravaged.

Seeing her reminded me instantly of the parent-teacher meeting where we met twelve, maybe thirteen, years before, when I broke the news to her that her son, Aidan, might have been suffering from ADHD, attention-deficit hyperactivity disorder, a condition characterised by hyperactivity, mood swings and violent impulsivity. I told her that afternoon it was a fairly common disorder and although it first manifests itself in early childhood, it may not be diagnosed until later in life.

It came back to me in a flash of instant memories.

I had checked out my suspicions with Doctor Moyne the previous evening before telling her. Moyne said he would make a note in his diary to visit her, to explain more in order to allay any anxieties she might have had.

I had always regarded Maura Ferris as a good mother to her son. She dropped him to school every morning without fail, collected him each afternoon. She occasionally stayed behind to talk about Aidan's progress, problems with homework. She regularly helped out with school fundraising projects.

I had always regarded Aidan as bright, if a little wild and inscrutable in Owen Durkin's company. He got away with his boldness, I suppose, because he had a smile that would melt a rock. Much like his mother, I remember.

He palled with Owen Durkin, a friendship I frowned upon. Like poles never attract, the saying goes. Wrong again, I used to say. The more I tried to intervene and separate them in the school playground, the more they wreaked havoc. Years later, I often wondered how Owen Durkin's disappearance had affected his best friend. Little did I know that Aidan Ferris no longer had the capacity to ask.

Maura Ferris waited patiently, with a firm hold on her petite black shoulder-bag, while I explained the situation to Karen and Josh. I told them it could be some time before I was free. They decided to dine without me.

Reception was a hive of activity that Friday night. A band belted out showband favourites in one bar, while a disco was coming alive somewhere deep in the bowels of the hotel. Couples courted openly while small groups moved from one bar to another.

Maura Ferris looked out of place, in a petrol-green knee-length coat and a pair of moccasins. She wore a headscarf, knotted and hanging loosely around her neck. It seemed to take me an eternity to get to where she stood, weaving and excusing myself as I manoeuvred sideways through the Friday-night revellers. Her hair was wet and flat and bedraggled. The shoulders and back of her coat were soaked. She looked as though she had walked from Claddagh Mines.

I held out my hand. "Hello," I said politely, "it's lovely to see you again."

She nodded and forced a smile. "Thank you for meeting me, Mr Freeman."

It occurred to me that I was still a schoolteacher to her, still the man I used to be thirteen years ago. "Please, call me Dave," I said. Immediately I could see she found my informality off-key. "Would you like a drink or a light refreshment?" I said.

She shook her head. "I don't have very long. Can we talk in private somewhere?" she said, uncomfortable, as I was, with the crowd and the noise.

"I have a suite here. If you like we could go up and use the living-room area."

"OK," she answered.

I showed her to the lift.

Maura Ferris didn't speak another word until I had closed my hotel-room door behind her. "Please, sit down. Make yourself comfortable. I can offer you a beer, or an orange juice . . ."

"Just water would be fine, thank you," she said, raising her hand, as if to suggest that already we were losing valuable time. "I have to get one thing straight before we talk, Mr Freeman. And if you don't mind, I'd feel a lot more comfortable calling you by that name." She waited for my reaction.

"Whatever you're happy with," I said.

"I wanted so much to speak to the woman that came out to my house with Josh Traynor this afternoon. But I couldn't. She very kindly gave me your phone number. But since I couldn't talk with you on the phone I thought it might be best if I came here. I hope you don't mind."

"Not at all. I'm glad you're here. Talking on the phone about personal things can be . . . painful." I could tell she wasn't comfortable. She looked overwhelmed, as if she might have run for the door at any moment. I resisted saying any more.

"My husband would *kill* me if he knew I was here tonight."

"Why?"

"Don't get me wrong. Doug is a good father. Or, at least, I used to think he was. We don't always agree . . . on things, like. It's very important that I speak with you, Mr Freeman. I have kept so much buried for so long. I don't know what happened to me today. But when I saw that woman, and the way she spoke to Aidan, and the way he was watching her, almost trying in his heart to reach out to her, I just felt I couldn't keep it in any longer. She is the first person in over five years who has tried to have a conversation with my son. Do you know what that means to me?"

"Karen is a psychologist, Maura."

"I don't *care* what or who she is. She spoke to my son today with respect. No one, not even Aidan's father has done that for years. I am the only one who talks to the boy, praying to God every time that he understands what his mother is saying to him. I tell him every hour that I love him. Have you any idea what it's like for your baby not to understand the words, 'I love you', Mr Freeman?"

She was becoming more flustered, as if a part of her was fighting hard to get the words out, while another part was reluctant to speak. I watched the tears as they welled up in her eyes and streamed down her cheeks. She dabbed at them with a tissue she pulled from her sleeve. "That woman made something come up inside of me this afternoon, Mr Freeman. And that is why I am here. I told my husband I was going to the hospital in Kilkenny to visit a neighbour of ours. I have marks on my body to prove what can happen to me when I lie to him, Mr Freeman."

"So why do you stay with him?" I could feel my arms trembling, as she brought my own memories flooding back.

"Because I married him. I suppose that means I have to love him, doesn't it? For better or worse, and all that. Perhaps that's a bit strong. I once loved him and I remind myself of how things used to be when we were a family. He's OK when he's not drinking." She dabbed her eyes. "Anyway, if I was to leave where could I go? What would I do with Aidan? That house is a roof over my son's head. He needs me. I can feel the love he's sending to me, even though no one, not even his father, can see it. I can *feel* it. I'm his mother. I have to look after him. If I don't who will?" She spoke in a hushed, almost embarrassed-apologetic way.

"Take your time," I said, pushing the glass of water closer to her hand.

"I wondered about what I was going to say to you when I met you, Mr Freeman. You probably think I'm a bit stupid . . . from the sticks. 'Maura Ferris is a big, thick country woman.' That's what a lot of them used to say. I'd hear them at Mass of a Sunday, watching me and branding me like I was a farm animal. Well, I'm not stupid. I mightn't be the best educated mother in these parts. I mightn't have all the words to make me sound intelligent, but I know what I want to say. I know now. I didn't always though. And there were times, when I did know and wanted to say so, that I was afraid to open my mouth. I've learned the hard way, made lots of mistakes." She looked at me with a pained expression. "What I wouldn't give to be able to turn back the clock. If I'd known then what I know now . . . I've learned a lot. If I could only have kept a note of all the hours I spent in the library, pretending I was shopping, or making excuses that I was visiting my mother; and all that time I was hiding in cubicles, reading about things like what might have been: places I'd love to visit. But I was there, I suppose, because I have a great imagination. I can close my eyes and go where I want. Maybe that's been my strength for ten years now. I've bought and borrowed books. Some of them I've had to hide from Doug, in case he thinks I might be getting grand notions about places I'd love to go. I've taught myself a lot of what I wish I'd known ten years ago. Sometimes it helps me to know I'm better than him."

"Than who?"

"Doug Ferris. He can threaten to beat me and throw me out all he likes, but the reason I smile in his face sometimes is because I'm cleverer than he is. I'm better. Knowledge is a beautiful gift, Mr Freeman. So many people seem to just take it for granted. I taught my husband how to read and write, Mr Freeman. Did you know that?"

I shook my head. "Well done."

"And what do I get in return? Nothing. Just abuse. And to be honest with you I worry that I mightn't be able to put up with much more, although the abuse isn't so bad now. He's just drunk a lot. He sleeps a lot, feels sorry for himself like no one else exists. I have hidden so much for nearly ten years now. Have you ever got the urge to go and do something you've always just dreamed about?"

I nodded and smiled.

"The time has come to be honest both with you . . . and myself. I've always had great respect for you. Maybe that was because you had the gift of knowledge and you shared it with others unselfishly . . . so much knowledge I used to envy you. I even told the priest in confession one night that I was jealous of how wonderful a man you were, and how pathetic my man was.

"You were a good teacher. Aidan liked you. He spent a long time asking me where you had gone off to and why you had left. He often asked me when you would be coming back. I used to tell him that you were such a good teacher that you had to move on to teach other children who weren't so lucky as to have someone like you teaching them." She tried to catch her breath, and squeezed the tissue. "I'm being deceitful to my husband coming here like this tonight."

"You're not being deceitful, Maura."

"I know what my husband did to you the other day, Mr Freeman, and I just want you to know I am so ashamed."

I waved my hand to her. "Don't worry about that. I'm fine."

"He arrived home and spent the evening out in the cattle parlour. Friends of his were coming and going all evening, so I knew there was something wrong. I didn't want to go near him because I knew he was in a foul temper. That's when I hate him and curse myself for marrying him. That's the time I could happily leave him and Aidan. Have you ever felt like running away, Mr Freeman?"

"Regularly. I suppose that's what I did ten years ago, isn't it?"

"I know you're not responsible for what happened to Owen Durkin. I didn't realise it had got as serious as I later found out. We don't get to hearin' too much out where we live. I wished many times that we could live in the town, that I could have decent friends and people to talk to. But it's not to be, is it?"

"One thing I realised, Maura, is that no one owns me. It took me a long time, years, to discover that. I'm sorry I didn't know that ten years ago. Back then, everyone owned me, the pupils, their parents, my wife, her mother. I imagined that I had to be available for everyone I came in contact with; I had to give a little bit of myself to each of them. It was only when I went away and looked back at my life that I realised I had nothing to show for it. I had achieved nothing. Sure, I passed on the knowledge I had to all those children. But it was only when I sat back and examined what was left after what had happened to me that it dawned on me that there was nothing."

"I never got the opportunity to tell you this, Mr Freeman, but I never believed the things I heard. I always thought you were a good and kind man."

"I didn't do anything to hurt Owen Durkin."

"I know that, and I also know you didn't do anything to hurt my son."

"Do you know what happened to Aidan?"

She clenched her fists and sat forward. "Eleven years ago, Doctor Moyne visited our house unexpectedly. Let me explain something to you. We had a lovely house back then. I took pride in keeping it nice and cooking meals and inviting our friends over on special occasions. We'd sit there, all of us, and play cards. Doug was a different man then. He rarely drank heavily. He dressed nice whenever we went out."

"What happened when the doctor arrived?"

"I remember Aidan was out in the garden. I'd been hounding him to do his homework. I remember telling him that the TV would not be switched on until he'd put his books back into his schoolbag, ready for the morning. We had an Old English sheepdog. Tara, we called him. I'd taken Aidan to Doctor Moyne a few days earlier, after you had told me that he might be suffering from attention-deficit disorder. I couldn't handle him he was so hyper and so bold. He used to tell me to fuck off at the least little thing. And the things he called me made me cry when I was on my own. He never slept at night *at all*. He'd refuse to eat the meals that I put in front of him. His father used to threaten to take his belt

357

to him. Not even that made any difference. His father wanted to kill him. Eventually neither of us could control him any more. I couldn't allow him to go to any of the other children's houses. After a while none of the other children wanted anything to do with him. Their fathers were calling here regularly accusing Aidan of beating up their sons and stealing their lunches. Doug even got into a fistfight out in the garden one evening with a man, a father of one of the other boys in Aidan's class. This man threatened to kick the . . ." She paused, hesitating over the word. "The . . . you-know-what . . . out of Aidan. Shite," she whispered. "Those were his exact words – if Aidan went near this boy again. Doug put him down with one swipe of his fist. I was watching from the window. It got very messy. The police arrived later that night and told Doug that this other man was pressing assault charges. Eventually it came to nothing once Doug had apologised and made his peace."

"When did you first notice anything wrong with Aidan?" I said.

"It's difficult to say. He had always been hyperactive from the time he could walk, he was always getting up to mischief, pulling the dog's tail, then later kicking the dog. Then later again breaking things around the house for no apparent reason. I suppose I just accepted for a long time that this was all normal. We have no other children so I had nothing to gauge the pace of growing up for children. Neighbours told me it was the 'terrible twos', then the terrible threes. But I couldn't accept it when he was four, five, even six. All our friends have perfectly normal, well-disciplined children. We had a monster living with us. He'd kick me and punch me, and break up things in the kitchen.

"I used to get down on my knees every morning and pray that when he walked out that door to school that he wouldn't be sent home. It was the only chance I got each day for a few short hours to be like other women my own age. I could shop, stop off in town for coffee and a cream cake, listen to other women talking about normal things, like buying clothes and going on holidays and looking forward to Christmas." She wiped her eyes again.

"What happened to him, Maura?" I said quietly.

"Doctor Moyne visited that evening. I'd been taking Aidan to see him every two weeks. It wasn't doing any good. Doctor Moyne had suggested changing his diet. We did that. Cut out sugar. We did that. We even stopped giving him soft drinks and any kind of sweets and things like that. We basically refused to give him money to spend unless one of us was with him. The doctor put him on Ritalin. It's a drug especially for children with ADHD. It had no effect whatsoever."

"None?" I said.

"Nothing. It might as well have come from a sweetshop. I remember going to the doctor's with him. Every time we went, I'd go with real hope in my heart that this time Doctor Moyne was going to give him something that would take away this curse. That's what it was, Mr Freeman, a curse. I was beginning to hate my son. Can you believe that? To *hate* him. I didn't want him to come home from school. I used to imagine a car knocking him down and killing him. That's how much I wanted an end to this nightmare, at *any* cost." She waited to wipe her nose and sip from the glass of water. Then she continued. "I'm sorry if this sounds disjointed and confusing. You have to remember, Mr Freeman, that I don't get out of that house much. My days and nights are spent nursing a baby. I get no comfort or assistance from my husband whatsoever. All I get is abuse when I don't have his dinner ready for him in the evening, or his shirt and trousers ironed for him before he goes to Sunday Mass. It's funny how things have changed."

"What do you mean?" I asked.

"Years ago, I wanted my little boy to die, so that I could have a normal life with my husband. Now, I would give anything for Doug to be taken, killed in a fall, a car crash, anything at all! I *want* him to die so bad, so that I can spend my life looking after my little boy without that man's insults and abuse."

"Does he hit you?"

"No. Well, not hard, like. Only now and again, when Aidan's asleep. That's why I try to keep Aidan awake until after Doug goes to bed. That way he won't . . ." She stopped.

"Won't *what?*" I asked.

"Won't force me against my will."

"And do you refuse?"

"Only when I know he won't beat me until I'm sick."

I closed my eyes and thought about what she had just said. I wanted so badly to tell her I had first-hand experience of what she was talking about; that I knew how she felt because I'd been beaten black and blue by my *wife*. But she knew Neasa. And I knew she wouldn't believe me. If the police had ridiculed me about it, what chance had I with a woman who knew my wife to be a pleasant, caring wife and a dedicated mother? None. "So what happened the evening the doctor visited you?"

"A few weeks before he visited us, Doctor Moyne had suggested a special school for Aidan. I thought it would be a good idea. But my husband refused to entertain the suggestion. He kept shaking his head and shouting no. The doctor begged him to think about it, that Aidan would eventually get right if he got the right attention and treatment from experts in that field."

"Did Doug agree?"

"No. He eventually told Doctor Moyne to leave. He told him not to come back unless he could hand us something that might make Aidan better. All my husband could think about was tablets. He kept arguing with the doctor, telling him his job; telling him that there must be some sort of medication this late in the twentieth century that would cure our son and calm him down. The doctor apologised and said there was nothing."

"And he left?"

"Yes."

"So what happened then?"

"Well, we didn't see him for nearly a month. I wanted to take Aidan for his fortnightly visit to Doctor Moyne's surgery, but my husband forbade me. He told me we were throwing away good money by going to see the doctor. He told me he'd prefer to see Aidan out getting some fresh air and playing football with the other children rather than wasting away his life and money in a doctor's waiting room. I told him we had to keep trying, that eventually Doctor Moyne would find some way to help Aidan."

"And did he let you take him to the surgery?"

"No. An argument started. I told him if he didn't give me the money there and then, I was going down to the post office in the town and I was going to withdraw enough money to take Aidan to the doctor."

"And what did he say to that?"

"He took me out into the front garden, where Aidan couldn't see or hear us, and he grabbed me by the throat." Maura Ferris raised her hand to her neck and swallowed. "He shouted abuse and cursed at me . . . an' he was shaking me. I couldn't breathe. He told me that if I didn't listen to him he would kick me out of the house and I would have to live with my son on the side of the road until I got down on my knees and apologised to him for giving cheek."

I was becoming angrier by the second. I had to calm

myself before saying anything. "So what did you do?"

"I waited until the afternoon. As soon as Doug had gone off to repair a car for a neighbour I rang Doctor Moyne and explained what had happened that morning. I told him I really needed to see him, that I couldn't continue living like this. I really wanted Aidan to go to a special school where he would be guaranteed the attention he needed. Doctor Moyne was glad I felt like that. I wanted my son out of this hell. And I had planned that as soon as Aidan would go to this special school that Doctor Moyne had told us about, I was going to leave Doug and get us as far away from this place as I could."

"But you told me a minute ago that he's not really that bad, that you would never leave that house."

She sighed. "I suppose when you've trained yourself to think like that for so long, it just comes out automatically."

"And where would the two of you go?"

"I had planned to spend a little bit of time with my mother. She lives in Pallasgreen, not too far from this special school. It would have been perfect really. I could have stayed with my mother until I got something sorted out with the solicitor, and still be able to drop Aidan off in the mornings and collect him from this school each afternoon."

"And why didn't your husband agree to this plan? It sounds as if it would have been perfect."

"Because he's a bully. My husband, Mr Freeman, is

a completely different man when he goes to church on a Sunday, goes up to receive the blessed Eucharist with his two hands outstretched, to the person he becomes when he gets back home afterwards and changes out of his Sunday suit. My husband is a bullying, evil bastard. The only reason I don't shoot him with the rifle he pointed at you earlier today is because I might miss. Then I would have to live with that for the rest of my life. And believe me, Mr Freeman, life is bad enough as it is without that hanging around my neck."

Maura Ferris spoke with a calmness that told me she had had this conversation before. "Have you told anyone else about how you feel?" I said.

She smiled. "Aidan. I tell Aidan everything, every day, often three or four times in the hope that he might understand me, how I feel; how much I hate his father; how I would love to move to Pallasgreen with him and start a new life. I don't mind looking after my son, Mr Freeman. He's part of my flesh and blood. I know God looks after me, so that I can look after him. It's just that his father makes my job a million times harder. And as God is my judge, right here and now, I wish he was dead."

Her voice cracked. She cried hard, bowing her head and rocking back and forth, with the tissue around her nose and over her eyes.

"I don't want to be rushing you, Maura, but can you tell me what happened after you rang Doctor Moyne?"

She nodded and blew her nose. "He arrived at the

house that evening around half four. I was glad to see him because my husband wasn't going to be there to silence me. I had just collected Aidan from school. I needed to have him there that afternoon so that Doctor Moyne could talk to him, so that the doctor could see maybe for himself what I had to put up with day and night. I looked forward to having the doctor to myself, just the three of us, for a half-hour."

"Did you ask him to call?"

"No. He suggested, 'Why don't I call out and see you?' He told me he had been thinking on and off about us and there was something he needed to talk to me about."

"Such as?"

"I have to explain something here before I say any more, Mr Freeman. I – *we* – were so desperate at that stage, we would have done anything, tried anything, that would have given us a normal life. Doctor Moyne was my only prayer. He knew us. He had been our local GP since we got married and moved into the area. I trusted him with my life." She drew a deep breath and held it, staring at the glass of water. "Doctor Moyne told me about a new drug that they were testing in America. He wanted my permission – *our* permission – to try it on Aidan. I remember thinking to myself that he seemed more nervous than I was, telling me all about it that afternoon."

"Did he tell you what it was called?"

Her face stiffened. "Promoxidine. It's a word that will haunt me beyond the grave, Mr Freeman."

"And did you agree?"

"Of *course* we agreed. What was the alternative? Here was a doctor – as far as I was concerned, a caring man – who wanted to cure my son as much as I wanted him to, offering us a slim chance at being able to put a stop to all this insanity. Of course I agreed, wouldn't you?"

Maura Ferris waited for my answer.

"Yes," I said.

"Thank you. Then I hope you'll partly understand why this drug gave me hope. Even if it was only for a short while, the feeling of regeneration inside of me was difficult to explain, Mr Freeman. This doctor had just given me a second chance at life. I would have tried anything at that stage. If Moyne had told me to put Aidan sleeping on his head for a week, I would have tried it. Aidan was almost thirteen by then, unpredictable, unmanageable. He tried to burn the house down only days before. I had become terrified of him. I was afraid to sleep at night. My husband was drinking like a fish. I probably would have ended up doing the same myself, except one of us had to be awake and watching at all times. I was *terrified* of my own son, Mr Freeman. Can you understand what that does to a mother?"

I shook my head. "Tell me about the drug he suggested."

"He spoke about it and told me it was being tried out in a number of places in the States. An experimental period involving selected doctors and patients who had volunteered. He told me that, all going well, it would be available here within five years."

"*Five years?*"

"That's exactly how I reacted. It was worse than no news at all. It was like as if he had built up my hopes and dreams in the space of a couple of short minutes, given huge hope, more hope than I could handle, and then not only did he take it all back, but he left me more despairing than I was when he arrived."

"And was that all he said?"

"No. He seemed to think to himself for a long time. I remember making him a cup of tea. I could hear him asking Aidan certain questions."

"Like what?"

"Did he get bad headaches? And things like that. I couldn't hear their conversation too well. Anyway I was so disappointed by what he had just told me, I was mad with him and with everything."

"So you brought him his tea. What happened next?"

"Well, it was like as if he changed his mind. He took a tiny jar out of his case and placed it close to my cup of tea on the small table we were all sitting at." Maura Ferris shivered at that moment. She rubbed her shoulders and arms. "He told me that this was the drug. He said to us he would like to put Aidan on it for a couple of weeks, just to see if it had the desired effect."

"Which was?"

"To calm him down. To make him normal again."

"And did you agree?"

"Course I did at first." She sighed. "But there was a little voice in my head . . . something inside me, telling me this wasn't good. I remember reading an article somewhere before that these kinds of experiments can have awful consequences. A voice inside me told me we'd be better off waiting a bit longer. I don't know why I said no. All I know is that the question was answered for me."

"So what happened then?"

"My husband arrived back just as Doctor Moyne was leaving."

"What did your husband say?"

"He asked Doctor Moyne why he'd come out to our house. When Moyne said he was just checking up on Aidan, my husband told him that he'd have to give him a better answer than that. Anyway, to cut a long story short, Doctor Moyne explained about this new experimental drug. He'd barely started talking about it when my husband insisted he wanted it. 'Give it to him, give it to him!' he kept saying to the Doctor. Moyne told him that I had decided against it. I knew then I was in trouble. I started to change my mind: avoid the beating I knew I would get for going against Doug."

"But you were only safeguarding your son's health by saying no."

"I know that. But my husband makes the decisions in our house. What he says goes. If you question anything he says, he gets mad."

"Even now?"

"Not so much. The occasional time he might threaten me. 'Don't have me take my belt to you,' he might say. But that might be all. Then he'd go out and drink. It's not that bad now. We sleep in different rooms. I just make him his meals and wash his clothes. That's the extent of our *happy* marriage today."

"So what did Doctor Moyne say when your husband insisted on giving this drug to Aidan?"

"He sat down again and spoke about it a bit more. Promoxidine," she said quietly, as if talking to herself.

41

I asked Maura Ferris if she minded if I took notes. She said she didn't. I checked my watch. It was shortly after ten that night that I started to jot down dates and times.

At the top of the page I wrote: Promoxidine.

My mind was telling me that something awful was evolving here. This was the nightmare that I had been trying to imagine since hearing of the deaths of the four young boys. It might well be an indication of what had happened to Aidan Ferris, of what had been responsible ultimately for leaving him in such a damaged, helpless state of life.

Another part of me found this unlikely, since Moyne had the reputation of being a top-class practitioner, with certificates of competency in many different areas of medicine and, more importantly, research.

These were dangerous surmises. No human being, neither trained *nor* unqualified, would be so wicked as to attempt such a foolhardy game. I found my mind racing with questions, whose answers would instinctively protect Ivan Moyne's mature responsibilty. Surely he would have known the consequences of experimenting on his patients? He must have known what the outcome would have been if his peers had discovered that he was 'testing' out a new drug that had not received the seal of approval from the Food and Drugs Administration in the States, and, more relevantly, the approval of the Irish Medical Assocation. It just didn't make sense since the consequences of such foolishness would have seen him struck off and debarred from medical practice.

It seemed idiotic to even entertain the notion that a man as highly qualified and respected as Moyne would engage in such high-risk exploitation and, ultimately, black magic.

All this was bombarding my brain as Maura Ferris continued to tell her story.

"Did he tell you what the drug would do to Aidan?" I asked.

"He seemed reluctant at first, but my husband made him keep talking. He kept on telling us it wasn't dangerous. He said that new drugs were being introduced every day all around the world, while other more familiar drugs that had been used for years were being taken off to be replaced by stronger, faster acting medication. He told us the Promoxidine would relax him. It was designed to work on that part of his brain that was causing so much hyperactivity."

"What happened then?" I said.

"He held out this jar of pills. My husband grabbed them and started cheering. 'This is going to cure you, Aidan,' he kept saying. He took the top off the little bottle and started to smell the tablets. 'They look like sweets,' he said to me. Something in me didn't want to take them from Moyne. I even watched him while Doug was waving them around the place like he was showing off a gold medal. My stomach felt queasy. There was something not right about what he was doing. But who was I to question a doctor? For all I knew, I kept telling myself, I was only imagining the worst, while what I should be doing was thinking about how they would help my son to develop a calm, normal lifestyle."

"Did he leave then?"

"No. He stayed for another hour or so, talking to us about other drugs that were being tried out for different complaints and illnesses. All the time he was taking us in, more and more. Eventually I would have taken them myself if he'd told me to. He was good at putting you at your ease and making you believe everything he was saying to you. Aidan had gone back out to play with the dog. Moyne asked me to call him in. Doug went to the door and shouted his name a couple of times. That's when I really began to feel uncomfortable."

"Why?"

"Because while Doug was gone looking for Aidan, the doctor took a syringe from his case. He told me he was going to give Aidan the first part of the medication in an injection. I remember we had to hold Aidan down. He hated needles and he screamed and roared. His feet and fists were flying and kicking."

I tried to write as fast as she was speaking. After a while, I was just jotting down words and phrases, while wondering what exactly I was going to use these notes for. I urged her to keep talking.

"He put the needle in the fire. I remember hearing it sizzling for a while. I asked him why he had to give him a needle. He told me it was how the medicine worked. It would start to take effect much quicker if the tablets were preceded by an injection." She stopped talking and looked at me. "I suppose you think I'm a fool, Mr Freeman."

I shook my head. "How were you to know? This man was a doctor. Most people trust doctors, even when it comes to treating their children. What were you meant to do? Did he leave then?"

"No. He sat down and took some papers out of his bag. He told us he'd like us to sign a couple of things. 'Nothing important,' he assured us. It just meant that the treatment was official. The papers were just for his own records. He called it 'the usual paperwork', so as he'd know on his next visit exactly what treatment Aidan was on . He said he'd file it when he got back to the surgery."

"Did you read the papers before signing them?" I said, feeling quite helpless now.

"No."

It was all she said.

"Why not?" I could tell she was guilt-ridden. Remorse was written across her face. Her voice broke up more with each question.

"Because we trusted Doctor Moyne implicitly. He delivered Aidan in our bedroom. His were the first hands to touch my little baby boy. He became part of all of our lives that afternoon. There was a bond there. Can't you see? He immunized Aidan when he was a small child. He prescribed for us all whenever we got sick. Wouldn't you trust someone who has seen you through difficult times?"

"I suppose so. It's just that . . ."

"For God's sake, we were being offered a cure, for all we knew. And who was I to doubt a man who had devoted his life to the cause of others? That's how I saw him. Anything was better than life as I had come to know it. This was what I'd prayed for, don't you see?"

"Yes. Had Doctor Moyne mentioned Promoxidine to you before?"

"No."

"So what happened after that?"

"Aidan seemed fine, as wild as ever for two or three weeks. I thought the medication was going to be like the Ritalin he'd been on some time before. I remember saying it to Moyne when we went for Aidan's first check-up."

"How long was that after he'd received the injection?"

"About three weeks. He was taking two of the tablets as well, one in the morning with his breakfast, the second before he went to bed at night."

"What did Moyne think during that first visit?"

"He seemed confused. At first he seemed to have forgotten that he had given Aidan an injection. Then he mumbled something about stepping up the tablets to four a day. Then he scribbled on his record sheet and said, 'Forget that. We'll keep him on two a day for another couple of weeks'."

"And that was it?"

"Yes."

"Did anything happen?"

"Not for a week. Then one morning Aidan couldn't get out of bed. That was very unusual for him. Normally he was up with the lark. It was midsummer then, I remember. Sometimes he'd be up and dressed hours before we were. He'd watch television, turning it up real loud; or he'd go outside with the dog if it was sunny."

"Can you tell me about that morning?"

"I could hear him moaning, saying that he felt sick. When I went into his bedroom he had the curtains drawn so the room was fairly dark, He had his hand up to his eyes. I pulled back one of the curtains and he squealed like as if I'd stuck a pin in him. He shouted at me to close them again. So I did. He told me he didn't want to go to school that day. Typical me, I was cursing him, because I'd spend the whole day, longer than usual, having to watch him in case he got up to any mischief."

"And did he?"

"No. He only got out of bed to vomit. And he did that a lot that day. He could barely crawl out to the bathroom. Eventually I had to bring a basin and a towel in to him, he was so physically sick."

"Did you call Moyne?"

"Yes. About midday. He was out to us within half an hour, looking very worried. I asked him could it be an allergic reaction to the medication. I couldn't figure out how it could have been since he'd been taking the tablets for a good while and they didn't seem to be affecting him badly. Moyne said no. Some people, he told me, had reacted differently to it than others. It would just take time, he said. He mentioned something about certain psychotropic medicine taking weeks to work. I'd never heard of them. He told me that this kind of medicine affected the brain and could change your behaviour, like. It usually heightened your sensitivity to everything, and that this could have a queer effect on your stomach and bowels for a couple of weeks. That was how he put it to me. He said that adverse effects were not unusual in the first few weeks. He told me to give him sips of flat 7-Up for the rest of the day and to skip that day's medication."

"And then?"

"It's hard to say, Mr Freeman. He got over the sickness, but he just seemed to be listless for the rest of that week. I told myself he was just weak after all the vomiting. But he stayed like that, ignoring my questions, just watching television and moping around."

"Did the pain in his head go away?"

Maura Ferris shook her head. "It became bearable, from what I can gather. I wanted to take him off the medication permanently. But Doctor Moyne told me to leave him on it, just to give him two tablets every other day. I remember thinking it was peculiar how when Aidan didn't take his medicine for a couple of days he would feel better. Strangely enough, that made me happy. But when I'd insist on him taking the tablets, he'd get a headache again and start crying."

"Why did you keep giving him the tablets if they were giving him a headache?"

"Because Moyne told me to. He said it was most like just an acclimatising period, that he'd get over the headaches and nausea after a week or so."

"Jesus Christ." The words were out of my mouth before I knew I'd said them.

"What?" Maura Ferris said.

I could only shake my head in disbelief. "I'm speechless. That's all I can say, Maura. Speechless."

She sipped her water, and for a while the room was silent, except for the traffic passing on the street below.

"Did it get worse?" I said.

"No. Not just then. Oddly enough, he improved. He slept more soundly that he had ever slept in his life. He studied harder. He was more relaxed. He ate his meals.

The only thing that concerned me was that he was sleeping everywhere: in the car, on the couch, on the bus. I found him asleep one afternoon in the porch. He'd gotten a lift home from school. That particular afternoon, he sat down in the porch and slept for over an hour."

"When did he really start to deteriorate?"

"About two months after he was put onto the medication. He started to have nightmares, really horrible dreams that he would wake up from and be hysterical for the whole night afterwards. He said monsters and snakes were trying to eat him while he was lying on his bed. His dead grandmother was beating him with a big stick." Maura Ferris trembled. "It was horrible, so horrible he had me almost believing the dreams were real.

"A couple of nights later, the pain came back. He crawled around the house on his knees, clutching his head in his hands, screaming and begging for me to take the pain away. *'Mammy, Mammy,'* he kept screaming at me, *'please take it away,'* he said. *'Please make it better again.'* He'd start to vomit again then. The pain lasted for days. I wanted to take him to the hospital. But Moyne disagreed. He said he could treat him at home. He kept reassuring me that Aidan would be fine. I could see he was anything but fine. He gave him injections, he said, for the pain. After a couple of days he seemed to stabilize him. But he wasn't the same. He wasn't the same ever again. That was the day when we lost our Aidan."

"What do you mean?"

"He never really recovered after that period. He seemed permanently drugged, almost semi-conscious. We had to speak really slowly if we wanted him to understand what we were saying to him. He just nodded and shook his head, and mumbled and blew bubbles whenever I spoke to him. I didn't really notice the speed of the physical deterioration. My husband began to notice it quicker than I did. He would be out working a lot so he wouldn't see Aidan from early morning until six, maybe seven, each evening. Doug could see the changes. He was kinda maddened by what he saw."

"Was he still on the medication by that stage?"

"No. I'd stopped giving him the tablets a week before that. He couldn't swallow anyway. He couldn't keep anything down by then."

"Were you giving him anything for the pain?"

Maura Ferris sneered. "Moyne told me to give him paracetamol for the headaches."

I closed my eyes to concentrate on stopping my hands from trembling. I tried hard to remember what I might have been doing during this nightmare, where I was and how I would have reacted to it if I had been told. I needed to hear more. "What happened then?"

"Another week and his speech had become slurred, like he'd been to the dentist and had got an anaesthetic. He dribbled a lot, didn't seem to notice it though. Within a couple of months he was dragging one whole side of his body. It was like he was after suffering a stroke and the right side of his body, from the top of his head to his toes, was dead. Then he started dropping things with his good hand, as I had started to call it. He couldn't hold his pencil to do the sums and little pieces of homework that were being sent home for him. Then he couldn't hold his fork to eat his dinner with us in the evening. His fingers slowly began to bend over, like claws. Soon after that started, he couldn't straighten them out."

"Did you go the police?"

"Why would I have gone to the police? What would I have said to them?" She stared at me. "Are you being serious?"

"Yes," I said, discomfited.

"Would you have taken your daughter to the police? Let me explain it like this, Mr Freeman. I had a doctor on one side who told me everything would eventually right itself, that my boy would get over this 'minor setback', as Moyne had described it. On the other hand, I had a deranged husband who threatened my very life if I went against his word. And you want to know why I didn't call the police? When your daughter ran a high temperature or vomited late at night, did you call the police? It must be difficult for you to understand all this, Mr Freeman. After all, you're a well-educated man, unlike us folk who live simple lives and rely on the grand education of others to get by. I'll say it again. Who was I to doubt a man as genuine as Doctor Moyne? He was my only hope, Mr Freeman. He was our ticket to health, as I believed with all my heart and soul. You don't expect someone like that to be depraved."

She stood up and closed her coat.

"I have to be on my way. There could be trouble if I'm late home. I wouldn't put it past my husband to ring the hospital to see if I'm there."

"Let me drop you home, please. I'll leave you to where the bus would drop you off. He won't know we spoke, I promise."

She agreed. It would take almost an hour to drive her home. I reckoned that hour might be invaluable.

42

Maura Ferris only spoke again once we were out of the city and driving in complete darkness. It was as if she didn't want me to see what she was saying. She spoke softly, at the same time looking away from me towards the passenger window. "I suggested going to the police. My husband wouldn't hear of it." She reminded me of someone who spoke with two voices; one voice she used most of the time while she was at home with her family; the other, a tone and a vocabulary she reserved strictly for people she was trying to impress. I got the feeling I fell into the second category.

There were long pauses in our conversation now. We were both tired, I felt. And I also felt she was embarrassed by the long confession she now had time to contemplate.

"Has your husband always been violent?"

It was a painful question. I felt it stinging in her answer.

"Not always." She thought again, wiping the condensation off her window with the side of her hand. "Not always. Why?"

"Do you remember the first time he hit you?"

"Yes."

"Did he apologise?"

"No. He simply said there was a lot more where that came from. They were his exact words. We had been at a wedding. I was seven months pregnant. I couldn't drink while I was pregnant with Aidan. So I suppose I ended up chauffeuring Doug around after he'd had too much to drink."

"What happened at the wedding?"

"He'd had too much to drink. I told him I was going home and that he could have a lift if he came with me at that precise moment. I warned him I wasn't hanging around. He told me he'd be ten more minutes. He was after buying two pints for himself. I reckoned it would take him about half an hour to drink them, and I wanted to go home."

"What did he do?"

"He stood up and hit me a smack of his fist across the face. I ended up with a black eye and a dislocated jaw." She turned her face towards me and pointed to a small darkened mark on her cheek.

"In front of everybody? He hit you?"

She nodded. "I suppose you could say I eventually came to expect it. I grew to know when he would lash out, so I learned carefully to avoid those situations."

"And no one standing there beside you did anything to help you?"

She tutted. "Of course not. It was private business between a man and his wife. No one around here was going to get involved in something they knew little about. 'Let them go home and sort it out between them,' would have been their attitude." She looked at me differently now, in the darkness of the country night-time. "I'd prefer not to talk about that those times, Mr Freeman, if you don't mind."

"Not at all. Talk to me more about Aidan, if you want to."

She breathed deeply and opened her window a couple of inches. "Aidan's condition deteriorated to the extent that he couldn't do anything on his own. I had to put things into his hand, and then take them out again. He eventually needed a wheelchair all the time. He wasn't able to walk. He couldn't talk coherently. He babbled and spluttered, and roared and squealed. Exactly like he is today. The rest is history."

"And what about Moyne?"

"Moyne came to see him regularly. He would tell me he had been speaking with So-and-So Expert, and Mister Big-Shot Psychologist, and that there was a possibility that his situation might improve."

"Did you believe him?"

"For a while I did. It might sound ridiculous after all I've told you, but I would have been happy just to get my hyperactive, unpredictable little boy back again.

That was all I wanted, for things just to be the way they were."

"And when did you know they wouldn't ever be?"

She tossed her hair and ran her hand through it. "I can't remember an exact moment when I knew this was permanent. I suppose it just slowly crept up on me. Then one day I looked at him and knew it wasn't going to change."

"Did you take him to any specialists?"

"No. My husband was against it. And I knew better than to argue with him. I suppose when it all settled down and Aidan reached a point where he wasn't getting worse and he wasn't getting better, that was when I accepted it. That was when I decided to just get on with life."

"And your husband?"

Maura looked at me, waiting for me to say something else. "What about my *husband*, Mr Freeman?"

"How does he see this whole mess today?"

She sighed heavily. "If my husband ever found out that I came here to your hotel tonight, he would kill both you *and* me."

She raised her foot and, angrily, kicked the dashboard three times; so hard, I slowed down with the fright. She pulled at her hair and whined.

"Are you OK?" I said nervously.

"No, I'm *not* OK. Do I *look* OK?" she shouted. "*Fuck him!* Such a cowardly bastard. I hate every bone in his body. If I could kill him without anyone finding out, do you think he'd be still walking about intimidating people and moaning about how God and his mother have destroyed *his* life? That shit has beaten me black and blue and spent every penny of the money we got!"

I waited a second. "What money?" I asked.

She seemed embarrassed again. "The trust fund that was set up."

"For Aidan?"

"Yes."

"By who?"

"Moyne called my husband one day. He told him he needed to talk to him. That a man would call to our house. A man who worked closely with Moyne. My husband was so angry he told Moyne that he would kill this man if he set foot on our doorstep. Moyne told him this man had some money for us, that he wanted to give us to help us in our problems. My husband is a very mercenary man, Mr Freeman. He loves money. Money speaks volumes to him. So he changed his attitude and told Moyne he would be waiting to meet this man when he arrived."

"And did he?"

"Yes."

"What was his name?"

"Dalton. Augustus Dalton. Everybody called him Gus."

"Who's everybody?" I asked.

"Everybody who worked with him. He was a big shot at the pharmaceutical plant. Moyne was chief executive of a factory in Clonmel that made drugs. An American company, called Blaine Odox. Dalton was his right-hand man. Dalton did all the dirty work for Moyne. It meant Moyne never really had to come out front. Dalton made all the statements for the company. Moyne stayed in the wings while Dalton became the face and voice of Blaine Odox."

"Where did Blaine Odox come from?"

"New Haven, Connecticut, he told us. That's where the mother company is based. Or at least *was* based. It was sold off to some big US bank nearly three years ago. They're in Texas."

"Fort Worth?"

"Yes."

"Are you sure?"

She nodded.

"How do you know?"

"When I knew something horrible had happened, I went to the drawer where Doug keeps all the house insurance documents and car insurance and tax details, not that he ever gets his insurance like he's meant to every year. And I read through the forms that Moyne asked us to sign that night he started to administer that poison to Aidan."

"Were you able to find out anything else?"

She shook her head. "Not a lot. Doors slammed in my face here when I went looking for help, someone who might be able to tell me what had happened and who I should go to to find out more. In eight years that's all I've been able to find out. I've written letters to anybody who I thought might be able to help. I've even written to a Senator who, I was told, *would* help me."

"And did he?"

"*She*, actually. What do you think?"

"Maura, I need to ask you about the other boys. The four young boys who died. Where they all being given the same treatments?

She shrugged. "I still don't know the answer to that question. I tried to get their parents interested in forming a support group. I told them there was strength in numbers. We could meet with local government representatives here in the area. Two of the families said they had no interest. The other two said they'd have a think about it and get back to me. That was four years ago."

"What happened to Ivan Moyne?"

"He retired and moved abroad, locals say. His marriage broke up shortly before he retired."

"I know. He had an affair."

"How did you know?"

"I met his wife. She's got Alzheimer's. She's in a home for old people close to Dublin. I should have been visiting her tonight."

"I'm sorry for messing up your plans, David."

It was the first time all evening she called me by my first name. I smiled. "I called earlier to say I wouldn't be able to make it. I'm meeting her tomorrow night. Do you mind me asking, what did Gus Dalton say the evening he called out to you?"

"He arrived shortly after eight. He seemed in a terrible rush. He sweated buckets while he spoke to us both. He told us that the Promoxidine drug had been withdrawn. He explained that Blaine Odox wanted to remunerate us for the anxiety and stress we had been enduring. He offered us a quarter of a million pounds."

My mouth dropped. I almost missed the turn for Claddagh Mines as the zeros flashed across my mind under the imaginary spotlights. "What did you say to that?"

"We took it." Maura Ferris waited to see my reaction. "My husband, as you know by now, makes all the decisions. Gus Dalton wrote out a cheque to cash, quarter of a million pounds, Mr Freeman, and handed it to us. He told us it was the least he could do to repay us for the hardship we'd come through. He suggested we invest it. It could be worth twice that in five years, if utilised carefully and strategically."

"So what did you do with it?"

"My husband blew every penny of it in the space of three years: first on stupid, hair-brained business notions. Then, when he tired of that, on horses and booze."

"What's left?"

"Of the money? About twelve thousand I managed to sneak out of the bank account, in dribs and drabs, and lodge somewhere Doug wouldn't find it. There wasn't a whole lot left. Not enough to do anything worthwhile with."

"And what did Dalton say about Aidan's condition?"

"He told us he wasn't a doctor. That Ivan Moyne would continue to keep a close eye on him. He told us there had been a slight hiccup in the drug's development. That was the first I knew of it that the drug wasn't even a drug yet. A minor setback, Dalton called it. Nothing major, he assured my husband. *Jesus Christ, nothing major?* I've got a young lad who barely exists, who should be out makin' a living for himself. He's just a deformed shell. I used to look at photos to remember how beautiful my boy was. Now I can't even look at them. My husband just bins them, or grabs them off me and throws them into the fire when he catches me crying over them." She coughed and caught her breath. "Dalton then had the gall to turn to me and tell me that most likely Aidan would be OK. As far as he understood it, the catatonic paralysis was only temporary. 'Within a couple of months he should be back to his good old, cheerful self,' he told me in a patronising, I-couldn't-give-a-shit voice. I'm sorry for cursing."

"That's OK," I said. "Can you get me those forms you signed for Ivan Moyne that evening?"

Maura Ferris thought about my question. "Why?"

"Evidence. If we're going to bring this case to court, I'll need those forms with your signatures on them."

"They're disclaimer forms, Mr Freeman. Basically, what they do is get Blaine Odox and Ivan Moyne and his little gofer Gus Dalton off the hook. Because we signed those forms we now must take full responsibility for allowing our son to be medicated. We also took quarter of a million pounds from them, remember? How is that going to make us look when we stand up in court to sue Blaine Odox?"

I had no answer for that question.

"Here," she said, nodding to the bus shelter, "you better drop me off here. Otherwise my husband will be asking questions." She turned to look at me. "I probably won't see you ever again. I know you're heading back to the States in the next couple of weeks, so I don't mind saying this to you . . ."

I listened, wondering what could possibly come next.

"From the moment I first saw you, standing at the main door of the schoolhouse, the first morning I dropped Aidan to school, I thought you were the most handsome man I had ever laid eyes on. I remember wondering if there was even the slightest chance that you might notice me and think of me as attractive.

"I remember being green with envy when I saw you out with your wife in the pub one evening. I wanted you for so long. I can also remember how devastated I felt when I heard that you had left the country. You asked me earlier if I would leave my husband? I would have left him for you. And only you. But I knew I could never have you. Your wife saw to that. That didn't mean I couldn't think of you and dream about you, which I did regularly. I often felt guilty for fantasising about you. But it's not a sin to think, since we can't keep ourselves from thinking." She placed her hand on my leg and ran it slowly up my thigh. "I've a good mind to ask you to keep driving on up this road to a little clearing in the forest about a mile-and-a-half from here. Just to be alone with you. Alone alone, if you know what I mean. That way I'd make sure you never forgot me." She waited, watching me.

I stared, eyes front, out the window, watching the rain as it fell more softly now, feeling her gently, then more forcibly, squeezing my crotch. Somewhere in my half-crazy, confused mind I imagined what it might be like lying with her on the sodden floor of the dark forest as the rain poured down on our bare bodies.

She smiled because she knew. "I best be going." She took her hand away. "Goodnight, Mr Freeman."

43

The rain had given way to a clear, starry sky by the time I had reached the hotel. My room felt weirdly unfamiliar in the pitch darkness, the full moon throwing shapes and stretching shadows across the floor, as I tiptoed from chair to mantelpiece to chair, conscious that there might be bags and suitcases strewn around, left exactly where I had opened them, waiting for my eyes to adjust and recognize the strange, silhouetted outlines that kept getting in my way.

Someone snored like a freight train in the distance, close to me now. My eyes cleared and surveyed the furniture and the outline of the room. Josh Traynor lay sprawled across the settee, the smell of stale alcohol stronger and more permeable with each loud rumble.

I checked the bedroom. I could barely just make out the curled shape in the large double bed. I watched for a few moments as Karen slept deeply.

"Hi, there."

The soft voice gave me such a fright I got weak. It came from deep within the darkness of one of the corners in the sitting-room. I recognised it immediately, but only after my blood ran cold. "Molly?"

"Sorry, I didn't mean to scare you like that."

In the darkness, I could make out her shape coming towards me, reaching out and rubbing my arm. A form of reassurance. I hated the darkness and the way it played on the conscious mind. I remembered telling her that during a phone conversation one night while we endured a power cut that had left the island in complete blackness for almost eight hours.

She put her arms around me and we hugged.

"What are you doing here?" I said, the surprise registering in my voice.

"I came back on the train this evening. I've been thinking a lot and I just wanted to see you. That's all."

I fumbled with a socket in the corner of the room closest to the window. It felt like an age until I eventually found the light switch. I squinted and looked at Josh, one leg across the back of the settee with the trousers rolled up to his knee, the other leg on the floor. I closed over the bedroom door and left Karen to sleep. A note on the small table read,

> "Waited up for you but the drink got the
> better of me in the end.
> Hope you had a fruitful evening, Love, Karen."

I smiled. Karen's writing was almost illegible.

"Would you like a cup of tea? It's all I have," I said, nodding to the kettle and coffee-maid service on the dresser.

Molly shook her head. "No, thanks." She sat down in the armchair, under the glow of the reading lamp. She looked awfully pale and drawn in the soft light.

"You really should get some sleep. How are you feeling?" I asked.

"Tired. But I wanted to wait up for you. I found out some things in Dublin. They may mean nothing." She took some folded pages from her pocket. "I visited the National Library today and yesterday. I was curious to see if they kept copies of *The Thurles Tribune*, and I was surprised to find they did. They keep most of the local newspapers and all of the nationals on microfilm. They just set up the first one for you and leave you there for as long as you want to stay. I went through dozens of back editions."

"What did you find?" I felt uncomfortable, expecting now that she had discovered something terrible.

She handed me the pages. More photocopies. I straightened them and laid them out on the table.

JOURNALIST DIES IN CAR CRASH

The piece had been written by Josh Traynor. It was a short article.

Sharon Jory, a former reporter with The Thurles Tribune, *was fatally injured . . .*

. . . a head-on collision earlier this week on the M6 motorway in Warwickshire . . .

I didn't bother reading the rest of the article. "What were you looking for?" I asked Molly.

"I don't know. I suppose I was curious to see if there were any more articles about you."

"Why?"

"Because you're my father. And for ten years I didn't have you. I didn't have any mementos, or photographs, or things I could hold that would remind me of you." She nodded to Josh, sprawled across the settee. "Can we go for a walk?"

I checked my watch. It was almost two in the morning. I nodded. "I'd love to."

We strolled arm in arm along the narrow, deserted streets. Neither of us spoke. We would stop and glance into a darkened shop window and then move on. Molly was the first to say anything.

"I always hoped that you'd come home. Do you know that?" she said.

"I always hoped you'd come out to the States. But I knew you couldn't." I stopped and turned to look at her. "I missed you too. You know that?"

"I know. I guess I just wanted us to be a family again. All of my friends used to talk about their fathers, and where they had taken them at weekends, and what they had bought them for their birthdays. I suppose that was what I missed most. I knew I could just pick up the phone and ring you but you were never physically there. And that was what I wanted more than anything else."

I waited before asking a question I had asked myself for ten years. I watched the steam off my breath as I blew hard. "What happened that day?"

"What day?"

"The day you went missing. And came home with your hair cropped and daubed with green streaks . . ."

Molly said nothing for a moment. She looked away and slowed her pace. "I came home from school that day. It was about half three. I rushed into the house looking for Mom. I needed money. She wasn't in the kitchen. I thought maybe she was out in the garden. She wasn't there either. So I tried her bedroom." She went silent again.

"And . . ."

"And she was there . . . in bed . . . with a man. The two of them were . . . they had no clothes on. I knew what they were doing. And they just looked at me. The man smiled. I ran out of the house. I could hear Mom screaming out my name. I put my hands up to my ears and kept running. I swore I wasn't coming back. I wanted to run away. I was crying. Some of my friends were waiting outside. I remember they asked me what was wrong. I didn't say anything. I just wanted to be on my own. So I ran up to my granddad's grave and sat there, crying and hating my mother."

I tried to conceal my shock. "Who was he?" I asked calmly. My wife had been bedding another man under my roof, in *my* bed.

She ignored my question. "I sat there all evening,

until it got dark. Then Owen Durkin came looking for me. He fancied me."

"How do you know that?"

Molly laughed. "Because he kept telling me all the time during school breaks. All the girls teased me. I hated it when they did that. I didn't fancy him. He used to drive me mad."

"So what did he say to you in the graveyard?"

"He told me he was running away with the gypsies, the ones on the outskirts of the town. He used to play with the three gypsy kids. He told me they were nice to him, more decent than the other kids in the town. Their mother used to ask him to stay for dinner. We shared our secrets. I told him I'd tell him mine, if he told me his. So I told him about Mom and her lover, and he told me about his mother's friend, the garda. And we swore we'd never tell another living soul."

"And did that include running away?

Molly nodded. "He asked me never to tell anyone that he was thinking of running away from Silvermines."

"And did he?"

"What?"

"Run away?"

"I guess he did. He hated Claddagh Mines. He used to say there was nothing to do. He used to say his father was always drunk, and the policeman was always in his house. He used to hate that, so he never went home until it was dark. He told me that evening that his mother was going to take him to see Doctor Moyne the next morning. He knew he was hyperactive like some of the other kids. His mother told him that the doctor had medicine to cure it. He told me that evening in the graveyard he wouldn't be going to Doctor Moyne's the next day. He asked me to go with him."

"Where to?"

"I suppose wherever he ran away to. With the gypsies, I guess. There was a time when I could never think of anything else. I used to hear people talking about him in the pub years later, wondering if he was dead. For some reason it didn't start really bothering me until I was fourteen or fifteen. Then I used to hear the old drunks whispering about the beating that Owen got from . . ." She stopped.

"Me?"

She nodded. "Yeah. And I used to shout at them that you had nothing to do with his disappearance. And Mum used to send me home from the pub for being rude to the locals at the bar: fat, smelly bastards who never went home, just drank themselves to death."

"And what used you say to them about Owen, in the early days?"

"Nothing."

"But you knew."

"Yeah, I knew. I wanted to tell you. I suppose I would have. But then you just disappeared as well."

"I didn't *disappear* . . ."

"You did as far as I was concerned," she said forcefully, almost cutting me off. Then she said softly, "I know now you didn't disappear. But I was only eleven years old then."

"I had to get out, Molly. I couldn't stay."

We walked slowly now, avoiding puddles like they were part of this slow, painful conversation.

"You hated me for leaving, didn't you?" I said.

Molly thought over my words. "I guess so. I didn't *hate* you. I suppose I wanted to go with you." She looked at me quite sternly. "Have you ever had a hero?"

I laughed. "A man called *Ironside*."

"Who?"

"He was a lawyer . . . and a detective, all rolled into one. He was in a wheelchair, but he never let that confine him. And he used to solve all these serious crimes . . . and chase the criminals in his wheelchair. And he never had a gun. Yet, they all seemed to be terrified of Robert Ironside. And he was driven around in the back of this windowless van . . . and he used to shout instructions to the driver to 'put the foot down' and 'move in on them'." We stopped walking. We were on the bridge, close to The Mill.

"Who was your hero?" I asked.

"Someone I knew years ago. He was gorgeous. I was head over heels in love with him. I remember thinking when I was back then, 'I really want to marry him'. All the girls at school used think so too. They used to tease me because I was closer to him than they were. I used to love when he'd put his big strong arm around me and squeeze me really tightly. And every time he squeezed me he used to tell me he loved me."

I watched the steam off her breath as she watched the fast current of the water rushing downstream.

"Then he broke my heart . . . because he went away."

"Owen?"

"No. It was you, actually."

I smiled. I could feel tears coming. "I remember that night when you hugged me tighter than I've ever been hugged." I put my arm around and felt it close tightly around her skinny frame.

We turned and headed back towards Langton's.

"You know I never meant to hurt you," I said.

She squeezed my arm. "I know that now."

"So where do you think Owen Durkin is today?"

She shook her head. "I don't know."

"And what happened you that night? Who daubed you in the green paint?"

"Owen. He told me that the gypsy kids used to do it all the time and then hide in the fields and scare people after dark. He had this mask. It was grayish-white with black stripes, and a big black circle under the chin. The green paint was luminous so I cut my hair real short with a scissors he got from his mother's bedroom and we painted each other. Then we waited in the graveyard for someone to frighten."

"Did anyone come?"

"Yeah."

"Who?"

"The man who'd been in bed with my mother that afternoon."

I could feel the arm she linked me with shaking. Her voice trembled. Her pace quickened. We were walking uncomfortably fast now.

"What was he doing in the graveyard?" I could feel the tension rising inside me.

"He was having a pee against the wall closest to the church." Her voice was agitated now, scared.

"And what did he do?"

"Owen let out a high-pitched squeal, like a crow, like a *caw*-ing-sound. It scared him I know because he jumped about a foot in the air and slid down the low grassy slope. Then he stood up and looked down at his trousers and started to curse. He turned around and spotted me. He must have heard me laughing. Before I knew it, he was on top of us. The grass was wet and slippery. I couldn't run. He grabbed me." Molly started to shake, her breath almost choking, as if she was reliving every second. "Owen ran. He kept shouting to me to run. But the man had me by the shoulder. He tried to grab me by the hair once or twice but his hand kept slipping because of the paint. He must have scratched my face because my eye was all swollen and my cheek was cut.

"I could hear Owen's voice screaming to me. Then it stopped. He'd gone off and left me there with this madman. The man was staring at me. He told me if I ever told either you or Mom what had happened he'd come back and kill me."

"Jesus. Did you get a look at him?"

"It was very dark in the cemetery."

She cried softly. She wouldn't let me put my arm around her. "So what happened then?"

"Owen came back and let a roar at him. 'Let her go or you're dead.' The man just started laughing so much he let me go. Then I heard the gunshot. Owen didn't hit him but he grazed the man's leg."

"What did the man do?"

"He hobbled away, cursing and screaming that he'd be back to get us."

"Did he ever come back?"

"No."

"Did you recognise him?"

Molly seemed to think about the question. "No. I don't know who he was. He kept stopping and looking back and screaming at us that he'd get us."

"Who pays for your apartment?" I asked quickly, hoping she might tell me.

At first she seemed reluctant to answer. "Owen."

"Owen Durkin?"

She shrugged. "Yes."

"So he *is* alive?"

"Obviously. . . yes."

"So you *have* seen him!"

"No."

"But how can he pay for your apartment without you setting up the purchase deal?"

"I have no idea. Money simply arrives into my bank account each month. One week later it goes to the building society to pay the mortgage. I had no say in it. It's a series of standing orders, which I was notified of one afternoon when I was in trying to organise an overdraft. I wasn't able to afford to rent the apartment any longer. The landlord told me he'd give me four weeks to come up with the money. I asked my bank manager if it would be possible to borrow money. He said no. My two part-time jobs carried no security, even though I was scraping by. One week later I received a letter telling me the apartment was mine for as long as I wanted to live there."

I was trying hard to digest this most unlikely story. At first it sounded cock 'n' bull, but then I asked myself why my daughter should want to lie to me. "Is he wealthy?" I asked.

"I don't know."

"Where does he live?"

"I haven't a clue. The letter was date-stamped in Ecuador. It took two weeks to get here. He said in the letter that he moves around. That's all. Dad, I couldn't tell you what he looks like today, what he does for a living, if he's married . . . *I just don't know!*"

"And he's never phoned or called?"

"Never."

"So you just have that one letter that you received in the post?"

"That's right."

"Jesus, that's weird. It sounds like the bloke's stalking you."

"He's *not* stalking me!"

Her tone had changed to one of anger. I decided to drop the subject. "Are you doing anything tonight?"

She thought for a moment then smiled. "Me? Doing anything? I doubt it." She sniffed. "No, I've nothing planned. Why?"

"Will you come out to dinner with me? I've asked someone out and I'd love if you'd come along."

"Who?"

"Ingrid Moyne, the doctor's ex-wife. I thought it might be nice to take her away from that Home for a few hours. I've booked a table. Will you come?"

"OK."

I watched her as she agreed, and couldn't blame her for looking suspicious.

44

Saturday.

I woke early that morning from a short, frustrating and unnerving sleep, tired and more than a little confused. For some strange reason I couldn't fathom, I needed to meet Gus Dalton before dining with Ingrid Moyne that night. Josh knew where Dalton lived.

I had a light breakfast and waited in the quiet dining-room for the others to surface.

Once they were seated, I assigned them their tasks.

Josh was to check out his contacts on Ivan Moyne. I told him I didn't want to see him again until he was able to locate the doctor.

I asked Karen to check with a local travel agent about return flights to Boston, the sooner the better. We each had open-ended tickets. She was to buy a third one now, one-way, for Molly who in turn was to shop and buy whatever she needed in preparation for her journey. The two of them, if necessary, would travel back to Boston ahead of me.

Josh made a quick phone call over his scrambled eggs and grapefruit juice. He scribbled an address on the back of a cigarette packet and gave me instructions on how to find Dalton.

We all said goodbye shortly before eleven.

By one that afternoon, I had parked outside a small, discreet semi-detached house in a sprawling housing estate on the outskirts of Clonmel. A group of children playing ball in the narrow cul-de-sac watched me lock up my car and check the address against my notes.

The tiny rusty gate creaked loudly as I pushed it open.

I rang twice and stood back from the front door, watching for a shape behind the opaque glass. I had never met Dalton so I didn't know what sort of a welcome, if any, to expect.

No answer.

I rang again. And again.

I turned to walk back to my car when I heard the door open behind me. I swung around. A small man with black-rimmed spectacles and graying, receding hair stood in the doorway. He looked gaunt, almost wasted away he was so thin. He wore a loose, grey cardigan and black, shiny corduroy slacks. And slippers.

"Gus Dalton?" I said.

"Who wants to know?" he replied.

"My name is David Freeman. I need to talk to you for a few minutes, Mr Dalton, if that's possible."

He studied me, looking intently at my shoes first, and then slowly on up to the jacket I was wearing, and the small black diary I was carrying.

"Come in," he said meekly. He watched the children who had congregated at his gate suspiciously.

Gus Dalton wore the looks of a man who had been expecting the law to call at his door for a very long time. He closed the door behind me and pointed to the kitchen and the teapot on the table.

"I hope I'm not disturbing anything, am I?" I said politely, as we went through to the kitchen.

He sighed, half-laughed and pointed to the small armchair by the fire. A small flame burned on a blackened log in the grate. "Let me take your jacket. Have a seat."

He hung my coat on the back of the kitchen door. "Cup of tea?"

"No thanks. I don't really have much time. I used to be a schoolteacher in . . ."

He cut across me. "I . . . know who you are, Mr Freeman. What can I do for you?" He sat on a small wooden chair on the other side of the fire. The house was dimly lit, sparsely furnished and cold. A small portable television sat on a shelf above the fireplace. Dalton was watching motor racing from Brands Hatch. He picked up the zapper and turned off the television.

I could tell he felt uncomfortable in my presence and was regretting his invitation.

"I need some information about Ivan Moyne."

"Why?"

"Because I'm trying to find him, that's why."

"And do you mind me asking *why* you're trying to find him?"

I said nothing for a moment, hoping the silence might dissipate the nervous energy and tension that filled the air. "I think you know why I'm trying to find him, Gus."

Dalton sat forward on the cheap pine chair, resting his hands on his knees. "I knew the minute I saw your shoes that you weren't a cop."

"How's that?"

"Because cops don't polish their shoes so thoroughly."

"Have you had a lot of cops visiting you?"

"No. But I've always been expecting them. For nearly eight years now, every time a car pulls up outside the house, I always get nervous. I know they will come someday."

"Why?"

He smiled. "Don't patronise me, Mr Freeman. I know why you're here. So let's just cut to the chase and get on with it. What exactly do you want to know?" He stood up. "You won't mind if I pour myself a cup of tea while you're talking . . ."

"Certainly not."

"Talk, Mr Freeman. It's why you're here."

"Four young teenagers, former pupils in my old school, died in mysterious circumstances over the course of five years. You know that."

He nodded. "Nothing to do with me, Mr Freeman."

"Call me Dave. Why do I get the impression you've had this conversation before?"

He stared at me. "*Dave*. It's obviously *just* an impression."

"I never insinuated that it had anything to do with you."

"I never implied you insinuated anything." He smiled patiently. "Let's not get too deeply into semantics here. Please, go on."

He was an academic, intelligent, razor sharp and quickly assertive.

"They were all patients of Ivan Moyne during his tenure as GP in Claddagh Mines. You knew that?"

Dalton closed his eyes. "What Ivan Moyne did as a general practitioner was none of my business. I kept strictly to my own priorities."

"You were a pharmacologist at Blaine Odox, were you not?"

"I was not a pharmacologist. My speciality was pharmacopoeia. I was an authority on drugs treatise, namely their preparation, their chemical make-up, properties and recommended dosages and manner of administration. More loosely, I would have been familiar with the full compendium of available drugs and those that were almost ready to come into the market. And I was *not* a pharmacopolist."

"What's a pharmacopolist?"

"A dealer in drugs, basically. I usually left that side

of the business to the doctors and the psychiatrists."

"But you wrote out a cheque for a substantial sum of money to Doug Ferris. You blackmailed him into keeping your little secret, didn't you?"

"Simply doing what I had been told to do."

"By who?"

"Who do you think?"

"Ivan Moyne."

"If you knew, why did you ask?"

I ignored the logistical nature of his question. "What happened with Promoxidine, Gus?"

I could tell by his blanched reaction that I had touched a sensitive nerve.

He sat back in the chair and folded his arms across his chest. "I was a highly accomplished scientific engineer in the world of drugs production procedures. Promoxidine was originally labeled Beta-5, protective code-label 5078B, when we started testing it. First on laboratory animals, then on cattle."

"Cattle?"

"That's right. Cattle, cats, rabbits, rats, dogs, mice . . . you'd be surprised what they test new drugs on before they prescribe them to humans. You'd be quite astonished how much we humans have in common with certain animals, Mr Freeman." He studied me with those unnerving eyes. "In fact, usually the last stage of testing is carried out on medical students. I wanted to shelve the Beta-5 project for another couple of years. I didn't like the reaction reports I was reading.

411

It was tested on bulls to see if it would calm them considerably during the breeding season. Have you ever seen a tormented bull, Mr Freeman?"

"No."

"There isn't anything on this earth that will calm an animal like that down, short of a tranquilliser from a rifle. We thought we'd try a variety of experiments on these animals using Beta-5."

"What was the result?"

"Brain damage. Insanity. It's difficult to tell until you get the results of a postmortem. By then it's too late. So I set about changing a number of the compounds within the make-up of the drug itself. That became Beta-5A. And the results were good. So much so that after continuous testing over a nine-year period, Ivan Moyne, who was a director at Blaine-Odox, took it into his head that the time had come to administer the drug to patients of his suffering from Attention Deficit Hyperactivity Disorder. I warned him against it, told him I would have nothing to do with such an insane experiment. A drug like that takes close to twenty years to perfect. He argued he had put so much money into this business he couldn't afford any more. He wanted a return for all his investments. The rest is history."

I sat silently, contemplating what he had said. I wondered what the conversation between these two eminent men must have been like that day when Moyne decided to prescribe.

"Do you ever hear from him?"

"Moyne?" Dalton shook his head. "I wake up every morning hoping he's dead, and pray every night that if he's not, he will be soon. The man destroyed my life, Mr Freeman. Not just my career, my *life* . . . and the life of my dear wife. The pressure and stress of this abominable business became too much for her. She developed cancer six years ago. She died inside a year. I have no children, Mr Freeman. I have no one I can call my own. I'm sure you remember how that felt the day they ran you out of Claddagh Mines. I sit here every day, *all* day. I am waiting to die. And I am getting impatient. And I hope that day comes quickly." He stood up, tears welling in his eyes. "Not quick enough," he muttered. "Now if you don't mind now, Mr Freeman, I would be grateful if you were on your way, please. I've told you all I know. I hope you can appreciate how difficult it is for me to talk about it."

I was about to ask one more question, but decided not to. I stood up.

He handed me my coat and hurried me to the front door, as if he had had a complete change of heart.

I turned to thank him from the garden gate, but he had already shut the door behind me.

45

I spent the remainder of Saturday immersed in my own thoughts, anger and confusion, sitting by the banks of the river, close to Kilkenny Castle. I tried on several occasions to feel sorry for Gus Dalton, a man who had lost *everything* except his own life, by putting myself in his shoes.

It wasn't possible.

I could not find it within me to forgive a man who knew the sort of physical and mental damage this semi-tested drug could do to the four young boys who died as a result of his negligence, and a fifth who was living out his final days in a semi-vegetative twilight state. Yet, something in me felt sorry for this pathetic little man full of big words and praise for his early conquests and discoveries.

It started to rain. I went back to my hotel room to pack. Something in me had radically changed that afternoon. I would ring Karen and tell her to book my return flight. I was going back to Boston at the earliest opportunity. I had had enough.

* * *

Beckett's was empty when we arrived. It was as I had hoped it would be.

Ingrid Moyne was a frail little thing, dwarfed by the nurse who accompanied her. The nurse had dressed for the occasion and didn't say a word all night, apart from the normal courtesies, and when she was spoken to. Occasionally, she tapped Ingrid's arm and asked her if she was OK.

She fussed around the old woman now, making her comfortable, getting her a drink and taking her order for dinner.

Ingrid enjoyed the fuss initially, but I could see her growing tired of it quickly. Her dress was pretty. I could tell it was something she had kept over in her locker at the nursing home; something she had worn out to stately occasions with her doctor-husband. It was pink and lilac chiffon, with a heavy long-sleeved woollen vest underneath. She wore pearl ear-studs, a Tara brooch on the collar of her overcoat and a matching cravat-style scarf, swept over her shoulder.

I was delighted I had invited Molly. The two of them hit it off immediately. It was as I had hoped it would be.

We chatted about the food, the nursing home, Molly's education and the weather.

Finally, once the meal was finished and the table cleared, I felt confident enough to broach the subject I knew only too well she was expecting would be discussed.

"Could I be bold enough to order a brandy, David?" she said softly. She smiled.

The nurse, whose name was Pauline, frowned.

I winked and smiled back. "Of course."

A VSOP brought another smile to her face. "I'm not allowed this very often," she joked. She sipped her drink, letting it warm her cheeks, and closed her eyes. "Wonderful," she whispered. "Now, let's talk about why you asked me here this evening."

Molly looked surprised.

Pauline looked intrigued.

I felt embarrassed. I was expecting Pauline to dive for her bag, produce a notebook and start writing in shorthand.

Ingrid looked at Molly, then at me. "Well? I presume you want to know about Ivan. Am I not right, David?"

I nodded. "I'm trying to locate your husband, Ingrid."

She shook her head vigorously. "You'll find that impossible to do. Ivan is dead. I know that. I don't have a death certificate to prove it, but if I had the Holy Bible here on the table in front of me, I would be prepared to swear on it."

She spoke with a lovely, lilting tone to her grand voice.

"You see, when Ivan left me for another woman, I

had started to get quite ill. Not physically *ill*, you understand. I just found I was forgetting things. I couldn't drive my car because my own doctor told me it would be too dangerous. Eventually I became quite bad, I suppose you could say, and he recommended that I should live at Sunny Hall. Ivan knew the directors so they were delighted to have me. It's not so bad. I just wish they wouldn't keep treating me like a stupid child all the time. Apart from that, no complaints."

"And did he keep in touch after that?" I said.

"Oh, of course. It was almost embarrassing. He would ring up every couple of days to see how I was. I had found out that his affair with that woman – she was only half his age – ended after a few months. She realised what she was letting herself in for, I presume, when they started living together. But he never told me it was over. But I knew by the messages he was leaving with the staff that he was broken-hearted. He missed me."

"And did you talk to him?"

"*Never!* I would have forgiven him for everything if he had just been man enough to admit he had made a catastrophic error and broken my heart. But he didn't. Typical bloody male, he kept up this façade, pretending everything was fine. But I knew he wasn't. I suppose I wanted to hurt him a lot, like he had hurt me. I'm sorry now I did. He's dead."

"How can you be so sure?" Molly asked.

"Because, dear, Ivan used to say the same thing

every time he called Sunny Hall. He would say at the end of the call, 'Have a peaceful night for me, dear', and he would insist that whoever was taking the message would tell me he had said this. So, of course, when he died there was a whole month without calls. I suspected something was wrong. Then the calls started, but I knew it wasn't him because the messages were always garbled and they never had those sweet little words at the end for me." She smiled and sipped her brandy. "Why are you looking for Ivan?"

"Because I need to know what happened to four young boys who died some years back . . . four boys I taught in school, Ingrid. And I think Ivan might be able to help me."

Her face changed. She frowned now. "Why don't you ask your friend, Josh? I'm sure he might be able to tell you a thing or two."

Suddenly the mood was different.

Ingrid Moyne shivered and asked for her coat. "If you don't mind, I'd like to be getting back to the Home before they turn the lights out.

"Ingrid, when did Ivan die?"

As she was standing up, she froze in a stooped, uncomfortable-looking position and looked up at me. "Sometime in . . . September, I think." She composed herself and seemed to dwell on her words. "I think it was this year."

Molly never spoke all the way back to Kilkenny that

night. Two and a half hours on the road. On three occasions I asked her if everything was OK; if she was feeling unwell; if there was something I had said that might have offended her.

Each time she shook her head and we were both silent strangers again.

* * *

It was almost midnight when I turned the key in the room. Karen was asleep. Molly climbed into the spare bed, fully clothed, and pulled the covers over her head.

I flopped into the armchair in the other room and relaxed, wondering if it would be worth the journey back downstairs for a late drink. I decided against it. Josh Traynor played on my mind. Ingrid Moyne had said he knew a thing or two. What did he know?

I was about to close my eyes when I noticed the red light flashing on the phone. I had a message on the hotel mail-answering service. I pressed 7.

It was Josh. He sounded excited.

"Teacher, you're not gonna believe this. We have located the elusive doctor. A friend of mine in Dublin owed me a little favour. He got crackin' on it this afternoon and called me back an hour ago. Moyne is living in Majorca. A small place called . . ."

I could hear the rustling of paper and Josh cursing himself.

"Here it is . . . Es Capdella. It's a small town close to

419

Paguera. I'm goin' out there tomorrow. I'll call you as soon as I get there. But I want you to catch the first available flight and follow me out there. Call into the travel agent on Monday morning. Dixon Travel. Girl's name is Jane. I've booked two tickets in my name. She's expecting you." The phone beeped loud, and I put Boston on hold.

46

Feliz Navidad.

A huge mechanical Santa held up the giant poster in the arrivals lounge that said, its letters in red and black buried in fake snow, *Happy Christmas.* "Ho, ho, ho . . ." the recorded voice said cheerfully each time he turned slowly from left to right, then back again. A real Santa, standing under the sign that flashed *TAXI*, lit up a Fortuna, adjusting his beard so that he could leave the cigarette hanging safely from his lips.

Palma International Airport, on a wet December afternoon, in the week leading up to Christmas, had never featured in a travel agency brochure, so I had no idea what to expect. Simple decorations hung from the high hangar-like ceiling, giving the place a neglected, half-hearted feel for a season that demanded debauchery and overkill.

I felt lost, like I had been washed up on an empty

beach. I had one bag – hand luggage – so there was no hanging around. Within fifteen minutes of disembarking I was standing in the deserted arrivals hall, deciphering Spanish signs full of arrows and exclamation marks.

The young boy almost tripped me up as he grabbed my bag from between my feet. At first I thought he had planned on swiping it. He wasn't going to get far. I glanced down at the heavy pullover and dark winter jacket that straddled the handles of my luggage and watched curiously as he made an effort to drag the bag behind him. *"Hey, watch it!"* I shouted, pushing him away.

He refused to let go. He couldn't have been any older that nine or ten, his skin nut-brown, his jet-black hair neatly cut short, his eyes huge and hazel in colour, like two blackened bronze coins.

"Esta manera! Ahora!" he chirped, pulling harder on the handles of my bag with all his might, and pointing to an exit. The bag slid along behind him.

I followed my bag, eager to please this child but adamant I wasn't letting my luggage out of my sight.

Once outside, he pointed to a gleaming white Mercedes taxi, its engine running, its owner leaning back on the bonnet, watched curiously, smiling as the small boy yelled commands and dragged the bag like an impudent puppy being trained to obey. He patted the boy on the head, said something in Spanish, and opened the back door for me. The smile was strictly reserved for the kid. I got a frown and a quick flick of the head that told me to get in. He flipped my bag in after me.

I took a thousand pesetas from my pocket and leaned out through the window. The small boy's eyes lit up. He took the money and danced in a circle, shouting, *"Gracias, señor. Muchas gracias."*

The taxi driver gently clipped his ear as he walked past him. He said something to the boy, causing him to stop the dance. He quickly pocketed the money and disappeared back inside the terminal through the dark sliding doors.

I sat back and luxuriated in the white leather upholstery, smelling its rich texture. I noticed from the other cars parked in the rank, mainly Seat Cordobas, that I had the grandest mode of transport. I felt almost as if I had been singled out for preferential treatment, almost as if I had been expected. I checked my bag and its small external pockets. Nothing had been taken.

I checked my watch, reminding myself how much I hated it. It was just quarter to three. I also had to remind myself that it was late December. Judging by the weather, I'd never have guessed. The rain had cleared in the space of ten minutes – there wasn't a cloud in the sky now – and the temperature was hotter than anything I had ever known for Christmas.

My driver exited the airport and manoeuvred a series of roundabouts and slip roads before joining a huge motorway. It was then I realised I hadn't given him any instructions as to where I wanted to go.

"*Es Capdella, por favor,*" I said, trying to sound linguistically flush. I could tell my pronunciation was farcical.

"Yes, I know," he shouted back to me in a crabby tone of voice.

How could he know? I hadn't told him. There was no address on my baggage. My mind kept tossing the question back to me. How did he know where I wanted to go? Unless Josh had organised a special taxi and forgotten to tell me. I was happy to dwell on that possibility even though something deeper told me he hadn't. I started to get nervous, twitchy. I squeezed the bag handles to steady my nerves.

My driver wore a multi-coloured fleece and a cravat, loosely tied in a simple knot. Each time I checked, his eyes were watching me in the rear-view.

It rained heavily for the forty-minute journey. Blurred neon-lit signs broke the monotony of the motorway, flashing their wares and distracting me momentarily from an increasing sensation of fear, like a tide that had turned and was making its way back in across the beach, slowly eating up the patches of sandy land that had once seemed safe to stand on. I felt as if I was walking blindfold into something macabre, something I had no control over whatsoever. From the moment I sat in this taxi, I had relinquished my power to the unknown. Even my driver was involved in this charade. His eyes told me he was implicated. I tried to ridicule my paranoia but to no avail.

I resorted to trying to make conversation with my driver, anything to keep sane, and to stop my mind from driving me nuts. I watched him, wondering what I could ask him that might generate a pidgin-Spanish-part-English conversation for a few minutes.

"Has the weather been good?" I asked cheerfully.

"Yes," he said, watching me again.

"Is it always sunny here in Majorca?" It seemed like a more general question that might spark a debate over our two very different climates.

"Yes," he said again, studying me now.

I would have settled for just a sentence now. I decided that maybe an introduction would help. After all, we had been sitting together now for almost an hour. "My name is Dave. What is yours?"

"Domingo," he said, staring now.

I gave up and sat back. Time to study him, I thought. I could make out a lot of hair. *Seriously* hairy arms, right down to his knuckles; a deep dark growth from ear to ear and a gargantuan moustache, trimmed beautifully like a well-pruned award-winning privet hedge. He spoke through the bristles of his moustache.

The rain hit the windscreen like a drumstick beating a cymbal. Wipers on manic. Then the front window just became a sheet of opaque plastic, a wall of wash. He slowed to seventy and turned on his lights. Speed didn't seem to bother Domingo, even when he couldn't see the Mercedes badge on the tip of the bonnet in front of him.

He muttered something and I noticed his headlights reflecting off the car in front. His radio squawked. A female voice screaming like there was a chip pan on fire behind her. He raised the mouthpiece and squawked back. The radio fell silent again.

I looked behind as he seemed distracted by something. Another white Mercedes, its full beams pumping, sat on our tail. "Do you know him?" I chanced asking.

"*Si!*" He answered abruptly, as if I had rudely interrupted him. "*My friend!*" he shouted.

I couldn't believe it, I grinned to myself. At long last he had said something unprompted. I decided to tempt fate. "Do your friends always drive this close to you?"

"Yes," he said. "He's telling me something."

The radio crackled. A voice, deep and clearly spoken, cackled monotonously for a few seconds. Domingo listened intently, nodding and muttering to himself. Then he picked up his mouthpiece and appeared to be confirming whatever proposal had been put to him. He replaced the handset and seemed relieved.

"Good news?" I said.

He looked in his mirror again. His eyes were wide open. He seemed to smile. "For you, my friend, *very* good news."

"Well," I said, waiting anxiously, "aren't you going to tell me?"

He ignored me now, watching me again with those suspicious, haunting eyes, almost as if he had said something he shouldn't have. I sat back again, hoping that Josh was in a taxi behind us and the final details of this very sketchy, very dubious plan had just been put to bed. The end was in sight. At long last, I told myself, we were coasting in on to the final lap.

"Is Josh behind us?" I asked.

Nothing. He wasn't even watching me now, choosing instead to understand me only when it suited him. I checked my files again, trying to hold onto that fleeting moment of cosseted safeness, which I sensed was slipping away from me again: treatment sheets, given to me by Ingrid Moyne; a full account of Maura Ferris's story that tied in perfectly with the details of treatments as documented by Ivan Moyne; the disclaimer her husband had signed, a simple piece of paper that inevitably had sentenced their son to death, and a list of emergency phone numbers to call as soon as we had arrived at Ivan Moyne's place of residence.

I marvelled at how Ingrid Moyne had preserved the treatment sheets down through the years, and wondered why she had never taken them to the police. Josh warned me not to forget this crucial paperwork. Without these papers, we had no case.

I couldn't stop myself from thinking about Ingrid Moyne's answer to my question as we all stood to leave the restaurant. Had Ivan Moyne been in touch with her immediately before his death? Did he mention he'd been unwell? It haunted me. I felt unsafe – uneasy – and vulnerable. For some strange reason – even if for just a fraction of a second – something in me believed her. I was determined for some strange reason now to convince myself that Moyne was dead. Her voice rang true the more I reasoned, but she was also very ill, I had to remind myself.

* * *

Josh had outlined the schedule that morning when he called me. We would wait until after dark, stepping up to Ivan Moyne's front door at precisely eight o'clock. Josh assured me Moyne would be in. He was always in. We had to nail him early in the evening. Leaving it too late would present us with an unfortunate problem: Moyne would be drunk. He got drunk most nights.

"Windmill," my hairy driver mumbled, pointing through the windscreen wipers. The afternoon was clearing quickly again. The blue sky spread out ahead, the black clouds lost somewhere behind us now.

My mind was feeling giddy now. I had spent the entire day telling myself I was insane. *We* were insane. We had no lawful right to be doing this. I knew that. I had no idea how friendly Moyne was with the local constabulary. He lived in the mountains, on the outskirts of a remote village. Perhaps he had security guards watching the house. I imagined a huge fortified mansion with observation posts and close circuit TV. I pictured electronic gates and huge, insurmountable walls with barbed wire and vicious dogs. But why? I asked myself. What was he afraid of to need that level of security? Not us, surely?

We passed a sign for Paguera, a small select resort, off the beaten tourist trail, mainly German residents, and some British mixed among the predominantly Mallorcan natives.

Es Capdella, 4KM.

The sign pointed into the sandy hills beneath a dark blue sky. The rain had stopped as abruptly as it had tried to run us off the motorway.

"Ten minutes," my driver said, becoming more cheerful with each rare utterance.

"What time does it get dark?" I said.

He stared back at me and shrugged. My question had been a bit ambitious. I tried again. *"Darkness?"*

He didn't understand.

"Night?"

It rang the right bell.

"Six . . . maybe seven."

"What is the temperature now?" I said.

"Nineteen . . . maybe twenty."

I decided to ask again. "My friend . . . Josh? Is he is the car behind us?" I tried to impress upon him that my question was important. "Who is in that car?" I pointed over my shoulder and watched his eyes. "Señor Traynor?"

He shrugged, his eyes flitting between me and the road ahead.

The skies had cleared and the view from the taxi as we weaved our way up the winding road that seemed to cling to the side of this desert mountain was breathtaking in a terrifying sort of way. Who the hell did I think I was? The question came out of nowhere. What if this poor man was innocent? What if this had been a careful, elaborate plan to disgrace him? What if it turned out to be a hoax? Surely Ivan Moyne would put an argument that would point to his absolute innocence. And what if he was innocent? I looked at my files again. They didn't seem so invincible after all.

What if he *was* responsible for the deaths of four boys? It seemed like such a long time ago. Surely it seemed perfectly reasonable to allow this old man to live out whatever was left of his life in the solitude of these hills. It was a prison of sorts, it occurred to me as I looked around at the parched, barren soil and the withered trees in this lifeless desert. He was harmless here.

And what about our chief witness? A woman suffering in the early stages of Alzheimer's. Early stages or not, it had been diagnosed. She was useless for this case. Her evidence wouldn't stand up in court. Unstable came to mind. If the law refused to let her change her will under her prevailing mental condition, surely she'd get laughed out of court. And Maura Ferris? She'd end up accusing her husband of signing away their son's life. She'd probably end up incriminating herself. What if the judge insisted on subjecting her to a psychiatric examination? She hadn't a hope in hell of coming out the far end intact. The more I gave room to these thoughts, the more I realised we had little evidence, if any at all, on which to convict Ivan Moyne.

I squeezed my document case and wondered why I hadn't thought of all this before I climbed the steps of my first plane earlier that morning. I was panicking and it wasn't healthy.

The car behind us remained at a consistent distance. I knew I'd feel better if only he would tell me who they were and why they were following us. I was about to grab my driver's shoulder and shout, *Stop*, when my phone rang. It was Josh. "Thank God," I heaved, when I recognised the voice.

"Where the hell are you, Teacher?"

He sounded nervous. "Just past the turn-off for Paguera, about two kilometres from Es Capdella," I said.

"Good," he cheered. "You didn't forget the papers, did you?"

"No."

My driver watched me intently as I spoke.

"How was the journey?" Josh asked.

"Long and boring. Three flights. Nine hours. I'm dizzy from looking into overhead bloody lockers. I never want to see another plane."

"Not tonight anyway, Teacher. Let's get this little job over with. Then you and me are going to do a bit of celebrating. I've notified the Irish Consulate in Palma. They're expecting us about ten. The consul's name is Thompson. Brian Thompson. Nice guy. It took a bit of convincing when I first spoke to him yesterday. I met him this morning, explained what's going on. He's with us all the way on this one."

I was more nervous, more uncomfortable than ever as I slid the phone into my shirt pocket. Sweat trickled down the back of my neck. How could it rain so heavily and still be so warm? I wanted to ask him. I opened the window another couple of inches. The air felt cooler as it raced across my face. So Josh wasn't following us. Who was it? I looked back. It was gone. With the exception of a beer delivery truck, the road was empty, its tar shiny hot in the afternoon sunshine.

My bushy driver drove his taxi hard once we had left the motorway. As we climbed the mountain road, he muttered something that suggested he was urging me to look behind at the scenery. Paguera unfolded in the unrepentant sunshine of the late afternoon, with its apartment blocks and industrial cranes overlooking blue water for as far as the eye could see. Even if it was a sight to behold I wasn't in an appreciative mood for admiring great scenery that afternoon. Quite the contrary, I felt sick. At any moment I knew I was quite likely to lean out the window and vomit.

I couldn't help noticing the state of the road surface. It looked brand new, as if it had just been laid an hour ago. Jet black and shiny smooth in the heat, it was like a wide role of duct tape below a giant overhanging slab of layered desert rock. The layers reminded me of a peanut-butter sandwich.

Domingo pitched the car on the continuous white line, driving faster as the road became steeper, short straights into acute hairpins, one after the other. He'd drop a gear, straighten the wheels and hit the metal harder again. I was about to explain that I was in no hurry when he almost drove off the road.

"*Bastardo!*" he yelled at the long strip of corrugated iron that had just saved us from a one-hundred-foot sheer drop, spit spraying the windscreen.

I clenched my teeth and squeezed my knees together. I prayed to the first saint I could think of.

Es Capdella appeared over a hillock, like a ghost town scene from an old western movie.

On a steep road leading to a small row of pretty villas he swerved and climbed up a steep kerb, and stopped. I handed him four thousand pesetas.

He grumbled and said, "*Hasta luego.*"

See you later.

47

Es Capdella is situated in the parched foothills of the Serra De Tramuntana Mountains, off the beaten track, nestled between Santa Ponca to the south, Paguera to the south-west and the fishing resort of Andratx to the west.

It's a sleepy little village, all its quaint buildings of natural stonework, beige and brown in colour, blending with and almost camouflaged by its barren, arid surroundings of desert countryside.

During late July and August, it's not uncommon for the temperature here to soar to the mid-forties on the Celsius scale. The dead, shimmering heat has turned everything in nature that continues to grow here into a survivor.

And only the strong survive.

I had to remind myself that we were within days of Christmas, and the temperature was in the mid-twenties. For as far as I could see, lemon and lime trees flourished in large, sloping gardens in the stifling, baking intensity of the perennial sun. Long straight lines of vines climbed hillsides to my left and right, their greenness starkly set against the burnt-orange stonework of the pretty villas with their flowerboxes and satellite dishes and discreet private swimming-pools.

On hearing the chimes of the local town clock, I checked the time. It was half three. Siesta time. I felt like someone's pet dog, now officially a stray that had been dumped miles from familiar surroundings.

There was no main street in Es Capdella. If there was it had no distinguishing features, not during this limbo-esque time of the day. I sat beside an old stone well under a granite arch, wondering if the cool, clear water was safe to drink. I decided against the notion.

The place had a monastic feel about it, almost contemplative. I could hear voices but see no one. The heat playing tricks on my mind? It wouldn't have taken much to unnerve me. From where I sat I studied the parched ridges of the Serra De Tramuntana. The jaded green bushy trees seemed to cling to the sharp inclines for dear life. Here and there, the hills had collapsed, leaving huge sandstone cliffs in their wake. Blood-red chunks of pointed rock dominated the summits.

Es Capdella seemed far removed from a way of life so many local natives had come to despise: tourism.

I walked the narrow streets in the silence of the siesta and wondered where he was. Ivan Moyne. *Come out, come out, wherever you are* . . . I gave my shoulder hold-all a reassuring pat of my hand. It contained documents he thought had been destroyed, papers that would finally imprison him. I was the Grim Reaper.

For all I knew, at that moment, Ivan Moyne could have been watching me. I tried to remember what he looked like ten years ago, and how that much time might have aged him. I could see his silvery grey hair, his neatly trimmed beard and the way he would remove his wafer-thin spectacles and finger them while he described various ailments. I remembered his potbelly and his short stubby legs, and how he seemed to have a penchant for tidy grey suits. Would I recognise him now, ten years on, when he opened his front door to me? Would I be able to see the shock registering on his face? Who would speak first? What would I say when he asked, "What do you want?"? I shivered. The salty sweat stung my eyes. My shirt and trousers were stuck to my skin. My ribs ached. My legs pained me deeply. I had to find somewhere to escape from this heat.

The bright green and golden brown shutters on the discreet roadside residences were firmly closed. This town was asleep, conserving its energy for cooler times of the day. I had to do the same. I had almost three hours to kill. Already I was exhausted.

And all this time, Ingrid Moyne's sweet voice rang in my head: 'Sometime in September,' I could hear her saying to me.

Two elderly women approached with leaflets. They seemed friendly. They smiled, looking at the bag I held tightly. They spoke in Spanish. I apologised.

They asked me, "Speak Spanish?"

"*Hablo muy poco español,*" I said. Very little Spanish. I kept grinning. They had two words of English. I had four words of Spanish.

"*Adíos,*" they cheered.

I remembered what Domingo had said to me, his final words. "*Hasta luego!*" I shouted. They looked back and giggled. And waved.

That elusive clock somewhere in the town pealed again. It was four o'clock. Two hours to fill. Rest up, a voice told me.

A vintage car passed me, disturbing the silence. It backfired in the narrow street, causing it to sound like an explosion. A dog barked hoarsely somewhere in the foothills. I could hear the faraway voices again. The giant cacti and the rows of tomato plants were confusing me now. I found myself gasping as I walked wearily to the crossroads of what appeared to be the town centre. A bureau de change stood on one corner. On another, what appeared to have been once an old derelict building had been renovated into new shoebox-sized apartments.

Josh had told me to relax. He mentioned a small roadside café with a shaded veranda. Stay there once six o'clock comes, he had told me. It was only ten past four. He emphasized the importance of keeping the reason for my visit to Es Capdella private. *Don't mention Ivan Moyne!* he kept saying on the phone.

I would never have been so stupid.

The main street, once I had found it, was indeed slightly busier. A tiny newsagent sold *Hello!* magazine. David Beckham stared out from its cover. The Corrs – three beautiful sisters and their somewhat misplaced brother – pouted on the front of the latest edition of *Marie Claire*. A small fountain spouted water, more like a hypnotic trickle, in the seating area outside.

From where I sat beside the fountain, I looked out over maybe thirty houses – greater Es Capdella. I reckoned on a population of a couple of hundred, max, allowing for another hundred hidden in the hinterland. One of them was Ivan Moyne.

I thought about him as I sat in the shade of a tall, skinny chestnut tree. Did he enjoy this freakish heat? Had he accepted that one day someone would come looking for him? Would he be even more surprised to discover that that someone was me? Was he aware that I was here? Would he give himself up peacefully? Or would he point an automatic rifle at my forehead from between the curtains of his bedroom window?

I tried for a moment to put myself in Ivan Moyne's situation. Knowing what I was going home to face, I believed I would have toughed it out, picking off the sheriff's posse, one by one, hoping that in the heat of the frenzied battle I wouldn't feel the crippling pain of the bullet that would drop me.

I sneezed and shivered, hot and cold.

I imagined a huge wall surrounding a palatial estate and its secluded mansion in the foothills of the Tramuntanas; the perimeter fences electrified, a picture of an Alsatian dog on the gate pillars. *KEEP OUT*. The house with its burnt-orange brickwork and sloping roof, with long skylights to capture the warmth of the sun, set well back from the road, inconspicuous among the groves of lemon trees . . .

I concluded that if Ivan Moyne was that well organised and security-conscious, he knew I was here from the moment I set foot in the arrivals hall at Palma airport.

48

The *supermercado* was closed.

I imagined the humming noise of its cooler, packed full of soft, ice-cold, fizzy drinks, laden down with cans of chilled, sparkling Fanta – so freezing cold it takes your breath away and gives you a pain in your chest and a cramp in your gut. I checked my watch. Twenty past four. It would re-open at half-past, I reckoned. My head pounded from the worst headache I had suffered in years.

Dehydration.

I had sipped champagne on the flight from London to Madrid, just to steady my nerves. It made me feel relaxed, slightly tipsy. Now I was paying the price for such stupidity. Josh had warned me to keep a clear head. Rest regularly. Move discreetly.

By the time I had said goodbye to him the previous day, I felt like a regular, all-encompassing combat commando.

Even the local Catholic church, Mare de Deu del Carme, was taking a breather, its huge mahogany door firmly closed.

I walked back from the church towards a bar I had spotted coming into town.

An elderly man strolled towards me in the distance. I became quite nervous. What if it was Moyne? Would he recognise me? He strolled slowly, like someone just out of bed. A walking stick and a straw boater. He had a moustache. So did Moyne. I pulled the peak of my cap low and stepped out onto the road to allow him pass.

"*Gracias,*" he muttered in a distinctly Spanish accent.

It wasn't Moyne.

I relaxed on the pretty terrace outside Cafeteria Bar Nou and ordered a *cafe con leche* from a pale, tired-looking woman. It arrived pronto in a tall glass, too hot to handle.

Bar Nou was a busy little place. Three cyclists in the corner of the shaded terrace nursed their chilled beers. Each of them was decked from head to toe like a wasp, black and yellow helmets, matching jerseys and Lycra shorts. Their bikes lay in a heap at the roadside. The exhausting heat had won out again.

I watched them enviously, sipping their drinks and cajoling each other in exhilarating mood. I was looking forward to a few beers with Josh later that night, I decided, to celebrate our prize-catch.

The flies attacked relentlessly in the shade. A

mosquito hovered over a discarded sachet of sugar. I brought the cigarette box down hard and flicked the squashed remains off the table.

I was tempted to look over my documents again, just for a sense of reassurance that I hadn't gone mad, but my host was watching me curiously through the open window of the bar, half-smiling, half-pondering. An elderly gentleman two tables away made me nervous as he eyed me suspiciously, thumbing through his newspaper, *Diario de Mallorca*, impatiently. He chain-smoked and poured a bottle of San Miguel into a pretty tankard. He was about Moyne's age, I calculated.

Perhaps he knew him.

Perhaps not.

I left the bag shouldered, its thin strap straddling my chest uncomfortably. I wondered how many times Ivan Moyne had visited this place; how frequently my tired host had brought him coffee to this very table; and would she be surprised if I showed her the contents of my bag, and told her that her friendly visitor had murdered four young boys?

I lit another Marlboro, my shaking hands fighting to steady the lighter. It was pure agitation and nervousness. As I lit the cigarette, a man's voice called out from behind.

"Hola?"

I coughed and dropped the cigarette, and knocked my glass of coffee onto the ground. It smashed. The sound of breaking glass brought silence to the bar and its terrace. Four men sitting at the counter inside looked around. I expected to feel Ivan Moyne's hand on my shoulder at any moment. I froze. Should I run? I couldn't run because I hadn't paid for my coffee. My host would surely call the police. What would the guardia civil say once they had examined the contents of my bag?

The man walked past me, staring at the mess under my seat. He called out again. *"Cómo está?"* He had blond hair. He shook the hand of a man at the bar and ordered a beer.

For one confusing split-second, I thought the plan had been irretrievably scuppered.

A rally car Renault 5 Turbo shot past the terraced bar like a Boeing 737. I jumped again. By now I was petrified. I told myself I wasn't cut out for this. Selling books and teaching kids how to play football, yes. Espionage? Not on your life.

Less than forty-eight hours before, Josh Traynor had spread out a map of Majorca on the bonnet of his Jeep and shouted down a phone at me that Moyne had been snared, thumping a spot on the map repeatedly with his index finger. Coma Calenta. "That's where the bastard is!"

I examined my map over a cappuccino and found the spot. Coma Calenta was a miniscule dot at the foot of Es Puig Batiat, a seven-hundred-metre high mountain, on the banks of a river called Barranc de So

N'Alfonso. Como Calenta seemed to be in a valley between the two mountains. I walked to the edge of the terrace to find my bearings. I could see the gap between mountains. I chanced asking.

My host told me it *was* Coma Calenta. My curiosity had proved to be a mistake. She arrived out with a cappuccino, smiling and singing, and full of chat as if she'd just set eyes on her long lost stepbrother.

Thankfully she had little English. She just rabbited on, pointing to different buildings and higher into the mountains in different directions. I smiled and nodded, pretending to take it all in. Eventually I excused myself and went in search of the men's room.

* * *

Quarter to five.

I had to get far away from Bar Nou, to let the paranoia and the bogey thoughts dissipate, even if only for half an hour, and decided to walk out to what appeared to be the other side of Es Capdella.

The small town was busier now. A small lorry, with its cargo of pot-bellied pigs, and its driver sucking on a blade of grass, snaked up the narrow, winding road I guessed would later take us to Ivan Moyne's house.

The driver slowed, as if to offer me a lift. He wore a poncho and a wide-brimmed mauve-coloured hat. He waved and shouted something. There was no smile. He was telling me either I was a fool for walking on the road, or that since he was going my way, there was a seat on offer, but I was still a fool for walking on the road anyway.

I waved my hand and smiled. *"No, thank you!"* I shouted, giving my English a Spanish cadence, as if it might help my Spanish driver to understand it better.

As he picked up speed, he mumbled and waved, dismissing me as he talked back to his pigs, as the ancient lorry groaned and backfired.

I looked around now in the misty evening, unsure of my bearings. The streets seemed narrower now in the last hour of this confined daylight. Further up in the foothills of the Tramuntana, I could see the evening mist settling on the orange reeks, some of it descending into the foothills like silent gunsmoke seconds after an old rifle's been discharged.

I passed the local post office, closed for the evening. Letters and parcels addressed to locals, I presumed, had been left outside on a deep window ledge surrounded by a tall black railing, well sheltered from the unlikely chance of a rain shower.

Obviously the postman delivered his daily bulk of mail directly to the post office, rather than wandering around the isolated area looking for individuals.

It dawned on me that crime was a rare affair in Es Capdella, something that urbanites in the tourist-infested towns had to contend with, that the natives of Es Capdella could watch on their satellite television sets and be thankful they didn't have much personal experience of.

I was curious, making sure no one was watching, as I thumbed through the letters, fanned out for quick examination like a deck of cards.

A police car slowed down to a crawl as it snaked past me on the road into town. Its two occupants watched me and said something. I waved again, with that smile that tried to say, "You needn't worry about me." I went back to my prying.

And there it was. *Doctor Ivan Moyne*.

The name I wasn't expecting to see, in a neat bundle of letters and cards, caught my attention like a flash of lightning. I counted four official letters, bearing the same insignia and design, all addressed identically to *Doctor* Ivan Moyne.

I couldn't fathom why he would risk exposing himself by letting the postmistress and her customers know so much about him. Then it occurred to me that perhaps Ivan Moyne was the local GP. I shivered. My stomach knotted. I felt like a neighbourhood vigilante, the sort locals seem delighted to have living close to them, but the same individual they silently regard as insane.

As I held this man's letters in my hand, I squeezed each one of the envelopes and wondered would he be stopping by at any second to collect them. A part of me wanted to wait for that moment, to see if Moyne could still recognise me after ten years. I wondered what would be the first thought that might enter each of our heads, and would it be the same thought?

At that very moment, something deep inside

wanted to warn Ivan Moyne of impending danger. Whatever it was that drove me to think like this refused to believe that this silent, helpful man, as I remembered him, was a cold-blooded butcher.

Each of the letters was addressed as follows:

> *Para l'atención de:*
> *Doctor Ivan Moynes,*
> *Es Capdella,*
> *Mallorca, SA*

The address seemed vague enough. The locals obviously regarded him as a medical practitioner. What I did next still shocks me when I think back. I picked up the four letters and, without looking around to see who might have been watching, calmly walked away as if the post was mine. To give the impression of familiarity, as I walked briskly in the direction of Bar Nou, I looked again at each of the letters. The address and postmark on each of them was identical. The shock I felt as I quickly studied the origin of each separate letter was tangible. I felt too close, as if suddenly I was trespassing in a private matter that was too complicated – one that had too many ramifications for someone who wasn't sure of his bearings.

Ivan Moyne had not been collecting his mail for a long time.

* * *

I was still sitting on the terrace of Bar Nou at half past six, half an hour after our planned rendezvous was meant to happen. I was scared now, afraid to move, having almost convinced myself a dozen times that I had seen Ivan Moyne walking towards me, scared stiff that any more meandering might get me into serious trouble. My headache was gone. Tiredness overwhelmed me. And the questions: What prevented him from collecting the letters? What was in each envelope that one should have cause to arrive each week? I tried to think back four weeks, recalling what I had been doing. Four weeks ago I was on Martha's Vineyard, preparing for a busy Thanksgiving weekend, hoping it would bring us boom profits in the shop. None of this had happened. So what made Ivan Moyne stop collecting his letters?

Every so often, I found myself looking at the envelopes again, as discreetly as I could without making it too obvious, in particular at the postal address in the top left-hand corner. The postmark was *Texas*. The address haunted me, like a recurring dream that was taking on a life now:

> The Franklin Global Group Inc.
> Fort Worth
> Texas 08175

I felt a chill, an unwelcoming shiver shoot down my spine. My mind flashed through the long conversation I had had with Maura Ferris. I realized now I was touching on truths. Something told me there and then to call Dan McKenzie.

Dan was a close friend of ours, a detective inspector. He

practically ran, single-handedly, the police force on Cape Cod. Dan was a voracious reader who spent hours on his off-days browsing through the bookshelves at The Meadows. His favourite pastime was medical malpractice. He knew more about dodgy doctors and shady surgeons and burnt-out psychiatrists than I knew about teaching. I was introduced to him by his goddaughter: Karen.

I stopped at a street corner which linked the road into town with the main street I had spent much of the afternoon sitting on. I took out my mobile phone. I checked the time. It was twenty to seven. It beeped twice to warn me it was low on power and needed recharging shortly. My heart started to race as I dialled Karen's mobile number, remembering the international code before the familiar digits. I cleared my throat and swallowed hard, praying that her phone would ring, *and* that she had it somewhere close to her so that she would hear it ringing.

I have always maintained that, when it comes to mobile phones, there exist two types of people: those who can't do without one, and those who can't remember they have one. Karen fell into the latter. Her phone started to ring. *One.* I clenched my teeth. *Two.* I wondered how I would get around the small talk quickly. *Three.* What was I going to say to her? *Four.* What was so important about Dan McKenzie that I should have to get Karen to call him? *Five.* She was not going to answer. The call became a voicemail option.

Now I had a choice: I could either hang up, or leave a message.

" . . . *Please speak after the tone . . .*" Beep.

Silence.

"Karen, it's Dave. I need you to do something for me. It's urgent, Karen." My words were fast-fire, quicker almost than my thoughts. "I need you to ring Dan McKenzie, Karen." There was a sense of panic in my voice now. "Tell him I need him to do a check on . . ." I pulled out one of the envelopes, conscious that another beep would cut off my message. ". . .The Franklin Global Group. They're in Fort Worth, in Texas. Karen, I'm not sure why I need this information. But something is telling me that Dan will know why it's important. Mention Ivan Moyne in the conversation." I checked my watch again. "It's quarter to seven here. So it should be almost one in Boston. Either get *him* to call *me*, or maybe you could give me a call as soon as he has something. *Anything*, Karen. I'm beginning to get the feeling that all's not right here; that something is terribly wrong . . ." I was on the verge of telling her about Moyne's post. "I love you, Karen." I rang off. There was no point worrying her more.

Twenty minutes earlier and I could have happily laid in the gutter and slept for twelve hours.

Now the energy was pumping again, adrenalin coursing through my veins. The evening was much cooler now, almost chilly. I threw a pullover over my shoulders and tied it around my neck. The dusk was heavy, with an orange-tinted sunset disappearing fast over the peaks of the Tramuntana. Music filled the bar now. Barry White and Teddy Pendergrass. Soulful songs with a thumping beat. Voices were loud and garrulous.

As soon as the sun had vanished behind the sharp reeks of the mountains, darkness began to reclaim Es Capdella, making it smaller, its outer reaches invisible. I could hear the crickets, and a monotonous, almost mesmerising, whistle that comes with the night-time in such a remote setting. I was no longer sure of my bearings. My host had been talking about me to the men at the bar. They had glanced around a few times, much drunker now I could see. She said something and they laughed.

I had been hanging around here now for two hours. I wondered about Ivan Moyne, and how he might have spent that time. A part of me was feeling sorry for him, wanting to forgive him and go home. He had been a brilliant and intellectual medic when I knew him; a bit erratic, but that simply exemplified his brilliance even more. I knew I shouldn't be thinking like this or feeling this way about the man. I resolved to try not to question what I was doing any longer. I decided I would remind myself, whatever lay ahead of us that night, that I was doing it for Maura Ferris and her son.

49

For someone advocating the benefits of low profile, Josh Traynor's arrival scared me.

He pulled up outside the terrace in an angry sleek black Audi Quattro convertible, the leather top folded back, the sound of Spanish dance music blaring. At first I didn't recognise him, until he yelled at me.

"Teacher, I hope you're not drunk!"

I cringed. The four men at the bar left their drinks to inspect this fifth entity, this quintessential love machine that epitomized Josh Traynor. I assumed he had hired it.

For some reason I expected him to tell me the plan was off; that Ivan Moyne had fled the island, or had disappeared.

He apologised for the delay. "I hope you haven't been waiting long." His grin told me two things. He'd been drinking heavily and he knew I'd been waiting for almost three hours.

"I got a couple of friends. They're gitanos. They've been watchin' Moyne's house all day."

"What are *gitanos?*" I asked, stifling my anger.

"*Gitanos* are Spanish gypsies, Teacher. They do anything for money. You pay the right price they'll stand on their heads and shake their maracas."

"How do you know all this?"

"I've been planning this trip for a little longer than you think, Teacher." He waved into the bar. *"Maria!"* he shouted. *"Hello, my love. Cómo estás?"* He blew her two kisses.

"What the fuck do you mean?" I shouted.

"I mean I've been doin' a little bit of scouting around. That's all, Teacher. Nothing to worry about. I'm with you all the way. Know what I mean?"

"No, I don't!" I felt confused and the feeling scared me. I grabbed his wrist as he waved to Maria. "What the fuck do you know that I don't?"

"Not an awful lot, Teacher." He pulled his arm away. "I just thought it might be a good idea to come over for a couple of days and observe the good doctor's movements."

"Why didn't you tell me?"

"Well, and please don't take this personally, you're a little highly strung. Highly strung people scare the fuck out of me. So I thought it might be better to come over here alone initially and lay the groundwork. Once that was done, it made your job a whole lot easier."

Maria called to him and laughed.

"Two beers. Rapido. Then we vamos!" He waved to one of the men at the bar. He stared at me. "You're looking at me as if I got three fuckin' heads." His eyes were bloodshot. His cheeks and nose were burning red.

"You've been drinking," I said calmly.

He laughed hysterically. "Of course I've been drinking, Teacher. You can't very well set foot in this holiday paradise and *not* treat yourself to a few drinks and a bit o'blow." His speech was slurred.

I grew more afraid with each sentence. "A few drinks is one thing, Josh. But you're drunk. *Pissed!* You look like you've been hammering the stuff all fucking day." I slapped the table.

"Hey, Teacher, calm down. I don't want people talking unnecessarily around here. I don't want these locals suspecting anything."

"Suspecting? For God's sake, Josh, it'd be a bit difficult to expect them to behave like nothing has happened when you arrive in that all-singing, all-dancing passion wagon, for Christ's sake!"

He looked proudly at the car. "Do you like it, Teacher?"

I nodded reluctantly. "It's OK, I suppose."

"Tell you what, when all this is finished you can take it out on the road and drive it to your heart's content." He raised his hands and lifted the beers off Maria's tray. *"Gracias."*

"Gee thanks, Josh. That's just what I always wanted. Listen, you dumb fucker, I didn't come all this way to drive your little sports car. I don't want to be here. I must have been fucking mad to let you talk me into this."

"Excuse me, if I remember rightly, *you talked me* into getting involved in this."

"Who the fuck owns that car?" I said, pointing.

"A friend."

"Where does this *friend* live?"

"Here. He's been doing a little bit of work for us. Managed to find out where Moyne lives. That's kinda helpful, isn't it?"

"Josh, we are not some kind of government agency, OK? We are *not* Interpol. We are not working for a private investigation bureau, all right? If you ask me, we are way out of our depth on this one. There's nothing to stop Ivan Moyne calling the Spanish police once we knock on his hall door and having us arrested for trespass and harassment. Has that crossed your mind at all?"

He nodded and drank without stopping until the litre glass was empty. *"Maria! Again, my love!"* He ran his hand through his hair and put back on the baseball cap. "Here, hurry up. It's your round."

I pushed my glass across the table. "Here, you can drink this one as well." I stood up and secured my bag across my chest. "So you're tellin' me that it's a coincidence that you've got a friend here, twenty minutes' drive from the man we've been searching for, and he just happens to tell you within the past fortnight that Moyne lives here?" I stepped out onto the street, into the cool night air.

"Wait a minute, Teacher. Where are you goin'?"

"Back to Palma, and out of here on the first available flight to anywhere remotely close to where I've just come from. In short, Traynor, as far away from you as I can get!" I walked away from the terrace.

He followed me. *"Dave, wait! Please!"*

I could hear him behind. I turned around. It was the first time Josh Traynor had ever called me by my first name. Hearing it shocked me. It sounded almost obscene.

"Don't go, please. I need you. I can't do this on my own. Look, the car belongs to a friend of mine. He's a Spanish waiter, lives in Paguera. I met him on holidays here years ago. He's the guy I was talking about, the one who located Moyne for us. He'd seen him a few times in the bar where he works in Paguera. Really, Dave, it's the truth. I *swear*! You'll have to believe me. *Please?*"

I thought about what he had just said. I thought of the documents I was carrying. I could see Maura Ferris back at home, wondering how we were getting on, and Aidan in his wheelchair. "OK. But you're gonna sober up *now!* Hear me? Your bar ladyfriend in there is gonna pour so many espressos down your fuckin' throat, you're not gonna need that sports car you'll be able to move so fast. Hear me?"

Josh nodded. "I hear you." He held out his hand. "Friends?" he said sheepishly.

The notion made me laugh. We shook hands and walked back to the table on the terrace.

50

My mobile phone rang just as Josh Traynor was excusing himself to go and pay the men's room a visit. He glanced back momentarily then disappeared behind the bead curtains beside the bar.

The voice on the other end was deep, with the rich, familiar tone and pleasant twang of a middle-aged man from Raleigh, North Carolina.

Dan McKenzie introduced himself politely as if he'd just called to my front door and was about to sell me a Bible. "I'm looking for David Freeman." His voice was authoritative, an obvious sense of urgency in place of its normally relaxed tone.

"Hi Dan, this is Dave here. Thanks for calling me back." I expected him to ask how I was getting on in Ireland. He swept past that, his voice louder now, determined and unbending.

"Dave, I've been talking to Karen."

I checked the time. Almost seven.

"We've done a check on this company in Texas. Franklin Global?" He waited.

I repeated the name. "That's right."

"Dave, exactly where did you come across this company?"

"On an envelope. I found four envelopes . . . well, I didn't exactly *find* them. They were addressed to a man I'm looking for here." The vigilante was beginning to break out in me again. I felt foolish.

"What *man?*" McKenzie asked.

"His name is Moyne. He's . . . *was* a doctor in a small town where I used to teach up to ten years ago." I could tell I had lost McKenzie. I was going to have to start at the very start for any of this to make sense. Even then, I wondered would it, since it wasn't making much sense to me anymore.

"Karen said you needed information. *What* information? I've got half a dozen computer terminals at my disposal. If you can tell me what you're looking for I can check if any names come up here. I don't think you're gonna have luck with Franklin Global though." McKenzie said, savouring his statement in that grand, embellished voice that I frequently wished was my own.

"Why?" I asked.

I could hear his unsteady breathing, and his muttering growl, as if he was reading off information to himself that he was unearthing. "Well, I don't have too much on them at the moment but I've got a pal who retired last year from the Bureau. He's gonna make a few calls and get back to me. All I can tell you at the moment is that Franklin Global are at the centre of an FBI investigation. They ceased trading years ago. Three of their directors were arrested and released on bail pending trial, subject to further State evidence. So far, not a lot's been happening with a court hearing because their main man, a multi-millionaire called Alfred Roizen, was gunned down leaving his two daughters to school one morning. Roizen appears to have known the FBI were onto something so he managed to get rid of a lot of the evidence the Bureau needed to nail these people. And since Roizen is now dead, the case remains in limbo. In fact . . ."

McKenzie was muttering into the phone again, reading information from the screen in front of him.

" . . . Sorry, Dave. I shouldn't really be talking over the phone like this. Who were the letters addressed to?"

"Doctor Ivan Moyne."

He noted the name. "OK, I'll call you back. I'm not sure how long it's gonna take my Bureau buddy to come up with information. He might not have anything when he calls back. He's gotta check to see if one of his understudies is on duty today. If he is, he gets access to the FBI hard drive. If he's not on duty, you get nothing, my friend."

I thanked him and was about to say goodbye when he interrupted.

"Dave, if you don't mind me asking you, what the fuck are you doing in Spain the week before Christmas?"

"I'm looking for the man I just mentioned. Ivan Moyne."

"What did he do that's taken you all the way to Spain to find him?"

"I think he may have been responsible for the killing of four young teenagers."

"Murder?"

"No, most likely manslaughter. I doubt he intended killing them when he did what he did."

"What did he do?"

Dan was a cop again. I could hear the drive and the lust for information in his questions. He wanted to hear more. It would have to wait for some night when I was home and all of this was consigned to the past. "I can't tell you now, Dan. I don't have time. I'll explain it all when I see you."

"I'm looking forward to that, Dave. Are you on your own there?"

"No. I've got an old friend from home. Well, he's American, but he's been living in Ireland close to where I spent my time teaching. That's how we know each other. He's a journalist. He did most of the hunting and tracking for me in this case. Actually it was he who found out that Ivan Moyne lives in Spain. That's why we're out here."

"What's this journalist's name?" Dan asked.

"Traynor. Josh Traynor."

"Where in the States is he from?"

"I think he said Nebraska. I can't be too sure about that. He told me about fifteen years ago."

"How come he came to Ireland?" Dan asked.

"Said he'd come over to check on his ancestry. He reckoned his grandmother was from Tipperary. He came for a fortnight. And stayed forever. You know the way it is. He's hoping to write a bestseller and get rich. Usual story."

"Has Karen got a photograph of him?" Dan said.

It seemed like a strange question. "Why?"

"Oh, just wondering. I'd just like to get a look at this guy."

"Why?"

"Why not?"

There was silence.

"She might have, though I doubt it. If she doesn't, the people he works with at the local newspaper should have plenty of them on file. I'm sure they could scan one and mail it."

"Great. I'll call Karen back right away and get her to set it up right now. Don't worry. It's just something we regularly do. He's probably harmless enough. We get told to do these things. It's part of the training, I suppose. Most Yanks love going to Ireland. They all believe they've got some Irish blood in their veins. It's just a bit unusual for them to stay on there. I don't know that many of them do. I'll get back to you as soon as I have something."

Josh was making his way back to the table slowly, watching me.

"Who was on the phone?" he asked.

"The guy who's looking after my shop back home in the States."

"What did he want? Not bad news, I hope?"

"No. Just wanted to know when I'd be back."

"What'd you tell him?"

"Couple of days." I finished my beer.

"At the most. You're gonna be a hero after tonight, Teacher. When we get this business wrapped up, every newspaper in Ireland is gonna have you splashed across its front page. You'll be the toast of every school in Ireland." He laughed and raised his glass.

I smiled at the notion. I couldn't help thinking of what Dan McKenzie had just said: 'I don't know that many of them do . . .' I placed my glass on the table. "What made you stay in Ireland?"

The question caught him unexpectedly. He smirked. "What the hell makes you wanna ask a question like that on a night like this?"

I shrugged. "Curiosity, I suppose."

Josh looked out into the darkness, listening to the sound of the crickets bleating, and the barking dog somewhere in the distant blackness. "I'm not sure. I guess it was a hunch." He stared at me. "Did you ever get a feeling like that, a kind of a sense of belonging? Something in your head, and your heart, tells you you've found your castle? That this is where I belong? Something like that." He shook his head. "Any more million-dollar questions, Teacher?"

"Where are you from?" I said bravely.

"I told you fifteen years ago, when I first met you. Western Nebraska. Hillbilly country. I came from a small scenic little place called Kimball, two-horse town in the Lodgepole valley, miles from nowhere. Any one who had any sense once they found Interstate 80 just kept on drivin'. I've tried to forget the name but it keeps comin' back to me." He stared at me suspiciously. "Know what I mean, Teacher? I'm sure after what you've been through back in Claddagh Mines that you've tried to forget the name. But I guess it kinda haunts you forever. Don't it?"

I shook my head. "I try not to let it. Why can't you forget about your little two-horse town, Josh?"

He raised his glass and finished the beer. "Lots of reasons, Teacher. But you don't need to know them. I got in with the wrong people, and I'm not talking about the local Baptist choral society either. I guess we all have things to be ashamed of. Some of us are lucky enough to be able to forget about them. Some of us get haunted." He stood up and pushed the chair back. "Time to go to work, Teacher. If we sit around here for much longer talking this bullshit, we're gonna miss the hen that laid the golden egg."

He walked away towards the car. I watched him. "Josh," I called after him.

"Yes?" He turned around.

"Why are you so keen to catch Ivan Moyne?" I said.

He grinned and tossed the car keys into the air, catching them and throwing them higher. "One hell of a story, Teacher. I'm a journalist. I survive by hunting people down, then splashing their names across the front page of my paper. I've never seen a page to refuse ink." He turned and, placing his left hand on the door of the Audi, jumped into the driver's seat. He started the engine, revving it hard, and waited.

51

"Are we far from his house?" It was all I could think of to ask.

"About two miles," he shouted. He raised the can of beer to his lips. The beer trickled down over his chin onto his neck as he slurped from the can. He was still extremely drunk and, consequently, unpredictable; and he hadn't told me everything, which led me to believe that I knew nothing. For that reason I was petrified. The wind lifted his cap and blew it into the back seat. He laughed.

I checked the speedometer. Ninety kilometres. Sixty miles per hour on a dingy little dirt track with no respect.

In the space of ten minutes I had come to hate the man I was sitting beside. I prayed for my phone to ring, watching the illuminated green hands of the clock in the centre of the dashboard. Quarter to eight. *Ring!* I kept saying over and over as the cool wind swiped my breath away and left me gasping in the cold night air to stop my heart from pounding. Then I heard, the familiar beeping ring. I grabbed the phone from my pocket and pressed *yes*. "Hello," I said, reassuring myself that I wasn't sounding too eager.

It was Karen. Her voice, high-pitched and excitable, was breaking up as we bumped and ground over the rough terrain in the foothills of what I presumed was Es Puig Batiat. I could hear water through my other ear. A river, the Barranc de So N'Alfonso was racing wildly to my left in the same direction as the car.

I needed to sound calm, no point shouting at her that I couldn't hear her. "Hello," I said again, more solidly this time. "Karen, can you hear me?" The signal seemed to improve for a short moment.

"Dave! Where are you? Dave? You're not safe . . ." she had been screaming down the phone. It wasn't all she had said, but it *was* all I could make out. The line went dead. I swallowed calmly and pressed my back hard against the plush leather seat.

Josh took his eyes off the windy road. "Everything OK?" he asked.

I nodded. "Karen. She was just wondering how we were getting on. The line was very bad. I lost her just as she was asking for you . . ." I looked at him quickly to check to see if he had been convinced by my lie.

He smiled. "How is she?"

"Fine."

I'd lied again. Another lie that might give me a little more time to decide what I should do. But there was no point in trying to make a decision if I didn't know the factors determining the necessity to change the plan. "Fucking bullshit!" I said into the wind that was spraying gritty dust into my eyes and against my skin, and the flying nits that had been drawn to the lights of the car, before realizing that death was imminent.

The whole night was going to be one big lie. I knew that. I no longer believed we were here to find Ivan Moyne.

I willed the phone to ring again, at whatever cost. I watched the bushes and the branches of the trees as they lashed the sides of the car on this narrowing road that climbed, turned, descended again and weaved its way gradually upwards to where we seemed level with a full moon and a clear, starry sky.

Far below, I watched the lights of Es Capdella and the fluorescent San Miguel and Dorada beer signs hanging out over the front of the terrace of Bar Nou. It looked like an aerial photograph now, as if we were flying over the town at five thousand feet. I decided that throwing myself from the car might not be such a good idea.

Despite the unsafe surface and the bad visibility caused by the mist that crept out over the hedgerows and wild shrubbery, Josh accelerated, as if unaware of the steep drop to our left. "Slow down, Josh. We're not in that much of a hurry," I said cheerfully.

He ignored me.

The road in our wake had grown bright. I looked behind, through the dust the Audi had kicked up, at a set of headlights. The full beams seemed to swerve to avoid the stones and the dirt we were throwing back into its direct path.

"Are they with us?" I asked.

Josh shrugged. "I doubt it. I wasn't talking to anybody. I've got a couple of guys ahead, waiting for us."

A couple of guys.

I felt a surge of adrenalin. The fight or flight syndrome. I was being given a choice to match my fear. Stay and confront whatever it was that Josh had planned. Or ask him kindly to stop and turn around. Drop me back to Bar Nou. I'll call a taxi from there. Sorry for the change of heart! The words didn't really fit the situation. I took out the bent box of Marlboro Light I had bought during my drinking binge the previous week. I had three left. I searched for my lighter while offering Josh one.

"I hate those cigarettes. They give you dimples you've gotta drag so hard," he shouted.

I'd left my lighter behind on the table at Bar Nou.

Instinctively, I leaned forward and pulled open the glove compartment, expecting a smoker to have a lighter, or a box of matches. I wasn't quite prepared for what fell out onto the floor of the car and rested between my two shoes.

Carefully, I picked up the gun. It was a standard

Smith and Wesson, .38 calibre. I rested it in the palm of my hand and looked at Josh.

He put up his hand. "Careful, Teacher. That thing's loaded. One bump on the road an' I'm history. You could blow my fuckin' head off pointin' it at me like that." He grabbed it off me and shoved it precariously between his legs, the barrel pointing out front.

I was speechless. "What's that for?"

"Any unwanted meddlers," he said, without taking his eyes off the road.

"Like who?"

He didn't answer.

"Where did you get that?"

"From a friend. He's a local policeman. He let me borrow it for the evening. He's not on duty so there's no problem. I just gotta make sure I can account for any bullets I use."

"Use *how?*" I said in disbelief. I imagined Moyne to be a frail, old man now, not someone who might put up such physical resistance that his captors might need firearms to arrest him.

Josh spoke methodically. "I don't know what surprises he might pull this evening, Teacher. He lives in a nice house. I hear he has protection from time to time. I don't know whether his security have a licence to carry firearms. We're simply taking as many precautions as we can think of." He looked across at me and slapped my knee. "Cheer up. It's nearly all over." He laughed.

The car behind us stayed at a safe distance to avoid

the stones and small rocks I could hear banging against our own undercarriage before flying into the air behind us.

Just as my mind went into overdrive, my mobile phone rang. It was five to eight. Five minutes ahead of our rendezvous arrangement. It was Dan McKenzie.

"Dave. Can you talk?"

"I'm fine, yeah. Any news," I said buoyantly, trying to disguise the nature of the conversation. Josh watched the road ahead. I could tell he was listening hard.

"Is Josh Traynor with you at this precise moment?" Dan asked, each word separate and emphasised. I could detect the tension in his voice. "Just answer yes or no."

"Yes."

"Are you in a car?"

"Yes."

There was an eerie silence for a moment that felt like an hour. Then he spoke even more slowly. "Dave, my friend. You are up shit-street. I suggest you find a way to get out of that car and as far away from the individual you are with as quickly as possible, preferably without his knowledge. Think you can do that?"

My mind was going into shock. I was sweating hard. All I could snatch from the conversation was "shit-street". I felt like I was holding a conversation with Mission control at the Kennedy Space Centre and I had just been told my rocket was about to burn up on re-entry into the earth's atmosphere. "What's up?" I was just about managing to keep up the façade.

Josh Traynor, sensing something was wrong by the sudden change in my voice, stopped the car. His eyes flitted between the rear-view mirror and me. Then he grabbed my arm. I almost shat myself.

"I'm gonna catch a quick smoke, Teacher. We're a little ahead of ourselves so if you wanna take your time on that phone call, there's no problem." Josh nodded and got out, moving away towards the front of the car. I could feel my heart pound simply by the twitches in my fingertips. The shirt I'd been wearing all day was stuck to me and smelled of sweat.

52

Mental torture is impossible to analyse. Yet, by its nature, its effects seem logical in their outcome. The harder you squeeze, the more you'll understand.

The critical faculty of the consciousness, the gateway to the human mind, is tricked into believing that, for being on its best behaviour, it will be rewarded. It's been duped. On bypassing the conscious barrier of realisation, the torture is then slowly inflicted onto the unconscious mind, where it leaves its scars and its effects, often for the rest of the individual's life.

I believe I was emotionally tortured ten years ago. I still bear the scars of that night, when my daughter arrived home in great distress; when my wife shut me out of their lives by closing her bedroom door in my face; when that same wife whom I married, assuring her of my unconditional love, stabbed me and forced me to lie.

Often these scars remain buried so deeply, the conscious mind forgets the incidents ever happened. And then, just when you least expect it to happen, an abreaction occurs.

An abreaction is the reliving of an emotionally traumatic event that occurred some time in the past. I say reliving, as distinct from recounting, as it's usually accompanied by visible emotional signs, as if it's happening for the very first time.

As I sat in the car that night listening to Detective Inspector Dan McKenzie, I found myself crying. Not because I was afraid; for some reason which defies me to this day, I was not afraid – not even slightly.

Tears streamed down my face onto my shirt as I forced myself to concentrate on the ordeal that seemed to be unfolding before me with every word this policeman spoke. I watched the glow of Josh Traynor's cigarette in the soft, mild night air: its bright red tip gave his face a chilling blush, then nothing. We were in total darkness now.

"No lights," Josh urged. "Locals around here get suspicious when cars stop in the dark." He shouted to the driver of the car behind, "Kill the lights!"

The darkness was supreme apart from the sporadic glow from his cigarette.

"Dave, can you hear me?" Dan McKenzie shouted.

His voice sounded weirdly uncommon to me now, as if I had been listening to the talking clock giving me information that seemed to change with every new line, details I couldn't assimilate as quickly as he was delivering. He'd spoken about Josh Traynor explaining how troublesome his childhood had been. I wasn't interested in his childhood. I wanted to know about the man who was standing twenty feet in front of me, with the handle of a gun jutting out of his jacket pocket.

"OK," McKenzie said. He took a deep breath. "I hope you're ready for this," he muttered under his breath. I heard him whether he'd intended me to or not. "Traynor's real name is Joe Taylor. He's fifty-two, divorced three times. We're not sure whether or not he's got kids. He's from Des Plaines, Illinois. A garage mechanic."

"He says he's from Kimball, in western Nebraska."

"He would. He's a pathological liar. That's according to the judge that tried him in court. And that wasn't yesterday. The police have him on their invitation list for a long, long time, Dave."

"Cut out all this crap, Dan. Why does the FBI have a record on this bloke?"

"Because he broke out of prison and they managed to chase him across five states before he disappeared under their very eyes. *Vvrooom!* And he was gone."

"What was he in prison for?"

"He was serving life for murder."

The word made me press the phone hard against my ear to stop it from falling out of my hand. It echoed in my head. My limbs felt numb. *Murder*. I watched him in front of the car, kicking up the dirt, tossing stones about with the tip of his boots, hands in pockets, whistling, occasionally stopping to check on little night-time noises. *Murderer*. Then he turned and walked away, into the darkness, until all I could sense was the sound of his footsteps. Then nothing.

"Dave?" McKenzie was raising his voice again.

"Yeah, I'm here," I whispered. "What happened?"

"Bank robbery. Turned nasty. He dragged a security guard outside. Held him hostage until he'd managed to get a woman and her kid out of their car. Then he shot the security guard and the woman. Ten-month-old baby survived."

My mind was trying to visualise. For some reason I still couldn't connect the man in front of me, stamping out his cigarette butt, with the psychopath Dan McKenzie was describing. "When did this all happen?" I asked.

"Almost twenty years ago. A little place called Chevy Chase. He lived there for a while, in Maryland."

I thought for a moment I was listening to a Showbiz Weekly update.

"Seemingly a storeowner seems to think he was just passing through. He'd picked up some supplies and mentioned to her that he was gonna have to get some more money. He asked her if there was a bank close by. She pointed across the street. Next thing she realises he's draggin' this elderly security guard out onto the street. He couldn't reach his own car so he picked on this young mother who was strappin' her young kid into his baby seat. When she went to try and rescue the kid, he shot her. The security guard tried to stop him. He shot him too. He stopped just outside town and left the baby sitting in a trashcan in a bus shelter."

Silence.

Random words flashed in my mind. With each flash my heart thumped. I watched him, trying to imagine him stretching his arm, holding out the gun, screaming and yelling. The picture seemed to change. Josh would never have screamed and yelled. He would have had a nickname for the security guard by the time he shot him. He might have smiled as he aimed. A quick observation followed by a smart remark. He never would have screamed and yelled.

McKenzie was still talking. It was more like a news report now. The cop had broken into law enforcement lingo. Words like *apprehended* and *vehicle* and *pursuit* were drifting in on top of the vision of Josh Traynor, or Joe Taylor, putting another one into the security guard as he lay lifeless on the ground.

A sudden jolt brought me back to the present. Traynor was walking back towards the car.

"I gotta go," I said quickly.

"Not yet!" McKenzie said. *"I need to tell you more!"*

"See ye later," I said, changing my tone to a cheerful one. The phone died. The panel of numbers remained luminous for a few seconds. Then came the total darkness. Jesus Christ.

"Who was that?" Josh asked, impatiently.

"My mother," I said. I cringed. The first reflex instantly

476

became the first words out of my mouth faster than my mind could stop them.

"Jesus, can your mother not find a more appropriate time to phone?" Josh laughed. "Did you tell her what we're up to here?"

"Of course not!" I wanted to give the impression that I found his question funny. He didn't laugh. We were moving again. He waved to the car behind, and its occupants who had sat quietly behind me all the time I'd been speaking to McKenzie, to take the lead and move ahead of the black Audi.

"So what were you talking about that took so long?" The tone in his voice sounded slightly hot-tempered.

I couldn't think of a suitable alibi. "Oh, you know what mothers are like. They just talk as long as you keep giving them space. She wanted to know why I hadn't called her in three weeks. I suppose they worry about us."

"Do you often talk to dead people?"

I looked at Josh. He was staring now. He looked back at the road and slowed down. "Your mother is dead," he said, almost reverently. "You told me ten years ago your mother died one year before your father."

"Did I?" It was all I could say. Confusion was fogging my mind. McKenzie's conversation . . . the night Molly came home daubed in green paint . . . her mother screaming at me like she did the night I stuffed a white towel into the hole in my chest caused by the broken bottle she had stabbed me with . . .

My mouth was dry. A pounding headache had started. My eyes felt like they were swimming with the sickening motion of the car and the way the road bounced up and down on two levels with each bump Josh drove through at high speed. I could hear the metal exhaust walloping against the stony road surface. "Did I?" I heard myself saying it again. My voice felt distant now.

"You're lying to me, Teacher. Your mother is *dead!* Who was on the phone?" he shouted.

"A friend." It took all my energy to say that. Then I leaned out over the car door and vomited into the wind that whipped my hair and cooled my flushed face.

53

Cold drops of rain fell on my face, sporadic at first then heavier and more consistent. I felt reclined, lying flat. The seat I lay on felt awkward and uncomfortable. I had been dreaming pleasant dreams, walking along the shore and climbing the foothills of the multicoloured cliff face below Gay Head light, on the west end of Martha's Vineyard, on a warm spring morning. Molly held one of my hands. Karen's arm was around my back, her hand resting on my back pocket. We were all laughing, then chasing one another. Then I broke into a run. I ran faster. Without warning I became terrified. Something was chasing me. I could hear voices. Molly was screaming. Karen was urging me to run faster. Their voices faded and disappeared.

The wave behind me grew bigger, like a huge wall suddenly about to collapse. The water felt solid and heavy as it dragged me backwards. I fell. Water filled my ears and my nose. I couldn't breathe. The foamy wash stung my eyes. I couldn't see. Everything got darker. The pressure in my lungs and in my head crushed me until I could move no longer. I opened my mouth. It felt a bit calmer now. The pressure receded, bit by bit, until I felt at ease, floating. The water didn't feel so cold and heavy any more. Then blackness.

I'd sweated while I slept. My face felt damp and cold, like a fever.

The car was stopped. I was alone, lying on my back staring up at the blackness of the sky and its millions of stars – constellations and formations everywhere, brightest directly above my head. I shivered.

"You OK, Teacher?"

I couldn't place Josh's voice for a moment. It came from behind the car. I listened. I could hear him talking. Some words of Spanish, mostly English. I tried to sit forward but each time I raised my head, it pounded me with pain.

I listened to a car approaching, its engine dying down, then silence again. Two doors closed almost simultaneously. Greetings exchanged. Fast-fire conversation between two native Spaniards.

"Esta todo listo para la grande sorpresa?"

It was Josh's voice. I recognised "grand surprise". The Spaniard replied. I couldn't understand what he was saying.

"Bueno, pires no dejamos que los clientes espereen," Josh said. My mind played with words I was hearing that I didn't understand.

Footsteps.

Josh looked down at me, lying on the reclined passenger seat. "Did you have a good sleep, Teacher?"

"Yeah. I feel like I've been run over by an express train. What happened?"

"I slipped a little pill into your beer earlier on. I reckoned you were gonna get a bit excitable. I just thought an hour's kip would do you good." He waited, watching me watching him. "Are you getting' up? We've got a bit of work to do."

I sat forward slowly and adjusted the seat to give my back some support. Two men, locals, I guessed, stood at a distance. The dimmed headlights of their car behind them made it difficult to see their faces clearly. They moved forward slowly then stopped. They stood almost solemnly, almost out of respect. My vision was blurring. Were there two cars . . . or three?

The man on the left turned side-on to say something to Josh. I could feel the shock as I recognised him: it was my taxi driver from the airport, Domingo. He spoke in Spanish. Josh appeared to understand. He waved his hand, pointing to an old lopsided gate to the right of the car. He kept urging them to keep their voices down. At one stage, he almost performed a dance, while emphasising the importance of complete hush, as he put it.

"What are we supposed to be doing now?" I asked.

"His house is just around that bend. In five minutes one of these *gitanos* is gonna create a bit of a commotion. He's gonna knock on the front door and tell him his car has broken down. He's gonna ask Moyne if he can use his phone to call the breakdown unit. That way, he'll get into the house and check if Moyne is alone or not."

I was utterly confused now. I tried to recall my conversation with McKenzie, less than an hour ago. I was sure it had happened. Or was I imagining it? The sleeping tablet made my mind dull, my head heavy. My headache pounded away.

Just as I released the seat belt, my mobile phone rang.

Karen's voice sounded like a tape-recorded message replayed at twice its normal speed. I had to tell her to calm down and start again.

"Dave, you're in awful danger . . ." she kept saying.

"How do you know?" I asked three times, each time louder and more forceful, until she heard my question.

Josh stood beside me. When I looked up at him, he was grinning.

"Sharon T Jory . . ." Karen repeated the name three times.

"What about Sharon T Jory?" I yelled. I didn't care now who was listening. Josh was laughing quietly.

"It's an anagram! Sharon T Jory is Josh Traynor. Rearrange the letters . . . they're the same person. Josh wrote those articles about you ten years ago . . ."

The words, like the blood in my veins, seemed to sink lower and lower. I felt myself going cold, shivering, until my bones ached and my eyelids snapped shut. I opened my hand and just let the phone fall into my lap. Karen's voice was still screaming my name. It didn't matter. This horrible confusion was all beginning to make sense now. Then I remembered what Ingrid Moyne had said: "You should ask your friend, Josh Traynor. He should know a thing or two."

I looked up at Josh out of the corner of my left eye. His gun was only inches from the side of my face, so close I could smell the freshly greased chamber. It had been prepared and primed.

"You know something, Teacher? You're not half as clever as I gave you credit for. I expected you to suss out what was goin' on a long time back. You're a dickhead. Just like all those morons back in Claddagh Mines."

"How could I have done that?"

"Well, I have to compliment myself on that, all right. I mean, I left very few clues for you to pick up on. Didn't Ingrid Moyne tell you not to trust me? After all, she did say her husband *was* dead. Yet you chose not to believe her. Why was that, Teacher?"

"Because she had Alzheimer's. The day-care manager told me she had been hallucinating. Why shouldn't I believe a medical professional?"

"Ingrid Moyne seemed to be pretty much in control of her faculties if she was able to hand you over the file with those kids' charts in there. All the documented evidence you would have needed to testify against Ivan Moyne and get him a long, long stretch in the slammer,

I would have thought." He held out his hand. "Give me the files. It's the only reason I brought you out here, *dickhead*!" He took a cigar from his breast pocket and lit it. He was making perfect sense. Of course Moyne was dead. I believed that now. If only I had believed it forty-eight hours earlier. "Moyne told me she had them. He searched high 'n' low. Couldn't find them. He knew she'd always have something on him while she had them files. He never stopped goin' on about them. 'Have you got the files yet?' was all he ever asked me.

"Right back at the very start he asked me to get them. Now how the hell was I meant to do that? I eventually accepted that I might never get hold of them. But then you came along, stuck your big fucking nose into where it didn't belong. That really pissed me off when you got up on the altar and spoke to those people like that. You know, Teacher, some people just can't leave well enough alone, can they? I gave this a lot of thought. I really thought my number was up at one stage, that I was gonna have to pack my bags and disappear again. But then it all changed when I heard you'd located Ingrid. Her Alzheimer's was music to my ears. Once I knew you were visiting her, you became the perfect courier. I was laughing all the way to the bank.

"Let me show you something, Teacher." Josh sat into the car, careful to keep the gun half-trained. He turned the key and popped a CD into the player. He turned the volume up until the music filled the night-time air. Jackson Browne's voice lifted the lyrics into song.

"One of my favourite songs, Teacher. 'Tender is the Night.' I just love the words." He started to sing along. He looked at me and stopped. "And what exactly do these beautiful words tell you about life, Teacher? They must have something very wise to say to you, you being an academic type, of course. What do they say to you?"

I looked at him for a moment. "Nothing."

"*Nothing?*" He tutted. "One of the world's most prolific songwriters composes one of the most beautiful songs ever, and you say, 'Nothing'?"

"No. I'm not familiar with his music. I'm sorry."

"He says, '*I'm sorry.*' *Shit!*" He laughed. "Well, it doesn't really matter. You've got shit for brains. D'you know that? Hell, even *I'm* cleverer than you! You know how good that makes me feel, Teacher? Do you know what's wrong with you? You're too nice, and that's your downfall." He killed the sound. "What d'you think they might put on your tombstone, Teacher? Ever wondered? Those precious few words that everyone's gonna remember you by? Two or three lines of carved epitaph that will sum up your life for ever more: 'Here lies Dave Freeman, a kindly, generous man who loved to help others.' But then someone's gonna slip into that graveyard late one night and write in brackets, 'But where the fuck did that get him?'" He took the keys out of the ignition.

"What that song says to me is quite simple. Staring you in the face if you'd only fucking look! What it's saying is that no matter how damn much you think you're right, you are, in fact, wrong."

Domingo and his friend watched from a distance, hands in pockets. Occasionally they muttered remarks quickly to each other.

"Have you *any* idea, Teacher, just how much I *hate* you?"

I could feel the loathing in the depth of his voice and the hostility in his eyes.

"That song is all about a wimp, a man who just never wakes up to the fact that life doesn't give us what we want. If you want something you gotta change the shit that life's dealing you. That might mean that life's also gonna change for the people around you. But *fuck them!* That's what I always say. It's always been about lookin' after number one." He thumped his chest. "No one matters as much as me. Anyone gets in the way of that piece of wisdom normally gets moved out of the way with whatever it takes."

"You're full of *shit!*" I shouted. I stared at him. His eyes bulged. He aimed the gun. His jaws trembled as he straightened his arm and pointed it directly at my forehead.

"I should just kill you now. But that would spoil the little game I want to play." He lowered the gun slightly. I could see the lacrimation, the tears in the corners of his eyes. His nose was running; or was it sweat? He didn't appear to notice. His stare was intense, unbroken by the bark of a dog in the distance, somewhere in the valley below.

"Move in through the gate, slowly. One silly move and I'll happily shoot you in the back."

I turned and kept my hands behind my back. I walked behind Domingo and his friend. Domingo turned to face me for a few seconds. His expression seemed to be saying something. His stern frown scared me more that the sharp nudges I felt in my back as Josh pushed me on, harder and faster.

As my eyesight adjusted to the darkness, allowing for the full moon that had slipped behind the reek in front of me, I realised I was walking into a graveyard. I tripped, almost losing my balance, against a stump of an old tombstone. The cemetery was ancient and derelict. I could make out about fifteen, maybe twenty, graves, spread across a hilly field, surrounded by a low stone wall, broken in places. There was no sign of a church, just the tiny, flickering lights of a house in the distance.

"Keep moving," Josh said from behind.

I followed Domingo, watching his step, moving to the left, then the right, avoiding the potholes and broken memorials.

"Stop!"

We all froze. Domingo looked back at me. I turned to face Josh. He pointed the snout of the gun at a tombstone. It was newer, more recent, than the others.

"Read it!" he snapped.

I bent down and knelt. Josh handed me a torch. I shone the beam on the simple words, which retained their gold-embossment. The message was brief. It gave nothing away.

In memory of Joe Taylor
Rest in Peace.

I could hear McKenzie's voice. "His real name is Joe Taylor . . ." Karen's frantic words re-echoed in my head. *Sharon T Jory is an anagram for Josh Traynor.*

I decided to stay on my hunkers. Something told me it would be harder for him to shoot me in this position. While the bullet might strike, I would have a better chance of surviving such a hit. I was accepting that I was about to be shot. I looked up at him, shining the torch in his face. He held his free hand up to his cheek to shade his eyes from the glare. "How many names have you?" I said.

"As many as I want, Teacher. Let's see now. I guess I've used at least a dozen different names over the past twenty years. I've had four different passports, seven different social security cards, quite a few hairstyles, the occasional beard and moustache, which I despise; but then one had to accept whatever disguise proves most effective. Why, I've even dyed my hair blond!" He laughed heartily.

"Who's buried here?" I asked.

"The one and only, that eminent quack himself, *Doctor* Ivan Moyne."

"Why did you kill him?" I said.

He seemed shocked by my question. "Who told you I killed him?"

"You have a criminal record. An elderly security guard, a helpless mother, an ageing doctor . . . how many more people have you shot in the back, Josh?"

"Cowards shoot their victims in the back, Teacher. I shoot mine in the head." He held the gun to my face. "Right there, between the eyes. I love to watch their eyeballs roll upwards and back, then inwards until they're looking at each other, and then when they fall backwards, their hands and legs wobble and shake like they're doin' a bit of rock 'n' roll or something."

"You're insane."

"And you're a piece of shit. And I intend to lay you to rest tonight, Teacher." Josh nodded to his left, my right. "There's your little bed o'maggots over yonder. It's kinda nice and mulchy tonight so I expect you'll sink a foot or two. I'll need to come back in the morning and pat you down a good bit." He looked back at the Spaniards. "Let the games begin. Isn't that what one of those crazy Roman emperors used to say in the coliseum?"

"Yeah. And he was just as fucked up in the head as you are."

"I don't like it when you're smart, Teacher. So keep that big brainy mouth of yours *shut!* Hear me?"

"I hear you."

I looked across the small cemetery, where the light of the torch shone on the mound of fresh earth in the corner and the dark hole beside it. I shivered, but for some reason told myself that I wasn't going to die that

489

night. I didn't care what injuries I sustained, life was going to continue at any cost.

The two Spaniards were gone now. It was just me, kneeling at Josh Traynor's feet. If he expected me to beg for mercy, he was going to be disappointed. I could feel my heart starting to race, surging the blood into my cold hands and aching legs. I wanted more strength, I kept telling myself, willing my unconscious mind to drive energy into my limbs; energy like I had never experienced in my life. Physical control and mental concentration were all I could afford to focus on now, apart from the questions I needed to keep asking, stupid, mindless questions, in order to keep Josh Traynor, the pathological liar with the psychopathic tendencies, talking.

"You know something, Teacher, when I heard that you'd come back to Claddagh Mines, I wanted to take a gun to you immediately. All of those people back there who resented you setting foot in that place, I despised you more than all of them put together."

"You wrote those articles about me, didn't you? Sharon T Jory. That's you."

"Yep, that's me. I remember sitting in a pub the night the police were lookin' for young Owen Durkin. A local guy, pissed out of his mind, kept muttering that you'd beaten the crap out of the kid. I even hated you then. So I reckoned that I'd have to come up with some sort of pseudonym to protect our friendship. I didn't want you walking around thinking I hated you. I devised this name, Sharon T Jory, when I got back home that night. I wrote the article next morning. Then I got thinking. What if that clever teacher sees through my little anagram game? But you didn't! I *really* thought you would. But you didn't, did you?"

"I didn't hang around to read your pathetic little newspaper articles. You're just a small-town, small-minded fuck-wit, Josh. Or should I be calling you Joe? Or *Sharon?* Or would you like to tell me what other names people address you by, you fucked-up moron! I'd say the people of Des Plaines were glad to see the back of you."

He was silent for a moment. "Do you want to know why I was so disappointed when you came back, Teacher?"

"Why, Josh?"

"Because I was giving your ex-wife one."

I froze. "Jesus, you're pathetic. How low will you go to have the final say, Traynor?" This bastard had been bedding my wife. The pain cut through me like three broken ribs. But why did I feel anything like this? I hated the bitch. "I don't believe you, Josh."

He laughed. "I knew I'd get to you somehow, Teacher. I'm not lyin' either. I've been banging that woman of yours harder than a storm door in a hurricane. She is something else in bed, Teacher, quite incredible. Beddin' her is like trying to break in a wild horse."

I knew why he was doing it. He wanted me mad. Then he wanted me to cry and beg. Then he was going to shoot me. He wasn't going to get anything.

"I was fuckin' her brains out while you were down at that little school of yours bein' the perfect teacher." He laughed. "And you know something else? That little daughter of yours . . . I've met her a few times when I've been to Dublin. I took her to dinner a couple of times . . ."

"Lies," I shouted.

"I've been back to that nice, posh apartment of hers . . ."

"Lies."

"I've even stripped her down to her underwear and played with those cute little tits of hers and . . ."

"Lies!" I grabbed his foot, but he unhooked himself and jumped back. He couldn't stop laughing. "I knew that would do it for you, Teacher. She's got such a cute little ass. Have you ever tried that with your ex-wife? She loves it from behind . . . and as for the screams! I thought one of the neighbours might call the fire brigade one morning she was screaming so much. And you know what she said to me afterwards? She said, 'Josh Traynor, you've got stamina. I wish you could pass on some of that magic to my husband.' Well, Teacher, I was shocked by her honesty."

I squeezed my eyes tightly closed, kept thinking of Karen and Molly. In my mind's eye I was leaving this all behind me and going home to Martha's; I was walking the beach with Karen, proposing to her. Now I was marrying her. We're having our own children: a brother and sister for Molly . . .

I let these thoughts flood my mind, forcing the

insulting shit-tactics this lunatic was firing from every direction to wash over me.

"What do you want to ask me, Teacher? You were always full of questions when we knew each other all those years ago."

"Why do you hate me so much?" I said.

"Why? Good question. But then, you always *did* ask good questions. I hated you because you were more intelligent that me. I could never have been as clever as you, and that always hurt me. I always felt inferior in your presence. You see, Teacher, they taught me a lot in prison. Not only did they explain to me that I was a compulsive liar, but that I was also an evil deviant. *Imagine* what that did to my self-esteem! I was gutted. They were basically telling me that I was no better than a piece of shit. Well, I decided I wasn't gonna hang around there too long. I like being with positive people. Prison officers are not really the most positive people in the world. Anyway, to cut a long story short, I was privileged to meet up with you. You seemed like a nice intelligent, modest type of person. But eventually you started to give me a major pain in my ass. So when the incident with Owen Durkin happened, I thought it would be beneficial to capitalise on it. I had no idea that I would be responsible for destroying your entire life and forcing you to be separated from your family and loved ones. Please forgive me, Teacher." He laughed in a cackling tone of voice. "I killed two birds with the one stone that day. I got rid of that little shit, Owen Durkin.

He let the air out of two of my tyres one night while I was attending a council meeting in the school. Not *one*, but *two* tyres. I was stranded and he just stood at a distance and called me names."

"What did he call you?"

"He called me a Yankee prick!"

I laughed, exaggerating my bellows. "He was right, Josh. You *are* a Yankee *prick!*"

The kick to my jaw felt like a brick hitting my face. I rolled onto my back, into the deep, dark, filthy hole, falling four or five feet.

I was lying in my own grave.

As I landed face down, earth toppled in on top of me. I smelled the musty, damp clay as it clogged my ears and my mouth, then my eyes and my nose. I scraped frantically at the soft, pasty muck, as it slowly rose up, inch by inch, and I fought for more breath.

I managed to turn myself around. My face ached. I could feel my jaw swelling. My chest was hurting again. I wiped the muck out of my eyes and stared upwards.

Josh Traynor looked down at me, surrounded by a pale, white light, silhouetting him from behind, giving him ghostly qualities. He pointed the gun at my balls. "Let me finish this story for you, Teacher. But first, I gotta do something . . ." He pulled the trigger. I jerked almost automatically. Before I heard the booming crack of the weapon, I could feel a searing pain cut through the flesh and bone of my leg and shoot upwards to my neck like an acute electric shock delivered with a hammer blow. With all five senses, I could feel the bones in my knee being destroyed in one split second. I could feel the warm urine soaking through my jeans, into the cold earth below me. I knew I was screaming with pain, but the intensity of my agony prevented me from hearing anything.

54

Freshly dug clay gives off a unique smell. It is a scent that causes the fear-emotion to go on its guard. Defence mechanisms, inherent deep within the unconscious mind, I believe, recognise the ultimate finality of life when confronted by certain signs. Clay is one of these signs. Apart from its life-nurturing properties, it is a symbol of death.

Clay represents the final resting place. It is the aftermath of physical death, when the power of the soul has become exhausted and the spirit has vacated the body like an old moth-eaten overcoat. The unconscious mind instinctively recognises the smell of freshly dug clay. Nothing could terrify me more than the smell of clay.

I lay in that hole, in the soft, cool rain, wiping the sticky muck from my face, trying to position my body in such a way as to lessen the piercing, scalding pain in my left leg. It was most bearable when I arched it and placed my foot on a rock I had found somewhere in that pit.

My entire body trembled uncontrollably. Spasms, like giant muscular jolts surged through me every couple of minutes, accompanied by secondary darts of pins and needles through my hands and right foot. Slowly my leg was losing all sensation. With every thumping beat of my heart, I could sense the gush of blood spewing out of the gaping wound in my swollen knee.

I was wet from the sweat. Or was it the rain? A ringing sensation in my left ear seemed to ease the red-hot pain that shot from my knee to my hip and up my back to my neck, which I could barely move now.

I couldn't see the blood, but I was aware now, physically, that I had lost a lot. More worrying was the fact that it seemed to be bleeding faster and more heavily now.

"Why did you do that?" I said, realising how much pain it took to talk, and how I seemed to bleed uncontrollably each time I moved anything, including my mouth.

"Because you left me with no choice, Teacher," Traynor said, almost sympathetically. He bent down and stretched out his hand. "Here, give me your arm," he said.

It seemed bizarre that the man who had just shot me was about to pull me out of my own grave only, I was certain, to shoot me again later.

Pain took over, searing hot agony. The spasms were torturous. I couldn't speak, nor was I aware of anything, couldn't see, while I moved in this fashion. My leg felt like it had exploded wide open and now there was very little left that I was familiar with.

Once out of the grave, he eased me backwards, laying me down on the soft, soaking wet grass. "You shouldn't have said those things. I wouldn't have shot you," he said apologetically. "Just remember who's holding the gun, Teacher."

"Yeah, sure," was all I could say. My mouth was bone-dry. I needed water. The rain had stopped just as quickly as it had started to fall. My eyes felt swollen, my skin cold and clammy. I knew I was in shock, dangerous if I didn't get treatment soon. Then it occurred to me again, what's the point? He's gonna kill me anyway. Maybe I'll bleed to death before he has a chance to bury me alive. "Are you gonna kill me?"

He shoved the gun into his trouser belt and placed both hands on his hips. "I guess I'm gonna have to, Teacher. Even if I don't, the hospital's a forty-minute drive from here. I don't think you'd make it. I reckon you'll be lucky to survive another thirty minutes with that hole in your leg. Anyway I'm too drunk to drive to Palma." He sat back against a small tombstone.

"So what are we going to do for the thirty minutes?" I said, trying to be sarcastic. I could feel my strength sapping with each deep breath I took. I crawled backwards until I could feel cold stone behind me. I pressed my back against it and stayed there. The moon was sitting opposite me, very low in the clear moonstone-blue sky. I guessed it must have been after nine.

"You decide, Teacher. I'm gonna be alive in thirty minutes so it makes no difference to me." He laughed and folded his arms.

"Did you kill Ivan Moyne?" I asked.

"Yes."

"And you knew all about the kids who died back home. You were aware that Moyne had prescribed Promoxidine to Aidan Ferris, weren't you?"

Traynor nodded again. "Yes."

"Why didn't you go to the police?" I was gasping for breath now. I knew I was dying. I was terrified.

"Because I saw an opportunity to make a lot of money. To give credit where credit's due, Ivan Moyne was quite a brilliant man. He was wasted in that little snots-ville town, call it what you will. He would have been better off in Harley Street, or in one of the city's universities. Jesus, reporting on the smalltown shit that came out of that neck of the woods used to make me sick with boredom. I can only imagine how brassed off Moyne used to be. The guy was a genius. He had the mind of an inventor, *a wizard*! It takes brains to invent medicine. Moyne *had* the brains. But . . ." Josh slapped his thighs, "we can all make mistakes. And in my language, that's OK!"

"What are you *talking* about? The man is a murderer. He experimented on five children with a drug that hadn't been sanctioned. The drug was not officially recognised. No official understanding of the side effects existed in any manual. It was only in the early stages of testing. *And he went and prescribed it? Jesus Christ!"*

"Calm down, Teacher. You won't even last half an hour if you keep ranting like that."

I sighed and tried to control my breathing to stop the shaking and ease the chronic pain. My chest and neck ached. I could barely move my hands and wrists. My leg was numb below the knee. "Are you going to just let me bleed to death?"

"Of course not. I'm going to shoot you again in a few minutes."

"So how did you manage to get involved with Moyne?" I was barely able to whisper now. I tried to conserve my energy for listening and remembering.

"Dougy Ferris, the guy who tried to beat the shit out of you that morning, he came to me one afternoon with this story. He claimed that the doctor was trying out a new drug on his young boy and that it was having some strange effects. The boy would be real quiet one moment. Next minute, he'd be having a seizure, screaming with the pain in his head. Then quiet again."

"And why didn't Ferris go to the police?"

"Because he got money. The day he came to see me he'd been drinking heavily. He was crying and ranting and cursing blue murder. He wanted to take his shotgun and go up to Claddagh Mines. He said he was gonna blow the fucker's head off."

"So what did you do?"

"I told him to be calm, that I'd sort something out. I told him I'd try and find out a bit more about this drug. So I did. I got on to a couple of contacts in Dublin. One of them is a vet. He lectures in the city. He called a couple of his friends and found out everything I needed to know."

"Which was . . . ?"

"Everything I could find out about Promoxidine. Gus Dalton has already filled you in on what that shit does if it gets into the bloodstream. Then I sat down and made out a little shopping list. Once I had that made out I went up to Claddagh Mines and sat in the doctor's waiting-room, waiting to see him." Josh laughed. "You should have seen his face when I said it to him."

"Said what?"

"I told him I knew all about the drug. I told him I knew he had administered it to a number of his patients, and that there had been rather nasty adverse effects, to put it mildly. And I gave him a choice."

"What was the choice?"

"That he could read all about it in a two-page special in one of the national newspapers, or he could give me half-a-million pounds to persuade me to keep my mouth shut forever."

"Why a half-million? Why not two million?"

"Clever question, Teacher. By modern-day standards, half-a-million's not a lot of money when you think about it. But take yourself back ten years. Wage packets are probably a third of what they are today. So ten years ago, half-a-million was quite a substantial sum. Anyway, I didn't want Moyne to go bankrupt; I just wanted enough to live comfortably and have a bit of fun."

"How did he react to your demand?"

"He almost had a heart attack, sitting in that big brown leather swivel-chair. Remember the one, Teacher, with the big tall straight back on it that came right up behind his head? First of all, when I told him I knew everything, he fell back. I thought he was gonna die on me, right in front of my eyes. Then he jumped forward and said, 'What do you want?' I knew we were in discussion mode then."

"Would you have printed the story?"

"Too fucking right I would have. I reckoned a story like that would have got me a job in *The Irish Times*. But let's face it, what's more enticing . . . a job, or half-a-million quid? Anyway, I was never gone on the writing. It was just a front. Something that stopped people from asking awkward questions."

"Did you escape from prison?" I asked.

"Yeah. Sixteen years ago. My lawyer wanted to appeal my case. He reckoned the sentence was too harsh. I got two life sentences, to run consecutively. That's rare, even by American standards. That means I would have been due for parole when I was one hundred and six!" He sniggered and wiped his nose. "I guess I should count myself lucky. At least it wasn't a capital punishment state; somewhere like Texas where they kill you by lethal injection. The humane killer, the State Governor once called it."

"That's too good for you, Josh." My body was convulsing now. I knew I was in deep shock. My vision was blurring. Josh was drifting in and out of focus. I was seeing two of him, then three. My eyelids felt so heavy. I rubbed my cold, wet fingers under them to keep them open, careful to keep the clay out of my eyes.

"What do you mean, *too good?*" he said indignantly.

"You're a psychopath, a nutter. You deserve to be tied to a railway track. Something that's nice and slow and painful; so that your victims can watch you dying real slowly, *real* painfully. Just like they did."

"Coincidence you should say that, Teacher. Because I'm actually sitting here doing just that; watching *you* dying real slowly. And if it's not painful enough . . ." He took the gun from his belt and pointed it down. "I could always shoot you in the other kneecap. That might balance the discomfort a bit, eh?"

I yelled at the very thought. *"No . . . please!"* I held out my hand, to shield myself.

He chortled. "I'm only kidding, pal." He put the gun back in his belt. "Now where was I? Ask me another question. I feel like I'm back in school and you're the teacher. Go on – ask me! I'm enjoying this."

"What happened to Moyne? Why did he leave Claddagh Mines?" I was slurring now, taking shallow breaths with every couple of words. The weakness was like a form of analgesic. Catalepsy was setting in, the final stage before unconsciousness and death. I tried to convince myself I was strong. But I knew my last breath was only a matter of minutes away.

"Moyne left Claddagh Mines eight years ago, almost two years after we ran you out of town. We kind of did the same to him. A lot of people knew he had been dabbling with strange medicine. No one was going to him with their petty little old-folk, small-mind conditions any more. All the hypochondriacs had found a new doctor in Thurles. Two of the four kids were seriously ill by that stage. So he just disappeared one morning. A local man rang me with the news. The house was empty. There was a *For Sale* sign up against the front wall. To the general populace of Claddagh Mines, Moyne had just vanished."

"And what about Ingrid?"

"She was already gone. She knew from the start he'd been dealing out shots of drugs he shouldn't have been. He got away with them. But then the Promoxidine thing broke. Moyne shut it off quickly by handing out big bucks to the families involved. They accepted the money and kept their mouths closed. I diverted attention away from it by printing a story about the toxic waste spill. The whole area fell for that one. By the time the various government departments had ridiculed any notion of a dangerous chemical spill, everyone had forgotten about the sick kids. But no one had forgotten about you. More importantly, no one was really interested any more in the kids who had died. Simple really, it meant they just kept pointing the finger at you any time someone mentioned 'the war'." He stopped and bowed his head, grinning and pulling his cap down low. "Then the good doctor's wife found out he was having an affair with Neasa."

I closed my eyes and my mind to what I had just heard. It had no effect now. I was drifting. Even the pain in my leg and hips had subsided. My head floated, almost pleasantly resting on a cushion. I felt like I was lying on a waterbed. While I could sense the different parts of my body, I couldn't physically feel anything. First Moyne, then Traynor. My wife was a slut. But I knew that anyway. I opened my eyes again and spent a few seconds slowly focusing. Josh seemed disappointed that his revelation hadn't delivered a harder blow. Right now, I didn't care about anything. I believed resolutely that I wouldn't feel the next bullet. That was if I lasted that long. I was almost dead and it felt strangely nice.

55

"What time is it?" I asked, barely audible. My voice had been reduced to a grating whisper. My vision was blurred beyond recognition now. My fingers were numb. My head pounded. My eyes were too sore to open, dry and sandy. I was left with my hearing and my sense of smell.

I was acutely aware of the sounds of the night. A gentle breeze in the trees behind the cemetery, amplified now in my shocked and frightened mind, sounded like giant waves crashing down on the sandy beach overlooking Nantucket in the dead of night. I was alone with the wind blowing from behind, watching the rollers begin their foamy race for the shallow waters, travelling diagonally, subsiding then building again.

My heart beat more slowly now, my breathing, hoarse and shallow and lazy. Somewhere in the distance, I could see an arc of light. I debated whether it was a passing car, or the start of whatever was waiting to greet me on the other side.

Was I dying? I asked myself.

A surge of warmth enveloped me, making my fingers and toes tingle. My heart seemed to slow even more. Endorphins, part of the body's natural defence mechanism, were coursing through my blood now to protect my body from having to endure further pain and discomfort.

I was starting to hallucinate.

Jack Lyons, my old science teacher was standing at a blackboard, close to the wall of the graveyard. He tapped a long, white stick of chalk on the table in front of him. *"Freeman, pay attention!"* he snapped.

I sat up straight. My pain was gone. I put my hands out, each side, to find a comfortable position and watched the lesson unfolding in front of me.

"Endorphins play important roles in controlling our emotional behaviours, such as those associated with pain, anxiety, fear and related affective states produced by pain and fear. Endorphins are the body's natural opiates; painkillers produced in the pituitary gland to protect us from dying of severe shock to the heart and brain . . ."

"Death is the inability of an individual organism to keep itself alive. Put simply, but inadequately, the point at which an organism ceases to be alive . . ."

He was wearing an Aran sweater. He had a beard and spectacles, black-rimmed. He spoke with an authoritative, yet kindly voice. He seemed to be stretching out his hand. I drew back, trying hard not to be touched. I didn't want to go yet.

He died five years ago. I remember being told in a letter. I couldn't remember who had written it.

Jack Lyons faded into the darkness. A jagged, broken-down wall stood in the place where his blackboard had been.

The moon was behind a packed, puffy cloud. I felt blind, apart from the glow of light that seemed to be coming from somewhere close to where I had imagined Jack Lyons to be. I squinted my eyes, trying to use as little of the iris and retina as I could, to preserve my visual strength. For what exactly I wasn't sure.

I could barely see beyond Josh now. He was still talking – mutterings and misgivings. Behind him, the glow was growing. The trees seemed to be coming alive with a shallow, embracing light, like the gentle, reassuring glow a fire might throw off from a great distance. It seemed to be getting nearer, each time I blinked and focused a little harder.

"What happened to Owen Durkin?" I said, unsure as to whether or not Josh could hear my voice. He did.

"That little shit! I was having a piss one night shortly after leaving your missus, in the cemetery. He jumped up wearing this spooky fucking mask that almost scared the shit out of me. I followed him back to the cemetery. I guess I overreacted. Found out then the little bastard had let the air out of my tyres."

"Who was with him?"

"Some skinny little kid. I don't know who she was."

"An eleven-year-old girl?"

"I guess so."

I wanted to kill at that very moment. But I couldn't. I was dying too quickly. "That was Molly, my daughter."

"No, it wasn't. Don't be stupid."

"It was. You were sleeping with my wife. Molly looked in the back window and saw you. She ran away because her mother was cheating on her father. Kids are impressionable like that. Course, with *your* shit for brains, that would never have occurred to you, would it?"

"Your wife was sleeping with everything she could get her hands on, Teacher." He laughed.

"It makes perfect sense now what went on in Molly's room that night. Her mother was warning her that she could never tell me anything about what happened during that whole day. From the moment she caught you in *my* bed. What did the mask look like?" I could feel my heart quicken.

"Who?"

"The kid who shot you in the leg that night. What did he look like?"

"How did you find out?"

"Molly told me."

"He was wearing this weird mask, standing there strutting his old daddy's shotgun. I didn't think he'd do it. But he did. Raised the rifle and grazed me in the leg, little bastard."

509

"What was the mask like?"

"A black 'n' white thing, tiny hole for his eyes. Black stripes on the cheeks, and a black curve just under the mouthpiece. A little tuft of brown straw-like hair, a kinda tuft sticking up over the forehead. Scary-lookin' thing . . . spooky witchcraft feelin' about it. He had all the kids running crazy, half o'them havin' nightmares for the rest of their lives."

"The Killcrow," I whispered.

"The *what*?"

"The *Killcrow*. It's an old tradition the gypsies shared with the Native American Indians."

"How did the gypsies get wrapped up with Red Indians?"

"They didn't. But gypsies are nomads with a similar culture to many Indian tribes. There could be a link way back or maybe just a cultural link. Imagine the army, and how it's broken down into companies and battalions. Imagine them as families, half-related because they all come from the same command, and some of them related because they're inter-marrying."

"So what does this *Killcrow* have to do with the gypsies?"

"The gypsies from Albania, Armenia, the Balto-Slavics . . . they travelled from country to country, inter-marrying, settling and resettling. Eventually they came to mainland Europe and started to germinate. The Killcrow protected those people on their journeys. He was meant to ward off evil spirits, which, according to tradition, stole the gypsies' children in the dark of night while they slept in their wagons and around their campfires." I was barely able to whisper.

"*Bullshit!*" Traynor shouted, and laughed. "What a load of hocus-pocus! Do you really believe all that shit, Teacher?"

"I'm not sure what to believe in any more, Josh. Can you afford *not* to believe it?"

"Where did you hear all that?"

"I'm a schoolteacher. I'm a bookshop owner. I'm also living with a woman whose grandfather was a north American Red Indian. A Sioux chief, no less. These people live simple lives for one reason and *one* reason only. They can't afford to let their lives become too complicated. If they do, they lose touch with their Spirit. Without their Spirit, they're nothing. Life holds no meaning without their spiritual connection to the greater cosmic forces of the universe."

"I can't believe I'm listening to this. I should just shoot you and go home. But then I want you to ask me a few more questions first."

"What happened to Ivan Moyne?" I was no longer looking at Josh. I watched the orange glow growing in strength, spreading out now behind him. It was a reflection of sorts, like the sun at dawn. While there seemed to be no sound, I could tell, even in my decrepit, semi-conscious state, it was getting nearer.

"I knew he'd done a runner. It didn't take me long to find him. Gus Dalton was left behind. He's a wimp. He had plenty of money. Blaine Odox paid him well, then paid him off generously when they closed down the plant. But he just seemed to become a hermit. Moyne pleaded with him to leave the country. He knew that by leaving him behind, he left the way open to be followed by the law."

"Or by you?"

"Precisely. You're ahead of me, Teacher. I get a buzz from that. So I just had to pay a couple of visits to Dalton. I threatened to take him to the law. His wife was very ill and he was afraid the shock of all this terrible business would be too much for her. So he told me late one night that Moyne had run away to here." Josh looked around and stretched, and breathed in the air. He seemed oblivious to the orange incandescence that was spreading out rapidly behind him. He yawned. "So I made a couple of visits. Got friendly with a couple of local *guardia civil*, paid them a few hundred quid each. Within three days they'd located the great doctor, right to his doorstep. Now that's what I call good lawmanship."

The light was growing brighter with each minute. The orange balls seemed to flicker now, blurring my vision and dancing in front of my eyes.

I was certain they didn't exist at all, that I was hallucinating, and my defence mechanisms were breaking down my thought-patterns so as to protect me from the lethal combination of shock and pain.

Or perhaps it was the two Spaniards returning to help Traynor finish me off. But why would they come through such a fractious, uphill route. The lights seemed to jump from tree to tree as they moved closer. I squinted again, counting three at first. Then there were six, or was I simply seeing double?

Josh was too wrapped up in his story to notice what was unfolding behind him. "I called to his house one evening. Naturally he was shocked to see me. I told him I wanted another half-million to stop me from printing the story. He invited me in and explained that he didn't have that sort of money any more. A combination of costly mistakes, along with Blaine-Odox's decision to relocate, had cost him dearly. His divorce had proved quite expensive. His affair with your estranged wife meant he had to triple what he had originally expected to hand over to his own wife when they separated. Did I mention that your wife was sleeping with the doctor too? Anyway, I told him I didn't give a cute fuck about his costly demise. Either he gave me the money or I talked."

"What did he say to that?"

"He thought for a moment. Then his disposition seemed to change in the blink of an eye. He told me to get out. I told him he was being foolish. I warned him I could get at least half-a-dozen affidavits within twenty-four hours. He'd definitely be looking at ten to fifteen years when the truth came out in court. He insisted I get out. 'Get out or I'll call the police,' were his precise words, spoken coolly and calmly."

"What did you do?"

"I left. I went to a bar and had a few drinks, and

thought about what course of action was required. I decided to let him stew on it for a few weeks. I reckoned he'd come crawling back to me and hand me the money if he knew what was good for him. As it turned out a year went by without anything happening. That was because I thought I'd been recognised by an old American friend I walked into at Dublin airport on my return. He was a cop from Illinois, grew up in the same little town as he did. Went to school with the bastard."

"So what happened?"

"I laid low for few months. Wrote as Sharon T Jory. Once I felt no one was coming after me, I went back to talk to Moyne. He'd started drinkin' very heavily. He bought a little place just down the road from here. I guessed that if I didn't hit on him soon that all his money would run out. Before I came out I paid Gus Dalton another visit. Naturally he was delighted to see me. I asked him to explain how Moyne was managing to live so comfortably. After a little persuading, Dalton explained that the Blaine Odox mother company in Texas, Franklin Global, they're called . . ."

"In Fort Worth, Texas . . ." I said, transfixed now by what was slowly materializing behind Traynor.

"Bingo, Teacher. You've been doing your homework again, *good boy!*" he cheered. "How did you find out?"

"Because there were four envelopes sitting on a windowsill outside the post office when I arrived in town this afternoon. They all bore the Franklin Global insignia at the top of each envelope."

"Clever. And what did that tell you?"

"It told me that either Ivan Moyne was too terrified to collect his post each week because he felt he was being watched or followed, *or* that he was dead."

"I left them there for you, Teacher. I just cashed in the cheques and filled the envelopes with old bills."

"Liar!"

"Why should I lie?"

"Because you didn't expect me to find them, did you?"

"It's not worth shit to me, Teacher. I don't care what you found."

"I could have gone to the police."

"Nearest station from here is Paguera. That's where my buddy works. Do you speak Spanish, *señor*? They hate the English-speaking tourists," he mocked. "They think we're all Brits. That's why it's handy to speak the lingo, *señor*."

I knew now that there were people in the forest behind Josh. I was also aware that the brightness of the moon on Josh's face was blocking any light he might have otherwise sensed behind him.

I counted three people carrying small flaming torches. They hovered from tree to tree, without walking, it seemed, waiting and watching, and then moving on to a closer tree, zigzagging and bending, stooping and dodging. Then there were three more, without torches, their shapes, darkly clad, illuminated by the light of the flames.

I had a choice of what to believe was happening. Either I was in the process of dying, the final stages of transition, and this was the 'welcome' party; *or* Josh's helpers – his *gitanos* – were returning, and they intended to finish me off and burn my body. But why were they being so stealthy?

I closed my eyes and prayed.

56

Eyes wide open.

My pain had subsided considerably. My leg was stiff and swollen to twice its normal size. It felt cased. The slightest movement caused a pain so intense I almost lost consciousness. I *had* no idea how long I had been sleeping, if I had slept at all. My awareness was sharper. The pain had abated somewhat, provided I stayed perfectly still. My clothes were damp through, cold and matted. I could smell the wet fabric of the jacket I wearing. My face felt hot. Very hot. I knew I was running a high temperature. I had flashes of all the possible outcomes and complications. Gangrene, septicaemia, amputation. Provided, of course, that he let me live. Somehow I doubted he would.

That was the first time I let my conscious mind entertain the notion of death. In my semi-conscious state I wondered how it would feel. Would it be more painful than getting shot in the knee? I couldn't imagine a pain worse than what I had felt for that split second when I heard the gun discharge. The bullet felt as if it had passed straight through my knee. I had bled from both sides, front and back. The wounds had now caked into a gooey mess. I knew I had lost pints of blood, and wouldn't live for much longer in these conditions.

Josh Traynor sat astride the tombstone now, drinking a can of beer.

The moon was gone, so were the torchbearers. I sat forward very slowly and winced as a red-hot dart of excruciating pain shot up through my left leg, hitting the base of my skull like a sharp pellet from a sling.

I felt somewhat let down, as if I had been half-expecting those ghostly strangers to alter the chain of events, which ultimately would result in death if help didn't arrive soon. What help?

I looked around and tried to focus on small distant house lights across the valley and in the foothills of the Tramuntanas.

Although, now, I wasn't prepared to let it all happen so easily. For a moment, I was convinced I had been hallucinating as a result of deep shock.

A hooting sound sent a shiver down my spine. It came from the direction where I had seen the flaming torches earlier. Then another, longer, more strained series of hoots reverberated around the huge valley below us.

Josh seemed oblivious, swinging his feet and

guzzling what was left of the beer. "What the hell is that sound?" he said casually.

I watched him drain the can. I was parched; my tongue so dry and enlarged and uncomfortable it felt like a gobstopper jammed in my throat. I couldn't swallow. Realizing I was awake now, he cheered. "Good morning, Teacher." He tossed the bottle into the hole.

"What time is it?" I said.

"It is five minutes past midnight. How are you feeling?" he asked, drunk and slurring.

"Never felt better, thanks."

"You've been out cold for a little bit. I was worried."

"Why?"

"I thought maybe you'd bled to death on me."

"Wouldn't be such a bad thing."

"I just had a quick feel of your pulse. I hope you don't mind me touching you like that. I was hoping you'd wake up soon. I was beginning to doze off myself. Come on. Keep asking me those questions. We don't have long more to wait."

"For *what*?"

He didn't answer. "Where was I?"

"You were talking about Moyne." I looked beyond him to the stone wall and the forest beyond. If I could just manage to get across the wall and into the deep shrubbery, I could lose him. He was drunk. That was my only ticket out of here.

He opened another bottle. "You were about to give me your theory, on why you think the good doctor is dead."

He waved the bottle at me, gesturing me to continue.

"I know he's dead, Josh. Ingrid Moyne told me on three separate occasions he was dead. And I believe her. She might be in the early stages of dementia, but each time she told me, it was in connection with something she was discussing quite coherently."

"Bullshit!" He drank down the bottle and lobbed it in after the other one. "I've been ringing that home every fortnight for months, imitating that posh doctor, Teacher, asking them how she is, finding out if she needed anything. I've even been sending them money. Hell, I even rang one night pretending to be her long-lost nephew from America!"

"You were obsessed with this Moyne business, weren't you?"

"Someone's gotta do it. Otherwise that old battleaxe is gonna suspect something's wrong. I didn't want anything to seem out of place. Know what I mean?" He peeled open another can of beer.

"What was the last thing he used to say each time he rang Sunny Hall, Josh?"

"What d'you mean, *the last thing?*"

"There was an affectionate little expression he would use each time he rang Sunny Hall to see if she was OK. He always ended the phone call with it, insisting that whichever member of the nursing staff he was talking to had to make sure to say it to her when they went to tell her that he had called." I watched him.

He stared at me, lost. "What was that?"

"He used to say, 'Have a peaceful night for me, dear.' It probably doesn't mean much to you or me, Josh, but when someone has been ending a fortnightly telephone call to the same person with those words for so long, they become very important, especially when you still love the person who says them."

"What are you talking about, Teacher?"

"Ingrid Moyne still loved her husband. He rang Sunny Hall every two weeks to see if she was OK. She refused to talk to him because of what he had done. But she still loved him. So when you started to ring, you didn't say, 'Have a peaceful night for me, dear.' So she knew something had happened him."

"So what? What's that got to do with me?"

"I'll tell you if you tell me what happened."

Josh got comfortable and threw away the unfinished beer. He was more nervous now, more edgy and unsure. "I knew Ivan had come out here. He told me he didn't want anyone to know where he was living. He was afraid that if she found out, after all that had happened, she'd send the police right to his front door. So I agreed not to tell her. It became a little secret between Ivan and me. And he knew it would stay a secret provided he kept paying me what we had agreed on."

"What was that?"

"Well, since he couldn't afford to hand over two million, I told him I'd settle for a couple of hundred thousand a year."

"For how many years?"

"Indefinitely. *Till death do us part*, you could say. Anyway, he got a bit stroppy and awkward to deal with in the end. Said he was getting anxious out here, getting too old and lonely to be living with people you can't understand. That's what he told me. He said he was thinking of coming home and handing himself over to the authorities."

"And that's when you killed him?"

"I told him I was catching the next flight out here to have a chat with him. I even told him I'd come here and live with him, rather than let him throw away this arrangement. When I got here, he was already packed. He even had the taxi to the airport booked. He wasn't taking no for an answer. He was going on about Ingrid, and how he wanted to patch things up and take her out of that place and nurse her at home. I couldn't let him do that. It would have meant that I would automatically be incriminated in his testimony. They'd want to know everything. So . . ."

"You killed him?"

He took a deep breath and shivered. "Yeah. I was faced with no choice. Believe me, I didn't want to."

"You bastard!"

He stared straight ahead, into the silent, dark valley. "He's buried over there." He nodded to the gravestone marked *Joe Taylor*.

"Who erected the gravestone?"

"I did," he said.

"Why?"

"'Cos it creates less suspicion when people see a new gravestone rather than none at all. At least when they see a name, they assume that's who's buried there. If all they see is a mound of freshly compacted earth, they're gonna start asking questions, aren't they, Teacher?"

"And what have you been telling people about Ivan's whereabouts?"

"That he was unwell. That he had to return to Ireland for treatment. That I'm looking after his little pad until he returns. Although I have told them he's very ill, and that that won't be for some time, if ever . . ."

"And how are you related to him, did you tell them?"

"I'm his son." He grinned.

"*Sick bastard*! Did you grin like that at the security guard you shot dead? Or the young mother you killed while her baby looked on?"

"Where did you hear about that?"

"From a friend of mine in the States. He's a cop. He did a check on you. Now all five of the States that have you on their wanted posters know where you are, Josh. Or should that be Joe?"

"Of course that makes you my accessory, Teacher. This bears all the hallmarks of a beautiful plot, Dave. They're going to think that you enlisted my services to bump off the man who fucked your daughter . . ."

The words didn't register for a couple of seconds. I could hear the laughter. He was gloating now, shaking his finger as I focused on his face. I could feel the rage boiling from somewhere deep within. *"Tell me that's a sick joke. Please?"*

He was laughing louder now. "I knew that would get Davey Freeman steamed up."

I could feel tears. My finger clawed into the wet, sticky muck, deeper and deeper until my fingernails and bones ached. I arched my head and closed my eyes. I prayed for the strength. He watched me.

"Do you want to know how it happened?"

"No."

"Well, that's tough shit, Teacher, because I'm gonna tell you. I know you want to know. Don't you?"

I shook my head and squeezed my eyes closed, bracing myself for what I was about to hear.

"I met her one night in Dublin. I was up on business, staying over. I knew where she'd be drinking. I heard her mother mention the name of it a few times. Seemingly they'd go to this place together if your *wife* was visiting her for a couple days. It was a nice place, off Grafton Street. Real trendy, full of tasty dolls dressed like sluts. They were just begging to be swept off their feet. I was drifting that night. I wandered in and – lo and behold – there she was with a couple of her college friends. She was well tanked up by the time I got there. Come to think of it, so was I. She introduced me to her three friends. I bought them all a drink. Then this bloke, this jumped-up creep came over and asked her if he could buy her a drink. He just wouldn't take no for an answer. So I stepped in, like any decent gentleman would, and told him to piss off.

He still wouldn't take no for an answer, kept comin' back like a lost sheep. So I followed him into the gents' a couple of minutes later when I noticed him heading that way. And proceeded to show him the error of his ways. Needless to say he didn't rejoin our company."

I was shaking uncontrollably now, desperate to claw my way away from him. I didn't want to hear any more.

"By the time she was leaving the pub, she could barely walk. I offered to call her a taxi. She accepted, on one condition – that I share it with her. She was all over me in the back of that car, pulling at my fly, unbuttoning my shirt . . ."

"Liar . . ."

"When we got to her apartment, she begged me to come in for coffee . . ."

"You're a liar, Traynor . . ."

"I told her I'd go up for ten minutes. As soon as I was inside the front door, your little girl started tearin' the clothes off me, Teacher. She had me on my back inside of two minutes, I swear. I've never experienced anything like it."

"Shut up, you bastard! You liar!" I try to get to my feet. I ignored the pain. I pulled and heaved. I couldn't move. I felt paralysed now. There was no feeling, no sensation or movement whatsoever, in my left leg.

He laughed. "That was some night, Teacher. She taught me things that made my eyes pop."

I cried silently now, keeping my head down, my eyes away from his. I knew it was all lies, every word he spoke. I willed myself not to listen. He went on. And then, like a prompt, I asked the question. I spoke slowly, without raising my head. "When was that?"

"When was what? *Go on, I want to hear you saying it . . .*"

"*When did it happen?*" I shouted so loud, in such a maniacal way, he went for the gun and pointed it.

"Patience, Teacher. I'll tell you when it was exactly." He scratched his stubble with the point of the gun barrel. "It was the Tuesday night before you came home last month."

I waited for a moment, until I could be sure of what I was about to say, before the hateful rage that was welling up within could spill over. I wanted to grab him by the throat and squeeze the last breath of air out of his lungs, and watch his face turn blue. In truth, I couldn't physically move. "That was the night Molly tried to kill herself." I tried to say it calmly.

He sniggered at first. Then he shook his head. "No," was all he said, over and over. Silence. Disbelief. "What are you accusing me of, Teacher?"

"I'm accusing you of being responsible for my daughter's attempt to kill herself. She was out celebrating her twenty-first birthday with a few friends. She decided to have a few drinks, one or two too many, and you saw your big chance, *you evil bastard!*"

He shook his head and tried to laugh.

"Did my daughter know you were seeing her mother?"

"Of course she did. What's that got to do with anything?"

"Because she was *drunk* when you seduced her and tricked her into bed, Traynor. When she sobered up she suddenly realized that she was in bed with her mother's boyfriend, for Christ's sake! How do you think she might have felt not being able to remember what happened?"

"That's not my problem, is it? I didn't know your daughter was a basket case, Freeman!"

"And you told her you'd kill her if she ever told her mother what happened, didn't you?"

"Don't be ridiculous!" He jumped down off the tombstone and walked to a few feet away from where I was sitting. "All I said to her was that this was gonna be our little secret. She enjoyed it, for God's sake. She was moaning and begging for it."

"Fuck you . . . you bastard!" I yelled so hard, the pain almost knocked me out.

Traynor laughed uneasily.

"When did you tell her that?" I said.

"When I was leaving."

"Did you find her in the bath?"

"No."

I closed my eyes to shut out the horrible images my mind was conjuring up, hoping that if he had intended finishing me off he would do it there and then.

"Who found her?"

"I don't know. I left her about three. She was a bit upset. But she told me she'd be OK. She was going back to bed. That's what she said."

"And what role did her detective uncle have to play in your little scam, Josh?"

"He was meant to keep an eye on you, Teacher. I never thought he was a good cop. So I knew he'd be a useless private detective. But since he was getting a share of the money, I could do nothing about him. You did me a favour, Teacher. You killed him for me. Thank you for that."

"Why was he in on the deal?"

"Because he was nosey bastard. He knew something was going on. He saw me meeting Gus Dalton one night. He bought me a drink afterwards, told me he'd heard the whole conversation. Bang. He was in, or he was going to the police to tell them.

"I guess he was a bit upset after what happened to his little darling niece. Let his guard down, and you copped right away you were being followed that night the happy family went to the theatre. You know Neasa hated every second of that evening with you. She told me afterwards."

"I was only doing it for Molly."

"The two of us are planning on heading for Australia when all this is tidied up and out of the way. I think she's kinda keen that Molly comes with us."

"That's not going to happen, Josh. Molly's coming back to the States with me."

"The only way you're going home to the States, Teacher, is in a big brown lead casket."

57

There were three of them.

In hindsight, I am certain of that now.

In the moment I opened my eyes and looked to see where Josh Traynor had gone, I saw them, standing directly in front of me, perhaps twenty feet away: three tall figures, silent and motionless, on a small patch of land where the top of the cemetery's stone wall met the perimeter of the dark forest.

At first, I thought I was hallucinating again. Then I was convinced the shallow beams of light the moon was throwing between the gravestones as it slipped down lower in the late night sky were playing tricks on my eyes.

I watched them, studied their shapes. Three men. I squeezed my eyes together, rubbing them with the backs of my hands, to get a closer look. They wore long, dark coats. As I watched for longer, I could see the long sleeves that covered their hands. Their boots were tied up, in a zigzagging pattern, around their ankles. The one in the middle, the smallest one, wore a light-brown belt around his waist, and a diagonal strap, like a brace, across his chest. They all wore identical headdress: not scarves, or hats. Hoods. I could see from this distance the different colours, but it was impossible to be specific in the darkness.

The tallest of the three, on the left, wore a beard and moustache.

My heart was pounding wildly. They seemed to move, almost float, back and forth – one moment almost invisible in complete darkness, next visible as the long beams of moonlight caught their spot. The two flankers were bannerets, it seemed.

For some reason, I didn't believe they were with Josh. But who were they? The way they appeared to move seemed to be an illusion. Each time I focused more intently, they looked perfectly still, statuesque almost.

I looked at Josh to see if he had noticed them. He was looking the other way.

It was all happening, unfolding before my eyes, in the space of a few seconds, maybe less. Then I watched them again for a few seconds. Two of them were watching Josh. The one in the middle never took his eyes off me for a second. I couldn't see the middle one's face. It was as if he, or she, was standing in the shadows of the other two, a foot or two behind them, smaller than them, his face hidden behind their broad shoulders.

I opened my mouth and was about to call Josh, when one of them, the man on the right, lifted his hand, raising his finger to his lips.

I froze.

They *were* real.

What happened next will remain with me, clear as if it had only just taken place yesterday, for the rest of my life.

The one on the right slowly lifted his arm. His draped sleeve blew gently behind him. Without turning around he raised his hand above his head and twirled it in a circular motion. Immediately, the glow I had seen earlier returned, and with the glow, a tingling, plinking noise that grew louder as the glow brightened.

Later when I would try to describe it to Karen, all I could think of was the sound of dozens of wind chimes.

Josh spun around. "What the fuck is that?" he said.

I watched him carefully as his eyes settled on the three men. I looked at them, watching him. He went for the gun in his pocket. I watched his hand fumbling, his eyes twitching. Just as he pulled it loose, a loud voice broke through the gentleness of the night and the sound of the chimes.

"Don't . . . move . . . another . . . limb . . ."

The voice, while commanding and direct, was soft and slow, almost melodious and unaccented, like a voice from a choir. It came from in the middle, from the man I hadn't been able to see. He was definitely not a Spaniard.

He stepped forward and, as he did, my jaw dropped and I froze.

The small individual, standing out front now, in between the two flankers, stood silently pointing at Josh Traynor. His face was masked, a façade of black and white stripes. He wore a deep hood, the steam from his breath drifted across the rays of light that broke through the branches of the trees directly overhead.

As I waited to see what would happen next, a dart of pain, horribly debilitating, shot up my leg. I screamed out and collapsed onto my side, clutching my knee.

From where I lay, I could see the three ghostly figures watching me.

"He needs to get to a hospital," Josh shouted nervously, stuttering as he tried to cover up his shock and disbelief.

"We will look after that," the main figure said. "We will also look after you." He turned and said something to the man on his left. I propped myself up, balancing on my wrist, to get a better view, aware only too well now that I could pass out at any moment.

The man on the left nodded and looked behind. He reached back with his cloaked hand. It was then I noticed other heads, other bodies, huddled together in the warm orange glow. One passed something to him. Whatever he had been given, he passed it immediately to the main figure who turned to take it.

At that moment Josh raised the gun and pointed it. *"You bastards . . . you don't scare me!"*

As he raised the weapon, I watched the dark figure

in the middle raise his hand high above his head and down behind his shoulder. Then he brought it forward, flicking his hand with amazing speed. I could hear a loud whirring sound as something passed at lightning speed.

Josh grabbed his neck with his left hand. The gun discharged, the bullet hitting a tree somewhere in the corner of the cemetery. Josh staggered around in a circle, clutching his neck now with both hands. He started to stumble towards me, muttering words and pleading with me.

Then I saw the knife.

It had entered his neck, just below the projection of the thyroid cartilage – his Adam's apple. He fell to his knees, his tongue sticking out and his eyes rolling back up under his eyelids. Blood gushed from the wound, spurting and squirting with each beat of his heart, and from his mouth into a pool where he knelt now, as he pointed to the knife, pleading with me. He collapsed across my right leg and became perfectly still, his head face down in the wet clay.

I looked back at the figures on the hill. My vision wasn't as good now. They seemed to be moving towards me, drifting in and out of focus. The harder I tried to pinpoint each of them, the more nauseous I felt. I was trying to say something but my words were coming out garbled and disjointed. My speech was just noise. As they got closer to me, I could hear my voice, distant and detached, begging them to help me, and pleading with them not to hurt me. I felt cold, ice cold. No sensations but a floating feeling as if someone else had taken control of my mind and body.

No words.

Just noise.

A warm comforting darkness enveloped me like a reassuring embrace.

And nothing.

58

Suffice it to say, my memories of the events of that awful night are still quite sketchy. I was later told I had lost almost five pints of blood, leaving less than the body needs to carry out its normal physiological requirements to keep me alive. I should have died that night.

But if my own experience was agonising, I can still only imagine what Molly and Karen had to endure unexpectedly. While I was being prepared for emergency surgery in Palma hospital that night and barely conscious, my mobile phone rang.

A man asked me if I was David Freeman.

He told me that Karen and Molly had been involved in a terrible accident while en route to Dublin. Karen was recovering. There had been a fatality. I remember lifting my hand to my face and covering my eyes. The anaesthetist had already given me the pre-surgery jab.

In my grogginess I couldn't say anything to him. Karen was in a comfortable condition in hospital in Naas. Molly, however, had sustained serious head injuries. As he spoke, she was been being transferred by helicopter ambulance to a special head injuries unit at Beaumont Hospital in Dublin.

Four weeks later, I was told their story.

Karen had arrived back at Langton's late that night, having arranged to meet Molly in reception. The Duty Manager described her state as "very distressed". The Duty Manager, a woman called Jill, asked her if she was OK. Karen insisted she was. Jill explained that Molly had gone to The Old Mill public house for a drink with her mother. From there she had intended to go back to her grandmother's house to say goodbye.

Jill informed Karen that Molly was expecting to be picked up from there. Karen found this somewhat strange, since Molly knew she had never driven Irish roads before, and the small roads to Claddagh Mines were like a labyrinth to a stranger.

Karen insisted she was fine and would find it, "no problem". She was eager to get back to the car, which was double-parked and unlocked. Jill thanked her and said goodbye.

Once out past the city lights, Karen froze when she checked her rear-view mirror. She recognized the staring eyes immediately. Neasa grabbed her right shoulder and held a syringe to her throat. She had been hiding in the back of the car, low down behind the driver's seat, waiting.

Karen tried hard to control her breathing to avoid swerving into the path of the oncoming traffic, while keeping her head painfully tilted to the right to avoid the sharp tip of the hypodermic needle pressing the soft flesh under her left ear. Karen asked a number of times where Molly was. Each time she was told to shut up and drive.

Neasa warned Karen that if she didn't follow her precise instructions she wouldn't hesitate in stabbing her with a deadly overdose of the anaesthetic, Novocaine.

Karen told me she could smell the alcohol on Neasa's breath. Neasa told her she was on her way to Amsterdam with Molly, to link up with Josh at Schiphol airport. From there the three of them were bound one-way for Australia.

Karen told her about the warrants out for Josh's arrest in the States. Neasa laughed at the notion. Then she became quite disturbed as Karen described the shooting dead of the young mother and security guard and, in her agitation, dropped the syringe.

Later, Karen described to me minutely how she pressed the accelerator down hard as soon as she realized that Neasa had dropped it. She knew the road would be in a bad state after the stormy weather we'd been having that week. She decided to take a chance, while Neasa was distracted, and punch in 999 on her mobile. She fumbled in her jacket pocket for the phone while Neasa, scrambling around the floor below the backseat cursed her and shouted abuse.

Karen never realised she was only seconds away from the dangerous skew bridge that crosses over the main Dublin to Waterford railway line, where the road narrows into an acute sharp-left hairpin manoeuvre. She passed the luminous road sign, *Dangerous Bridge Ahead*. In a split second, black and yellow stripes straight ahead were reflecting in her full beams. At that moment, Karen realized she wasn't going to be able to stop in time.

Karen recalls blinking hard, opening her eyes wide and, almost instinctively, checking the mirror one last time. She assumed Neasa was still down behind the seat searching for the syringe.

Karen had just enough time to press her full weight back into her seat and to check her belt was secure. The last thing she remembers is hitting the footbrake and noticing that the speedometer was at seventy.

In the blink of an eye, she gauged that the wall was about bonnet-high. She closed her eyes on impact, felt a sickening thump, as if a huge bomb had just exploded in front of her knees. Sudden impact winded her. There was no screaming, just a sensation of sheer uncontrollable weight in rapid forward motion, and then free-fall.

Neasa shot forward between the front seats, like a ragdoll off a catapult against the hard dashboard and on through the windscreen into the spitting-rainy darkness, like a garment being sucked through a mangle.

The car jolted and thumped, side-over-end, clearing

the bridge and flying into what felt like a deep, black ravine. It seemed to fly forever, Karen said later, then nosedive, until it came to rest on a steep bank.

The impact had ripped the car asunder.

Karen remembers feeling the sharp shards of prickly, broken glass, as they rained down on her head and face and onto the back of her hands as she raised them to shield her eyes.

Then there was an utterly pervasive silence. Deafening was how she described it.

She opened her eyes once she was sure the car was still. She could feel her face bleeding. Or was it her head? she remembered asking herself.

The roof of the car had been crushed, almost flattened beyond recognition. Karen's seat had buckled, forcing her forward so that her nose almost touched the bent steering wheel. It took her what felt like an eternity to struggle free from the wreckage and crawl away to a clear patch of grass. Her greatest fear at that moment was fire. She was terrified, listening to the gentle, uneven hissing, that something somewhere was about to explode into flames.

On the grass verge beside her, sloping steeply to within inches of the railway track was a single shoe, a black and white trainer. Beyond it, Neasa lay face down, arms outstretched on the glass-littered slope.

She had been decapitated.

The silence was interrupted by a dull, knocking sound from the boot, then a weak, muffled voice. Karen told me she crawled back to the driver's door, praying that the release switch for the car boot would still function. It clicked. The boot lid sprung up. The voice was clearer now, closer. Karen crawled up the steep slope to the back of the car. Clawing her way for support she managed to stand up. Her first reaction was to scream.

Molly was lying gagged and bound hand and foot, doubled up now after the impact and bleeding heavily from a deep gash above her eye. Karen untied her and held her until she could see the blue flashing lights illuminating the night sky.

* * *

Neasa Maher died in tragic circumstances that night, in what some might say was a fitting end to a sad and selfish life. She could have taken Molly and Karen with her.

I know now that my wife was a very sick woman, as distinct from all the times I simply just hated her for her irrational reasoning and violent outbursts. The plan she hatched that evening to smuggle my daughter out of the country in a drug-induced stupor and to remove Karen from the equation by killing her and making it look like a tragic road traffic accident, was nothing short of the work of a psychopath.

Neasa was planning to make it look like careless driving on Karen's part in wet, wintry conditions. How Neasa hoped to get out of the car alive and then get Molly to Dublin airport without anyone suspecting anything is beyond me. Maybe she had organised to have a second car waiting for her somewhere along the route. I don't know. Her plan was doomed from the moment she dreamt it up.

Karen was certain that Neasa was very drunk that night. Alcohol has a knack of making you believe your own delusions of grandeur. It certainly had that effect on Neasa on the occasions I drank with her many years ago.

I often wonder what she had hoped to achieve by kidnapping our daughter and trying to kill Karen. Was she really in love with Josh? Had she really been so unfaithful to me while we were still living together?

I sometimes wonder if, somewhere in the recesses of her twisted, sick mind, Neasa was pleading for a new start. Suddenly Josh Traynor's infectious madness and wild ways had swept her off her feet and shown her a way out. Josh had become her ticket to that new life she dreamt of. I believe she was going to attain it at any cost. Whatever had been tormenting her all those years finally took its toll in an ironic twist to a sad story's end.

* * *

Outwardly, these days we are a quiet, affable sort of family; warm and welcoming to a small, select group of close friends who have helped us to cope with the intensity of what each of us has come through.

But once the front door closes and the darkness descends, bringing with it the ghostly memories, the three of us talk and share, like fishermen pulling in the nets quickly ahead of a great storm that has caught them off-guard. We look for reasons and support each other, and listen and talk . . . and hug and cry. We've done a lot of crying.

Molly has been undergoing treatment to help her cope with the years of self-blame, denial and confusion. Karen has been able to help her release the awful repressions she had buried all those years ago, when she found her mother in bed with her father's best friend. Josh had threatened her that he would track her down and kill her if she ever told her story to anyone. His threats, and the consequences of ever breathing a word about what she saw, were so overwhelming, she forced herself to forget the whole incident, to repress anything that was even remotely associated with her impressions of a time when her young, growing mind should have been showered with love, not evil.

This repression became so deeply buried that Molly's mind refused to recall it. Karen explained to me that Molly's subconscious mind had been protecting her by hiding these evil memories. They became untouchable and therefore invisible, like a small bronze coin lost in a forest floor covered with brown-fallen leaves. The symptoms of her repression, unknown to Molly, caused a huge build-up of paranoid anxiety. The intangible repression finally became too much and, like a huge river of water pressing against the walls of a dam, broke through, driving her over the edge.

Josh had tried to seduce her the night they had been drinking together. Once he realized Molly wasn't interested, he tried to rape her. He forced her onto the settee in her living room, pinned her legs down with his weight and ripped her blouse open.

Molly summoned all the strength she could muster and sank her teeth into one of Josh's wrists as he tried to hold her hands above her head.

She's not certain about what happened next. All she remembers was a high-pitched scream coming from Josh as she felt the warm taste of blood in her mouth, followed by a blinding blow to the side of her head. Then blackness and nothing,

When she regained consciousness, she was lying on the floor of the apartment, her clothes soaked in blood.

She thought about phoning the police. Instead she walked into the bathroom and ran the hot water tap, placed the stopper in the plughole and glanced at her reflection in the mirror.

She told me the feelings of worthlessness had been haunting her long before that night. While the bath filled, she started to drink the whiskey she had often thought about throwing out. Neat. She gagged a few times as she forced herself to swallow it. The first few gulps burned her tongue and throat.

To this day, she still does not remember the rest.

It was only when Molly was sure Josh was dead – that he could no longer come back to kill her – that her mind decided it was time to release the repression and consign it to the past, giving her back her life.

The past is something, we've all decided, won't darken our lives for much longer, which is easier said than done. It belongs with yesterday I have to keep reminding myself. Needless to say, when a frightening moment stops us dead in our paths, or a heart-stopping memory surfaces unexpectedly, we help each other to deal with it.

59

Oak Bluffs, Martha's Vineyard
Four months later

Spring, with its promise of new life and its cheerful optimism, is my favourite time of the year, poignant more so this year than ever I can remember.

Golden Pond, like a secret hideaway that never changes and always welcomes, is my place of refuge and hope, with its baby ducklings and its nests high up in the branches of the old trees that have always been here, it seems.

I still awake each morning, remembering the horrors of what seems like years ago. Faces and blood and death are still vividly alive each time I close my eyes at night. But I know that will pass in time.

Karen has been an indefatigable strength, helping Molly and me come to terms with all that has happened. *And* she doesn't charge for the therapy.

Molly is settling into life on the island. She's been helping me out in the bookstore, urging me to rest when my knee acts up. A surgeon in Boston has urged me to think about knee replacement surgery. It's not a priority.

Molly has adopted an Irish Red Setter pup.

A day hasn't gone by so far that I haven't made a point of telling her, "I love you too."

And such is *my* priority – to make up for all those years she could only tell over the phone, "I love you, Dad."

She has met a boy. Or should I call him a man? I suppose by referring to him as a boy, I get to feel she's still my little girl. They're keeping it all very clandestine. Often when I see them, I have to remind myself that she's no longer a child. Those days are gone and can never be brought back. Robert is his name. He's just received a scholarship for a college in Seattle. Eventually, she says, she might follow him out there. "See what life brings," I've heard her say a couple of times.

And she's right.

The Irish police no longer bother with us. They closed their investigation at the end of January.

I often wander back in my mind to that night in Spain. My memories are hazy and unreliable. I blacked out shortly after Josh Traynor – as I will always know him – collapsed face down across me. That's as far as I can remember. When I awoke, I was in hospital being treated for a very serious gunshot wound. I have no recollection of how I got there. Nor can I recall the doctors and staff questioning me about where or how I had been shot.

The three men on the hill, and the orange glow, and the sounds of wind chimes, blur the more I try to rationalise what they might have represented or their reasons for being there.

In my recuperation, I have taken time to read about the *gitanos*, the gypsies of continental Europe, and their history and traditions.

The Killcrow is referred to frequently in their beliefs and rituals.

With fear comes a warped, stifling paranoia. Many ancient beliefs that continue to thrive today are based on fear. Often what people feared most they held in high respect. The Killcrow, while a symbol of power, was also a safeguard and a sign of refuge. The Killcrow protected his people. Such status was only passed to those who were deemed pure in heart.

I accept now that I will never fully know the truth; how Traynor had upset the *gitanos* to the point that they pursued him to his death, as I believe they did. Relaying my story has been neither easy nor an enjoyable experience. Pieces of this unlikely jigsaw remain missing. I've reached the conclusion now that it's best not to recount it any more.

Karen believes that Ivan Moyne had been treating the *gitano* people on the island. Perhaps it was repentance; that he had been caring for them out of a sense of guilt for what he had inflicted on five small boys before he had left Ireland. Perhaps this was Moyne's way of atonement for his sins.

Neasa was buried next to her brother and her father,

following a small ceremony, in the cemetery opposite the church of St John the Apostle, in Claddagh Mines.

She had been out for a drink with Molly on the night of the fatal car crash. Molly says her mother had begged her to meet her. Molly agreed. They had a few drinks in the bar in Langton's.

Neasa had been extremely irritable and uneasy all evening and, shortly before ten that night, became engaged in a serious stand-up argument with her. Molly insisted she was returning to the States with me. Neasa objected vehemently, telling her she belonged at home with her mother. At one stage Molly stood up and threatened to leave. Molly is convinced that Neasa slipped a pill into her drink. She doesn't remember much after that.

Karen had left the keys of my hired car in the ignition while she rushed into the hotel looking for me. She can only assume that Neasa must have seen her enter the foyer and taken the opportunity to go outside with Molly who was finding it difficult to walk and talk by then. She must have helped Molly to the car and on a quiet night in Kilkenny, while no one was looking, bundled her into the boot and left her there in a semi-comatose sleep.

A search for Josh Traynor's family or next-of-kin turned up nothing. One month following his death, he was cremated in Spain, during a simple service attended only by a police witness and a Catholic priest.

* * *

Gus Dalton went out on New Year's Eve and bought himself a brand new car. That morning he had received a letter informing him that he was part of a police investigation into procedural irregularities at Blaine-Odox. He drove high into the foothills of Slieve na mBan, connected a plastic pipe to the exhaust of his car and gassed himself. A local man out walking his dog found his body three days later. The police have since closed their enquiry.

Maura Ferris finally stood up to her husband and refused to be bullied or beaten any longer. During a violent confrontation on Christmas night, she shot him in the chest with the same rifle he had pointed at me that afternoon I had visited with Karen and Josh. She told the police it hadn't been her intention to kill her husband. She pleaded guilty to manslaughter. She remains on bail, her case pending, provided she continues to live with her mother in Limerick. Aidan, her son, is now in professional care.

Ingrid Moyne passed away peacefully in her sleep late on Christmas Eve. Vera Tubridy wrote to inform me that I was one of the last people she enquired about.

I proposed to Karen on New Year's Eve, just as the bells struck midnight. She is in the process of setting up her own private practice here on the island, intending to commute between Oak Bluffs and Boston, where she spends two days a week as an intern clinical psychologist at Massachusetts Children's Hospital. We plan to marry in September. Molly has insisted on being Maid of Honour. I wouldn't have it any other way.

Come the good weather, we hope to extend our small house. The bookstore has never been so busy.

I sometimes wonder what direction all of these lost lives might have taken if I hadn't received that telephone message that night in November. I try not to dwell on it. In reality, I left in my wake a litany of disasters just waiting to happen. I know I was the catalyst; the volcano had simply lain dormant for ten years. It consoles me to know I was instrumental in saving my daughter's life. Perhaps it was her way of telling me she needed me more than I realised.

I tend to play down what happened. Most of my friends here on the island don't know I was shot. To explain it would require a long and painful account that would simply rake up thoughts and memories I am trying to consign to the past. I doubt seriously if anybody would remotely believe my account. I even find it problematical to explain to Karen and Molly the events of that night on the island of Majorca.

If outsiders ask me what happened, I simply say I hurt myself in a climbing accident. To tell them I barely managed to climb out of my own grave might sound ridiculous.

I have my theories. These I keep to myself. Suffice it to say that I truly believe that Owen Durkin is alive and well; that the young man who would now be heading into his twenty-fourth year was instrumental in saving *my* life that night last December. I can't be certain if he was there – one of the three illusory, ghostly figures who had watched me, like guardians, from the top of the hill – but I sense that he wasn't too far from me.

Many might say such a notion is far-fetched. If I had been listening to someone recounting such a story of his own experience, I might not have believed him. I know now that he saved Molly's life. Later again, he saved mine.

I have good reason for believing this.

On returning to Martha's Vineyard after a weeklong stay in hospital in Palma, a package was waiting for me. Needless to say, my shocked expression on opening it was to be anticipated. Neither Karen nor Molly could understand it. Wrapped neatly in crepe paper and placed in a box of straw was the mask of the Killcrow. There was no note, sender or detail, just an address on the package, scrawled in red ink. It hangs in my shop for all to see. When asked what it represents, I tell them it means purity of heart. It is as if the responsibility has now been passed to me.

A miracle is an expression of love. Sometimes that's all it takes to overthrow evil.

* * *

Life is wonderful, just as I had always hoped against hope it might be someday. This is our home. I no longer dwell on what was Before and After, preferring to spend all my available time and energy living in the present moment, doing the simple things in life; things that, one day, Karen and Molly and I will be able to look back on and regard as happy times. Already I can tell they've started.

What do I like most about my life now? I suppose that I don't have to dwell on how much I missed my daughter all those years ago. A day never goes by that she doesn't say to me, "I love you, Dad". And while it often reminds me of what each of us has come through I always smile.

"I love you too, Molly."

THE END